Walk in Love

Dear Janet,
 Thank you for your interest —

 Sincerely,
  Margot Dolgin

Walk in Love

Margot Dolgin

Writers Club Press
New York Lincoln Shanghai

Walk in Love

All Rights Reserved © 2001 by Margot Dolgin

No part of this book may be reproduced or transmitted in any form or by any means, graphic, electronic, or mechanical, including photocopying, recording, taping, or by any information storage retrieval system, without the written permission of the publisher.

Writers Club Press
an imprint of iUniverse, Inc.

For information address:
iUniverse, Inc.
2021 Pine Lake Road, Suite 100
Lincoln, NE 68512
www.iuniverse.com

ISBN: 0-595-15018-7

Printed in the United States of America

In memory of my father, Don Alfredo (Arbelaez). His three grandchildren who knew him too short a time, but forever love him, still refer to him as Papito (little papa). Upon seeing my first born, a son, Dany Walker, he affectionately greeted him with 'hello Papito'. Somehow it became the children's name for their grandfather. To their delight and mine, he was an avid storyteller. As a child I remember him as a great horseman, who rode like the wind. He passed on much too young, his wavy dark hair not yet gray. I still hear your laughter daddy.

PREFACE

The romance of a pastoral pre-gold rush California, when the Dons reigned over vast Ranchos, and the love of family was predominant. When San Francisco was a Mexican hamlet called Yerba Buena Cove.

Chapter 1

APRIL 1844

Three women stood tightly huddled on the deck of the merchant ship Skylark as she proceeded Eastward; all sails set passed the steep headlands that announced the entrance to the Bay of San Francisco.

As she lay slowly through the gate, a thick shaft of fog fell upon her path. A chilling wind flit at her riggings as well as through the women's long dark capes and ample skirts. The murky green waters were rife with bursting white caps.

The Skylark altered her course to starboard. Gradually the mist began to fade. Suddenly to their right, a small shoreline village encompassed by darkening hills emerged. Yet framed by haze it appeared to waft above the water. Here in the bay opposite Yerba Buena Cove is where their ship would lay anchor.

After having endured a fifteen hundred-mile voyage around Cape Horn, Belle Bradbury and her two grown daughters had at last arrived at the remote Mexican outpost, destined to be home. Fifteen-year old Iris shuddered in her mother's half embrace. Sobs caught at her disdainful words.

"Welcome to the Country of California. We must look pretty pathetic standing here in this cursed fog! Where in blazes did it come from? Only moments behind us is a bright red sun dipping into the sea. The sky aflame with the most beautiful sunset ever. It was hell's fire taunting us! That's what it was. An ill omen Mamma. An ill omen!"

She commenced to cry, all the while shivering from the chill. Her mother's arm drew her deeper into the warmth of her breast.

"Come now girl, after having survived eight months at sea you're not about to be done in by a little fog." Belle endeavored to humor Iris, though the tone of her voice was not totally convincing. "Why, we're practically old salts. "We've touched two oceans, passed the equator twice, been clobbered by everything in creation, and we still made it. We're home."

"Home?" Iris wailed. "How can you possibly call this place home? Our home is back in Boston. We've come to the edge of the world Mamma. And the fog, it's frightening. It wrapped itself around us like a shroud as soon as we sailed into the bay. I want to go back. I don't care if I vomit for eight months straight from seasickness. I just want to go back home!"

"This is home," her sister Heather half whispered. "For all it's worth, this is now our home."

Iris was quick to snap back at her. "No it's not! It never will be. It's the remotest outpost in the entire world. I don't know why we bothered to put on our best bonnets and frocks. Who's going to gave a hoot? With or without you I should have stayed home."

"We no longer have a home," Heather angrily admonished. "You've known that all along. Why are you carrying on now?"

"Please girls," came Belle "this is no way to begin a new life by bickering. And certainly no way to meet our Uncle Johnny."

"Uncle Johnny!" groaned Iris. "We don't even know if he got Papa's letter, or ours for that matter, or if he even exists. It's been at least twelve years since he visited us. I was only three, Heather five. Who can remember? He's our only uncle in the whole world and he saw us once in all that time. Why pretend he cares now? Face it Mamma, we are three total strangers in this miserable country of California. At best the backside of America. Imagine being part of a backside!"

"Stop it!" Heather scolded. "Uncle Johnny will be there with open arms. Papa promised. Don't you dare doubt it for a moment."

Iris scowled. "Just because he wrote ever so often, doesn't mean he's going to be elated at the sight of us. More likely he will loathe the idea of being saddled with three civilized ladies, and kin at that. We know nothing about Uncle Johnny other than what he bragged to Papa in his letters? It is not exactly heart-warming knowing that he was a fur trapper killing animals in the wilds, consorting with savages. Now suddenly he turns up owning a cattle ranch in California, of all places." She began to sob. "Now that we've reached our precious Pacific shore, the idea of us living in such a place is more dismal than I ever dreamed. How could our own Papa have been so blind as to hand us over to a mountain man, who doesn't even want us?" Tears spilled down her face.

"It's not that way at all, Iris," Belle soothed. "I truly believe that Uncle Johnny has at last made a good place for himself. Otherwise Papa would never have considered placing us in his care."

"And you know right well that we were welcome long before Papa died." Heather firmly added. "Why do you insist on making matters worse than they are?"

Iris commenced to sob all the harder. "What could be worse than this? Welcome you say? Welcome to what? To the wilderness?"

"We've come a very long way, Iris." It was Belle. "Now that we're finally here is no time to have doubts."

"I'd rather it were Papa waiting for us ashore," Iris cried. "Why did he have to die in that awful way? In debt and disgrace, leaving us penniless, save for a few miserable possessions and that last letter sealing our fate." Her sobs became muffled in her mother's tender embrace.

"Please don't cry," Belle gently offered "dwelling on it time and again is not what he wanted. It was his last wish that we go on to a new life. Isn't that what we promised ourselves when we started this voyage? Papa's gone, but in a way he has somehow directed our course, as he always did. As far from all the world as this place may seem, this is where he wanted us to live."

"Why here of all places?" Iris moaned. "There's nothing here, Mamma. Nothing to look forward too ever again. It's cold and wet and we're standing here shivering in our shoes, absolute foreigners about to step on some desolate shore. How can you pretend it's some wondrous adventure."

"Coming around the Horn was indeed an adventure," Belle insisted. "I'm proud of us."

They were hit with rain, squalls, sleet, snow and one hundred-knot winds tearing at the riggings. Wasted with seasickness they were lashed to their bunks, the cabin knee deep in water. Still, they had seen incredibly crimson sunsets, huge orange moons, an infinity of stars, the Magellan Clouds, and the Southern Cross, the most brilliant constellation in the heavens. They experienced the utter silence of the sea, water so calm that it shone like glass. And there was the strange sight of those sleek porpoises that at times mystically accompanied them.

"Actually, we're three plucky ladies," smiled Belle. "We've been through too much together to give way now. I feel good and even a bit prophetic about this place called Yerba Buena." She mused a moment, seeming to fondly study the shoreline village, though it could be barely traced through the fog. "It means Good Herb, from the wild mint that abounds. I like the sound of it," Belle affirmed.

"You would." Iris choked between sobs. "Let's be honest Mamma. It's Tobias Knight that you really like."

Belle continued, avoiding the inference. "Considering, we have a great deal to be grateful for. There wasn't a moment throughout the voyage, when we weren't given the best of treatment. Even during the worst of times. Yes, Tobias was there for us, for all of us," she accentuated. "We were also fortunate that Captain Honeywell turned out to be the rare exception that he is."

The Bradbury women were luckily spared the sight of sailors being flogged, keelhauled or unduly abused, as was the case on most ships.

"We've shared something few women ever experience," Belle continued. "And there's more to come, good things. I feel It."

"I dread to think what you really feel, Mamma," Iris sarcastically offered. "Papa must be spinning in his grave."

"Stop it!" Heather was provoked. "There's no reason to be disrespectful. We're going to be guests in Tobias' house until he can bring us together with Uncle Johnny. I suggest you keep your ugly inferences to yourself."

"You mean we have to continue being beholden to him?"

"Not beholden, grateful." added Heather.

"It's Mamma who's grateful." Iris sneered. "She's thirty three years old, middle aged, and she's found herself a man, without even trying. What about us Heather? Once we step off this ship we're going to be stuck here forever. Two dried up old maids. I just know it," she cried.

"You have to give it a chance, Iris." Her mother soothed.

"Do I have a choice?"

"No!" Heather sharply added.

"Try to remember Iris" it was Belle, "that each place we've stepped ashore, we've not only been treated hospitably but with the utmost respect."

"God awful primitive places!" snapped Iris. "And we've been gawked at like freaks."

Once the Skylark rounded Cape Horn, with its steep projecting headlands and its perilous gales, proceeded by lightening, and sailed up the western coast of South America, the Bradbury women were at once struck by the reality of reaching a shocking new culture.

Having passed the beautiful South Pacific Island of Juan Fernando, the Skylark continued north up the long coastline of Chile to reach Valparaíso (Vale of Paradise), their first port of call out of Boston. Valparaíso was surrounded with hills, with distant snow-capped summits and cool Northern winds. Once a poor fishing village of huts and barefoot inhabitants, Valparaíso now teemed with commerce. The women were amazed to find innumerable trading ships anchored in the bay, two from Liverpool England.

After months of being confined aboard ship, Belle and her girls found themselves aching for the feel of terra firma and civilization. Their wobbly sea legs were at once apparent as each of them needed assistance down the slopping gangplank. Belle was gently guided by Tobias while her daughters clung to the arms of two of the ship's officers. The women were led through a labyrinth of barrels and crates piled high on the dock by sweating workmen who froze at the sight of them. Fast behind, were sailors from the Skylark on their first leave. They quickly ambled down narrow streets to some darkly lit bar, all the while being accosted by anyone of the numerous beggars. Belle shuddered at the sight of a young dark skinned native mother with her two frail little girls clinging to her soiled skirts. 'But for the grace of God, go I,' she thought, her grasp at once reaching for her own daughters, who quickly responded prompting their escorts to step back. Tobias, who trailed guardedly behind the Bradbury woman, gave the poor wretch several gold coins, leaving her joyously aghast.

Belle and her daughters, with their pale porcelain skin, bright blue eyes, and flaming auburn hair managed to stun the populace. Being meticulous dressed in corseted black mourning attire, with tight string bonnets, only added to their conspicuous appearance. Their shocking experience on the dock was short-lived as Tobias gallantly whisked them into a hooded carriage. They rode past crowded streets toward the placid undulating green of the outskirts, to arrive at the home of an affluent Spanish couple, whom he visited each time he sailed around The Horn. Although the graciousness of the family spoke for itself, Tobias patiently acted as interpreter. Iris could not complain, but she did with snarling asides to her sister. She resented him for being so adept at everything; too quick to take care of their every need. 'Take over' was the word she used. What she hated most was his attentions upon Mamma. 'Besides,' she had snidely interjected, 'Valparaíso is neither Boston nor Boston Harbor.

"Well Monterey was most pleasant." Belle vainly offered.

She referred to the seat of California, where they briefly embarked before sailing the 150 miles north to Yerba Buena. Monterey sat back in a cove with a white beach, green lawns and abundantly wooded with pines. At first sight, from the vessel, the scattering of white-plastered houses with their red tiled roofs seemed rather quaint, a far cry from the congestion of Valparaíso. They were piloted ashore to be presented at the governor's office where they would obtain permission to remain in California.

Once on land they found no streets, fenced vegetable gardens, wild horses grazing at will, few shops and a plaza with a mariachi band giving their arrival an air of festivity. A run down fort, with two rusted cannon and a dozen or so poorly garbed soldiers faced the marina. All this was centered around a Mission complex with a small stone chapel grandly referred to as a Cathedral.

The Governor was both gracious and giddy as he bowed and kissed each of their hands. Documents were signed and sealed with an enormous smile. Ladies as beautiful as the Bradbury women were welcome to stay indefinitely. He introduced them to several Yankees married to daughters of the country. Though most hospital, none of the women spoke English, their husbands having learned the language of the land.

They were ultimately feted at the home of a prosperous American merchant, Thomas O'Larkin. What a nice surprise to find that his wife Rachel was an Easterner, whose mores and manners were wonderfully familiar. Their one of a kind house of Colonial architecture had a decided New England flare. Its exquisite furnishings, center staircase and upstairs fireplace, was sadly reminiscent of what the Bradbury ladies left behind.

Aside from their pleasant visit with the O'Larkin's, Iris' depression compounded upon learning that Monterey was considered the most civilized place in all of California. The fact that there were many outlining ranchos, each with their own jubilant lifestyle, was of little consequence to her. She sulked all the way to Yerba Buena.

"We're fortunate to have arrived in spring," Belle futilely attempted. "Everything has been so green all the way up the coast."

"So what happened here?" Iris grumbled. "Here, we're cursed with fog."

"It will lift Iris," Belle's voice brightened "My goodness girl, have you forgotten what it's like to have solid ground beneath your feet again? And real home cooking? No more salt pork or beans or that awful concoction they call pudding. Imagine the taste of fresh fruit and vegetables and cool spring water. Fancy the feel of sleeping in a real bed that doesn't sway."

Heather shivered. "And no more rats teeth in our biscuits. Or having them chew at our carpetbags."

Iris slowly raised her eyes to the minuscule flicker of a few far away lamps dimly pulsating from the scant amount of dwellings on the focusing shoreline. 'Shakes at best!' she thought. She could not help but compare that sparse skyline with the bustling grandeur of Boston. How could she not cry? Papa was dead and all that was promising had been dashed away one lovely Sunday afternoon, a little less than a year ago. She had been arranging a centerpiece of roses for the evening meal while excitedly anticipating a young attorney caller. Suddenly they were reduced to this. They might well have been three outcasts unjustly sentenced to some far off penal island. The thought caused her to give way to even more traumatic tears.

Belle's throat tightened. She could feel the vibration of Iris' sobs hammer deep inside her breast.

Heather reached out and softly touched upon her sister's quivering shoulder.

"Hush, Missy. Hush now." She soothed, choosing to call her by their father's special name.

Heather was barely two years the senior but she might well have been two decades older, tending to be solicitous to her own mother, who at first glance appeared as young as her daughters.

All three women were striking copies of one another, slim stately ladies, with the same coloring, so much the same, yet dissimilar in disposition. One immediately concluded that Missy was her father's favorite. Iris' cloying behavior continually prevailed upon Papa's softness. At fifteen she was still sitting on his lap babbling about some inconsequential happening.

From the time the girls were tots they were unmindfully introduced as, 'This is our little Missy, our baby. And this is Heather, the quite one.' And so it was. Yet it was Heather who most resembled Papa. Like him her nature was both gentle and introspective, and perhaps even sadly repressed. How she longed to draw upon her sister's boldness. Now Papa was gone along with an unrequited love. Still it had always been there, deep inside for his first born. Iris cried uncontrollably at the funeral, while Belle's quite strength succumbed to occasional soft tears. Heather remained as breathless as Papa's corpse conspicuously hidden away in a closed casket. Later she lapsed into a profound lethargy that took on the tone of illness. Though the trip to California was secretly planned by Papa months before his suicide, it was considered an ideal cure for Heather's malady. Sending the sick on long voyages was the mode of the day. Mostly, they would be as far as possible from the scandal of Colon Bradbury untimely death.

It seemed inconceivable that a man as straight forth and spiritual as Papa could actually take his own life. Yet he had booked passage for his three ladies on the Skylark and written his younger brother Johnny an endearing last letter months before his death.

Their lovely Georgian home with its furnishings was given to creditors. Colon's piano, which he prized, was first to be sold. Belle managed to salvage a few precious items, as her husband's favorite rocker, a French mantel clock, a set of silver, a few modest pieces of jewelry to be given to her daughters, and the sum of $382.26. She secretly nested the money away to be used for some future frivolity. Never did she dream that it would one day serve as the meager beginnings for a new life for the girls and herself. Lastly there was Colon's wedding band which hung around Belle's neck on a fine gold chain.

Miraculously it survived the roaring flames that had rendered him a charred shell of a body, a bizarre end for a man who had swallowed poison. When his remains were found in the counting room of the mercantile house where he worked, it was the gold band with its simple inscription that identified him.

There was something foretelling in finding Colon's ring gleaming on his finger even though he was burnt beyond recognition. It gave Belle the courage to go on with his last wishes.

In reality she knew no other course. Having been orphaned as a child and married at fifteen, her husband, who was years older, assumed the role of father as well as spouse. There was no choice but to dry her tears, and adhere to his final request. So California it was.

There was Iris' hysterics to contend with and Heather's withdrawal, both warranting added love and attention. Heather, who was already repressed, sank deeper into herself. Too often when Colon was alive, Belle had watched Heather's lovely face fall as Missy brazenly pushed her sister aside to claim their Papa's affection.

Having started with her father Iris soon learned to use her wiles on all men. Leaving Boston's promising social life was almost as devastating as Papa's death. Once on board she was shortly pleased to discover that fate had thrown her into a world of young, hungry-eyed men. To her dismay she soon learned that the crew was kept forever busy, save for Sundays when they appeared particularly fetching in their loose hip-hugging white ducks, their checkered shirts, black neckerchiefs and trampoline hats. Even worse they were forbidden to speak to the passengers.

Iris focused on the officers, most of whom were too old, unattractive, or married. Still, their solicitousness resuscitated her spirits. The Bradbury women were afforded the best quarters available and their meals were served at the Captain's table, at first, a succession of feasts. Once they hit the high seas the true impact of their voyage took place. The violent storms, the depletion of the ship's supplies, the voracious rats, the bugs and fleas, the unrelenting motion of the ship took their toll.

"All that for this!" Iris was overwhelmed with despair as she stood there on deck shivering, a chill whipping through her billowing garments down to her skin. She squinted disdainfully at the dark undulating hills that hovered over the tiny village of Yerba Buena, all the while sobbing.

"We've arrived at a nothing place at the end of the earth."

"A pastoral place."

A masculine voice magnified. It was Tobias Knight, the agent and owner of the vessel. In the ensuing months he had become Belle's ardent suitor.

"Believe me ladies, Yerba Buena will emerge quite beautiful by dusk once we've passed this fog bank."

Iris' eyes narrowed with contempt at the sight of Tobias. He was dressed in his California attire. Beneath a black broadcloth cloak, were black trousers with a red satin sash and a black gold trimmed short fitted jacket. He wore elaborate deerskin boots and a large rimmed black hat. It was a dashing contrast compared to the terry trousers and pea coats worn by the crew.

Belle sighed at the sight of him. Iris was seething. Tobias and her mother were obviously finding it difficult not to touch. From the moment they met something electrifying happened between them. They were close in age and each had recently lost their spouse. This was the coincidence, not the common bond. To Iris it was disgusting that her own mother while in mourning black could be so easily charmed by this brash good looking stranger.

Tobias' wife was ill most of their marriage and Colon Bradbury, though kind and responsible, did not bring out the spontaneity and giddiness that Belle failed to show even in girlhood. With Tobias she had secretly shared a demijohn of brandy, danced to the surgeon's fiddle, and sang nightly duets in the stateroom. How easy it was to fall madly in love with this Yankee Californian. She experienced not only an elatedness of life but also an unbearable desire to make love to him. The very thought was at times too overwhelming to endure. There were two daughters and one year's mourning to be honored. She wondered why any of it mattered, for Colon's face and the memory of their lives together became less and less a reality. Ironically, it was he who had booked them on the Skylark. Belle did not know whether to feel guilty or guided.

One thing was certain. She knew that she and her daughters were safe with Tobias'. Her eyes did not once leave his face as he endeavored to pacify the recalcitrant Iris.

Often throughout their voyage he described the magnificent beauty of sailing into the Bay of San Francisco. So here they were. His rhapsodizing somehow failed to mention the possibility of them heading into an impenetrable fog. He spoke of great verdant headlands flanking a magnificent bay. With deer and elk standing majestically on the precipices, of woodlands and splashing falls, of sparkling white gulls and geese and egrets circling a cerulean sky, of barking seals suddenly emerging out of the waters to greet them.

'A pastoral place indeed!' Iris scoffed to herself. 'Liar.' They were immersed in the deepest, coldest fog imaginable. How could he stand grinning, seemingly oblivious to the total grayness of the day, of the chilling moisture that permeated their very bones? What she failed to realize that unlike her, that interminable voyage around the Horn had brought Tobias home, not away. To top it all, he had Mamma right were he wanted her, in his house, in his own bed. Iris was scowling so deeply that he could almost read her thoughts.

"Truly my dear, when it clears the Bay of San Francisco and the country that surrounds it are incredibly beautiful. I grant Yerba Buena may be a bit modest but as soon as word gets out that a Yankee ship is in the harbor, the whole place will come alive with the Rancheros, both men and women on their magnificent horses." He smiled. "The sand hills will be an endless mass of rumbling carretas, the California ox-cart."

Iris shrugged. She had become indifferent to the use of Spanish, which had first come as a shock to the ears. The carretas were wooden carts drawn by yoked oxen. It's two huge wheels were solid wood hewn from a tree trunk, a foot thick at the rim with a hole for an axle. They would be brim full with hides and tallow, the California money.

He continued to enthuse. "Our launches will be sent to all the Ranchos around the bay. The Skylark will suddenly become busier than any Boston store."

Surprisingly the Spanish Californians would appear en masse, arriving from all directions, on horseback and by launch. The Dons would be extravagantly attired, along with their elegant wives and handsome brood of sons and daughters.

"It should please you to know," smiled Tobias. "That aside from selling our wares, the Skylark will be hosting a fiesta, right here aboard ship. Nowhere will you meet a happier more hospitable race of people."

"We'll see." Iris shrugged pretending indifference.

Already they had previewed the large store-room with its show cases and scales, with its drawers brimming with rolls of rich fabric and laces, with embroidered shawls from Canton and ivory and tortoise shell combs for the hair. There was china and crystal, silver utensils and the finest of furnishings, a piano and pool table included. There were seeds and spices, tools, gunpowder, wooden spoke wheels, window glass, and much more.

Tobias was generous in bestowing Belle and the girl's gifts from the showroom. Becoming lost in that maze of merchandise was a wonderfully exhilarating respite from the boredom of being at sea. The exquisite embroidered shawls, rolls of fine fabric, French perfume, and hand mirrors were but a few of the items that would be packed away with them upon departing the Skylark. For all his generosity Tobias could not win over Iris, while Heather was immediately charmed by this magnanimous gentleman, with sparkling gray eyes and a trim mustache. Inadvertently he helped sublimate the loss of her Papa; being at times more attuned to her needs. Enthusiastically he answered all her questions about the country of California. Besides, he had made her mother happy again. To no longer see Mamma morn, lifted her from her own despair.

Tobias continued. "You can be certain, that our lamps have already been sighted from the Presidio. It's an Old Spanish fort that sits on the first bluff entering the gate."

"In this soup?" mumbled Iris.

As Tobias surmised, the few inhabitants of Yerba Buena Cove had gathered and were already scurrying down the sand hills through the marshes that rimmed the crescent beach. The profusion of wildlife scuttling through the thick brush and towering fronds or fluttering overhead in mass flight seemed happily conjoined with the exhilaration ashore. As the Skylark moved deeper into the Bay the hills and shoreline took on clarity. Beacons were excitedly waving in the near distance.

Iris sighed, muttering. "Looks far less civilized a place than Valparaíso or Panama."

Belle retorted, seeming to scold. "Just think, you know such places exist."

Tobias deliberately interrupted. "The pilot is in the long boat ready to take you ladies ashore."

Heather hesitated, her eyes anxiously scanning the ship fore and aft.

"You're looking for Will, aren't you?" Iris slyly remarked.

She was referring to the young man they had picked up in Panama, Wilhelm Medina an American who became ill and disheartened waiting long weeks for a ship to arrive on its way to California. Once on board, the whole of his time was spent in his cabin. His thin body was curled up like a fetus in a lower berth, fighting the ravages of jungle fever, overexposure and near starvation.

At first they took him for a native, barefoot and straw hatted, his olive skin deeply tanned from weeks of living outdoors, sleeping on the beach or huddled in some church ruin. He subsisted on fruit, half raw pigeons and fish, or whatever he could find when he was not too sick to swallow.

The first sight of the Skylark found him shaking uncontrollably and choked with tears. Once on board he totally succumbed to his illness, as though it were at last safe to be sick. Through the murky depth of his delirium a woman's hand tenderly touched him, wiping his face and brow with a cool cloth and feeding him small sips of soup and liquids. No one knew, not even the ship's surgeon.

Iris was quick to catch the look of concern on her sister's face whenever the young man's name was mentioned. There were identifying papers in his carpetbag, plus a gold timepiece on a heavy gold chain. On the inside was the inscription, 'To Will, with all my love always, mother.' There was another timepiece similarly inscribed, but to 'Gus', causing them to immediately conclude that there was a brother who possibly did not survive.

Iris watched Heather stand by ashen upon first seeing them carry the young man aboard. He looked ragged and emaciated and so terribly alone. For an instant in passing his black eyes raised and seemed to blankly stare into Heather's face. She did not know if he was fully conscious of her presence for he was quickly swept away, leaving her aghast.

Somewhere in the interim she had managed to be at his side, ministering to him, gently comforting his feverish ramblings. And no one knew. Least of all, Will.

Chapter 2

Belle could hear the throb of naked feet tearing through the darkness toward her room. The door ripped open then slammed tightly shut behind the continuing scamper of frenzied steps. Iris pounced beneath the covers and instantly adhered herself to her mother's side. Heather was fast behind her, causing the large brass bed to reverberate. Belle felt the tangle of arms about her waist and the shock of ice cold feet. There was a conjoining of shudders as both girls reacted to the unrelenting howl of a wild animal close outside, a coyote stalking the house for a second night in a row. The rapacious predator, though sounding fierce with his baying and scratching, could be well sated by devouring one of Tobias' securely cooped hens.

"My God, Mamma" Iris cried from beneath the comforter. "You've brought us half way around the world to a wilderness."

"Hush Missy," Belle soothed. "We're perfectly safe inside."

"Where in creation is your precious Don Toby?" Iris mockingly used the name affectionately bestowed Tobias Knight in the California tradition.

"You know very well where he is," Heather countered. "He has promised to bring us our Uncle Johnny, and he will."

"If he's such a big man in these parts" Iris sarcastically emphasized, "why didn't he send someone else to fetch him, his Indian servant, for instance? I'd wager that savage is right outside our bedroom door listening to every shivering detail, actually relishing our plight."

Both mother and sister simultaneously hushed her. The savage Iris' alluded to was Miguel Pedro. His Spanish Christian name was given to him by the Franciscan Padres at the Mission San Francisco de Assisi; fondly referred to as Delores. He was born and raised at the Mission. Most of his thirty-three years were spent in prayer, rigorous labor, inflexible discipline and absolute segregation of the sexes. At no time did his life ever resemble that of his Ohlone ancestry, that long ago free-spirited tribes of hunters and gatherers that inhabited this very shoreline by the Bay. Though he spoke the Castilian Spanish of the fathers, his comprehension of English was enough for him to be taken aback by this milk-skinned girl's cruel condemnation of him. After all, they had come by way of Don Toby whom he deeply honored. Tobias had entrusted the three women unto his care so that the dashing in the night and the gasps of fright automatically sent him scurrying from his cot. He indeed stood listening outside their bedroom door, but only out of concern, not contempt.

"Your Don Toby abandoned us the moment we set foot on land." Iris insisted on raving." Just rode off and left us in this desolate place with no one or nothing to do!"

Heather scolded. "That's not true. We've been greeted by practically every member in this cove settlement."

"You mean those few dumpy looking ladies and their scraggly off springs and spouses?"

"That's cruel of you. We're strangers here and these people have taken it upon themselves to make us feel welcome by bringing food and gifts to our door. Things we might not have enjoyed aboard ship. What do you expect, anyway? We're certainly not up to socializing being so wasted from our voyage, and as thin as paper."

"Socializing!" Iris squealed. "Are you blind? There's nothing out there to be social for!"

"What do you want from these people anyway, Iris," Heather angrily added, "isn't their goodness enough for you? Why can't you get it through your head that Tobias did not just leave us like that at all? He saw to it that we were made welcome and comfortable. In fact, his going after Uncle Johnny could very well have waited until he got his land legs. But no, he was thinking of us first, as always."

"Us! He's thinking of bedding Mamma, that's what!"

"Iris!" Belle sat straight up in bed. "I forbid such a thought!"

"You can't forbid me my thoughts, Mamma. I don't care if he ingratiates himself in a thousand ways. His desires aren't any less primitive than those of Miguel Pedro with his blue-eyed mestiza daughter."

"Stop it!" Belle hissed. "What has gotten into you? You not only debase Tobias' character, but you're intent on having yourself heard by that gentle caring Indian, who happens to love his daughter very much."

"Why not? He can boast to the world that he bedded a white woman. Probably some demented back woods creature. And what happened to her anyway?"

"The girl's mother is dead." Belle's anger came forth in harsh whispers. "As for your business, which it isn't, they were married! In church."

"And this you know already?" Iris was sarcastic. "Must have heard it during one of your cozy interludes on board ship."

"Es—Estrellita," Belle had difficulty enunciating the name, "is a sweet, gentle young woman, whom Tobias and his late wife Hannah treated as one of their own. She and Miguel Pedro have been a part of this household for eight years, since the girl was six. And you Missy, are in no way going to hurt them with your cruel sarcasm. Remember it is you, not she, who is the guest in this house. Just be grateful we have a home at this time."

The caustic words has ceased as well as the howling animal outside. Probably off somewhere digesting his prey.

There was a soft skirmishing from behind the door, a deliberate movement from the stealthy Miguel Pedro who heard every word. He had been hurt before, many times, even whipped as a youth at the Mission. Because of Tobias, he and his daughter had fared better than most Indians. Mexican rule had decreed that the Missions be secularized. The neophytes were scattered. All they had known was despoiled. Suddenly there was no direction, no place to return that was again home. Some joined old tribes; most became field hands or servants in the many outlining Ranchos.

For a while Miguel Pedro and his tiny mestiza daughter lived on the Martinez Rancho across the Bay. By some miracle, Tobias Knight heard of them and brought them to live with him, first in Carmelo, close to Monterey, then in this house, which he built for his bride. Here in Yerba Buena Cove, on the shores of his ancestry, Miguel Pedro and his little daughter at last found a life.

The so-called insensitive savage would repress the tears and pain deep inside himself, but he would be quick to cut out that wicked white girl's tongue if she dare hurt his Estrellita, his Little Star.

Suddenly Iris sat up screaming. Something shook at the bed, unsettling Belle and Heather as well.

"It's only one of the cats." Belle pacified, her heart yet palpitating. "Now, go to sleep."

Tobias proudly owned six cats. The gray-eyed calico was patting a place at the foot of the bed. Cats were considered a luxury in this rat-infested hamlet. Those fat beady-eyed rodents were everywhere, more excessive at dusk as they ran havoc through dusty often time muddy streets.

"And you were so relieved to get off the Skylark!" Sneered Iris to her sister, both understanding the connotation of that remark.

Heather reached down and gently gathered the purring creature in her arms. "I don't care. I'm still happy to be off the ship and in this house, safe and warm. It is much more than we expected to find. Papa's rocker and our mantel clock would look pretty silly in a tent."

Of the twenty or so structures in Yerba Buena, Tobias Knight's house was considered quite elegant with its hillside view of the Bay of San Francisco. The wooden dwelling with its Spanish style red shingled roof opened unto a large center hall surrounded by a parlor, a dinning room, four bedrooms and a large cook house in back. All were furnished with superb pieces shipped around Cape Horn. It was a lovely house that somehow still permeated with the presence of its demised lady. The china cabinet filled with porcelain and crystal, the silver, the lace curtains, gilt framed paintings, the needlepoint pillows carefully placed on the settee, an embroidered shawl draped over the spinet and a family bible all typified the late Hannah Knight.

There was her flower garden colorfully contrasted against the sand hills and chaparral. She had brought the seeds with her on her first voyage from her New England home. The profusion of hardy geranium and fragile faced pansies were obviously her favorites. There were lilacs, nasturtium, hollyhocks, sweet peas and wild red roses trellised to shelter a shrine of the Madonna.

Sad, sweet little touches prevailed everywhere, but none so heart rendering as the daguerreotype of a tiny baby girl in a coffin. Tobias whisked it into a drawer shortly after their arrival, but not soon enough. Nonetheless, Belle knew. He had related the heartache of losing a child. And of his wife's utter despair that caused her to be even more withdrawn, though she undoubtedly loved him.

Here in Hannah's house, Belle began to perceive Toby from a different perspective. He too had suffered, as she, but on board the Skylark there was not the reality of tangible things, of him having lived with a woman who was his wife. Yet this is where he choose to bring Belle and the girls, what he had to offer.

Belle found herself torn with questions, from the profound to the foolish. Where would she put Colon's rocker? There was already a mantel clock and candlesticks finer than hers. What most disturbed her was the realization that Toby had given her his and Hannah's bed. It was one of the largest and loveliest rooms in the house. Belle was not aware how deeply he had agonized over the decision.

Upon their arrival, Miguel Pedro was immediately instructed to remove Tobias' things to a smaller rear bedroom. The girls shared quarters close to hers while Estrellita slept in a pretty little room across the hall. Miguel Pedro and Kane-Paul, the Kanaka cook shared a bunkhouse a few yards from the main structure.

"I'm with Heather," Belle emphasized "grateful to be off the ship and in a warm safe house. Count your blessings. Now, off to bed."

"May we sleep here with you Mamma?" In the dark Heather sounded like a little girl again. She was yet cuddling the purring cat.

"Of course you may. God bless you girls."

Tenderly she kissed Heather's forehead. Belle turned to Iris only to find she had moved over to the edge of the bed, her back defiantly toward them, the comforter over her head.

"Goodnight, Missy" Belle whispered.

"Goodnight Missy." Heather followed.

Iris did not answer. They finally dozed off only to be awakened by a light rapping at the door, followed by an even more gentle voice. It was the girl, Estrellita.

"Doña Belle."

Their eyes opened to night commencing to defuse into dawn. The timid voice persisted.

"Doña Belle. They are almost here."

Estrellita could hear a flurry of movements and voices. The door cracked open. The small oil lamp in the girl's hands immediately illumined Belle's face.

"We need a few more moments to make ourselves ready."

"There is time, madam." The girl vacilated between English and Spanish speaking both languages, not only fluently but surprisingly literate. "One of the vaqueros has ridden ahead to announce their arrival."

"Vaq—?"

"One of the herdsmen—cowmen. She corrected herself fumbling with the translation. "I must light the fire and get out the aguardiente. Those are the instructions."

"What is that?"

"Aguardiente. A native whiskey. Muy Fuerte. Very strong, like firewater."

Belle shook her head. "At this hour of the morning?"

Initially aguardiente was distilled at the Missions, having come by way of Spain and Mexico. The crystal clear concoction was made of grapes, pears, apples, and doubly distilled. When burnt sugar was added, it became a translucent yellow, and fiercely strong, the padres having given it an added spiritedness. The words agua, water and ardiente meaning burning, is not to be confused with the later day aquadiente, a Gold Rush misnomer.

Belle smiled. "Well, It is a celebration. Thank you."

The Bradbury women were washed, dressed, coifed and totally unnerved as they took turns pacing the parlor, warming their hands by the fire and primping before the oval mirror above the mantle. Their outfits might be considered a bit ostentatious for a dawn meeting, but they had not traveled fifteen hundred miles around two coastlines to meet Uncle Johnny attired in their night gowns.

Heather stepped to the windows and drew back the curtains. That single gesture was the unveiling of magnificence. Tobias' hillside house afforded them a spectacular view of the bay, arching from west to east, spilling into the northeast and south. The expansive stillness of the dark bay shimmered with crimson and gold shafts of sunrise. The headlands far to the left faded into the mammoth Pacific. Tamal Pais, the great looming mountain on the North side of the bay, heightened into shades of ebony and deep purple, a swath of mist wafting at its shoreline. A small verdant island, not far from the entrance of the bay, was profuse with pelicans. The many lagoons and shadowy marshes glistened like quicksilver, as did the arcane group of shell mounds on the shore, remnants of another age. The stillness of the sand dunes appeared as velvet, diminishing westward to a long stretch of ocean beach that met with the Pacific. The dimming sky was a cobalt blue pierced by the pulsating brilliance of the last lone star. Myriad of birds silhouetted in patterns of precision flight.

"It's breathtaking!" Heather sighed. Her voice faded to a whisper. "It's like no other place I've ever seen. How I wish I could paint. Someone should capture it on canvass, as it is now."

Iris screeched. "Listen to her Mamma! Uncle Johnny is going to be here any second and she's painting pictures!"

Heather turned away from the windows. "Really Iris, you're so insensitive at times."

"Now, now girls." Belle interceded. "Let's sit down and calm ourselves. Fretting is not getting them here any sooner."

Estrellita stood before them, seeming to have materialized from a flitting shadow; at times part apparition, for she was there and gone without a stir. Her slight frame was both fragile and tawny, the barest hint of breasts commencing to cover the leanness. Her deep amber-gold skin and black waist length hair were a stunning contrast to her liquid blue eyes. Their large almond shape could stare unblinkingly, then again the lids might meekly fall. The cheekbones swept tightly to the temples. The fine high-bridged nose was slightly aquiline, and the mouth was a full perfectly etched bow. Her whisper of a voice commanded rapt attention to be heard.

At the moment she stood conspicuously alone. Miguel Pedro's absence managed to compound their shame. It caused them to impart an added geniality toward the girl.

"May I make you some chocolate?" Estrellita's eyes scanned the three women, seeming to address them all at once.

"Yes. No. Not now," came simultaneous answers.

"Did you say 'yes' Señorita Iris?"

Iris squirmed uncomfortably.

"That's all right dear." Belle took the initiative. "We'll wait. Thank you."

The girl was swiftly gone, unaware how unnerving her presence had been. Belle's eyes restlessly raised to the chandelier. The six crystal-shaded flames quivered synchronously, causing shadowed configurations on the wall and ceiling, confusing fire with glints of sunlight. She could not know that Estrellita had affectionately continued Hannah's homecoming ritual to Tobias. The chandelier had made its way around The Horn in one of the most tumultuous storms imaginable, tragically losing a young mate. Miraculously, it arrived at Yerba Buena unscathed, but for a few loosened nails in its securely packed case. To Hannah this symbolized something wonderfully auspicious. 'Come back to me safely now,' she would say with each parting kiss. Always he did, to the welcoming brilliance of those flaming crystals and to her. Yet, for all the waiting, for all those lone nightly prayers of safekeeping it was she who died. And another woman was now here in her place, waiting for him, mesmerized by those flames and not fully understanding why. Shortly Tobias would be home again and Belle could barely contain her feelings of elation. The last few days were the first time they had been parted since they met.

"I hear horses!" Iris jumped to her feet.

"Let's be calm now," Belle anxiously advised. "And behave like the ladies that we are. Not three little faces at the window."

Iris sat at the edge of the settee next to Heather, both seeming to wring their hands. Belle endeavored to appear composed, standing primly in the center of the room.

There was the sudden sound of men's voices, the heaviness of booted steps together with the metallic clink of spurs.

Miguel Pedro passed the parlor without giving them a glance. His gaze was focused upon the door. He opened it onto a tumult of masculine greetings and laughter. They could hear Tobias endearingly hail him as Miguelito. Amid the din there was another strangely familiar voice.

Tobias was first to enter, fatigued but smiling broadly. His eyes immediately met Belle's. There was a subtle exchange of tenderness.

"Ladies, I would like to present Don Juan Ricardo Bradbury, your Uncle Johnny!"

Iris and Heather leaped up in unison to stand side by side with Belle, three pairs of eyes transfixed upon the doorway. Instantly they were taken aback by the incongruity of what they expected to appear as Papa's younger brother.

Uncle Johnny dramatically emerged, a towering frame of a man, flamboyantly garbed in some kind of swashbuckling attire. A black broadcloth serape, heavily trimmed in red velvet and gold fringe capped about his shoulders. His slightly above the knee leather breeches were slit at the outer seams with a row of gold filigree. His botas, the red embroidered leggings of fine deer skin were thrice wound with a silken cord that terminated in swinging gold tassels. Inlaid gold and sliver spurs with huge glistening rowels were attached to two-toned red and black boots with elaborate gold toe pieces. This spectacular outfit was topped by a tan, deep rimmed, round crowned vicuna hat held on by a red ribbon tied in a flounce at the side of his neck. He at once loosened the red sash and removed his hat. His long light hair was drawn back in a queue, tied with a red ribbon. With a flourishing sweep of his sombrero he bowed. In those few quick moments they were not only introduced to Uncle Johnny but to the lavish style of the Californio. He then posed erect, a wondrous smile upon that bronzed face with its crinkling light eyes. They could not repress their gasps of astonishment. It was Papa! A younger, more handsome, taller, broader version of Colon Bradbury. It was Papa's familiar voice that had echoed from the hall, yet more so, for it was both booming and lyrical.

Iris could no longer contain the enormity of her emotion. She ran crying into his arms. Heather and Belle followed. He managed to hold them, all three in his bounteous embrace. He could feel the reverberation of their tears and laughter against his broad chest. Here were his brother's children grown, his brother's wife, all beautiful ladies, and kin.

"My cup runneth over!" He roared with laughter. "And my thirst. Bring out the aguardiente!"

*

Chapter 3

Tobias had barely secured the cabin door when he whirled Belle into his arms. Their bodies were at once hotly adhered to one another, their mouths ravenously kissing.

"My God Toby, what are we doing?" she breathlessly whispered, her palms upon his chest halting their passion. "We'll surely be missed."

"I don't care. I just have to be alone with you. There's no privacy in my own house. I never wanted to get back to anyone so badly in my life."

'What about Hannah?' she thought. Her mouth tightened, repressing the contentiousness of such a question. How could she think such a thing, now of all times? Suddenly she wondered if he had made love to his wife right here in this cabin. It was difficult enough living in Hannah's house, her wraith-like presence constantly hanging over them, a house replete with loving touches, and love. Belle shuddered. At the same time she could not help but chide her own foolishness. Hadn't Toby removed all of his wife's personal affects, down to the small miniature he had fondly carried in his vest pocket? Belle saw it the second week at sea; that lovely picture of Hannah and Tobias on their wedding day. She recalled the utter sweetness of that child face with its wide set eyes and timorous smile, all frothy white and angelic. Yet wasn't she once such a bride, equally as young and demure? In truth, it was the sight of Tobias that bothered her the most. The proud, demonstrative, incredibly handsome groom that he was, his arm affectionately embracing his bride. What a contrast to her own wedding picture, a miniature oil painting. She sat there looking so frightfully young and meek while Colon stood rigidly beside her, a somber expression upon his face, his hand paternally touching her shoulder. She had to remind herself of the devotion that had existed between them, and of the two beautiful daughters that were the sweet outcome of a dull dutiful union. Poor Hannah had given Toby a baby girl that died in infancy. Now she too was gone. It was neither of their faults that their spouses were dead, or that they had fallen madly in love with one another. Why doubt destiny? It was the present that mattered. A wonderfully wild, tender moment not to be questioned or wasted. The realization impelled her to throw her arms about his neck and impetuously kiss his face, his eyelids, his brow and languish upon his mouth, inciting both their passions. They might well have torn off their clothes to make love that very instant. But the uproar of revelry prevailed upon them. Laughing, chattering voices merged with the brassy music. Guitars, fiddles, flutes and cymbals accompanied the stomp of dancing feet. That, plus the incessant shuffle of steps and voices outside the cabin door were too distracting to dismiss.

As Tobias promised, the Skylark was brimming with a multitude of paisanos from all the outlining Ranchos. Proudly he had led Belle through a maze of excited faces, not only partying, but also buying and bartering, heaping their precious purchases on separate piles on the deck. It was a joyful kind of mayhem that culminated in the customary fiesta, in bounteous amounts of food drink and dance. And here they were closeted like two lustful youngsters in Tobias' cabin. For all their passion, they instantly tore apart as Don Toby's name was called out, an unrelenting pound upon the door. They held their breath. Considering all that was happening above and below deck, the owner and agent of the Skylark was nowhere to be found. Finally the knocking ceased. Belle was first to speak.

"See how important you are? And impetuous." He drew her firmly back into his arms.

"I don't want to go out there. Not yet."

"Nor I."

"Next Port of Call, you're coming with me." His kisses were upon her ear even as he spoke.

Since each Rancho and Mission had its own landing called an embarcadero, the Skylark would be making stops around the Bay and along the coast.

Ecstatically she sighed. "I don't remember ever in my life feeling like this. I haven't stopped grinning since you walked in that night with Johnny. He was wonderful to behold. But you, my darling, made my heart stop. Here I am, the mother of two grown daughters, still wearing my black widow's frock and shamelessly in love with another man."

"What's shameful is the idea of your sweet sensuality never having been savored. What a waste. Colon was a such fool."

The mention of her dead husband's name caused her to slightly stiffen. Tobias felt it and gently raised both her hands to his lips and kissed them.

"Whatever. I'm still compelled to dress in black," she meekly reminded him.

"Let's rid you of that damn dress then, right now."

She pulled back a bit. "Just because I had the nerve to wear this magnificent necklace and earrings you've given me, doesn't mean I'm no longer in mourning."

Cupping her face with both his hands he kissed her as passionately as possible. She was yet sighing when he released her.

"Take it from me you are no longer in mourning. And you have every right in the world to wear beautiful jewels."

She could feel the palpitation of her own heart as her fingers lightly caressed the diamond and sapphire necklace. It brilliantly contrasted against her high collared black dress. Matching pendant earrings dangled from her lobes grazing the sides of her slender white neck. Her blue eyes seemed more luminous in the presence of sapphires.

"Where did you find such a treasure? Tell me a pirate ship."

"Will a Manila Galleon do? I knew instinctively that I was buying it for someone I would someday love. I do love you Belle. And I want to make love to you so badly I ache."

For an instant they were caught in each other's gaze. Belle had to lower her lids. She too was overwhelmed with desire. It was obviously there in her eyes for him to see. Still he felt it in the trembling of her body aligned against his own. While at sea, whenever possible to escape Iris' prying eyes, they would slip away to his cabin, only to find themselves weakly withdrawing in the heat of passion. They had found one another. Wasn't that enough? Why doubt providence, or conjure the foreboding of both their demised mates? Toby was hers and she his, here, now.

But the tumultuous sounds of the fiesta seared right through the heavy paneled walls of the cabin. At times the voices outside their locked door were so near that conversations were alarmingly audible. It was not conducive to making love. Not for that crucially tender first time.

"I want you," he whispered, "but not like this. I want it to be perfect, Belle, and it will, I promise."

As always the sensual look in his eyes caused her to blush like a girl. The thought of making love to Toby left her shaken. How could she not compare him to Colon? Her poor dead husband paled pathetically next to Tobias.

That first night with Colon was devastating. She was a virgin of fifteen, trying her utmost to be the caring dutiful wife. She had felt excruciating pain and embarrassment. Meekly he apologized for his clumsiness. He never improved.

This she had confided to Tobias. It was not an uncommon occurrence, in this mid nineteen hundreds, for a wife to passively lay there as her husband quickly satiated himself. It was not going to happen that way with them. And least of all in this cabin on a hard narrow bunk with the uproar of the fiesta. His hold softened, leaving her free to step away. She straightened her black muslin skirt about her legs as she sat herself on the small settee that fronted his desk. He was at once on the floor beside her, his hands fondling her thighs.

Lovingly she touched upon the necklace. "You're such a treasure hunter." She jested. "I can't believe all the things you manage to accumulate from all over the world."

He laughed. "I admit to being obsessive about finding things and putting them together with appreciative people."

"You're the one who is appreciated. I saw it today in all those smiles and embraces. They love you, even if you do make a pretty profit at times," she teased.

"No matter how fierce The Horn, or how boring the voyage, I never cease to feel a thrill upon sailing into the Bay of San Francisco. As you can see, the crowds seem to pour in out of nowhere. It's hard to believe, but after our fiesta, the Captain and crew will be feted ashore for days on end. First there's work to be done. A huge amount of hides and tallow are piled high on launches, waiting to be brought aboard and stowed. That is a story within itself."

For all their wealth in land and cattle, there was a time when the Californios had windows without glass, earthen floors and crude furnishings. Merchandise long promised from Spain and San Blas never arrived. The enterprising Yankees were quick to take up the slack, at an enormous profit. The California hides, once back East were made into leather goods, then shipped back to be resold to the paisanos. So many Boston vessels come around the Horn that Boston was often referred to as the United States.

"It's amazing," added Belle, "how everything is just as you described it at sea, but more so."

She shook her head in disbelief recalling her awakening that early morning. The sights and sounds of that dusty little village of Yerba Buena suddenly became metamorphosed into something resembling a giant pageant. Like a small army rising out of the sand hills, the Rancheros emerged in full regalia, the accruements of their magnificent horses equaling their own flamboyance. Jewel-like reflections bounced rampantly upon the horizon; the glint of gold and silver from the saddles and bridles, but particularly from the huge shimmering rowels upon the masses of spurs. Following behind were the great rumble of the carretas, with the unremitting squeak of their large wooden wheels. Hoards of Indian drivers bellowed at the oxen and prodded them with long poles. Many more walked along side, prodding and screaming.

All of this activity merged with the sound of singing and laughing, and the barking of countless dog. The pale blue sky was dark with birds, squealing and chirping as they soared over the mixture of mirth and mayhem.

"Never in my wildest dreams," Belle enthused, "did I ever imagine such a place existed. And all these happy resplendently dressed people, emerging from all around the bay, to join each other like one mammoth family."

"That's about it Belle. Almost everyone here is related or interrelated. I've traveled the world over, but never have I experienced what I've found here, in this country of California. There is a love for family and life itself that dominates all else. The 'mañana' that you will constantly hear, is not procrastination, but a real satisfaction with today. And you my darling Belle, you and your daughters shall at once know the joy of being a part of a huge family."

She realized that he was referring to Johnny, now Don Juan Ricardo, and the trip they would soon take to his Rancho and the family that awaited them.

"You'd better help me with my Spanish. The only thing that comes to mind is carreta, which has got to be the noisiest most primitive vehicles ever conceived."

"Carreta?" He teased. "Well it's a beginning. By the way, the hides and tallow they carry will bring about a three hundred percent return. That's a damn good profit!" His eyes boyishly beamed. "And then I can go buying all or again. The ladies particularly like the embroidered shawls and will pay as high as sixty dollars for a tortoise comb. An unmerciful price, but that's a long time around the Horn. Truly, I try not to be as avarice as some. Still these people are so hungry for our Yankee wares, that they'll buy almost anything." He chuckled "There was even a time when bootlegged books were the precious item."

"Bootlegged books? Come now."

"I swear Belle, it's true. The paradox of the Spanish Californian was that for all his wealth, pride, and elegantly spoken Spanish, few could read. Those literate few who could, were compelled to hide their books. General Mariano Vallejo had thousands of volumes stashed away. That was before secularization, when the Mission Padres had complete control. They were against any literature that did not conform to their religious teachings. Vallejo was excommunicated at least twice, while still a young man." He laughed. "Well, the Missions system is over. I wager Vallejo is still reading away in his Swiss House in Sanoma. Whatever education does exist has been handed down from family to family. In truth, there are no professions to be used, less learned. They have herds of cattle and horses. These are men who excel on horseback and out of doors. Life is simple, and without stress."

Ironically, there were still some Mission Indians, as Miguel Pedro who was more lettered than the so-called blue bloods. It was common for Tobias to find an X at the end of a contract. Although a man's word as well as his handshake, were good enough.

"She had to laugh. "I've come to believe that anything is possible in California. For starters, we met and fell in love on our voyage here. What's more miraculous than that?"

His mouth was fast upon hers, longer and more passionate than before. For a Yankee he was akin to the hot-blooded Latin.

The din from the fiesta was all about them. There was dancing on the decks and in the stateroom. The cabin and everything in it seem to be reverberating. The hanging oil lamp was swaying. They might well be out to sea. Somehow they would have to slip out of there unnoticed and join in the fiesta. And they had not even made love. The compulsion was to stay wrapped in each other's arms. Since their arrival in Yerba Buena, Tobias had become even more amorous. How much longer could they wait? Lovingly he studied her face. That soft pale skin was so often flushed by his sensuality. Years of being married to Colin had conditioned her to being reticent in their intimacy. The concealing of naked bodies beneath a gown, robe or cover was customary in their relationship.

"I guess we'd better join the party," Belle reluctantly offered. Her hand grazed the exquisite necklace shimmering above her bosom. "I feel so frivolous."

Belle gave a strained little laugh. What she in fact felt was guilt. Having touched upon the necklace, her hand also brushed Colon's wedding band still worn on a fine gold chain beneath the heavy smocking of her neckline. Her own plain band had been switched to her right hand, uncomfortably so, adding to the dilemma of having this wonderful man enter her life.

"Be frivolous," he insisted. "This is California, my dear. Women are not afraid to be themselves. They dress as they please. Not to mention the men, whose style would stun a Bostonian in his tracks. There is no one to decree fashion. It just flourishes. In the States I wear my black frock and tall silk hat, come around the Horn and instantly I am Don Toby."

Her hands tightened on his. "Why me, Tobias? When you can very well have some exotic young Señorita. I saw so many beautiful women out there today eyeing you. Why me, the mother of two grown daughters?"

"Fate, the kinship between two Yankees, electricity. All that truly matters, and more."

She leaned over and kissed his hands again and again. "I want so to make you happy." Her eyes watered.

"You have."

"I feel like such a misfit. All those gorgeous women with their dark hair, wearing red satin shoes and spangled gowns, in the afternoon yet. They dance so provocatively, that I had to turn my eyes away, New England prude that I am. The girls and I must look pretty dull in our Boston best. I'm glad they decided not to wear their black frocks. Did you notice they wore the shawls you gave them and those high combs?"

"Don't worry, they're beautiful enough to hold their own. Just like their mother."

Tenderly he reached out and stroked her plaited hair. "I would love to see your hair loose about your face and shoulders, a pink Castilian rose behind your ear. You shall have two dozen in your wedding bouquet."

"What are you saying?"

"I want to marry you as soon as possible. Captain Honeywell is ready to perform the service as soon as we say. We can't go on this way Belle. I'm ready to move you aboard ship to get you alone."

"It's still too soon. Not a year."

"Women marry soon here, Belle. They're not to be left alone and unloved, but cherished. Not that our ladies are incapable of taking care of themselves, because they are. As you will well see when you meet Johnny's wife, Doña Rufina. She rides a horse like the wind and can handle a reata and bullwhip as well as her brothers. Still, she looks as fragile as porcelain. The California woman, if not born a Don's daughter, has made her way overland or around The Horn facing the same dangers as a man. Just as you did, Belle. I watched you aboard ship through the worst of times. You came through like an old salt." He smiled. "A seductive old salt, at that." He was kissing her neck, sending shivers up her spine.

"Weren't we suppose to be going back to the party?" Her words were quickly muffled by his kisses, his hands cradling her breasts, tenderly toying with her nipples now grown erect.

"Marry me, Belle. Marry me, so we can make wanton love every damn day of our lives, wherever and whenever."

Relentlessly he kissed her upon the throat and neck. Though equally overwhelmed with passion, Belle managed to pull out of his arms to soberly study his face.

"There is nothing I want more than to be your wife. My God, our whole meeting was a miracle. But there are considerations."

"Aside from this widow nonsense, if you mean me leaving you to go back to sea? No, we're not going to be separated. And you're not going to be one of those wives who accompany their husband aboard ship. A woman needs to be settled in a home with her possessions, with family and friends, and especially her husband. I'm seriously thinking of changing my life style." He paused, sadly recalling the long separations and the loneliness that finally depleted Hannah's spirit. "I promise you, Belle, once we wed, we'll never sleep apart."

"But you love what you do. You just said so."

"Not more than a life with you. We'll work it out, Belle. Trust me."

"It's too soon. Even brother Johnny, who is about as unconventional as they come, advised me to fullfil my mourning period. How much longer can it be? Three months?" She smiled at the mention of her brother-in-law. "That scoundrel, he immediately caught on about us."

"Caught on?" Tobias bellowed. "What did it take? I could barely keep your name out of the conversation as we rode that long distance from his Santa Clara Rancho. I understand his concern, you being his brother's widow and the mother of his nieces. Yet he knows right well the kind of man I am, reputable and caring. And I'll make a damn good father to the girls."

"The girls." She sounded exasperated. "That's another problem to be faced. Heather absolutely adores you, but Iris—" the sentence went unfinished.

"Don't worry about Iris. She'll come around. Right now she's in her glory out there surrounded by dozens of available young men, dark eyed and handsome. Not to mention the eager English and American bachelors settled in Yerba Buena. Believe me, she hasn't given us a thought all day. I wager she's out there in the midst of them already dancing. Once it begins it goes on until dawn and then some, to continue ashore with fireworks and all. As many times as the Skylark has challenged the Horn, I can't help but shudder wondering if she'll survive the thunder of Spanish heels."

He paused to stare at her exquisite face, those bright adoring eyes, the mouth, full and moist seeming to purse in his presence, begging to be kissed.

"How, how in heaven, am I going to survive us?"

Chapter 4

Tobias was only half-right. Many a male gaze was fixed upon Iris, hungry for a flash of those startling blue eyes, and that coquettish smile. But her attention was fully upon Uncle Johnny whose arm she proudly held with both her hands.

"I can't help but stare at you," she told him. "It's as though Papa was resurrected a younger, stronger man."

"Well, I am a lot younger. Almost killed our Mamma, ripping out of her frail body when she had given up on ever having another off spring. Been surprising the world ever since." He winked. "I'm also taller and broader and a darn sight ornerier. Remember that."

"Papa was a saint."

"Not me Missy."

"It's been so long since you two saw one another that you'd have been shocked at the great change in Papa. His hair had become almost all white and sparse. And he was so terribly thin and bent. He had so many worries, which he kept deep inside. We were never aware of his anguish until after he died. It was so awful losing him. I thought I'd never stop crying. He was so sad toward the end. He seldom laughed and when he did, it was never aloud, like you. It was sort of a soft smile." She contemplated a bit. "Suddenly I can't remember Papa's teeth. He did have teeth. Maybe not his own but—"

The earnestness of Iris' hindsight observation sent Johnny into spasms of laughter, displaying strong white teeth to the fullest, not exactly a sympathetic response considering she was describing his dead brother and only sibling.

She frowned. "But it's true. Papa had become a withered old man much too soon."

"It happens Missy, to us all. No, I take that back. These Spanish Californians seem to be ageless. Perhaps it's the pure Pacific air." He gave that mischievous wink. "Maybe it's all that good clover fed beef and the aguardiente. Truly, you find many of them in their sixties and seventies with thick dark hair, no bald heads and perfect teeth. And they live forever, eighty, ninety even a hundred years." He pointed to an old gentleman nimbly dancing with a young Señorita. "That is Don Victor dancing with his granddaughter. He's eighty if he's a day. I've seen scraggly-bearded mountain men of thirty that looked older than he. What a difference when you're trying to survive in the wilderness compared to this pastoral land."

"Well, you seem to have come though unscathed. Papa said you were once a trapper for the Hudson Bay Company. Is that how you got to California and ultimately became this flamboyant Don person that you are? I so want to hear about your days as a mountain man," she enthused.

"That story is to be saved for some starry skied night at the Rancho, which by the way is in the throes of preparing a great fiesta in honor of my two beautiful nieces and their lovely mother. Friends and relatives are being summoned from all the Ranchos as far as Monterey. It will last for three days and nights non-stop, full of sumptuous food and games and dancing. In fact, I want you to dance right now." His voice endeavored to rise above the sudden din of a fiery pulsating tempo.

"The waltz I can do in my sleep. What in heaven is that?"

"The jota, not much different than the Virginia Reel. But much more inciting. I wager you'll catch on in no time, considering all the available teachers at hand." Abruptly he spun her around to face the dancers.

"Well, which partner will it be Missy? Take your choice. Surely there must be one in particular that has caught your eye."

She grinned, her smile matching his. "Of course. Don't think I've given you my undivided attention. I've looked them all over, especially that one over there. That broad shouldered one in red velvet breeches with that exceptionally form fitting jacket glittering with gold braid. He moves like there's a whole slew of muscles under that costume he's wearing. He stands so straight and I do think he s a bit taller than the rest. Or are his heels higher?" Her eyes flirtatiously shifted back and forth from the young man in question and Uncle Johnny. "I'd venture to say that he's the most gorgeous man I've ever seen, except you, of course."

"Of course."

"He hasn't stopped staring at me. Do you know him?"

"It's difficult not knowing someone, considering almost everyone is related in some way or other. I'd say you have extraordinary taste in men, just as your old uncle here has in women. As a matter of fact, I just happen to know that young man very well. His name is Don Cristóbal. And he's one of my wife's seven brothers. He's all of twenty two and is sporting a new mustache and a rather affected swagger."

She gasped. "You're brother-in-law? Now that's interesting. That means Don Cristóbal and I are related, doesn't it?"

"Sort of."

"Does he speak English?"

"Possibly six or eight words, haltingly."

"Oh no! Aside from the few English-speaking people we met in the village, the whole of this country is Spanish or Mexican. I noticed Yankees speaking Spanish to one another. Even the money you people use is peculiar."

"Well, fancy that, considering Yerba Buena began as a Spanish crown colony. The Portola and Anza expedition didn't exactly come by way of Boston."

"Portola? Anza? Who are they?"

"History, little girl, history. I'll tell you about it one of these days."

"What do I care about history? It's the now that I'm concerned with. I have this gorgeous man staring at me from across the room and you tell me he has a total of six or eight words to wrestle with?"

"Oh, I'm sure both you and Don Cristóbal will fare quite well. Look what has transpired already, and you have yet to utter a word. Believe me, you're well on your way with those eyes and ankles and that swishing thing you do with your skirt. It's Heather that has me worried. Where is she, anyway?"

"Heather has a knack for becoming invisible. She actually knows how to fade into the draperies and woodwork. Or would the word 'hold' be more appropriate? She's such a dreamer, Uncle Johnny. You'll find that out. Men become confused by her elusiveness. Honest they do."

"Heather is shy and gentle" he sighed. "Why do I see your Papa and me in you two girls?"

Iris smiled broadly. "I'm you, Uncle Johnny, the wicked one. And at this moment I don't give a hoot about Heather, not with those smoldering dark eyes threatening to devour me. What do you suggest I do?"

Quite suddenly, almost forcefully, he led her away from the sideline where they were standing and spun her across the floor inches away from the astonished Don Cristóbal.

"Jota, Missy! You jota!"

It amused him to watch Don Cristóbal quickly reach out to gallantly catch Iris in his arms. Johnny could not help but laugh aloud at his young brother-in-law's bemused expression. Johnny had thrown him a rose, a thorny one at that. But this Don Cristóbal would have to learn for himself. At the moment the young man was ecstatic. Gently he attempted to lead Iris through the tempestuous tempo. She looked to the other ladies flourishing their brightly colored skirts right up to their knees. Scandalous in Boston, but at once appealing to Iris' lack of inhibition. She was quickly caught up in the dance.

Johnny was intent on finding Heather. He remembered last seeing her in the storeroom helping an elderly Señora drape herself with silver lace. He was certain his niece deliberately found excuse to avoid the festivity and particularly the men. It troubled him.

"You're much too lovely," he thought, "to be withdrawing into yourself. Damn It! I'm going to see that this nonsense changes. You are every bit as desirable as your sister. If it's the last thing I do I'm going to see that you meet the right man and fall madly in love. Not for a moment to be outdone by our manipulative Missy."

He came to an abrupt halt upon spotting Heather standing at the starboard. She was staring out at the bay, seeming much too forlorn. He was about to approach her when she suddenly turned away from the water and responded to a presence that was not his own. To Johnny's amazement, her face shone with a look of joyous surprise. Someone else had called out to her first. A tall lean young man with dark hair stepped out of the shadows to be instantly at her side. Johnny was taken aback. It was no one familiar, certainly not one of the crew. His outfit, which was a trifle loose, was one of Tobias' Boston best. Of course it had to be the young man Toby mentioned, the one they picked up in Panama, Wilhelm Medina. Johnny shook his head. "Well that's one on me, Heather girl." He could not help but smile. "You sly Bradbury women." he thought. "Each of you has quietly managed to select yourself a man. Something to do with all that sea air I suppose." He shrugged and made his way back to the party, which was overflowing onto the decks.

Contrary to Johnny's quick conclusion not one word or look of awareness had passed between Will and Heather before that very instant. When Will finally awoke from his delirium, it was the ship's surgeon whom he first recognized. Or so it seemed. He now stood before Heather a totally different man than she had nursed. It was shocking to see him so fastidiously dressed and shaved and combed. His long wild hair was trimmed to his jaw line and swept back from his brow in deep waves that half covered his ears. The black broad cloth coat and breeches, the crisp white shirt and thick satin tie meticulously bowed, spoke of a lone Easterner conspicuously misplaced in this far away country of California. She could only stare back at him speechless. Will spoke first, his dark eyes awash with tenderness, his voice a deep whisper.

"Thank you, my dear. Thank you for taking care of me."

Chapter 5

He stood there high spirited and laughing, Don Juan Ricardo Bradbury, broad shouldered and bronzed skin, hatless, the ash of his thick tousled hair gleaming gold in the afternoon son. Behind him, as far as the eye could see, was the immense expanse of countryside that was his Rancho. He had just returned from the day long inspection of herds of cattle and horses, of the bounteous domain of fifteen leagues that came by way of a land grant upon his Roman Catholic baptism and marriage to an 'heja del pais', a daughter of the country. How could he not help but be conspicuously self confident and joyous, this one time wanderer and mountain man?

He threw his wide brimmed yellow vicuna hat at Iris' feet, daring her to take up where the dancing had ceased but an hour before daybreak. She yawned and snuggled deeper into the cushioned bench shaded beneath the slope of the red tiled roof. The two-story, whitewashed adobe with its running balconies formed a huge U around the inner garden, and patio, which opened onto hillsides spangled with wild flowers. The garden was lush with the brightness of flowers, fern-like foliage and citrus fruit trees that followed a serpentine path to a center fountain of concentric shells. A rush of sparkling water cascaded downward from one to another reaching a round reflecting pool of fine sculpted masonry. White fat-chest doves, golden eyed black birds and twittering sparrows soared overhead to eventually flit their wings in the water. An assortment of dogs and cats wandered about or lie lazily in the shadows.

Aside from Iris and Uncle Johnny there were a small group of women and children at the far end of the garden. The ladies and their maids sat on benches working on drawn lace or hoops of embroidery laying upon their laps. The late afternoon breeze carried the fragrance of flowers as well as the subtle sweetness of guitars, softly strummed by two Señoritas. Toddlers scampered about barefoot and naked, boys and girls alike. The children darted about in games, their sporadic shrieks causing Iris to shudder, her hands gripping at her temples. For one who only had an occasional sip of her Papa's sherry, she drank an excessive amount of alcohol. She had danced almost constantly, daring to keep up with the tireless hijas del pais. The ladies were known for being able to dance for hours on end moving from one partner to another, of all ages, from grandson to grandfather alike.

Through those three days and nights of fiesta, Iris seemed ignited with unflagging energy. Though Don Cristóbal was her most constant partner there was an unending line of caballeros to take up the slack. Still, the seductiveness of his gaze remained upon her as she uninhibitedly moved about the floor, her skirts flying, her shapely limbs a delectable sight. Each time they returned to each other's arms, their passions heightened. He would kiss her palms at length, his smoldering eyes looking deep into hers. The very young, romantic Don Cristóbal was totally enamored. Iris felt triumphant, until now.

The fiesta had ceased and Don Cristóbal was nowhere to be found. She brooded even further when he failed to return to the house with Uncle Johnny and Hector, his majordomo. Where was he? As if that were not enough, her mother and Tobias had left the Rancho very early that morning to supposedly meet a launch carrying supplies down the coast to Monterey. 'A likely story,' she sulked. And Heather and Will, another obviously absent couple now wandered the countryside afoot. She felt abandoned.

Uncle Johnny could not help but smile at the sight of Iris curled up on the bench, her arms cradling herself, slightly rocking in a manner that depicted the debilitating pangs of a hangover. This was the girl whose vivacious had failed to dim for an instant during the last three days of festivity. The outcome of her excessiveness was amusingly predictable to him.

"That was practically raw liquor you were poring down your throat, Missy." He teased. "Some chili sauce, a dash of lime and a raw egg in one swift gulp will do the trick."

Her hands dramatically seized her throat. "What? Do you want me to die? No wonder they take so many siestas in California. How else can one recuperate from the fiestas? Or did I get the two words mixed up?"

"You said it perfectly." He grinned. "I'm famished from making the rounds. How about something to eat?"

She cringed in revulsion. "Don't mention food! Those two tittering Indian girls you assigned as my personal maids were there at my bedside with the first shaft of light, offering me chocolate and that flat bread you call a tortilla. I waved them away only to be later offered a thick vegetable soap and a monstrous piece of beef. Which by their grotesque pantomime I gathered was just freshly butchered. I almost retched. I can't eat or drink a thing, least of all blood red meat. Still, there they were, insisting on bathing and dressing me, slipping on these beaded moccasins and brushing my hair back like this."

Her long flaming hair was sleekly drawn back from the brow and worked into a single thick braid twined with bright blue ribbon and left to fall over one shoulder.

She was attired in a gray brocaded skirt that was capable of standing on its own, a short sleeved white blouse with a scoop neckline and a blue three cornered shawl, its points crossing over her breasts. It was a stunning contrast from the tightly corseted girl that stepped off the Skylark but two weeks past.

Unlike her mother and sister she was quick to completely abandon her Eastern clothes to be regaled in this comfortable kind of costume that befit the California woman. She changed three times during the party, adding different combs and shawls and flowers as well. Each time she appeared a little more daring in her dress than the time before.

Today she looked quite unassuming in comparison. She was not certain if she even liked the look or the two fawning, dark skinned domestics that she could not understand.

"There's an incredible amount of help here" Iris commented. "No wonder there is nothing to do but fiesta and be indulged. Your Indians do everything for you. How much help do you have?"

He thought a moment. "Two, three hundred."

"My God, Uncle Johnny, it's like being a plantation owner with your own slaves."

"These people are not slaves!" He was adamant.

She was taken aback by the sudden severity of his tone as well as the unsmiling face that added instant age.

"These are servants that encompass our family. Right off Missy, I want you to understand something about these people. All this land as far as you can fathom, originally belonged to their ancestors. They were peaceful people, the hunters and gatherers of an ancient time, countless small tribes with different dialects. Not at all like the Plains Indians or the mammoth assemblage that constitutes the Cherokee Nation. I doubt if we have more than a handful of the very old that were not born and raised in the Missions. Their language is predominantly Spanish, their faith Roman Catholic. Their teacher's were the Franciscan Padres. They endured an incredibly rigid life believing that one-day all the vast lands and herds would be theirs. It was a promise the Padres very well meant to keep. With Mexican rule the Missions were secularized, supposedly to become Indian pueblos with land lots divided among them. It never happened. Seventeen thousand Indians from twenty-one Missions were discarded like rubbish. Some of those lost souls endeavored to return to scattered tribes, but as a whole they became a misplaced people, having lost their own land for the second time."

"Well, you certainly managed to get your share, didn't you?"

He angrily snapped. "Either way, it never would have reverted back to the Indians! Yes, they work hard. They have the skills required to keep such a place going. They may not be the blue bloods, but they are the blood-flow that keeps the Ranchos alive and functioning. I, for my part, try to respect that, and expect those about me to act the same. Do you understand?" He was shouting.

She shrugged, her face flushing. His voice and look were intimidating, causing her to uncomfortably stir, to needlessly fluff the back cushions of the bench. God help her, she thought, if he had heard her cruelly refer to Miguel Pedro as a savage. All of a sudden Uncle Johnny emerged the Indian lover, doting on his help while Hector, his Indian Majordomo, seemed at times merciless with his own kind.

"Remember, Missy, we treat them humanely," he emphasized. "Each and everyone of them has something of himself to offer and is possessive of his own particular skill. He or she, does what they do best like the girls that served you chocolate and attended your needs. You will not find them in the field anymore than you will find the tanner or mason, blacksmith or herdsman in the calaveras, the slaughter-house."

Iris cringed back into the shadows. She deliberately looked away to suddenly find herself squinting out into the horizon.

"What's that all about?"

She was referring to a caravan of carretas and pack horses slowly moving across the hillside accompanied by dozens of Indian women and children on foot, followed by a slew of running, lapping dogs, their sharp barks ringing in the distance. She sighed with relief to again see him smile.

"That, my dear is our laundry. They are a bit early. Usually they leave at dawn and return at dusk."

"That's all laundry?"

"Indeed it is. They take it down to the warm springs, called 'agua caliente', pound it clean on smooth rocks, then drape it on the bushes to dry, all over the countryside. A wonderful comic sight. As it dries they have a picnic lunch, strum their guitars and sing and play. A unique way to deal with drudgery, wouldn't you say?"

"Looks like mounds and mounds of white things."

"White is my wife's favorite color. Blanca is the word for white. White clothes and bedding extol the fact that the Patróna, the mistress of the house, can well afford all the laundresses she wishes. Yes, you are right, there are servants for all our bidding, to allow us to fiesta, to ride, to indulge in sports and games. To allow the Patrón," he grinned "that's me, the master, to be unencumbered of exhausting toil so that aside from surveying my land and herds, I can be the loving husband, father and gracious host. Being hospitable is customary in California. Total stranger are provided food, lodging, a horse and if needed is discreetly left money on his night table. It is understood that life is to be shared. This is automatically accepted whether one is rich or poor. Time and again you will hear the expression 'mi casa es su casa,' my house is your house. And it is meant from the heart." He gave a half smile. "I take it you're disappointed to find that your blackguard of an Uncle has finally mellowed. There is no denying it. I was an arrogant young man, as well as misplaced in my New England lifestyle. The odds were that I'd be cut off in my prime in the wilds if not in some barroom brawl. I've changed, but not enough to wonder what would happen if this genuine hospitality were taken literally." He reflected a moment. "Yes, I grant I'm a foreigner myself who came to this wonderful country to ultimately reap the riches. But it's different, because I didn't just take, but became a part of the culture. As shocking a transition as it may seem for a mountain man, I take my role as Patrón quite seriously. In fact, reverently."

He hesitated wondering if he should continue. "This will undoubtedly come as a surprise to you, but very early this morning while it was still dark, Rufina and I arose to face the day. From starlight to sunset the Patrón and the Patróna go about their individual duties. I with the field hands and vaqueros, and she supervising her many maids accordingly. But first, all of us together get down on our knees before the shrine of the Madonna in the corridor and recite the Alba, the Morning Prayer of thanks for a safe awakening and an even safer day."

Iris indeed gasped, just as Johnny had anticipated. It was impossible visualizing him, of all people on his knees praying at four in the morning. He had carried his role of the Californio above and beyond the ostentatious dress and resplendent Rancho. Savoring her surprise, he continued.

"After having a light breakfast, we go our separate ways to meet at midday for a hearty meal, followed by a siesta. Then back to work. I spend the greater part of my day on horseback. It suits my nature beautifully. I would never have survived working in a counting room stooped over in the shadows like your Papa. The freedom of being able to gallop across the immensity of ones own land, soaring rhythmically on the back of a magnificent Arabian is exhilaration beyond belief. With a well-trained horse and a reata a man is indispensable, making play of the fiercest bull or black grizzly. Yes, my dear, as much as we are indulged by our help, we are not slothful. I take enormous pride in being Don Juan Ricardo Bradbury, and to have found a woman, as warm and wonderful and as devastatingly beautiful as Doña Rufina. Well that surpasses my wildest dreams."

For an instant his mind regressed to another time. To that merciless winter in the wilds as he lay feverish and alone, covered by snow. In his dissoluteness, tears freezing upon his face, he reached out to God to hasten his death. Instead, he survived to experience a new life with Rufina.

There was a soft smile on his face as his thoughts wandered to his wife of four years, to the memory of their first meeting in Monterey. She managed to see past his heavy, unkempt beard and long unruly hair. His blue eyes shone even brighter in her presence. They belied his trapper's outfit of worn leather breeches and a long leather shirt.

A group of them had come down from Yerba Buena, after having visited the Jacob Leese house. It was the only decent structure in the miserable Cove colony, yet geographically ideal for yet another Hudson's Bay Company trading post.

While in Monterey, they found themselves invited to a fiesta. The gregarious group of trappers became an uneasy lot upon taking stock of their own wretched appearance, compared to the lavishly colorful style of the Californios. Still they were treated graciously.

Johnny, who stood out from the rest because of his height, distinguished himself further with a quick display of mountain-man know how, by setting a young man's leg after a severe fall from a horse. He endeared himself to all, both men and women.

Iris could tell he was thinking of Rufina. It was the way his face suddenly lit up whenever her name was spoken. Doña Rufina, Patróna, whatever, it was enough to incite envy as well as anger in Iris.

Upon first meeting Johnny, Missy instantly claimed him for herself. There was so much laughing and teasing in Yerba Buena and on the launch that brought them here, that she mistakenly assumed that here was another Papa, another man to be easily manipulated. Or so she thought, until their launch arrived in Santa Clara. Uncle Johnny suddenly took on new importance when he was greeted en mass by a dozen vaqueros with extra horses to be ridden to the Rancho. The vaqueros who wore black, large rimmed hats, red scarves around their necks and multicolored serapes, rode with a fierceness and agility she had never before seen. Their horses either pranced proudly or soared. There was no in-between pace that allowed the Bradbury woman to relax in their saddles. Tobias and Will pulled back to ride with them while Johnny galloped ahead his vaqueros in wild pursuit, dust rising as they rode.

Surrounded by the verdant Santa Clara hills, they rode for an hour. From ridge to valley through thick brush and great towering pine and oak. Everywhere there were streams and creeks glistening through the foliage. And there was a welcoming abundance of wild flowers of every hue.

At last they reached the wide looming high gate, which announced that they had arrived at the Rancho. It was another four miles ride before the sprawling white Casa emerged. It nestled regally midst velvet green meadows, deliberately sparse of surrounding trees, the view clear to catch marauding Indians.

Followed by his galloping vaqueros, Uncle Johnny was first to sight the house. Spotting Rufina in the distance, he bore his spurs deeper into the side of his mount and raced faster still. There she stood, conspicuously beautiful, dressed in white, surrounded by the numerous family members having already arrived. Parents, grandparents, brothers, sisters-in-law, nieces and nephews, cousins and a mass of servants had rushed out to greet them. All smiling, all waving. For Belle and her daughters, as well as Will, this happy assemblage of greeters was a shocking surprise. It was their introduction to California hospitality and to family.

Johnny reared his horse but paces away from his waiting wife. He leaped from his magnificent Arabian and drew Rufina deep into his arms, his mouth at once finding hers. His kiss was full and long and totally oblivious to those who watched, to the yelps and laughter of the vaqueros.

When he at last released her, to meet the dismounting guests, they were at once taken by her exquisite beauty. There was a genuine sweetness in her smile and in the way she warmly embraced Belle and her daughters. For they were her husband's family and now her own.

Doña Rufina's white attire was a breathtaking contrast against the gleaming silk of her blue-black hair and fair alabaster skin, the cheeks akin to roses. That mass of ebony mane was drawn smoothly back from the brow and plaited in the traditional single braid laced with white satin ribbon and sprays of small white blossoms, the whole of which cascaded over one shoulder to the waist. She was as striking a woman, as Don Cristóbal was a man, with the same flashing dark eyes and high cheekbones, round aristocratic brow and chiseled nose. When she smiled, her full sensual mouth revealed perfect white teeth. And there was a lyrical sound to her voice and laugh. She carried herself distinctively straight and poised revealing an inherent kind of Castilian pride. Her white dress fit tightly over her slim, full-breasted body. It hugged its way to her knees where a wide ruffle afforded her room to step. The hem skimmed the ground, trailing from behind as she walked. On her small feet she wore white satin heels.

Though she was beautifully attired to meet her guests as well as her husband, one special touch was endearingly meant for Johnny alone. She wore the pearl necklace and earrings he had brought from Baja California for their first anniversary. Pearls that took on the luster of her skin. He had placed them about her neck and then they had made love. The sight of those pearls had become Rufina's subtle invitation to him. Each time she wore them there was a knowing secret smile that passed between them. It was there, now. How could she not help but appear both radiant and proud? Aside from every possible physical attribute she was also Patróna of this resplendent Rancho and absolutely adored by her husband.

Iris found herself seething with jealousy. That sulking searing expression was uncomfortably apparent to her mother and sister who gave her a simultaneous nudge. It was Don Cristóbal's courtly attention that ultimately made her smile. As well as the many other handsome males, brothers and cousins alike who eyed her with admiring smiles.

As was the custom, Doña Rufina took them on a tour of the house, through the many rooms whose grated windows opened onto balconies, to the huge ballroom with its French chandeliers, with its piano and harp. But foremost she proudly led them into the bedroom. Her limited English was unable to explain that it was very much the custom to furbish the master bedroom as opulent as possible, sparing no expense. The bed, being the focal point, had an ornately carved and polished headboard that peaked halfway up the white washed wall. The coverlet was made of thick white satin trimmed with silver and white lace and a profusion of pillows to match.

Johnny winked, facetiously adding his own quick-witted comment. "No doubt about it, this is my favorite room of all time."

For an instant his eyes were caught up in his wife's unwavering gaze. Her look incited visions of her nakedness moving beneath the silk of that black hair spilling about her hips and thighs. How well she knew that gleam and it caused her to slightly flush before her guests. He laughed and kissed her upon the mouth then lifted their two tiny daughters in his arms at once, fondling and kissing their cherubic faces. Señorita Juana was three and Señorita Teresa was fifteen months. Each was meticulously ruffled in white, with red satin ribbons streaming from their dark shiny braids. They bore their mother's sweet pink cheeks and dark luminous eyes.

"Well, Missy," Johnny finally spoke. "What do you think of our Rancho?"

"It's big enough. And it has a long name, that I don't understand at all."

"ISLA DEL VAGABUNDO. I wanted to call it MI ISLA, my island. But Rufina insisted that EL VAGABUNDO, the vagabond, suited me more. It translates into ISLAND OF THE VAGABOND." He laughed. Sure loses something in translation."

"As I noticed each time I'd ask you to translate one of Cristóbal's endearments. They sound so romantic rolling off his lips and so ridiculously gushy in English"

"Spanish is full of soul and poetry. A language you'll just have to learn if you're to live here."

"It'll take forever. It's so frustrating hearing all those people around me happily chattering in a strange tongue. I just hate it. And if I do utter a word it comes out so stilted. How does one acquire that roll?"

"Hey, I managed, as did others. As you will see in the many marriages of foreigners to native daughters. To the consternation of the

Californios their ladies have a preference for the ojos azules, the blue eyed men."

"Well, I'm captivated by dark eyes. At night by candlelight Cristóbal's are as black as onyx. Yet in the sun they are alive with gold. I think I'm smitten, Uncle Johnny." She devilishly sang her words. "Really smitten."

"We'll see." He had strong trepidation, for Cristóbal not Iris.

"Where is he?"

"Cristóbal is out riding with a little cousin from Monterey. She arrived with her family rather late into the party last night after a long ride and choose to go to sleep."

"She?"

"A cousin of fourteen whom he cherishes as a little sister. He stays with the family quite often when in Monterey. Her parents, Don Rigoberto and Doña Marta are his god-parents. It is considered a great honor to be chosen to co-parent a child. The god-parents are deeply respected."

Iris shrugged. "It may come as a surprise, Uncle Johnny, but I was christened. For the life of me I can't tell you who my god-parents are. So what's so great about having two adults stand by while they pour holy water over some squealing infant? Who cares?"

"Well it means a great deal here, Missy. Family and tradition truly matter. It gives one a deep sense of security and serenity. Perhaps it is the very essence that endows this race of man with his robustness, with his longevity and joy. Love is a pretty potent elixir." He paused seeming even more serious. "Without it a man can wither away. I know." His eyes were firmly upon hers. "I want you to understand that you are now part of a very large and loving family. Don't ever take it lightly." He remained aware of her sulk. "The family will remain here a week after which time they will be returning to their Rancho in Monterey. Cristóbal will be joining them to remain a bit, as well as take care of some business on my behalf."

"What? Why?" she cried "See? See how it is? He couldn't even tell me himself that he would be leaving. What is this precious little cousin's name?"

"Señorita Blanquita or Blanca if you choose."

"Blanca? Blanca like the white laundry? You mean her name is white?"

He burst into uproarious laughter. "Somehow it has a more lovely connotation in Spanish."

"It must," she scoffed. "So when do I get to meet Señorita Blanca?" She exaggerated the name.

Johnny took his good time answering her question. First he bent over, picked up his hat on the ground, put it on his head and jauntily tied the red sash beneath his chin.

"When you exchange that scowl for a smile. You must have been a real pain for your Papa."

"Papa adored me, no less than you love your two little girls, or a son if one comes along."

The remark rendered Johnny momentarily stunned. Strange that she should mention a son, considering that there was great doubt that Rufina would ever again conceive a child. She was badly torn and bled profusely after her last birth. A thing that filled her with melancholy considering that a family of ten or twelve were quite normal for her race, not to mention the enormous pride bearing a son to carry on the Bradbury name. Johnny had felt a great loss over the possibility but quickly comforted himself on the fullness of his life in general. Though slow in coming he was able to give Iris a big smile.

"Three ladies in my life is more than enough. And now I find I have two more in my brother's daughters. Somehow I feel that I have slighted Heather. We did waltz several times at the fiesta, but I barely know the girl. Here, you and I have almost come to blows, but Heather is so much like her father. I never really knew him." He shook his head. "But you Missy, are a real pain in the backside."

"Is that anyway for a Don to speak?"

"Probably not, but there is still a streak of the mean old mountain man lurking inside of me. For some reason I haven't discarded my long leather shirt or my moccasins."

"Moccasins?"

"There was a time when I lived with the Shoshone, followed their customs, spoke their tongue and—"

"And bedded their squaws," she brazenly added.

His eyes narrowed. "No wonder your Papa turned white."

"Only teasing, Uncle Johnny." She demurred from beneath fluttering eyelids.

"It's a good thing Cristóbal can't understand you. You are wicked you know that? Now keep smiling, just like that. And make it real, if you can, because Don Cristóbal is here now, in the garden with Blanquita."

Her eyes quickly flashed to the other side of the fountain where a flurry of birds rose in the wake of their steps. First they paused to converse with a group of ladies who were quick to enthuse at their arrival.

"That is her mother and two sisters." Johnny informed Iris.

She could only see the side of the young woman as she leaned over to kiss her mother. Little cousin Blanquita did not appear the child Johnny described. She was dressed in a most fetching blue riding habit and elaborate boots, a large rimmed hat concealing her face.

Don Cristóbal who immediately spotted Iris and Johnny gave a courtly bow to the ladies then excused himself to make his way across the garden to focus upon the incredibly sweet faced Iris. Don Cristóbal took her hand and affectionately fondled it for a moment before lifting it to his lips. His deep lyrical voice spoke her name, making it come forth as music.

Johnny grimaced at her blatant display of demureness as well as the unwavering stare that promised to devour the captivated young man.

Suddenly Blanquita moved into the picture. Fondly she embraced Johnny, kissing him lightly on both cheeks. Next she turned to be introduced to Iris, to the beautiful Bostonian with flaming hair whom Cristóbal had expounded upon throughout the greater part of their ride.

"I want you to meet your cousin Blanquita." Johnny intoned in such a manner as to subtly caution Iris to be civil. "Yes, your cousin through marriage. We are all family here remember?"

Iris, whose attention was upon Cristóbal, looked up to give Blanquita a patronizing nod. As she did her jaw dropped in dismay. This fair skinned girl, with the radiant smile, was so shockingly familiar to her that Iris could barely contain herself. Her height and form, her every feature, the gleaming black hair and the large startling blue eyes, belonged to Estrellita, the daughter of that savage Miguel Pedro.

Chapter 6

Will and Heather wandered the extended garden that adjoined the casa. They walked the winding paths, bordered with small shade trees and blossoming bowers. Mainly there were the roses, the pink Castilian ones that Rufina favored for her hair, or subtly slipped into her cleavage, but mostly gathered as a bouquet for the blue mantled Madonna in the corridor.

They stepped into the arbor. A configuration of knotted grapevines created a canopy of shadow and sunlight. Here stood great gnarled fig trees, flaming pomegranates, Mallorca oranges, lemons and limes with their delectable citrus scents. Peaches, plums and nectarines clustered heavily on leafy branches. It was a magical place, amass with the flutter and warble of birds. Further still they found themselves encompassed by a vista of pastures, of undulating green hillsides profusely dotted with black Spanish cattle grazing on wild clover. Masses of mustangs raced across the horizon, manes and tails flying, throbbing hoofs spurring clouds of dust. Everywhere there were wild flowers, hedges of fragile blooms in white and yellow in varying shades of blue and purple. This time of the year the hills were aglow with stretches of poppies reaching out for miles. That bright iridescent orange was a breathtaking sight for ships sailing the coast. The enthralling view of those flaming California hills was seen by all as they stood in awe on the deck of the Skylark.

Heather shaded a small white ruffled parasol over her hatless head. Her thick auburn hair fell in deep waves down her back and shoulders, at times succumbing to the gentle stirring of a light breeze. She dared to loosen her hair and discard her tightly staid corset, a welcome but wicked gesture for a young woman of her traditional New England background. But this was California, how could she not? Still her conservative gingham dress looked preposterous flaring about her newly acquired boots of red and gold tooling.

Will too was a mismatch of attire. The wide-brimmed black vicuna hat, the large red kerchief around his neck and again the magnificently elaborate boots were incongruous with his austere Yankee frock and breeches. A timid and comical transition for them both, but a beginning.

Often he took her hand to guide her through the cragginess of the terrain, his arm at last feeling free to settle about her waist. Eventually she too slipped her free arm about him affording him shade from her parasol. As they moved in half embrace she became aware of the weakness that yet sated his system; the unrelenting traces of a ruthless jungle fever. He sighed deeply, taking in the sweet fragrances of spring as well as the deliciously pure Pacific air.

Will was at once captivated by the serenity of the day, as well as Heather's tender presence. There was little time to be alone. The celebrant crowd with their spirited music and dance finally dispersed at daybreak. The tumultuousness, though well meant, was too much for him to withstand.

Heather intuitively sensed his need to be apart from the crowd. The devastation of Panama was yet rankling at his heart. It would be a long time before he would again feel festive or even social. Yet somehow with Heather it was all right. She understood. They had grown quietly close, yet each knowing little about the other, she far less than he.

They sat themselves upon the deep grass of a glen surrounded by tangled clusters of wild berries, the gleaming black studded ones and the enormous red stawberrles bidding to be tasted. Heather perched her parasol on a bush where it balanced like a giant white mushroom. They each gathered a handful of berries to be immediately devoured. The sweet-tart juices trickled through a conjoining of laced hands. They became as giddy as children. In that moment Heather realized that it was the first time she had heard Will laugh. It was a wonderfully spontaneous sound that even surprised him. His capacity for laughter had been suffocated somewhere in the thick of that far away jungle.

Will took out a handkerchief and paternally wiped her chin and the stickiness of her hands. All the while he studied the loveliness of that flawless face exposed to the fullness of the sun. She flushed in the caress of his palm, her light eyes mirroring in the darkness of his own. In that instant she was overcome with both ardor and panic.

'I don't want you to ever leave my life,' she silently declared. Her feelings of passion were so intent, so unfamiliar to herself that she could not help but lower her eyelids with embarrassment.

His steady gaze seem to read her thoughts. Will had a way of staring at her that she could not quite decipher. It was both sensual and searching. As though he were questioning their sudden closeness. Inwardly he was.

She was instantly drawn to him the moment their eyes met on the Skylark. She was certain that it would not have been any different if they had been strangers passing on a crowded Boston street. The fact that his semi-conscious was aware of her presence secretly tending to him in his cabin, magnified both their feelings.

Yet only now, today, did they truly touch. Will did not dance with her at the fiesta, but instead watched and waited for her to return to his side. Mostly she was with him, dining, talking sporadically through the din, awed by the exuberant dancers and singers, except when each retired to their room to rest.

Will particularly showed signs of fatigue and chose to remain in his room the greater part of the fiesta. Still, sleep was an impossible fete considering the sounds of conviviality. Heather could not know that this quite debilitated youth was by nature robust and exuberant, capable of taking her wildly and tenderly in his arms and into his bed.

Panama had taken an enormous toll. There was a great deal more that he could not share, least of all with Heather. Yet ironically he had come to trust her the most. Through the seriousness of his thoughts he mustered a faint smile.

"You haven't asked me anything about myself, Heather. I could very well be a rouge."

"You're not though." She sweetly assured.

"No, I'm not, but I am a stranger in your life who has taken up a great deal of your time. Still you accept me without question."

"What's to question? Will I trust you. You'll tell me, whatever it is, when you're ready."

She realized that he must yet be in mourning for a brother by the name of Gus. That part the inscription on the gold timepiece had revealed. She felt guilty for having known without his consent.

He was momentarily felled by her sincerity. "You know that I care for you, don't you?" He finally managed. "It was the last thing in the world that I thought could happen, me caring for someone, for you." he paused "My brother and I left New York for one purpose only." He bit his lip grasping for the next thought. "I didn't dream that I'd end up burying him in some God forsaken jungle. Even so, what we set out to do is now in my hands."

Will's eyes suddenly became unfocused as he stared out in the distance. It was the first time he had mentioned his grief. To have it come concurrently with his admission of feelings for her seemed ambivalent. Somehow she understood. Gently her hand slipped into his causing him to again look at her, his large palm tightening over her small tapered hand.

"I care about you too, Will. So much so that I can't help but feel your loss. I want to help you in any way I can. Even if only to listen."

"You have no idea how strange this all is. You, of all the people wanting to help me."

"I don't understand. Why is that so strange?"

He gave her an awkward smile. He was slow in speaking. When he halfheartedly did, it was not the answer to her question, but another waiting to be asked.

"What in heaven were Gus and I doing in that God forsaken jungle? Adventure?

Yes, I guess you could call it that." The words came unconvincingly. "We became fascinated with the history of it all. Once having been there, it is difficult to conceive that any human being would ever want to step into that dense stifling under world of a place. But there were hundreds, perhaps thousands that passed before us. As early as the sixteenth century there were Balboa and his men, to be followed by the infamous Conquistadors inching their way with their tons of Inca gold, silver and pearls loaded on mule-trains to be carried from the Pacific to the Caribbean. Their Galleons were glutted with treasure. There was that indomitable Englishman, Sir Francis Drake who sailed the Spanish Main, defying the Spanish harbors and jungle." He shook his head in disbelief. "There were even several expeditions of Scotsmen, who founded an obscure colony. Incredible as it seems, we met dark skinned natives bearing names like Macgregor and Mackinsie." He gave a sad smile. "And then there's the story of two dumb brothers from New York. Why waste months sailing around the Horn when we could cut across the isthmus touching two oceans in five days. We saved time all right," he sighed "but lost a precious life."

He commenced to choke. Not wanting to dismay Heather with a show of tears he turned away and stared out at the far away hills for an interminable length of time. She remained very still grasping his hand til he chose to again speak.

"In Balboa's time there was talk of building a canal across the Isthmus of Panama. It is still a dream. Perhaps one day it will happen. In their diggings they will unearth countless skeletons, beast and man alike." He paused, his throat again tightening. "Gus included."

She was at a loss for words, having suddenly realized the enormity of the pain he had harbored for so long. All the while he spoke their hands remained tightly locked. Breathlessly she waited for him to continue. His eyes were still upon the horizon.

"For a moment, when we stepped into the arbor I was struck by the beauty of birdsong. I don't know why, but I found myself regressing to the sounds of the jungle, to the cries of exotic birds and beasts, and the shrill of the cicadas. They are insects, billions of them, incessantly screeching into your ears. Until you begin to believe that the blare is coming from inside your own brain."

Will's hands suddenly clasped tightly over his ears in harrowing recall. The feel of Heather's hand gently stroking at the back of his head and at the nape of his neck coerced him to relax.

"It's all right Will," she soothed. "It's all right."

Slowly he raised his eyes and looked straight into hers. She was experiencing his anguish. His hands touched upon her shoulders, fondling them gently. He was more composed though a trifle ashamed. Still he continued.

"I didn't mean to burden you like this. It's just that I desperately needed to tell someone. How can you bury your only brother deep in some damn jungle and have no one to share your grief?" He was sadly silent for a moment. "Our two native guides dug the grave, then solemnly mumbled some half Christian incantation. I guess it was their way of offering solace." Tenderly he studied her face. "Your compassion at this time in my life is much more than I expected."

"I want to comfort you, to share your memories of Gus. If I may?" She said this knowing full well that she too often repressed her own hurt, choosing to withdraw, when in fact she wanted to be heard and held. This she understood in Will.

He stretched back upon the high grass propped upon one elbow facing her. "Where do I begin?" He took a calming breath. "We're from a family of six girls, Gus and I having tumbled out of Mamma fourteen months apart. I was the older and Gus the wiser, the reader, the planner, the doer. He had devoured the history, studied the maps and booked the passage from New York to Chagras. There was a fierceness in his actions." His voice suddenly strengthened. "Perhaps in mine also." His eyes narrowed in deep recollection. "After a pleasant twelve day sail we sighted Chagras. It's on the Caribbean side of Panama. It appeared lush and beautiful, trees rising from the shore. There is a gray stone Castille, the fort of San Lorenzo. It has a moat, high rambling walls and a placement for guns peering through rusted holes, the vestiges of another time. We were fortunate to have arrived in the dry season, which was bad enough. With our two guides we rode up the Chagras River by dug out canoe. It's a river of snake like twists and sudden falls. What could have been twenty miles in a straight line took on two hundred. We came to Cruces and rested the night. At dawn we tackled the eighteen miles to Panama City. We rode on miserably saddled mules through treacherous terrain. Everything steamed, dripped and reeked from the constant mold of vegetation and the infectious vapors from the swamps called the miasma." Will's recall inadvertently caused him to gasp for air. Once composed he resumed his story. "There was the shock of suddenly facing steep cliffs, in the midst of the jungle. Those long ago Spaniards had painstakingly chipped mule steps into the cliffs to transport their treasure." He faintly smiled. "I remember Gus laughing aloud at the sight of them. 'There you are, Will,' he said 'a monument to avarice. The undauntedness of greed has afforded us a staircase in the thick of the jungle.' Will shock his head. "I dread to think how we'd have managed without those mule steps. Mostly we walked along the riverbed, all the while welding machetes, our arms and back aching. With every step was the feel of slime and mold crunching beneath our boots. And there were mammoth colonies of swarming insects under every fallen, decaying tree. There are plants that sear at your skin like acid and others with blades as sharp as swords. We were constantly wary of crocodiles, scorpions, tarantulas and vampire bats that suck your blood as you sleep. The mosquitoes were huge and equally blood thirsty."

Heather's expression remained calmly intent, though his description of the jungle and his need to relate the experience caused her to quietly cringe. Her heedfulness prompted him to continue.

"We slept wound up in netting, our bodies drenched from the humidity." He paused to breathe deeply, his gaze upon the vista. "Each moment that I am here in the serenity of this place, it becomes more and more difficult to believe that Panama ever happened. But it did. That damn jungle feeds on you, body and soul! It claimed Gus."

Heather finally gave in to a shiver that caused him to reach out to her.

"I didn't mean to burden you with my story. It just suddenly spilled out. Forgive me."

"It's all right Will. Truly, it's all right. I'm here for you."

He eyed her tenderly and slightly smiled. "I must admit if Gus had lived we'd now be laughing about our high adventure. But he is indeed gone. Our last time together was—" his voice trailed.

Their hands were again knotted, even more tightly than before. His gaze shifted away from hers to once again stare blankly out into the distance. He took a deep breath before continuing.

"Gus was overcome with jungle fever. It was impossible to continue. There was quinine and brandy in our knapsacks, which we consistently sipped. At one point he shook so badly that I had to lie down beside him and hold him in my arms like a baby. Between the heat of his body and the jungle it felt like I was being engulfed by an inferno. We stuck together with perspiration. Through it all, Gus never complained. You know what he said? 'Let's kill the bottle of brandy, Will. Let's get good and drunk.' And we did, sharing it with our guides. We started singing, all of us, our own songs in our own language, a lot of drunken gibberish, sounding through the jungle, inciting the screeching of birds.

Suddenly, in the middle of all that uproar, he died. He'd been laughing and singing. All at once he was gone." Will choked back the tears. "We buried him at the foot of some ancient mule steps that rose up above his grave like a colossal headstone. I stood there crying uncontrollably with the sounds of strange birds mimicking my cries. For an instant I looked up and saw a sliver of moon, a bright orange-moon. Or did I imagine it? It was so rare to ever see the sky through all that vegetation. But there it was. It was Gus saying goodbye."

He at last gave way to a sob, his head lowering to his chest. The memory of his brother was heavily upon him. Heather felt his pain and she too wanted to cry. Both her hands were fondling his. The two of them remained unstirred and silent for a long while. Will finally spoke.

"I haven't found the courage to write my family, especially my mother. She adored Gus. How am I going to tell her when she pleaded with us not to go?"

"You're not returning with the Skylark?" There was a sound of relief in her voice as well as an unmindful selfishness. She had failed to comfort his question.

"I'll stay here a bit and try to regain my strength. More likely I'll return on the next merchant ship that sails into the harbor."

Her heart sank from the thought of losing him. Perhaps there was time enough and feeling enough between them for him to ask her to leave with him. She lowered her eyes for fear that he might catch a glimmer of her dissoluteness. Here he had poured out his heart to her and all she could think of was herself, of losing him. She took a breath and straightened, seeming more in control.

"You've been through a great deal, Will. First of all you must regain your health. Right here is the perfect place. After a while, it will come to you what you must do. I'm sure your family is anguishing over some news from you. You're right, it will be difficult telling them about your brother. At least write and let them know you're safe."

"How do I do that without mentioning Gus? I can't tell you how often I wished it were me instead of him."

"Please don't say that. I'm truly sorry about Gus, but I'm glad that you are here safe, that we met."

"Are you?"

He thoughtfully studied her face. There was such sincerity in her expression that he had to bite his lip for what he might well have told her about their meeting.

"Here we are," Will continued, "two transplanted Easterners, who had to traverse the whole of the Continent, to ultimately meet. Destiny, is it all destiny? Gus and you and me?"

"Perhaps, I don't know. When we lost Papa it was so shocking and painful. Strangely enough, it was the very thing that brought us to California, and to our meeting."

"You loved your Papa very much, didn't you?" There was something strangely cold in his question.

"Oh yes, much more than he realized. He was such a dear good man. It was a terrible loss, so sudden. You see, I do understand how deeply you hurt."

Quite abruptly he sat up, his hands slipping away from hers. He stared out at the sprawling landscape as though deliberately avoiding something better left unsaid.

"Look at those vaqueros out there."

He pointed to dozen or more riders racing wildly in the distance, their red kerchiefs flaring, and their huge spiked rowels at the end of their spurs glinting like mirrors in the sunlight. Jubilant shouts echoed back and forth over hillsides.

Heather found it difficult to respond. Obviously something in their conversation had upset him. She was suddenly ashamed of her own aggressiveness. Never before in her seventeen years had she so much as touched a man, other than Papa. And here she was stroking, fondling and all but flaunting herself at Will. It happened so easily, so instinctively. And now she was filled with misgivings. He had opened himself to her and then briskly cut off his feelings. Did she imagine his fondness for her? She stared out at the vaqueros diminishing in the distance, barely seeing them for the threat of tears.

"I always considered myself a fair horsemen," Will remarked "but those caballeros start from a gallop. The bareback vaqueros are as superior a horseman as the saddled ones with all their finery. They must surely be the best equestrians in the world."

"Yes." Heather weakly added. Finally she mustered the courage to ask. "What did I say Will, that offended you?"

He looked at her, his face softening. "Forgive my rudeness. It's just that some months prior to our journey to Panama we lost our father. Unfortunately, I can't go on about it with great affection. It's best if we do not speak of it again. I don't want my problems to change things between us. Believe that, Heather dear. Believe that I've come to care for you very much. I have no idea at this point in my life where it can possibly lead. I can't make any promises, which is not at all fair to a respectable young woman such as yourself."

She could barely repress her tears. "It's all right Will. Whatever comes of us, I am your friend, for always."

"I want more than friendship. Right now, this moment, I want so desperately to kiss you."

"Then—then kiss me." She could not believe her own words. Never had she dare be so brazen. But there was no time for formality, no time at all.

Gently his palms cradled her face and slowly lifted it to his own, the softness of his mouth at once seeking hers. She remained almost breathlessly still, all the while aching to throw her arms about his neck and kiss him back with unrestrained passion. But this was the first kiss. The first feel of a man's body aligned against her own. He moved in so close that she could feel the tautness of his muscles beneath his clothes and his heartbeat. For a moment they both felt faint from rapture. The tenderness of his kiss and touch took care with her inexperience. His mouth slightly parted only to draw away. His hands slipped from her face to look deep into her eyes misty with love. A look she recognized in him. Will was first to steady himself, sighing as he did.

"I think it's about time we head back to the house."

"Yes."

Her voice was soft and acquiescent, but a lie. She wanted to stay right here, slip down upon the high grass and make love. Suddenly her face was as scarlet as the strawberries. She jumped to her feet and ran homeward, leaving Will to retrieve the small white parasol tittering on the hedge.

A group of vaqueros riding past burst into uproarious laughter upon seeing a most peculiar sight. A tall lean looking Yankee, strangely garbed, was loping through the field with a lady's dainty parasol held high overhead.

Chapter 7

"For Gods sake Iris, stop that screeching!" Heather reproached her sister's high-pitched squeals of excitement, which came concurrently with rambunctious leaps across the bedroom floor.

Iris was reacting to being serenaded by a trio of throbbing guitars and passionate Spanish love songs led by the thoroughly enraptured Don Cristóbal. The elaborately dressed caballeros sat astride beautiful white Arabians, directly below their balcony. Heather was quick to turn out the two dimly lit oil lamps.

Iris groaned. "Did you have to leave us in pitch black?"

"Yes, I did. Just look at you, near naked in that thin nightgown and darting madly about the room for all to see."

"I'm going out on that balcony," Iris insisted. "Where in blazes is my robe? I can't see a dang thing!"

"Stop exaggerating!"

Shafts of moonlight streamed through the two narrow windows shadowing the ornate grillwork on the white washed walls. Heather rushed across the room and shut the dark brown casements.

"Now you did it Heather!"

"Give me a minute, while I light a lamp."

"Hurry up!"

In an instant there was a dim flicker of light. Iris was at once struggling with her robe and slippers, her impatience causing a tangle of arms and sleeves.

"Heather quickly, run down the corridor to the Madonna and steal me a rose!"

"I will not. That's a blasphemous idea. Haven't you any shame?"

"Oh, come on, Heather, I just have to throw him a rose. That's the way it's done here."

"I don't care and I don't approve of your encouraging that young man. His intentions are obviously honorable. I will not have you trifle with his affections."

"You sanctimonious prude!"

"I am not a prude."

"Not for yourself, you're not. I've seen you with Will. I think you're capable of obscene things. I didn't think that of you, Heather, but I do now. You flush every time he's near, or even when his name is mentioned. Look at you now."

"Go to bed, Iris." Heather was indeed flushing. It angered her to have Iris ridicule her feelings for Will. "Just go to sleep Missy and shut your mouth!"

"No! How do you expect me to ignore the fact that I'm being serenaded? Imagine he sings too. Listen to that voice. It sends shudders up my spine. I'm absolutely wild crazy about Don Cristóbal!"

"Wild crazy is a perfect description."

Iris was too elated to be dissuaded by Heather's admonishment. Once neatly robed she brushed her long hair to fall seductively over one shoulder and down upon her breast. Anxiously she reached for the balcony door only to have Heather pull her away.

"You're in you bed clothes, Missy!"

"So? Isn't night dark enough for you? I'm dressed like a damn nun compared to all the flesh I've seen displayed by these so-called Spanish ladies"

"We're still New Englanders." Heather scolded.

"Turn out that stupid lamp, because either way I'm going out on that balcony."

She tore away from Heather's tight grasp upon her wrist and again started toward the balcony only to turn back to quickly rummage through her valise. Finding a lace trimmed handkerchief she dabbed it with exquisitely scented French perfume. Turning to Heather she smirked.

"Compliments of Don Toby."

With a defiant swirl of her fine blue robe she moved out onto the balcony that wound around the house affording each of the upper rooms its own exit.

At the sight of her emergence Don Cristóbal's deep melodic voice truly soared. Each phrase, each heartfelt intonation was focused upon Iris. She stood there leaning over the railing, her eyes steadfast upon his. The moon was full upon her face causing the lustrous cascade of auburn hair to appear as dark as ebony and her pale skin the likes of alabaster. The sight of her stirred even deeper emotion to Cristóbal's already fervent lyrics.

Iris waited until the last note of his voice, the last strum of the guitar before making a coquettish gesture with the perfumed handkerchief. She fluttered it a bit before throwing it down to Cristóbal's waiting grasp. He caught it and tenderly raised it to his lips in a long passionate kiss that emulated what he might do if it were she. The sweet exotic scent of perfume caused him to slightly reel. He then tucked the precious item inside his jacket close to his heart.

"Mi querida," He called out to her in wonderfully rolling syllables. "My darling." He added in heavily accented English.

"Querida." Iris seductively repeated, unknowingly having used the feminine instead of the masculine use of the word. Cristóbal was even more enthralled by her efforts. He threw her a kiss. At that point Heather abruptly yanked her back into the room, tightly closing the thick balcony door behind them.

"What in blazes are you doing?" Iris could not contain her hysterics. "Tomorrow Cristóbal leaves for Monterey. I don't know when we'll get to see each other again. Since Mamma insists that we live in that dismal, dirty little hamlet of Yerba Buena with Tobias, our precious cousin Blanquita will have him all to herself!"

"Stop it, Iris! Stop being jealous of his sweet little cousin."

"Sweet little Señorita Blanquita," Iris sarcastically emphasized. "I'm sick of the sight of her! And the way everyone protectively fawns over her, like she were some darn princess. I'll tell you, there is something obviously very suspicious about that girl."

"Don't cause trouble Iris."

"That girl is the spitting image of our Estrellita, except she's much fairer. What is the big secret that seems to be deliberately ignored? I refuse to believe that you haven't noticed or aren't a bit curious."

"It isn't our business."

"It's really strange," Iris strutted across the room. "Really strange that Señorita Blanquita is called Miss White. Blanca, meaning white. You know the fair one. That would truly be a coincidence, wouldn't it? Two sisters having identical daughters born at the same time. One fair, the other dark skinned because the father was an Indian. Personally I didn't see the slightest resemblance between Blanquita and her mother and sisters, who by the way are all brown eyed."

"I saw many Californians at the fiesta with light eyes and fair skin. Stop creating a problem with this girl."

"The problem already exists, Heather dear." Iris stressed.

"Stay out of it, Iris. We're guests in this country. Uncle Johnny would not approve of your meddling. Nor would anyone else. What would Cristóbal think of you?"

Iris angrily pounced upon her bed only to be swiftly mollified by the persistent of guitars faintly strumming through the night. She lie upon her back, her arms hugging the soft beautifully embroidered pillowcase. She could not help but smile at the thought of being serenaded by one of the most attractive and seductive men she had ever met. It was not only thrilling but quite a conquest.

She first heard him sing at the fiesta. His voice and guitar accompanied his sister Rufina as she danced the Fandango. Her long gleaming black hair hung loose and flying as she sensually moved across the floor, her red high-heeled shoes rhythmically stomping. The strength of her legs belied their grace and agility. As enchanted as Iris was at first hearing Don Cristóbal sing her resentment toward Rufina only compounded. Everyone seemed mesmerized as she dramatically danced, her filmy black gown glittering with sparkles. The smooth silk-like flesh of her shoulders, her arms, her naked legs flashing through folds of billowing fabric were deemed beautiful by all who watched. Back home in Boston the sight of such a woman would have at once labeled her a whore. It was not righteousness that rankled Iris, but jealousy.

She was disturbed by Uncle Johnny's unbounded pride in his wife, the way his gaze remained fixed and glowing as he studied every sensual step and gesture, tantalized by the wild whip of her long shimmering black hair. At the end of her performance he walked to the center of the floor and passionately kissed her for all to see and applaud. Iris' recall of the fiesta ultimately turned her scowl into a smug little smile. She could not deny that it was the most exciting party she had ever attended, with the most devastatingly handsome and romantic man she had ever known. The brassy mariachi band seem to play non-stop, keeping pace with the tireless dancers of all ages that crowded the salon.

There was a constant replenishing of food that gorged the long white clothed tables. The whole roasted beefs and turkeys, huge steaming platters of corn tortillas, enchiladas and tamales, created wonderful aromas that tempted the appetite. A variety of preserves were dished in equally colorful bowls. Bountiful assortments of fruits were beautifully arranged in elaborate Indian baskets. Two Indian girls of twelve, waving long branches above the tables, protected the banquet from the flies.

Although there was a great deal to drink, wines, brandies, aquardiente, and an exceptionally strong beer called cerveza ruerte, the paisanos did not drink until intoxicated, in a way adhering to the old

Spanish custom of moderation. Not so for the celebrant crew of the Skylark and of course Iris, who managed to show the worst of wear.

The week following the fiesta came as a well needed respite. At times too much of a respite. She found herself spending untold hours being bored by the well-meaning ladies. She and Heather would ride and embroider, play a great deal of whist, were patiently taught to pick at the guitar and on several occasions were taken swimming. Swimming was something neither girl had ever done, nor ever contemplated doing. To their amazement the California women were expert swimmers, far excelling the men. In their long thin woolen nightgowns, that covered the whole of their bodies, they would dive into the bay or into lakes to emerge with their long hair and bodies soaking, the nightgowns clinging to them in a manner that might well be skin. Who could guess that Johnny and Rufina often swam in the nude, sometimes on moonlit nights, but always to the exclusion of others?

Why was it that Rufina and Blanquita were such thorns in Iris' side? Each had treated her most lovingly, had welcomed her as kin, which meant everything in this family oriented country. Still the idea of Blanquita disturbed her more. Everything about that girl lay heavily upon her mind. Especially now that the serenading had ceased and she lie in the dark while Heather seemingly dozed. Iris was struck with the realization that tomorrow was only hours away. Suddenly she sat upright in bed and loudly declared. "I want to go to Monterey!"

"You've been to Monterey," Heather weakly mumbled.

"Not with him, I haven't. Besides, it was a short uneventful stay. The O'Larkins were nice enough. Now that I think of it, she's such a prude. Can you possibly imagine her doing the Fandango? Sure, they fed us well enough and fawned over us as if we were long lost relatives. As if being Protestant was everything. There was no partying, not even aboard ship or at the Governor's house. No fiesta, nothing."

"God forbid, Iris! Aren't you fiesta'd out by now. Go to sleep"

"How can I sleep?" Iris anguished. "Do you have any idea what is going on inside my head and my heart?"

"I dread to think," Heather sighed. "Please, don't tell me."

"The only reason Mamma is being so stubborn about us staying with her in Yerba Buena, is because she wants to be with him." Iris emphasized 'him'. "Our own mother is using us, Heather. Our presence makes it all good and proper that she live in his house."

Exasperated Heather finally gave into sleeplessness. She propped herself up on one elbow and faced her sister's bed but a few feet parallel to her own. She could see her quite well for the brightness of the moon shafted itself across Iris' pillow. How young and innocent she appeared and how thoroughly she needed to have her neck rung.

"I don't believe that to be true, Iris. And I definitely refuse to have you dare discredit out Mamma's integrity with your ugly innuendoes."

"Well, I have my opinion. You know good and well we could stay here with Uncle Johnny. Why make us live in that hovel of a settlement, with nothing to do?"

"How can you say that? We haven't even had the time to explore the place or know the people. The few we met were truly hospitable. Tobias' house is charming and comfortable, and it looks out on that glorious bay."

"Oh, pish posh on the bay!"

"You can carry on all you want, Iris, but if Mamma wants us there, then I'm with her."

"And with Will" Iris hissed. "Will is staying in Yerba Buena with a Yankee family, I hear. So you'll get to see him. Of course you want to go back. What about me and Don Cristóbal. What's going to happen to us?"

"We'll be coming back here for the Rodeo. I'm certain there will be untold other events." Heather pacified. "And I don't doubt for a moment that Don Cristóbal will be courting you when he returns from

Monterey. Actually Iris we haven't been in California long enough to honestly know what's going to happen to any of us."

"What if Mamma decides to marry Tobias? Then what?"

"Then Mamma will be very happy and we'll be happy for her, won't we Missy?"

"A real pish posh on that one Heather. Am I suppose to get excited about having Don Toby as a father?"

"Yes you should. He's a good man and they do care about each other. She's thirty-three years old. That may seem ancient but she can't very well sit in a rocking chair the rest of her days. So let her have her life and we'll have ours. Can we go to sleep now?"

"I'm not sleepy."

"Goodnight Iris."

Heather turned back on her side and whipped the comforter over her head, pretending to recapture her sleep. But she was more wide-awake than ever. Iris proposed some rather startling questions. She had spoken badly about Blanquita, who indeed was an enigma. There was no denying the incredible resemblance between she and Estrellita.

There was their future to consider. More likely Mamma and Tobias would marry and perhaps Iris might actually settle down with the already captivated Don Cristóbal. What about Will and herself? He made it quite clear that he ultimately intended to return home. She lie there sleepless, anguishing over the thought. What would become of them?

Chapter 8

"What did you say in that eloquent sounding Spanish of yours?"

Belle reacted to Toblas' slow but fanciful response upon being greeted by Don Louis and Doña Carmen, the Patrón and Patróna of La Mirada. Their solitary hillside Rancho, which lay several miles south of Monterey, overlooked the Carmelo Bay.

"Eloquent" he laughed. "If only you could hear me with their ears. My Yankee accent with its grammatical blunders definitely had something to do with all that smiling."

"And what accounts for them so enthusiastically embracing me? Kisses upon both cheeks and all." There was a coyness as well as a suspiciousness to her question. "I realize that in California, I am referred to as Doña Belle. But right now, whose Doña Belle do they think I am?"

"Why mine, of course. My Doña Bella."

He affectionately emphasized, Doña Bella, the name also being an adjective for beautiful. His arms swept about her waist and pulled her close to his side as they followed their hosts to the large resplendent room that would be their sleeping quarters for the next three days.

"But Toby," she protested. "It's not true. I'm not your wife. What would they think if they knew?"

"What is there to know? These are my friends. We were joyously accepted for what we are, a man and woman in love."

Belle had no response. She wanted this as much as Tobias, had agreed to go away with him without question. Suddenly in the presence of all those smiling faces she felt tinges of embarrassment and deceit. He promised her privacy and here they were the center of attention. Yet their host and hostess took pains to afford them times of togetherness, respectfully uninterrupted moments that become the pleasure and inspiration of the entire household. The widower Don Tobias had taken himself a bride and they were genuinely happy for them both.

Belle was quickly swept up in a new role. How easy to play the part of Toby's wife. He was by her side, tall and strong, his arms warmly embracing her waist, his eyes, his smile a constant assurance. It was a kind of security she never fully experienced before. It entailed something far greater than the material comfort of her Boston home and the respect of being Colon's wife. Suddenly the idea of being a woman filled her with tremendous self-esteem. It was difficult remembering herself as that sadly frail widow with her two bereaving daughters trudging up the gangplank to first set foot on the Skylark. Their presence was happily received by the shipload of lonely men, many of whom were homesick boys.

As they stepped off at Yerba Buena, they again found themselves in a domain of men. Awe struck gazes, graciously tipped hats and beaming smiles, were the immediate response to their appearance. There was the grandness of Johnny's Santa Clara Rancho and an introduction to Spanish hospitality and now La Mirada.

All her life Belle had adhered to the rigidity of provincial customs. From girlhood to widowhood she had dutifully acquiesced to whatever was expected of her. With Colon's death she resigned herself to growing old and dying as a widow. After all, she was thirty-three years old with grown daughters. What else could she expect? How could she have possibly conceived that there was anything more, least of all a man like Tobias Knight? But he was here by her side, revering her womanhood, allowing her to feel unashamed of her own sensual needs and pleasures.

Time and again they had come incredibly close to making love, ceasing only at her guilty insistence. The months of mourning were spent almost totally in his company, on the Skylark and now here in California. How ironic to have it become the happiest time of her life. She had been too elated to grieve, too consumed with feelings of love and passion. She experienced the joy of having found the dearest friend she had ever known. Why be concerned with the proprieties of a Boston that was thousands of miles away? She yearned to be with Toby more that she had ever wanted anything before.

Those long months of longing, of fantasizing, were close to culmination. She was constantly distracted with desire, yet haunted by her own irreverence. She was almost at the end of her morning period. Why was it so difficult to wait a trifle longer? Already she had replaced her somber black frock with a fetching green riding habit and a matching wide rimmed vicuna hat trimmed in silver, worn jauntily over one eye. If that were not enough she wore shiny black and gold-tooled boots and a bright red scarf fringed in silver around her throat. Everyone, man and woman, wore bright red scarves tied in a side knot to fly loosely in the wind. It is a wonder her mirror did not crack at the sight of herself. She felt both shock and elation upon viewing her own image. That drab black dress and tight string bonnet was recklessly discarded with her old self.

Tobias had changed into an outfit that befits the finest of caballeros. She could not help but gasp at the sight of him. In his snug fitting attire with its gold trim and buttons, the extravagant boots and spurs, the black vicuna hat and red scarf, he appeared a devastatingly handsome figure of a man.

What might have sounded far-fetched back home was in fact quite real in California. Belle could barely believe the changes that had taken place in her life, so many so soon. But she was not about to turn back, ever.

Belle had to brace herself upon kissing her daughters goodbye. They remained aghast at the sight of their demure widowed mother brazenly dressed in green, her red neckerchief fluttering as she rode off with Don Toby. The girls could not believe their eyes, especially Iris. Mamma's girlish laughter rang in their ears long after the two riders disappeared over the sand-hills. Not for a moment did Belle look back. How easy it all was with Tobias at her side. A tender look or touch would dispel all doubt.

Upon arriving at La Mirada, and being enthusiastically greeted by the entire household, Belle paused unsteadily in her pace. She looked to Tobias, her eyes anxiously asking that he placate their scandalous actions.

"You're a grown woman, Belle." He hotly whispered into her ear as they moved through the arched corridor, where both sunlight and shadow shafted their course. "It is time to allow yourself to be thoroughly loved."

She almost reeled in his arms at the taunting reality of his words, as well as his warm titillating breath upon her neck and ear. "I've already made love to you a thousand times over in my mind, as you have me." His hands tightened around her waist. "You are already my esposa, my wife."

She flushed profusely before their hosts, causing them to grin more broadly. For here was a couple who were very much in love, and that in itself was a celebration of life. 'My God!' Belle thought, 'another fiesta?' To her relief, what ensued, was a, 'valecito casaro', a little home party. There was the delectable food and drinks, and of course the music and dancing. The festivity dispersed by mid-night.

Still one could tell that Don Toby and his Señora were tired from the arduous journey and wanted to be alone. The sweet sensuality of Spanish guitars accompanied them to their chamber door, at which time, they fell more in love with each other. Here at La Mirada they found themselves conveniently distanced from their doubts, at last free to consummate their wildest fantasies.

They were serenaded behind the closed door of a beautifully furnished bedroom, made even lovelier by the scent and sight of flowers, baskets and vases of flowers. Melodically romantic cords accompanied by seducing male voices echoed from the corridor. Belle and Tobias, who felt heady from the wine and the joy, were caught up by the music. The mood itself was intoxication. How exquisite to be able to touch without restraint, to languish in each other's arms and ravish one another without doubt or condemnation.

Their shadows silhouetted against the white washed wall, two figures fusing into one; slightly parting as garments stripped away to uncover the smoothness of naked bodies. For the first time in her life Belle stood fully unclothed before a man, half shadowed yet brazenly unashamed. Her pale body resembled alabaster.

Though slim, she was surprisingly curvaceous beneath those voluminous skirts and high-necked bodices. Her waist was wasp-like, having from the age of thirteen been subjected to the tightest of corsets. Her full breasts seem to swell warmly into his palms. Her limbs were long and lovely, fittingly curved at the thighs and calves in a manner he had failed to fathom. Till this moment, her slender ankles and the briefest show of a heavy stocking covering her calf, was all he had gleaned. His sighs of delight were one with rapture.

He loosened her hair and followed its fall to her waist, full and luxuriant. Her blue eyes took on darkness and brilliance. They glistened with tears of sheer joy.

Open palmed she reached out to touch upon the broadness of his chest, at first with a timidity and then with pleasure. Her fingertips delicately glided across his torso with its sprinkling of curly dark hair. He slightly shivered. He could not remember ever having been touched with such tenderness.

She found him much more muscular than she realized, a man often helping to lift and haul his own cargo, a man indifferent to status. Unlike her gaunt desk-bound husband, Tobias' body was taut and sinewy, his forearms strong. Her hands ran down the length of his arms to his large palms, which clasped over hers. In the semi-shadow of this room, with its faint oil lamp, there was the look of youth, each seeming to have transgressed in time. She was the girl he would have undoubtedly loved, if they had met years before. And he was the young man of the dreams she dare not dream. He lifted both her hands to his lips and kissed them. This was the tender prelude to a greater passion.

Tobias lifted her in his arms and carried her to the large sumptuous bed strewn with satin pillows. As he placed her down upon her back, her long hair cascaded across the bedding. He lie above her propped on both his elbows. For a long quiet moment he rapturously stared into her half shadowed face, all the while smiling. When he finally spoke it was with a softness that intoned the deepest of feelings.

"You're mine, all mine." He assured her "For now, and for all our lives."

She sighed and he felt her slightly tremble.

"What is it, Belle?" He gently asked, suddenly sensing her timidity.

"All at once, I feel fifteen again," she nervously laughed. "It's been a long time since I've made love—and even then—"

Her cheek aligned with his, her arms tightened about his neck. She was both hiding and hugging. Her voice was that of a little girl. "I want so to be right for you, but I feel like everything has sort of sealed up. I'm ashamed to be acting so virginal at my age."

Softly, he caressed her, his hands smoothing down over her back and waist and hips, drawing her closer to the hardness of his body.

"There is no hurry, Belle. We've time enough to savor every morsel, every juice."

His words caused a tingling up her spine. Never had she had a man speak to her so intimately. Even his words caught her breath. Suddenly all those months of urgency, of frenzied passion took on a profound tenderness. There was time to thoroughly touch, to indulge ones sights and senses and taste. Here were two adults; adhered to each other's nakedness in a manner that each had not known before, experiencing the ultimate of passion as well as love, in one and the same person.

Though he truly loved Hannah, Tobias had his sexual liaisons before and on rare occasions, during their marriage. Though his wife was a sweet caring woman, she could very well forgo the nuptial bed. It had disheartened him terribly to have her dutifully endure his passion. How desperately he wanted her to want him.

Until now, Colon had been Belle's only lover. He would approach her gently, but far too quickly and always in the dark, their nightgowns concealing the greater part of their bodies. Dutifully and even shamefully she would comply, feeling that the utter intimacy of their conjugal act had a sense of lewdness she dare not admit to herself. It was always so pointedly executed, as though there were no other loving part to her but that hidden place between her thighs, and the hardness of her nipples clumsily squeezed until they hurt. Too often she craved for more, had dared to move a different way, or hold him tightly against herself. But it was always the same, a quick frenzied act that satiated Colon. One that he politely thanked her for, followed by a ceremonious kiss upon the brow. He would then turn on his side to sleep, a cold space between them. She was left to clean up the sticky glob that was the culmination of his pleasure.

Never did she dream that one day a man would actually make her desire that hot surge of wetness deep inside herself. The anticipation of tonight bore a shamelessness, a completeness all its own. How easy it was to mesh the nakedness of arms and legs and torsos, an entirely new but all familiar fit. The tenderness of their kisses became hot and devouring.

"This is the way it's supposed to be." He whispered, alluding not only to his own feelings but also to the sweetness of her responses.

Tobias' mouth slid down to tenderly kiss her throat and breasts and trail down the tiny mound of stomach, and further still to explore every inch of her body, exhilarating in her sighs and quivers. Her hands embraced his head, fingers wildly meshing though his hair as he moved about her body even down to her feet and toes.

For the first time in her life Belle dared to take the initiative. It was her turn to ravish him. To wondrously emulate every detail of what he had done to her. She could feel him writhe beneath her mouth and touch. How much more ripe and moist could they possibly become? They were but moments from bursting. Tobias drew her deep beneath him, flesh fusing with flesh, heartbeats synchronously wild, to at last realize the ultimate intimacy.

"My God!" She sighed almost crying. "You belong. You slip into me so easily. I must have been waiting for you all my life and didn't know."

"Then give me you."

His mouth and breath were hot upon hers, both sweet and sensual. He commenced a gentle rhythm of thrusts that suddenly grew in momentum and frenzy. And she moved with him all the way, again and again her own abandonment welding with his every movement, again and again abating only with the depletion of all their senses, two ecstatic gasps in the night. Except with Belle, muffled tears and sobs continued into the broadness of his chest, already wet with perspiration.

"My darling, what is it? My God, what is it? Did I hurt you?" He was stroking her head, kissing her brow and the tears upon her cheeks.

"I'm all right," she whispered "truly I am. It's—it's—" she hesitated "I never felt like this before. I never in my wildest dreams realized how it could be. Everything seemed to go afire at once. Every fiber in my being seem to rejoice and explode in the same instant, throbbing into my very brain."

"That's the way it's suppose to be Belle." He was smiling broadly. Though she could not see his expression in the dark, she could tell by his voice.

"Now I know how men must feel when they go crazy with passion."

She was laughing amidst her tears. He realized that her sobs were in fact the shocking reverberation of her passion having at last culminated in ecstatic joy, and for the first time.

"It's wonderful, isn't it" she was yet breathing heavily.

His soft kisses covered her face. At last he paused to answer her. "Yes, it is."

"We fit so beautiful." Belle whispered "completely so." Suddenly she laughed aloud. "Can you imagine this ever happening in prim and proper New England?"

"With you, yes. Single, married, or widowed, it wouldn't have mattered. I would have still claimed you as my own."

He kissed her full and long upon the mouth, his arms drawing her even closer. She snuggled into his embrace brimming with love as well as gratitude, realizing that it was she lying with him naked in bed, and not some young beautiful hija del pais.

In that instant, Colon's shadow slipped away forever from her mind and heart. He was gone, and suddenly she was free to experience life at its fullest.

Chapter 9

A dozen or more horses galloped two abreast, at times being forced to move single file, through the densely brushed trail that was imposingly called El Camino del Rey, the King's Highway. The name was borrowed from the grand highways of Spain constructed by the decree of King Ferdinand.

Its remote California counterpart was a dusty footpath that the Franciscan padres used to travel from one California Mission to another, reaching all twenty one, from San Diego to Sonoma, in a good hard days journey between each. The gray robed fathers with their long hooded cloaks, dutifully adhered to the rule of St. Francis, by walking all the way, clad in sandals.

With the secularization of the Missions, it was rare to come upon a padre trudging the El Camino. If so, he more than likely was warn and aged, a few straggling neophytes accompanying him on his long lonely course.

The Mission trail which once broadened into great Avenidas adjoining the pueblos, had once been kept cut back by the multitude of Mission Indians. The neophytes were long gone. The sight of soldiers escorting priests, along with manacled runaway Indians, drunken sailors gathering in the many grog stops along the way, carretas and mules laden with hides, wares and wine, were lost to time and overgrowth.

The El Camino had thickened with trees, with pines and oak so full and knurled that riders often had to stoop atop their horse. The flutter and chirping of birds were everywhere. Thousands flitted through trees and into the deep brush. The excitement was enhanced by the throbbing gallop of unshod horses and the ring of human voices. Small animals dashed underfoot, rabbits and hare, squirrels and fox.

It was a placid kind of wilderness that never failed to concur to the silent threat of coming upon a huge grizzly bear, considered more ferocious than any lion. Yet merely game for the Californio, whose riata, though little more than a coarse kind of rope, was a magical weapon in the dexterity of his hands.

Led by Hector and flanked in the rear by the rest of the vaqueros, Tobias, Belle, Iris, Heather and Will rode homeward to Yerba Buena. After having passed the decaying Mission of Santa Clara, their next stop was 15 leagues away to the Mission of San Francisco, or Dolores. Here they would dismount and attend a service, or more accurately, a celebration; a spiritual celebration.

Even though there was an over night stay at Rancho San Mateo, the women were anxious to dismount. Unlike the Spanish Californians, who seemed to spend the greater part of their lives mounted on beautiful spirited mustangs and Arabians, Belle and her daughters were accustomed to traveling quite comfortably in carriages driven over Boston's cobble-stoned streets.

Rufina saw to it that they were appropriately outfitted for their long ride. From their boots right up to the wide brimmed vicuna hats which protected their skin from the sun, as was the manner of the ladies of the country. To be sitting crosswise with both legs hanging over the right of their mount, a firm sash about their waist was definitely not their choice of travel. It was astounding to learn that the hijas del pais thought nothing of riding seventy or more miles, leaping over stream and gorge alike, dismounting for a brief respite at some welcoming Rancho along the way.

Hector, who was paces ahead of the rest, was first to sight the Mission. Abruptly he reigned his horse, causing it to dramatically rear.

He whipped off his black sombrero, held it to his heart and with his right hand reverently made the sign of the cross, all without losing the thin black cigarillo that consistently dangled from the side of his mouth.

Mission Dolores sat in a fertile valley embraced by the foothills, southeast of the Bay of San Francisco. A valley gleaming from the flow of rivulets formed a creek close to its own small lake. The site had been name by a scouting party that shortly proceeded the founding of this sixth Mission. They had come upon a small stream on the feast of Our Lady of Sorrows, Nuestra Señora de los Dolores, the name Dolores meaning sorrow.

For all the beauty of the topography, with the lush fragrances that wafted through the pure Pacific air, the myrtle, mustard seed, rosemary, mint, chamomile, wild rose and sweet tangy pine, for all that the Mission had once been, there was indeed sorrow.

One's attention at once focused upon the thick walled adobe church, reminiscent of the other Mission churches, equally in ruin. Its facade of ten colonnades and a stretch of balcony across the front were typically Spanish. Its peeked rooftop was composed of tiles, a great many broken and missing. At the very apex of the roof rose a cross, a stark black imprint against a cloudless blue sky.

Adjoining this main structure was a rambling cluster of long open corridor buildings that formed a quadrangle facing a plaza. It was difficult to imagine that this desolate deteriorating complex was once a teeming, thriving industrious congregation that tended to the needs of thousands, soldiers, citizens, foreigners, traders, padres and Indians alike. Dolores once supplied all. In truth, the neophytes were the sole laborers.

Of course the team of usually two padres that foresaw the teaching and management of the Missions believed in putting in equally long and arduous hours. They were educated men who were capable of teaching every facet necessary to build and maintain a Mission complex, from the manual to the spiritual. Now there was no resident priest, no daily mass or services. A Pastoral visit was rare.

Several families and several single males from Yerba Buena made their home at the Mission. Five or six Indians sat or lie in the shade of the crumbling archways. After a lifetime of inexhaustible labor and dedication to the church, they were too old or beaten to leave. Still they subsisted by cultivating small garden plots of vegetables. Several scrawny-looking cows lazily crossed the courtyard indifferent to the multitude of gray squirrels running through their legs. There were hundreds of those little creatures poking out of every hole and crevice. And there were rabbits galore and untold pigeons roosting in the side shrines, in the carved headpieces of doorways, on cracked tiled roofs and in the belltowers. Family of quails, each mother leading her tiny offspring's waddled one behind the other.

High atop a fissured adobe wall an incredibly haughty peacock pranced back and forth, to at last stop and pose. With an air of complete omnipotence he unfurled his huge splendiferous tail, plumage composed of iridescent eyes in cobalt blue, vivid green and purple, awash with gold. He stood there vainly shimmering in the sunlight, seeming to gloat upon the sad spectacle that spanned out into the horizon. Not only the sight of decaying buildings and aqueducts, but withered vineyards, barren orchards, and empty pastures.

Iris, her mouth agape, surveyed the scene. She remained momentarily caught up by the sight of the cross, which for some reason sent a shiver up her spine. For the first time in days she was reminded of Papa, of his horrifying demise and of the solemn church service that followed. Her eyes lowered to the three large bells hanging beneath the cross. Each was recessed in its own bell tower between colonnades and suspended from thronged hide. They had been cast in Mexico and named in honor of three saints, Joseph, Francis and Martin. As she stared, the one directly below the cross began to loudly ring startling them all, the horses the small scurrying animals and the myriad of birds that suddenly rose en masse. The loud clap of wings almost dimmed the persistent toll.

"This is a celebration?" Iris yelled above the din. "It looks more like a dirge to me."

"Not likely." Heather pointed out to the canopied carreta in the courtyard. It was decorated with flowers and ribbons, the oxen equally bedecked.

"It is a Holy Communion." Tobias moved his horse in closer to the girls, the bell ceasing mid-sentence, leaving him shouting.

"What's that?" Iris asked.

"You will see shortly. Let us follow Hector into the plaza and hitch our horses."

This they did, the ladies allowing themselves to be helped from their saddles. Tobias tended to Belle, who had to lean on him for support. "I feel so weak." She whispered repressing a giggle.

He knew well why and squeezed her arm both affectionately and assuringly. It had been three wild days of making love, not to mention the arduous hours on horseback. His hold did not leave her for an instant.

Hector was quick to lift Iris down from her horse, black eyes and smile flashing, his thick white teeth sensually biting his cigarillo.

Will, who seldom failed to be far from Heather, was fast to dismount and unfasten her sash. He lifted her down in a brief embrace that not only caught Iris' eye, but her anger. How in blazes had she ended up being helped by Hector, when she craved Cristóbal's arms?

"Heather." She called out contriving a lame excuse to draw her sister away from Will. "Help me, I seem to be knotted." She pointed to the red scarf tied at her throat. "It's choking me!"

"If it isn't, I will!" Heather whispered under her breath, being well aware of Iris' bit of manipulation.

Will's hand tightened on hers as she moved away from him to her sister's side only to have the red scarf suddenly and quite easily slip away.

Heather found herself crunching it in her fist, then letting it fall to the ground.

Hector was quickly there to retrieve it and gently place it in Iris' palm. 'Again Hector', she thought in revulsion.

"Señorita." He smiled staring deep into her eyes.

There was something about his smile that unnerved her. As well as the way he always managed to be there. For once in her life she failed to flirt. He frightened her.

"Thank you. Gracias." She added haltingly in Spanish, then angrily turned to her sister. "Cristóbal gave me this scarf. He took it from his own throat and placed it around mine. You damn well knew it. Yet you deliberately squished it and threw it on the ground."

"Did I?" Heather feigned innocence.

"Girls!" Belle was upon them. "Please keep your differences to yourself, especially today, here at this holy site."

"Ladies." It was Tobias. Father Santillian has come out of the church to welcome us."

The thickly carved double doors of the church were wide open, and standing there on the steps was a very young and attractive priest beckoning them to enter. To their surprise he was ostentatiously garbed in white satin vestments gleaming with intricate gold embroidery, the loving diligent work of Mexican nuns. What a strange incongruity that such a desolately poor church be officiated by one so regally dressed. But it was only for this day of celebration. His garments would then be carefully packed and he would change into his dark secular frock and return to Santa Clara.

"That's a priest?" Iris exclaimed. "He's gorgeous and so young!"

"Father Santillian is only twenty four," Tobias offered. "He is a secular priest, newly ordained. Perhaps three or four months ago. He has come from Santa Clara to give Estrellita her First Communion."

"Our Estrellita?" Iris blinked in surprise.

The name immediately brought to mind Blanquita, who had ridden away to Monterey with Cristóbal. She could have easily remained indifferent to Estrellita, though the sight of her enormous blue eyes filled her with uneasiness. But no longer, not since she had met Blanquita. Iris was determined to unearth the mystery that surrounded these two young women, one fair, the other dark skinned. Both of them had the same startling blue eyes, the same silky black hair, the identical features and forms. Suddenly Iris's scowl turned to a coy conniving smile, one that Heather immediately recognized. Demurely she questioned Tobias.

"How do you say sisters in Spanish?"

"Hermanas," he answered.

Heather gave Iris a sharp pinch that yielded a squeal.

"What is it between you two?" Belle came back sternly, all the while endeavoring to modulate her voice.

Tobias interrupted. "Come, let us go."

Procession-like they walked to the church, Tobias in the middle escorting both Belle and Iris. Will, who caught on to the bickering little asides of the two sisters, moved-in to quietly placate Heather. Whatever the disagreement, he was certain that it was Iris' fault. Heather made a point to spare Will the particulars. He had enough to contend with without being pulled into their petty squabbles.

What Iris was intimating, as far as Blanquita and Estrellita were concerned, could very well magnify into a major problem. Iris' so-called curiosity had escalated into a vendetta. It frightened Heather to think of the damage that could be wrought to these two innocent, unsuspecting young women. Whatever their heritage, it was not any ones business. Yet deep inside, even she had commenced to wonder. Obviously they were related but discreetly distanced. One raised as a servant the other as one of the jente de razón, a person of reason or intellect, alluding to the blue bloods.

A smiling father Santillian greeted them with warm hugs and awkward blessings that befit a newly ordained priest. The vaqueros reaction to his presence was so overwhelming that he might well have been St. Francis himself. One by one they knelt before him, kissing his hand as well as the hem of his garment, all the while repeating the salutation handed down to them by Father Junipero Serra, Amor a Dios, love to God.

Although Father Santillian could not help but be taken aback by this enormous show of esteem, he understood, for Pastoral visits such as his were indeed a rarity. For over a decade there had been no resident priest to say Mass or give communion, to officiate at baptisms and weddings, to hear confessions or administer the last rights to the dying. The most sacred of Sacraments barely existed for this predominantly Catholic Country of California.

Belle and her daughters, as well as Will, were stunned by the sight of those rough swaggering vaqueros suddenly falling to their knees, their hard weather beaten faces transformed into expressions of bliss. As if the miraculous presence of this unseasoned Cleric was the last fragile link with spiritual salvation.

Father Santillian gestured for all of them to follow him into the Mission Church. Solemnly they entered to find a dark cavernous place lit only by a lone set of flaming brass candelabras standing on a sparse alter, and thin shafts of daylight through grilled recessed windows. Centered between the flicker of candles stood an ornate golden crucifix, a rich reminder of another time. It had been loaned from the Mission of Santa Clara for this special occasion. Like the candelabras, it conspicuously contrasted a church in desperate need of repairs.

The Mission carpenters were long gone and the pillages had been unmerciful in their greed. All had been defaced except for the Indian artwork yet vivid on the ceiling. The roll of adjoining beams, which were done with vegetable dyes in red, ochre and tan were painted in a jagged herringbone design.

Once Dolores had been filled to capacity with neophytes, their bodies not only exuding heat, but a certain vibrancy that seemed to permeate the adobe interior. Today the temperatures fell as they moved through the near empty church, its stinted light slashed wlth cold shadows. How opposite from the warmth and freshness of the spring day they had left outside. Their eyes had to adjust to the darkness.

They were not at first aware of those few already kneeling in silence on the earthen floor. The Carlson's and their two fidgety young sons rose to greet them in hushed tones. They were an American family from Yerba Buena, neighbors that were extremely close to Hannah and Tobias, and of course Estrellita and Miguel Pedro. They were the first to welcome Belle and the girls shortly after their arrival in California.

The vaqueros slipped silently into the church, black hats in hand, heads bowed and unassumingly knelt in the rear.

The small group of Yankees took their places close to the altar. There were no pews, only a hard earthen floor for kneeling. Rufina had provided each of them, with a small, embroidered mat. Still Iris' sighs and sulks disturbed those closest to her, which were her mother and sister. They were not even Catholic, she fumed, why were they being subjected to something so uncivilized? It was difficult enough sitting through the rigid services back home, but this was torture. Disgruntled, Iris looked about for Estrellita. To think they were going through all this for a half-breed serving girl.

Estrellita remained solemnly alone in a small high windowed sanctuary room awaiting Miguel Pedro's signal for her to emerge. It was he who had rung the bell of St. Francis, having arrived shortly before the Bradbury women and their party. He then hastened through the shaded corridor, now hauntingly devoid of sounds other than the echo of his own steps. He was struck by the memory of it all, the utter emptiness of the rambling buildings. The convento, the workshops, the storerooms and dwellings were stilled forever. Once Dolores was an unbelievable busy place with shops for melting tallow and stretching hides, with carpenters and blacksmiths, weavers, basket makers, with butchers and wine makers, Indians all. Except for the few padres that worked tirelessly at their sides, demanding as much from themselves as their wards. Whatever was needed or wanted was here, and plentiful. All those decades of prayer and toil of sacrifice and promises had culminated in chaos. What had happened to all those lives? Where had everyone gone? He must not allow himself to anguish over yesterday's pain. He must concentrate on this glorious day, which belonged to Estrellita.

He opened unto the small chamber where Estrellita knelt before a defaced statue of the Madonna. He had to sigh, for she appeared even more beautiful than when he first saw her in her Communion dress, while still in Yerba Buena. Her eyes were full upon him, the color of summer skies; a dark skinned angel dressed in white silk and gossamer. She was attired in a slim white dress, white satin slippers and silk hose. A white sheer fingertip veil hung from her head, hugging her face and tied in a white satin ribbon beneath her chin. Her graceful hands nervously fingered a pearl and silver rosary, each pearl an Ave Maria, which she whispered again and again as she waited.

Mrs. Carlson fondly helped Estrellita with her communion attire while still in the village. Time and again she stepped back to admire her, sweetly kissing her upon the brow when it was time to leave. The Carlsons proceeded her, leaving on horseback while Miguel Pedro proudly drove her to the Mission in the flower-decked carreta. Their voices harmonized in the Te Dium Laudamus as they slowly journeyed across the sand dunes, interspersed with scrub and chaparral, bright orange poppies, blue lupine and huge wild strawberries.

How very different today would be from Miguel Pedro's own First Communion, which he shared with a huge assembly of Indian children. All somehow transformed into dark skinned angels upon receiving the fragile white wafer that at a given moment during the litergy became the body of Christ.

There was a choir of thirty voices accompanied by guitars, violins, trumpets, flutes, clarinets, drums, rattles and rasps. A great melodious sound reverberated past the trusses to the very heavens. And there were bells. Shiny brass bells, of every size and resonance. The sweet intoxicating scent of incense wafted in misty puffs throughout the atmosphere reeling at the senses as well as an occasional body. Added to this was the perfume of rose petals that were scattered over the entire congregation at some momentous instant during the service. Untold candles flickered from all sides and from votive wheels that hung down from the rafters. The capricious flames caused the sainted statues to take on an aliveness, to smile and even weep. At a given moment a host of snow-white doves were released. Their soaring and fluttering of wing added to the spectacle.

This was the recollection of Miguel Pedro's First Communion, as it was for many a feast or holiday, a succession of litergic extravaganzas that were the complete opposite of the neophyte's otherwise austere lifestyle. It was pageantry never again to be repeated. He had a feeling of great emptiness upon returning to the Mission, feelings that had no place in Estrellita's quiet joy.

Miguel Pedro acted as sacristan, by thoughtfully preparing for the Mass that was a part of Estrellita's First Communion. The altar was adorned with a white linen cloth and mixed bouquets of flowers from Doña Hannah's garden. And of course, there were the candelabras and magnificent gold filigree crucifix. The once exquisitely carved tabernacle had been pillaged. In its place was a small white brocade tent with a curtain to house the chalice that held the Holy Eucharist. One host was reserved for Miguel Pedro to partake in the Communion with Estrellita.

He would also act as an altar boy, something he had done many times through those Mission years. At the end of the Mass, he and his sweet voiced daughter would join in the much-practiced Te Deum.

"It is time mi hijita."

A joyous sob emanated from deep within his throat. Mi hijta was an endearing term, which translated as 'my little daughter'. He handed her three long stemmed cala lillies, tied in a white bow, which she drew to her breast, the small silver crucifix from the rosary glistening over the back of her hand. Taking her by the elbow he proudly led her away.

As they entered the church he slipped from her side, prompting her to walk alone down the center isle. All eyes turned to this wisp of a girl, angelically garbed in white, her face radiantly beautiful. Her gaze remained transfixed by the alter, by the wonder of the hidden chalice beneath its white tent, the flaming candelabras and the exquisite gold crucifix, like none she had ever seen. To think it had once graced a Cathedral in Spain. Now it was here, especially for her. For the first time in her young life she felt beautiful and blessed. Her lone walk culminated at the bottom of the altar steps.

Father Santillian stood before the altar, arms outstretched facing them all. He was a magnificent sight, his white and gold vestments giving him an even more ethereal appearance by candlelight. Reverently he gave her a blessing and bid her to kneel.

As she did, tears began to well in those rapturous blue eyes. Miguel Pedro, who hastened to the altar from the side shadows, had arrived to catch that look of spiritual ecstasy that manifest itself in the sheen of her tears. He too softly cried. If only her mother could have lived to truly know the child she bore, a wondrous child, as no other. Surely Maria Inocencia's presence must be here this day, for them both.

Father Santillian raised his hand to bless the congregation, then turned to the altar to begin the Mass. To those who were not Catholic the Mass was a long boring ritual performed in tedious sounding Latin. And there was the incense and the sharp little bell that awakened one from their wanderings.

Time and again Iris found herself glass-eyed and reeling. "This is depressing," she mouthed to her sister.

"Suffer" Heather angrily mouthed back.

At last father Santillian turned to face them, the chalice in one hand, the fragile white host raised above the gold rim in his other hand, more Latin, more invocations and the piercing tingle of the bell.

Estrellita knelt throughout the Mass, her focus upon Father Santillian, upon his every word and gesture. At last he stepped down before her, a soft smile upon his face. She parted her lips and he gently fed her the host. There was a look of indescribable bliss on her face; one that confirmed that she was indeed steeped with a Godly presence. She had received the sacred Eucharist for the first time in her life.

It was now Miguel Pedro's turn. He knelt beside his daughter. For what seemed an eternity to Iris, they knelt there the two of them, father and daughter in rapt prayer. They were Ohlone Indians, their heritage seemingly lost to them forever, save for a fragment of Christian teaching left over from Delores. It was all they knew spiritually. Even though it too was eventually taken away, this moment before the tabernacle gave them a sense of belonging, of having a God somewhere who had not abandoned them.

Father Santillian returned to the altar to place the precious chalice behind drawn curtains. There was more mumbled Latin followed by a succession of blessings. Finally he gave a gesture prompting them to all rise.

The weary women had to be helped to their feet. Belle felt her knees buckle beneath her. All three of them were glad to find that the occasion had come to an end, though Iris made her feelings most evident with her sighing. Still, they were compelled to wait standing as Estrellita walked to the altar and reverently placed her bouquet of lilies before the tabernacle. Another long prayer ensued, which provoked Iris even further. Hadn't this thing been carried to the limit? She was hungry and tired and unbelievably bored. Suddenly even Tobias' house at Yerba Buena seemed desirable.

There was more, for at last came the moment for father and daughter to sing. Miguel Pedro began his solo, his deep baritone revealing not only the monotone Latin chant learned from the padres, but a trace of his own Indian heritage. Estrellita's small dulcet voice at last joined him in perfect harmony, their a capella strangely echoing through the near empty church. To the congregation, it was an inexplicably moving sensation, as well as chilling.

Estrellita at last turned and lovingly scanned those in attendance. She seemed to float as she moved down the center of the church followed by the small group.

Randomly they stepped out into the brightness of the day, at once squinting. There was the immediate feel and scent of fresh air, a delicious contrast from the pungent smell of incense and the molding dankness of the church.

Miguel Pedro, was the first to greet his daughter, seeming to transmigrate from one place to another in seconds. He touched her hand briefly then stepped away. His feelings for her were most private.

Tobias, who had always acted as another father, embraced her warmly kissing her on both cheeks, as did Belle, Heather, the Carlsons and even Will. Mumbling something meaningless Iris gave her a feeble hug and a feigned smile.

"Well, it looks like we're heading for home now," Tobias announced to the group, very much including Father Santillian who suddenly appeared on the church steps. "Kane-Paul has prepared a feast in honor of Estrellita's First Communion."

Iris actually showed a look of relief. To think they were at last heading to a comfortable destination and food. The entire journey on horseback was brutal. Who on earth had deemed that women sit sidesaddle clinging for their lives? And that dreary stop at Dolores had to be the worst respite one could conceive. She found herself actually craving for a hardy swig of aguardiente, though it promised to sear through her entrails.

Respectfully they all stood by and watched as Miguel Pedro helped Estrellita into the festooned carreta. They would wait a bit before mounting their horses. The splayfooted oxen pulling the wooden cart, with its four-foot diameter wheels, was a cumbersome sight compared to the graceful mustangs. As beautifully as it had been decorated, it was the only mode of transportation afforded Indians. Unless one was a vaquero, the law forbade that an Indian ride a horse. To do so would warrant severe punishment, though outlaw bands of Indians rode with wild abandon.

"What now?" Iris moaned as they watched the carreta rumble away. All eyes remained transfixed as it slowly diminished before them. "I thought we were leaving."

Heather gave her a sharp look, which quickly turned to surprise on suddenly seeing her sister cozy up to Hector, a man Iris loathed. Heather strained to hear Iris' effort to communicate in Spanish.

"Estrellita ye Blanquita—hermanas?" she slyly questioned.

Heather could not help but gasp. Hermanas? No wonder she asked Tobias how to say sisters in Spanish.

Hectors black eyes looked deep into Iris' disturbingly innocent orbs. He took an exceptionally long drag from his dark cigarillo compelling her to wait for an answer. Finally he shrugged.

"No se. Señorita."

Heather rushed over and grabbed Iris by the wrist. "No se, means I don't know."

"I know what it means." Iris snapped. "I'll bet he no say."

"Save the pun." Heather seethed. "Just save it!"

Chapter 10

"But Kane-Paul." Belle endeavored to persuade. "You've worked much too hard preparing Estrellita's Communion party. You've cooked every single meal since we've been here. My daughters and I want to be of some help. In fact, we'd enjoy it immensely. There are certain New England dishes we'd love to share.

"No."

Kane-Paul was most adamant. His strong sinewy arms were crossed firmly over his massive chest. He was a dark hulk of a man in his late thirties, with thick black curly hair, gleaming black eyes, a wide flat nose and a generous mouth with large white teeth that usually shown in a ready smile. Today he was surprisingly stern. He was dismayed by what Belle had proposed.

Although he was but a small boy in the Sandwich Islands when the ban existed that forbade men and women from eating together, and free eating was now accepted for over a decade, he was yet taunted by the word 'tabu' or 'kapu', which meant forbidden.

There was a time in the Hawaiian Kingdom when a woman daring to kindle a fire from a man's fire was instantly condemned to a sacrificial death. The idea of men preparing food still prevailed strongly in Kane-Paul's mind.

"Cooky no do by lady nice," he emphasized in his pigeon English, with verbs first and nouns before adjectives.

Belle found herself sighing with exasperation. The girls and she were yearning for some New England fare, particularly an old fashioned apple pie, something special that she could prepare for Tobias. They brought back baskets laden with luscious fruit from the Santa Clara Rancho. And here this mammoth figure of a man stood stubbornly guarding the kitchen door.

Only Miguel Pedro was allowed entrance. Estrellita helped with the serving and prepared an occasional cup of chocolate. Even so, the sight of a woman in his kitchen was most unnerving to Kane-Paul. He realized that times had changed and that they were thousands of miles away from the Islands, but old beliefs learned in boyhood were difficult to release.

Also, for many years prior to settling in Yerba Buena, he had been a food steward on a whaling ship. There too, he proclaimed the galley as his personal domain. He still rang a dinner bell and religiously donned his old frayed sailor's cap upon entering the kitchen. Although Tobias had brought him many a new crisp white cap, he insisted upon wearing his old one filled with the nostalgia of his sea-faring days.

As an islander he had a natural love for the sea and signed up at an early age. It was quite common to come upon the sight of a Sandwich Islander at almost any port in the world. Unfortunately, a ship in dire need of a crew had shanghaied many of them, but not Kane-Paul. He had made up his mind very early in life, although his first and fondest boyhood dream was to become a Paniolo. This was the name the islanders gave the cowboys who were very similar to the Californian vaqueros. Curiously, both had been influenced by the influx of Spanish and Mexicans. That dream quickly faded with the arrival of the Protestant missionaries; who were not much different from the Franciscan father's rule over the Californian Indians.

The name Paul came from St. Paul. His Epistles were very big in the islands. His shipmates added Kane, which meant man in his native tongue. His own melodious native name had long ago been discarded with Christianity. The dancing, singing, kite flying, gambling, the wearing of flowered leas and near nakedness was replaced by strict religious teachings. The natives were taught to read and write, often time forming their letters in the sand.

Kane-Paul still read the bible, which he kept under his pillow. The marker, a dried palm leaf from his homeland was placed on a passage out of St. Paul, which he invariably quoted or misquoted to suit his purpose. Something he chose to do for the occasion, pointing a thick dark finger at Belle as he did. "Go. Be filled with the fruits of righteousness."

Belle shrugged. Fruits of righteousness? The interpretation was good enough. She would give it her own connotation. It was totally right that she bake an apple pie, if it meant doing so at the Carlsons.

"I'm a bit tired" feigned Iris, as she watched her mother and sister don their bonnets. "I just want to rest awhile. Take a siesta, so to speak."

Heather gave her sister a suspicious look. She was certain that there was something-devious going on inside of Iris' head. How well she knew that disgusting expression of innocence.

Belle hastened Heather along. Once covered with a shawl they quickly whisked away the basket of fruit that sat outside the kitchen garden. The two women moved stealthily in the sunlight like two thieves in the night.

One way or the other, Iris was determined to question Estrellita. Ever since she had laid eyes upon Blanquita, her curiosity had become all consuming. She wanted to know the sordid truth. What else could it possibly be but something salacious? How convenient to be given the perfect moment. Her plan turned out to be far easier than she anticipated.

Iris had been lounging on her mother's bed, but a short while after their departure, when the strains of music commenced to waft through the house. At first so softly that she thought it her imagination. Someone was playing the piano. She had never heard it played in the short time they had lived there. Iris was stunned, even more so, to hear the piece her Papa so often played and sang in church. The words

'Saving grace how sweet the sound,' suddenly accompanied the playing. It was Estrellita's delicate voice. Iris sat up in bed. "How dare she?" she gasped.

Iris slipped from the bedroom and into the parlor, gathering her skirt so as not to create the slightest rustle. She stood silently, angrily behind the young woman seated at the piano. Her ominous presence caused Estrellita to abruptly stop playing, her lovely hands frozen on the keyboard. Without turning around she knew it was Iris. She felt it, as those of her ancestry might have instinctively sensed impending peril. Slowly she turned to face Iris who stood only inches away. Estrellita meekly rose coercing Iris to step back.

"Forgive me, Señorita, Iris I did not mean to disturb your siesta."

"Where did you learn to play the piano? Where in heavens did you learn that song?" Iris demanded.

"Doña Hannah, Señorita. She taught me when I was very young. She placed my hands on the keyboard when they could barely reach a cord."

"Did she now? What made you decide to suddenly play today?"

"Please forgive me, Señorita. I did not know that you where here."

"I think it strange that I have not heard you play before. Are you doing something that you shouldn't be doing as a servant?"

"Oh no Señorita. It is not forbidden me."

"Are you telling me that it is all right that you sit down at the piano and play when you choose?"

"Doña Hannah always encouraged me to play at will. It pleased her. Today would have been her birthday. It was my gift to her. The piano has been closed now for over a year out of reverence for her death. I wanted to bring music back into the house. To touch upon the sweetness of her spirit."

Iris became irritated by the sincerity of Estrellita's response. "The piano sounds out of tune to me, as does your voice. I don't ever remember hearing that song sung quite that way."

Like Miguel Pedro, there was a unique tremor to her voice when she sang, hauntingly reminiscent of some eon age. Estrellitas's face became flushed. She did not mean for anyone to hear her, least of all Iris. How she missed Doña Hannah, the motherly warmth of her embrace, her hours of attentiveness. So often there was only the two of them, sharing each other's company, as Don Tobias' voyages stretched out into long lonely months. She was the one who found her dead, right there on the settee propped up with pillows, watching, listening to her play and sing. To think that the very last thing Doña Hannah heard was the sound of her music and her sweet voice. How could this arrogant, milk faced girl possibly understand? Estrellita moved as though to withdraw from the room, but Iris stood in her way.

"Wait," Iris came back." I wasn't criticizing you. It was really quite lovely. It's incredible, you barely have an accent, and none at all when you sing. You know, if your skin were fair one would take you for white. How do you feel about that?"

"I am very proud of what I am, Señorita. Very proud."

"Very? How do you account for your blue eyes? They are not the eyes of an Indian. Are they your mother's eyes?"

Those very blue eyes were upon her unfaltering. "They are my eyes, Señorita. The ones God chose to give me"

"How commendable. It seems to me that God also chose to give you parents, a mother and a father, to conceive you. Your mother couldn't have been an Indian. That makes you a mestiza. Isn't that the word?"

Estrellita again made a gesture to move away only to have Iris stop her course. As she did, she found herself eye to eye with Iris, whose own blue orbs were coldly staring her down. Estrellita lowered her eyelids and attempted to back away only to have Iris aggressively persist.

"Surely you must know who your mother was? You act and speak as if it were Doña Hannah herself."

"That is blasphemous, Señorita," gasped Estrellita "Doña Hannah was as a mother to me. The only mother I knew. She is in heaven with that dear soul that gave me life."

"Dear soul?" Iris laughed mockingly. "So the two of them are in heaven yet, blue eyes and all."

"Con su permiso Señorita." Estrellita made an attempt to leave.

"With my permission? I didn't give you my permission." Iris' hand tightened around Estrellita's wrist, restraining her. "It was a simple question that I asked. If you are so proud of your duel heritage, then why the big secret as to your mother's identity?"

Estrellita's head dropped to her chest concealing the small tear that ran down her cheek. "Con su permiso Señorita."

Iris was not prepared to give up so easily, but was instead startled by Miguel Pedro standing in the doorway. The sight of him set Iris aback. Her face became scarlet and she quickly released the girl from her grasp.

"Mi hijita." He called out.

Estrellita raised her eyes to meet his, then ran to be held in his embrace. Tenderly he led her out into the garden.

Chapter 11

Miguel Pedro handed Estrellita a basket and instructed her to fill it with vegetables from the garden. Yet dazed, she held it in both her hands close to her breasts. With her eyes lowered concealing their extraordinary color, he could again see the outline of her mother Maria Inocencia; the head so perfectly round, the long raven hair cascading over the fine sculptured cheekbones. They were the same height and lean, a subtle sway in their steps, seeming to walk as one, the basket caressed rather than carried.

It was a beautifully woven piece of Ohlone craftsmanship with small iridescent shells and wisps of colored feathers, the tulle so tightly coiled that it could contain water. In handing it to Estrellita it became more than a diversion from the devastating experience that had occurred in the parlor. 'Be proud, mi hijita,' he silently said, 'Yours is an ancestry that spans the ages. Their spirits still soar through all of nature. Their voices are heard even now, in the birdsong, in the roar and whisper of the wind, in the great Sundown sea that ebbs and flows upon the shore and whips white upon the rocks, in the mystical baying of that lone coyote through the blackest of nights.'

She raised her eyes to search his, seeming to give credence to his thoughts. As she did, their brightness became as one with the clear cerulean sky and the wild blue lupine that strew the hillsides. As much as he loved her, at times the reality of their color filled him with searing memories, too painful to convey, least of all, to this blameless girl.

Unable to speak, he again gestured for her to fill the basket with vegetables, ones he planted for Doña Hanna. He had created a small version of the Mission garden, with potatoes, peas, lentils, leeks, cucumbers, peppers, squash and melons. Along with the flower garden with its Madonna shrine, it had given Doña Hannah a great deal of pleasure and solace. She and Estrellita shared many hours, not only tending to growing things, but sitting on a bench that faced the bay. Here Estrellita had learned to read and write. She listened to Doña Hannah recite poetry and relate stories of another world where the Yankee ships sailed to and from. Often times they would sew or petit point, but always they scanned the harbor for that one special ship that would sail through the gate with Don Tobias.

Quite suddenly Estrellita lowered her eyes, at once realizing that something about her gaze had wrenched at his heart. Her father had miraculously emerged to rescue her from Iris' deplorable questioning. The very questions Estrellita herself might have asked of Miguel Pedro, but did not dare. Without words each felt the other's despair. Sadly she bowed her head and moved away, the basket adhered to her heart.

Miguel Pedro's eyes soulfully followed after her. His silence concerning her mother must remain so forever. He fell to his knees in prayer at the foot of the Madonna, pretending to work at the array of flowers planted at her base. The statue was positioned facing north, her immobile gaze fixed upon that great mystical mountain across the bay. Its peaked summit reached toward the clouds and the stars, unfazed by the opaque fog that could suddenly sweep in great rolls through the gate.

The Indians called the mountain Tamal Pais. They believed that it belonged to the spirits. It was there that the mighty God Coyote supremely reigned. A place so revered, that none of them dare ascend the summit. To do so would be to die. Yet there it stood since the beginning of recollection, for all to see and be touched by the strength and solace of its presence.

To Miguel Pedro, the very sight of Tamal Pais was the conjuring of bittersweet memories. Somewhere beyond its undulating grandeur in a warm verdant spot the Indians called Nanaguani, were the souls of those buried in the forgotten graves of Mission San Rafael Arcángel, the hospital extension of Dolores. There, his mother and two tiny sisters had died and were buried with a multitude of neophytes. From the beginning the Indians of Delores perished in greater numbers than any other Mission. There were far more deaths than births. In a nine-month period two hundred and thirty six Indians died, the majority from an epidemic of measles. Almost all had succumbed to the white man's diseases, small pox, measles, tuberculosis and the shameful Mal Gálico, the venereal disease that unmercifully depleted his race. Neither the therapeutic steam of their tamascals or the medicinal herbs was enough to heal them. Even the Yerba Buena, the plant most used was of no consequence. It was a scourge that came by way of the low-grade soldiers that were recruited from the prisons and slums of Mexico. Suicides wrought by untold broken hearts took its proportionate toll. The Mission hospital dedicated to the Archangel Rafael no longer existed.

Time and again Miguel Pedro found himself gravitating to this garden site, to take in the majesty of Tamal Pais. Even when mists moved in from the ocean and obscured the whole of the headlands and mountain like a phantom shroud, he remained spell caught.

Why did he ache to be across that bay when there was no one left waiting for him? Yet somehow, the spirits of those he loved subsisted in the writhing fog, in the winds and the rasping cry of the gulls. He could hear his mother's soft voice whispering his name, and his sisters' little girl laughter. He anguished for them all. Mostly he grieved for Maria Inocencia. She lay in a lone grave apart from the rest. Maria Inocencia, the love of his life had died at Delores.

That day of Estrellita's Communion, as all of them stood on the church happily congratulating her, his eyes momentarily shifted to the left of the church, to a shed that was once a baptismal and a mortuary.

Further left was the cemetery, its tall grass, unruly weeds and wild flowers obscuring the graves of early Spanish dignitaries and their families. What seemed forever forgotten, were the thousands of Indians buried a-strata beneath those esteemed graves, in a fetus position, skulls heavenward, to allow room. The bedraggled living had coped as best as they could, wrapping the dead in shrouds and bowing their heads in prayer, as time and again the duo of weary padres gave their last blessing. On a chart entitled Spiritual Results at Mission San Francisco, was recorded the deaths of over five thousand Indian in its fifty-seven years. In truth the small cemetery was a massive graveyard of Indians, men woman and children, entire families felled by diseases that nearly wiped out their race. Who would ever know?

But he would not forget. As was the custom of his ancestors, the names of the dead were never again spoken. This he learned from his old Shames grandmother whose face bore the tattooed dots of ancient ways. That gentle old woman was the first of his family to die. He still wore her stone amulet around his neck and slept beneath her rabbit skin blanket, and traversed with her in his dreams. For her wisdom and love were always with him.

Shortly after his mother and sisters died, his father ran away never again to be dragged back by soldiers, put in stocks and shamefully flogged before all to see, his small son included. It was believed that along with several other runaways, he had crossed the bay in a tulle boat to hide on Alcrataz Island, also known as Turtle Island. Perhaps, he was yet alive, now an old man, a bit closer to the great Tamal Pais and the family buried at Mission San Rafael.

Miguel Pedro dropped his head to his chest and passionately gripped the weeds in both his fists. There had been untold heartache. They were not warriors but a peaceful and loving people. Why was his race not left alone from the beginning? This he asked himself not truly understanding the pureness of his own blood. He was as the padres made him a Christian and Spanish speaking. It was impossible to totally alienate himself from their life long teaching, or the Christ image he learned to love and implore in prayer. It was all he had left to spiritually sustain him and to pass on to his daughter.

He was baptized by Father Esténega himself, named after St. Michael the arch angel and Pedro, in memory of the first Indian buried at the Mission, a little boy of four who had fallen into boiling water. Miguel Pedro grew up to be one of the father's favorites, assisting him at mass, having personally been taught to sing by reading those large colored square notes that were common to the neophytes.

It was as a boy that he first laid eyes upon Estrellita's mother. Three times a day they would come with their families to the cookhouse with a vessel in hand to partake of the pozole made up of meat and vegetables. Sometimes there was gruel and meat, sometimes only gruel. Year in and year out it never varied. Nothing changed from the arduous and stoic routine of the Mission life. It seemed that nothing could, except that somehow that little girl, three years his junior, had caught his eye and eventually his heart.

Slowly he watched her grow into maidenhood miraculously reviving the utter dullness of his life. That glorious feeling that consumed his work and prayers his very dreams, was love. She was the girl he ultimately married and the mother of the beautiful blue-eyed mestiza daughter he refused to deny.

A mountain man had ruthlessly raped Maria Inocencia. As a scout for a fur trading company he had braved the Sierra Nevada to take stock of the sea otters that proliferated the Bay and coastline. He happened upon the lone unsuspecting girl and mercilessly ravaged her.

She was fifteen at the time. Like all other Indian girls at the Mission, she had been taken from her family at seven and made to live in a dormitory called the monjerio, the nunnery. Usually one of the soldiers wives acted as their mistress guarding them every waking hour and locking them in at night.

Maria Inocencia was sent to Yerba Buena to help an ailing officer's wife at the Presidio. She was to cook, clean, launder, and tend to the five small children. Whatever the need, whether it be food, provisions or help, the Mission yielded to the demands of the idle military and their families.

One early morning, barely past dawn, she left the fort with a large basket of laundry balanced high on her head, and walked to the Laguna Pequeña, the small lagoon but a brief distance from the cow pastures. She knelt on a sandy strip of shoreline flanked by a high wall of thick fronds, and washed on a large protruding stone, that glimmered black from the wetness.

At first she worked silently adhering to the Mission ways that she had been conditioned. Quite suddenly she sat back upon her knees and took in the splendor of the great bay that spilled out of the Pacific. The headlands shown a deep purple against the clear morning sky, and there were masses of birds in flight.

For the first time in her life she was filled with a sense of calm and freedom. No bells, no mass, no marching silently to and from meals and work. No one to direct her every move or restrain her from bursting out in song. She caught herself humming as she washed. Suddenly she was singing aloud. She sang that which she knew, the Gregorian chants, which were so much a part of her life. The Kyria Eleison, the Panis Angelicus, the Ave Maria, all in that haunting monotone that had been learned since childhood. Somehow, here, merged with nature, the words and music took on a different sound, one that was reminiscent of a people that once moved freely through this very place.

As a child she was singled out to sing in the choir, her sweet soprano at once recognized as a gift from God. She was given a few solo stanzas, which she solemnly sang grouped among the woman neophytes. With time she was given lengthy passages. The Panis Angelicus in particular brought out pathos in her voice that mesmerized an already hushed congregation.

Somewhere through her solo Miguel Pedro's deep compelling voice joined her in song, allowing them a closeness that was otherwise forbidden. As they sang there was a melding, far deeper than music. There was a joining of hearts. How very much she had come to love him without words or touch. But their eyes met, shy stolen gazes, each longer than the last. There, alone on that wondrous morning she was seized with an enormous feeling of love for Miguel Pedro.

She smiled at her reflection in the water. Her young face was even prettier than she realized. She seldom saw herself mirrored. Sometimes as she diligently polished the copper kettles and bowls she would catch glimpses of herself, but they were always distorted images. Or there was someone watching ready to scold her for seeming vain. But indeed, she was pretty. Certainly she must have been aware of it by the look in Miguel Pedro's eyes. She smiled at her own reflection; her honey dark skin and long black hair at times rippling. Her mouth was full and shapely, her teeth so very white. Perhaps she was a bit vain at that, staring at herself so admiringly.

She was not the only one staring. Maria Inocencia was startled to suddenly have another image appear in the water. One that filled her with fear. Immediately she recognized that mangy looking mountain man whom she had spotted several times at the Presidio. He looked every inch the wild man that he was. He had eyed her hungrily. So much so, that she shivered each time they passed.

He loomed behind her seeming incredibly taller than his six feet. His torso was naked and matted with a thick unsightly brush of dark blond hair. Her heart and breath caught as she slowly turned on her knees to face him, allowing the skirt she was washing to drift away.

In an instant he dropped down beside her, one strong arm around her waist, a large callused hand tightly covering her mouth, stifling her cries. He dragged her into the high fronds, which cracked cold juice beneath their bodies. She fought fiercely, but was no match for his tremendous strength. He straddled her, then pulled her skirt up high above her head so that her torso, arms and face were swathed in a tangle of restraining fabric. He ripped away her under garments, his hands immediately groping between her legs to crudely handle her pelvis. She felt the frenzied strength of his thighs separate her limbs. An excruciating stabbing pain tore deep inside her as he thrust himself again and again, angered by the tight virginal body that refused him full access. Ruthlessly he had torn her hymen causing blood to gush. In that very instant he gave out a loud animal cry that startled the birds in the rushes causing them to take off en masse.

Once sated the full weight of him collapsed upon her. She lay there nearly unconscious, barely able to breath or stir, pinned to the earth by the whole of that foul insidious demon of a man who had used her in the most demoralizing way possible.

Even after the heaviness was lifted she lay there almost lifeless. He knelt over her, pulled down her skirt and took one last mocking look at what he had conquered. He laughed aloud, cuffed her hard upon the cheek and walked away forever. Yet, those cold cruel eyes remained with her. They were the palest blue she had ever seen and wild. A handful of his light thin hair was yet clutched in her fist long after he was gone.

She curled up like a fetus and covered her nakedness with her skirt. There she lay uncontrollably sobbing, in shock and shame, her groin burning and bleeding, her limbs feeling as though they had been torn from her torso. My God! What had happened? Only moments before she had been ecstatic with joy. How could it have been so quickly taken away? Her life was ruined.

Maria Inocencia stumbled back to the Presidio, dazed and disoriented, unable to explain her condition. Had she come close to a grizzly and escaped, or a mountain lion? No one was witness to her rape, nor did she dare mention it, even in confession. She was immediately returned to the Mission where she lay for two weeks in the infirmary unable to eat or sleep, all the while staring into space.

Ironically, during her short absence Miguel Pedro had gone to the padre to ask for Maria Inocencia's hand in marriage. He leapt with joy at the padre's approval. He could barely believe his good fortune and immediately went to church to kneel before the statue of St. Michael to give thanks. To have Maria Inocencia return to the Mission and be confined to a sick bed made him all the more anxious to love and care for her.

Once she was up and about, the customary procedures followed. The padre introduced the couple to one another. It was then that they exchanged words for the first time. While Miguel Pedro's eyes were rapt with emotion, she could not look back at him. What presented itself as timidity, was in reality shame.

As the courtship ensued, through a grillwork window of the nunnery and the wedding drew near, Maria Inocencia became more and more withdrawn. Before going to the village, there were instances, when their eyes met and seem to melt, now she avoided his gaze. Miguel Pedro could only interpret her somberness as virginal apprehension. He too was filled with anxiety, for she would be the first and last love of his life.

They knelt as bride and groom before the altar aflame with candles, with the crucifix staring down upon them. As was the custom, they were tied together with string, a great white gauze veiled over the two of them as they said their vows. This youth of eighteen and his diminutive bride of fifteen were married. At last they were free to touch, to love, to live in the privacy of their own little house in one of the villages called Las Rancherias, owned by the Mission.

For all the days of his life, for all the love and anticipation harbored in his heart, Miguel Pedro would never forget his wedding night. His sweet lovely little bride suddenly cringed back into the shadows sobbing.

"Mi amor. My love," he tenderly called out to her in their familiar Spanish. "What is wrong? I hear tears of despair instead of joy. How can it be?"

"It is not you, she finally choked out. You, I have always loved. Always wanted. I cry for the evil inside of me. For my unforgivable lie!"

He reached out to gently stroke her long lustrous hair yet strewn with wild flowers. She cringed back even more distraught.

"Evil?" he sadly questioned. "How could it possibly be? I have watched you since we were children, from afar, from the corners of my eyes as you passed, as you knelt in church, when you carried sweet lemon water to the workers in the field. Always you were in my thoughts and dreams. I could hear the sound of your laughter and song even when you were not near. I was filled with your presence. And now, you are my wife. I am your husband querida. I promise I shall never hurt you. There shall be the gentlest act of love between us. How very much I have longed for you Maria Inocencia, for this very day." Again he reached out to touch her, but she crept deeper into the shadows. "I love you dearly," he assured. "You must believe that and trust me, no matter what."

The tenderness of his voice and words only caused her to cry even harder. How could she speak of the enormity of her shame? How very much she had longed to be his wife and bear his babies. Instead she could only offer heartache. He deserved to know the truth, no matter how difficult.

"It is not you" she finally managed, her voice trembling. "It is me. I have deceived you. Come to you dirty, another man's child inside my belly. Can you understand that?" Her voice strengthened with anger and self-loathing "Another man has had his way with me and given me a baby! A white man! Now go! Go run to Father Esténega and have him annul us and beat me until I am aborted! Let me die!"

Miguel Pedro felt his heart tear in its cavity. His breath seem to cease and his body chilled. He shook his head 'no' refusing to believe what he had heard. Not his sweet virgin wife, not his Maria Inocencia.

"How can it be?" he finally spoke, each word a sob. "Since the age of seven you have been watched and guarded every moment, locked away in the nunnery at night. How? My God! How could such a thing have happened?"

"That—that one time I was sent to work at the Presidio. I was there, but a few days when a man, a wild man from the Mountains—a white man—he—he took me!" Her sobs were so fierce that her words were barely audible. Still, she endeavored to continue. "He took me. Brutally took me! No one heard or came. I fought with all my strength. I was no match for him." Her chin dropped to her chest, her eyes avoiding his. "When he was through with me, he ran away. I can't remember his face, but his eyes are still with me, taunting me in my dreams, so that I am afraid to sleep. They were the wildest, palest eyes I have ever seen. A clump of his hair was still in my hand long after he was gone. I buried it in the sand beneath the fronds, then vomited on the very spot. To think that that horror is my baby's father. The baby that should have been ours." She spat. "I curse them both!"

She crouched deep into the darkest corner, her arms tightly wrapped about her legs, her head buried in her knees. Her cries were gasping choking sobs, so fierce that he feared her heart might burst. Cautiously he crept beside her and gently lifted her in his arms. He felt the reverberation of her cries deep within his chest. He commenced to rock her, this sobbing little girl lost to the entire world. What had she ever done to deserve such a fate? All her life she had been so incredibly good. He watched her kneeling in prayer like an angel. It was wrong that she be beaten or ostracized or punished in any way. Who in God's name was this beast who defiled this sweetest of all creatures? If he know, Miguel Pedro would kill the white bastard in the most tortuous way possible. That day in church he had vowed to love and cherish her all the days of his life. In the name of God and St. Michael he would keep that vow. She was his little wife. He was all she had. He could not turn away from her, not then or ever.

For one who had to be coaxed to eat, Maria Inocencia's belly became excessively large in her final months of pregnancy. The fierceness of her labor had caused her to faint only to be revived to an even greater pain. Still, nothing surpassed the shock of what emerged from her frail body like a stigma. Those blue eyes had come back to torment her.

Once alone, pretending to be asleep, she staggered from her birth bed to cut deep into the tendons of her wrists rendering herself bloodless. Maria Inocencia was one of the last neophytes to be buried at Dolores. A few months later the Mexican government took over Spanish rule. All was scattered.

Miguel Pedro and Maria Inocencia's baby girl became as one family. Strange that he had come to love the child, when other Indians in his circumstance would have not hesitated in killing a baby conceived of a white man. With Estrellita's birth, Miguel Pedro found himself clinging to a precious part that was her mother. This he could not bare to release, for it was all that was left to him of the woman he loved. The goodness, the gentleness that was Maria Inocencia was a spirit coalesced in her child. This he at once sensed as he lifted her newborn baby in his arms.

Miguel Pedro turned tenderly to study Estrellita as she knelt on the ground gathering vegetables in the basket. The intensity of his thoughts drew upon her so strongly that her eyes raised to meet his. It was a look of love returned. Beyond the startling blue of her eyes shone a beautiful soul. She was indeed her mother's child.

'What is it, my Papa?' She silently asked. 'What is it that you hide from me? You do not mention my mother, ever. And I dare not ask. Is it so painful for you Papa? So very painful that I will never know? But my heart tells me you loved her deeply, and that she loved you. All that love that you felt for one another is here in me. God in heaven please let it be enough to one day heal your hurt.'

Chapter 12

Iris quickly donned her bonnet and shawl and hurried from the house. She was not certain how much Miguel Pedro had heard. The sudden sight of him terrified her, especially since he caught her menacingly gripping Estrellita's wrist. Those scalding black eyes seemed to sear right down to her bones. She shivered at the thought of him. On tiptoe she scurried from the house, carefully shutting the front door so that it would not slam, which it did on a many a windblown day. Frantically she pulled at her shawl as it caught on the front gate. It snagged as she tore it away.

Her first impulse was to run to the Carlsons. Their house was a small, wooden, structure downhill from Tobias' fine home. It was no easy feat. Her mother and Heather had managed, she certainly could. But why stop there? Iris found herself looking down a steep dusty street filled with board covered gullies, all the way to the Bay. The former path had widened from the constant use of loaded carretas. It was a far more hazardous descent than she realized. The day of their arrival they were compelled to use a miserable little mule cart to carry them up to Tobias' house. It was an even more frightful down hill ride to the anchorage to attend the party aboard the Skylark, and then again to a launch which took them part way to Uncle Johnny's Santa Clara Rancho. Suddenly she was on her own. Breathless she stopped to cling to a scraggly tree. As she did, the grandeur of the view captured her gaze.

Flowing to the right and left was that great shimmering arm of water that was the Bay of San Francisco. The undulating mountains to the East loomed purple and green against a clear sunlit sky. In that moment, Miguel Pedro remained captured by the sight of Tamal Pais, which lay to the north. Iris could not begin to fathom the spiritual depth of this so-called savage. She could only fear for herself, for some foreboding repercussion. The sight of the Bay and the freshness of air offered her a moment of calm. Westward sand hills and chaparral rolled endlessly to a Pacific shore. To think that she along with her mother and sister had actually braved that mammoth sea. Such a long weary voyage and for what? She shook her head wondering if she would ever again see Boston. Still, the expansiveness and beauty of the landscape was breathtaking. So much so, that it made a mockery of the inconsequential cove hamlet that was Yerba Buena. Disdainfully she studied the scattering of wooden structures.

"Shacks!" she scorned aloud, her eyes scanning the whole of the village in seconds. "Nothing! Nothing, but shacks."

This is where she was stuck, with no theaters, or restaurants, or shops, save for a miserable merchandising store where the clerk slept in the back room. There was not even a church, which might at least offer some semblance of a social life.

Tobias described an old adobe house that served as a customs house. The so-called Plaza or Town Square had once been planted with a potato patch by a Mexican called Candelaria Miramontes, which helped feed the ragged garrison at the dilapidated fort.

The highlight of the hamlet was obviously Ridley's Liquor and Billiard Saloon, which doubled as some kind of headquarters for both Californians and foreigners. She had heard that Bob Ridley would often entertain the patrons at night with his rollicking fiddle playing.

"Welcome to Yerba Buena!" she pouted.

She ached to be in Monterey with Don Cristóbal. Time and again she heard it referred to as the social center of California, with a population of over a thousand whites. The lives of the Monterenos was a succession of fiestas, balls and tertulias, the upper class social parties, where a beautiful young Easterner like herself would be at once welcome.

Their brief stop at Monterey before sailing for Yerba Buena was a total disappointment to Iris. Everyone else, her mother and sister included, had acted enthralled at the very sight of the place, while still aboard The Skylark. Iris wondered how they could have forgotten the grandeur of Boston so quickly? Had those long months at sea, left them so desperate for civilization, that they were ready to embrace a place as primitive as Monterey? She sighed heavily. How ironic that this miserable cove hamlet suddenly had Monterey seeming like a great metropolis.

Iris since learned that Thomas O. Larkin, whose house they visited, was the newly appointed American Counsel. Through and through Yankees, he and his wife stuck to their principles by remaining stanched Protestants, as well as sending their children to be reared in the Sandwich Islands. The idea of a United States Counsel in Monterey offered Iris a nostalgic link with home. She could cry from the thought, instead she became distracted by the rattling sound of a mule cart making its way up the steep bumpy hill.

"Good day, Miss Bradbury."

The elderly driver managed to tip his hat and smile all the while being jostled upward. His English accent and cordial manner did not coincide with his unkempt attire and dusty crunched hat. They had never met, but of course he knew her name, although he might very will be addressing Heather. Everyone in Yerba Buena Cove had heard of the Bradbury women. As did the two young awe-struck men with equally ill fitted outfits, who tipped their hats, smiling broadly as they tediously trudged up hill on foot.

Iris was suddenly struck with the realization that male eyes were upon her from everywhere, for this was predominantly a village of men, augmented by the crew of the Skylark, with real cash money to spend. Men galore! She giggled.

Aside from being young and pretty, her simple rust stripped day dress with its long pointed waist and white collar and cuffs appeared the epitome of fashion. Her straw bonnet with its silk rosettes and fluttering colored ribbons, was indeed a sight for sore eyes. Although Iris could not remember donning it as she fled the house.

Upon first stepping onto the dusty hillside road, Iris had slightly raised her skirt, clutching it with one hand while she groped for tree trunks and hitching posts along the way. She hiked it up higher still, upon becoming aware of admiring masculine eyes.

She left the house in haste, haunted by Miguel Pedro's menacing glare. Why should she care? He was an Indian servant with some obscene secret. The adoring gaze of men, if any, quickly placated her guilt. She felt quite smug. The few women she met in Yerba Buena looked toil worn and dowdy. Their clothes were a mismatch of outdated styles, and their waists had thickened from years without a corset. Most had taken to wearing a rebozo, a shawl like scarf that covered the head and shoulders, and was favored by the Indian women. 'Who needs the Carlsons?' she thought. It was time to visit the village. She gave the gapping men a coquettish smile and continued to skid her way down hill, while they held their breath. Their eyes were upon her as she passed the old adobe Custom House and the Plaza, which vacillated from being a huge muddy hole to a sandpit, according to the weather. There were no tress to cling to along the Plaza. Still she persisted, at times almost losing her footing. Each man was ready to dash to her aid in an instant.

On any given day the wind would be blowing from the Bay, inciting stinging clouds of dust and sand. It would have relentlessly played havoc with her voluminous skirt and petticoats, Boston bought or not. Aside from that fog shrouded evening when they first sailed through the gate, and a light rain, the weather herald spring. It was well into May, a month the Californios called Maria.

Although Iris at once realized that her short-heeled square toed shoes were no match for the hill, flat ground had its own hazards.

Splintered planks made up the sidewalk, portions of which kept slipping into the mud. Tobias and Rufina had given Belle and the girls beautifully tooled boots, which she wore at the rancho. The muddy street flanking the saloon, along with a cluster of shacks, sat parallel to a lapping shoreline.

In the late thirties Jean Jacques Vioget, a French surveyor, engineer, sailor and saloonkeeper was consigned to make a map outlining streets and property lines. He owned the only instruments in Yerba Buena. No name streets now angled up sheer hillsides, through valleys, into lagoons and the Bay. Nothing resembled the straight line drawings on Vioget's map. Iris could not imagine anyone planning a block square plaza when no one of worth would ever consider living in such a remote hamlet, a place that took almost a year of one's life to reach.

She soon wondered what had made her think she could take a leisurely, self-serving stroll through the village without falling on her face. The precariousness of the planks made folly of her attempt at walking gracefully. Ordinarily she would have carried a parasol, as was the custom even here, for the hijas del pais believed in preserving their porcelain fine skin from the sun. How did one balance a parasol while maneuvering across rough-hewn boards? She wondered why she bothered to make that steep descent, ridiculously skidding all the way. Gentle courteous hands emerged from nowhere to guide her along her course. So many men, ill garbed, save the sailors who were in their white ducks. As for the male populace of Yerba Buena, not one of them had a decent shirt or tie. Hats were crunched, hair and beards wild. Yet all were surprisingly gallant. The sight of her brought back nostalgic memories of ladies left behind, of how they looked, walked, dressed and smelled.

Iris found herself standing in front of Ridley's Saloon and Billiard Hall. So this was it, she sneered. The place was packed with men from Yerba Buena and the Skylark alike, drinking, smoking, wagering at cards and billiards. An extravagantly painted sign gilt in gold was attached to the false front of the structure. Someone's wasted artistry proudly advertised the establishment, which as far as she was concerned, resembled a shed.

Three rickety steps led to a narrow porch lined with different sized barrels, sacks and jugs. A slab of a bench was aligned to the building beneath grimy windows. Two men lazing on the bench bound upward upon seeing her, their hats in their hands. Gawking and grinning patrons peeped out through the dirty windows.

A particular young man caught her attention. He was leaning against a beam on the porch, eyeing her at length as she tittered across the planks. When their eyes finally met, he straightened himself to his full six feet two and whipped off his hat to reveal a thick shock of tawny shoulder length hair. His 'good day Miss', caused her to smile. She was warmed by his Yankee accent, a reminder of home. Also, he was clean-shaven, which made him appear less slovenly than most. The steady gaze of his clear hazel eyes and his disarming smile silently told her that he had laid claim on her. How could he not? Breath abated he had watched her make her way down into the village, first having sighted her from a distance, a vision to the sorry lot of them. She moved closer, carrying herself in a regal manner, though each unsteady step promised to have her sprawling in the mud. Every man watching was ready to leap to her rescue. As far as any of them were concerned, nothing so lovely had ever before walked down that mud caked street. She was like a delicate flower somehow having risen out of the mire. Her rosy cheeks, creamy skin, large gleaming blue eyes, fiery hair and shapely form were a thrilling sight to this hamlet of women starved men.

For some reason, her focus was on the tall Yankee who managed to draw her attention. He felt his knees weaken as she stopped before him, her head tilting back so that their eyes met. God she was ravishing! Not only her young flawless face, but also her figure. He had forgotten how tiny a woman's waist could be, or how delectable the bosoms. She drew her shawl over her breasts. What he presumed to be shyness was in fact a seductive gesture. They remained momentarily caught up in each other's gaze and smile, these two Yankees several thousand miles away from home.

Needless to say, his good looks and height were most appealing, although she managed to conceal her utter disgust for his awful attire. His dark gray trousers were baggy and dusty. He wore a rumpled vest over what seemed to be a red collarless shirt. The two top buttons were opened, revealing a patch of light brown curly chest hair. And of course, there was the red scarf tied around his throat. His cowhide boots seemed molded from mud and quite common compared to those of the caballeros. The only object of worth, was a large gold timepiece tucked into his vest pocket, the chain looped into his trousers. Perhaps at some point in his young life it might have been worn with a proper outfit. Iris could not help but compare him with that fastidiously dressed young lawyer back home, with his broadcloth suit, immaculate shirt and silk cravat, or the elegantly costumed, Don Cristóbal. 'What a waste', she thought.

He caught her exasperated sigh. Self-consciously he began to button the two top buttons of his shirt, which was not a shirt at all, but long underwear, which he had slept in the night before.

"It would be my pleasure to acquaint you with our humble pueblo." He sincerely offered.

Iris' eyes narrowed. 'That has to be a factious remark' she thought. 'The place is a hovel.'

"Our biggest building, that two story brown adobe facing the plaza, is the last leg of The Hudson Bay Company, an English trading post. There's a Custom House, a restaurant of sorts, two grog shops, two grocery stores, a blacksmith and Ridley's."

His voice commenced to fade. What was he saying? Yerba Buena was a slum for the likes of such a cultured young woman. What was she doing here anyway?

"And a merchandising store," he added. "Probably the most suitable place for a lady." He managed "May I escort you?"

In an instant he had jumped down from the porch and was standing beside her. She still had to raise her head to look into his face.

"Perhaps," she coldly answered.

Did he actually believe that she intended to enter that ramshackle saloon, a young woman with her background?

This was California, wasn't it? The backside of America, a country that had a culture all its own. She had seen hijas del pais almost naked beneath their dresses, legs exposed as they danced, breasts jiggling. They swam and rode as well as the men, and puffed away at those ghastly thin black cigarillos in gold and mother of pearl holders. All the while being revered by the men. Even more amazing was the fact that the unmarried women were not only virgins, but also considered virginal.

The good-looking Yankee offered Iris his arm. She stood there studying him. Suddenly she realized that what she had at first thought was a collarless shirt, was in fact underwear. She was mortified and it showed.

"Excuse me miss," he advised. "I think it best if you take my arm, least you find yourself stepping into tide flat slime right up to your pretty bonnet."

He almost said 'ass' but bit his tongue. Damn! It had been too long a time since he had spoken with a lady. He stood there grinning down at her, feeling like a complete oaf, still offering his arm.

Slightly cringing, she placed her palm upon his forearm. The feel of her touch sent a tingling surge up his spine. My God, how long was it since he had a woman? The sweet scent of her perfume was intoxicating. Enough to send a man spinning. Pride coerced him to straighten, his stance emulating a peacock. At that moment every damn male in Yerba Buena was gaping with envy.

"Well?" she was sarcastic. "Do we stand here posing for the populace, or what?"

"Forgive my manners. It's been a while since I've feasted my eyes on anything so beautiful, if ever." He cleared his throat. "I forgot to introduce myself. I'm Jeremy Ethan. And of course, you're Miss Iris."

"Miss Iris Bradbury", she emphasized, realizing that first names were considered appropriate here. Even the servants at the Rancho referred to her as Señorita Iris. But how did he know she was not her sister? He at once concluded that Heather who seemed spoken for was not about to be wandering the village unescorted. He was intrigued by Iris' boldness.

"Of course, Miss Bradbury, if you wish. Well, Miss Bradbury, I guess you must be anxious to see our general merchandising store. Actually, it's much more. You'll be receiving your mail there as well as meeting neighbors and friends."

"Oh, joy!" she thought. She just spent months on end on the Skylark, with a huge storeroom brimming with every conceivable ware, a great deal of it somehow having been stuffed into the merchandising store. She sighed. What else was there to do in this confounded place? Jeremy Ethan was not half bad considering the prospects. In fact, he was quite good looking, she thought, if it were possible to block her mind from the idea of being escorted by a man in red underwear. She shrugged. Who was there to impress? That she had managed to do with little effort.

She allowed him to lead her along the sometimes-sinking planks. At one point he all but carried her across his arm reaching around her waist to slightly lift her from slipping into the mud. She found herself taken by the sudden strength of his arm, as it seemed to embrace her and save her at the same time. Her open palm instinctively supported herself against his chest. She found pleasure in the feel of his muscular torso beneath his vest. Iris gave a demure gasp upon closely contacting Jeremy. But her gaze told him otherwise. Those fluttering eyelashes failed to conceal that she was a consummate flirt. He had known a fare amount of women in his twenty-four years, ladies and tarts alike. Too many, to be fooled by Iris' tempestuous toying. Still, her very presence excited him beyond belief.

Once inside the cramped store, Iris immediately disengaged herself from Jeremy's arm. Yerba Buena or not she was not about to have herself presumptuously coupled with a total stranger. She did not belong to him, and that was to be understood.

As Jeremy expected, Iris' entrance caused an immediate stir. All eyes in the store at once focused upon her. Hats quickly come off, and those few lazily congregated around the potbelly stove rose in unison, causing a clamor as they did. The two chess players, deeply absorbed in a crucial move, stood as one.

Iris straightened to give the eight or ten men, several sailors included, a simpering smile. As much as she enjoyed being the center of attention, this place with its motley collection of men was most disconcerting. Disgusted her eyes quickly scanned the shop. The small interior was crammed to the ceiling with merchandise. She found herself surrounded by a display of every conceivable ware possible, bibles and whiskey being a big seller. Barrels abounded as a storing place for untold items. Baskets, sacks and wooden crates were heaped against the walls, creating a winding path to the counter, where the clerk stood, mouth agape, staring behind the scales. Even the rafters were chock full of hanging items, from saddles to lanterns to chairs strung upside down. More merchandise was stored in high shelves necessitating a ladder. To think that she had once dreamt of shopping in the salons of Paris. How had it come to this? She shuddered to herself.

There were two spittoons filled to the brim, chewing tobacco and savagely bitten cigar butts floating atop. A sight so sickening that Iris was unable to hide her revulsion. To make things worse, there was an indescribable stench to the place that made her want to retch even more. The dampness and mold the cloud of tobacco smoke and the men's sweat, merged with thick black coffee brewing atop the stove all day, was too putrid for her to withstand. Suddenly the cold breeze from the Bay was inviting. She looked to Jeremy indicating she wished to leave.

A pleasantly anxious voice interceded. "Welcome to Yerba Buena, Miss Iris." It was the clerk, a young man with a sparse red mustache and bushy sideburns on a boyish face. He too was in red underwear and baggy pants held up by suspenders.

"This here is Chester Perkins." Jeremy offered, then turned to smile at the store full of men. "Gentlemen, the lady with me is Miss Iris Bradbury. An Easterner like myself," he proudly added. "She is our newest and loveliest resident."

'With him?' Iris fumed to herself. 'A resident? Of this miserable outhouse of a trading post?' She was insulted.

Jeremy caught her expression as well as the slight shiver of indignation. Defiantly she tightened her shawl over her bosom. It did not take much to realize that Yerba Buena was a great disappointment to her, even though she had made a heroic effort to venture down into the village. It seemed ages that he had been in the company of a young woman of Iris' background and breeding, his mother and sisters being equally refined. There was Lucy Chadfield, a sweet tantalizing redhead whom he had loved. She turned down his proposal of marriage, refusing to accompany him in his adventures. He was heartbroken. In retrospect, she was right. It would have been a hard, unrelenting life and lonely. But he would have loved the hell out of her.

How ironic to come all this way to meet Iris Bradbury, the very image of what he left behind, and equally as haughty. A real challenge. This time, he promised himself, he would marry the girl. Grab her up before anyone else. The way he felt at the moment, the likes of Don Cristóbal or any other would be suitor was of no matter. Iris Bradbury was his.

As uncaring and callous as she could be, Iris was immediately attuned to his feelings and intentions. There was something silently possessive about him that both pleased and frightened her. She was overcome with a sensation she never quite before experienced.

Immediately she endeavored to shirk the feeling by looking away from his persistent gaze. She pretended to be captivated by a bolt of denim, when she longed for silk. Still, the hotness of her thoughts rendered everything, save Jeremy, a blur.

My God! What was she thinking? A man like Jeremy Ethan was merely someone to while away the boredom, nothing else. Slyly she looked back at him at once making eye contact. His eyes did not leave her for an instant. There was something totally consuming in the way he relentlessly watched her every movement. His full mouth with it's slightly crooked smile promised sweet passionate kisses. She could actually feel the depth of his desire, and it disturbed her.

Many men had looked at her longingly in her young life, but no one quite like Jeremy Ethan. It was both frightening and exhilarating. No! Nothing was going to happen between them. Absolutely nothing! If she were destined to remain in this God forsaken Country, it would be with the likes of Don Cristóbal. At least he could offer her a life of opulence and romance. Unnerved by Jeremy's gaze, Iris turned to the group of men yet standing.

"It's been a pleasure gentlemen," she feigned. She gave Jeremy a quick indifferent look, then started for the door knowing full well that he was fast behind her. She reached for the door handle. His large hand was there first, causing their bodies to be closely aligned, though not touching. She felt a tingling up her spine, which caused her to pull back as he proceeded to open the door. She wanted out of this place, not so much from the clutter and stench, or even the gaping men, but to run away from Jeremy, from the feeling, that failed to coincide with her self-indulgent plans.

As Iris stepped on the threshold, ready to hurry out into the street, she was stunned into a stationary position by a loud frightening roar accompanied by a shaking and rattling. She was terror-stricken by the sight of everything swaying en masse from the rafters. Articles fell from their shelves and from the ceiling. Bottles crashed. Some rolled across the floor before shattering.

The surprisingly constraint cry of "tremble, tremble", came one upon the other. Some hastily crossed themselves and mumbled the name of Santo Emilio, the patron of earthquakes. Iris threw herself into Jeremy's arms. He could feel her quiver with fright, desperate for his protective warmth. As he fondled her, he was at once aware of how very young she truly was, and inexperienced.

As an Easterner, she had never felt an earthquake in her life. The experience was devastating. Trembling she clung to Jeremy, her head hidden in the broadness of his chest. She remained there clinging to him even after the shaking had ceased. When she finally raised her head and looked into his face, the fear was yet evident in her eyes now brimming wlth tears.

"Sweet lady", he endearingly humored, "you do make the earth shake."

"I want to go home!" She cried, drops spilling down her cheeks.

"I'll take you home, Miss Bradbury" he tenderly assured, his hands gently caressing her back and arms.

"I want to go home to Boston!" she wailed.

Check mate." Came the shout of a triumphant chess player.

Iris was shocked by the incongruous reaction of someone having just experienced an earthquake. El tremble del tierra, as it was called in Spanish, a trembling of the earth.

"Welcome to California, Miss Bradbury." Jeremy Ethan sounded jubilant. "What a wonderful way to get a women into your arms."

Chapter 13

After trudging up the narrow footpath that ascended around tall green grass and a profusion of wild flowers in full bloom, Heather and Will reached the top of Loma Alta, the High Hill. It rose out of the water's edge at the north edge of Yerba Buena.

They were at once met by a whipping wind that bellowed through their clothes and hair, causing them to cling to one another, all the while laughing with exhilaration.

To have reached the summit was to immediately realize a panoramic vista of spectacular beauty. From atop this place they could view it in its entirety, the enormity of the Pacific Ocean merging with the Bay of San Francisco. The great glistening Bay was rimmed by the far away purple hills of the Contra Costa, the translation meaning the 'opposite coast'.

Heather recalled that on the day of fiesta and buying, the Skylark had sent several small boats and launches to fetch those living in the Ranchos of the Contra Costa. From here, those shoreline hills seemed incredibly far away. Tamal Pais, with its towering outline resembling the placid form of a sleeping woman, seemed to draw upon them with its closeness. About four miles from the entrance to the gate, northwest of Yerba Cove was the small island of Alcatraz. Three miles further, northeast, was the much larger Angel Island. Both appeared almost snow fallen from the rush of pelicans.

Today the water was choppy yet a bright blue-green, rife with white caps. Still they could spot the quicksilver movements of seals surfacing to bark, their hoarse sounds echoing across the Bay. Far out past the gate, two whales surfaced to breathe and blow, emitting fountains of froth. They then dove into the deep to reveal gigantic tales.

Further still they could clearly make out the peaks of those lonely cluster of rocks fondly called Los Frayles, the friars, after the founding monks. Windswept and craggy they preceded the entrance to the gate by twenty miles. Upon sailing past, one was in awe of the great mass of bird rookeries and huge lumbering sea lions blackening the white rocks with their presence. Today its jagged outline stood sharp against the cloudless sky. More often than not it was rendered invisible by mists.

"It's all so beautiful," Heather exclaimed. "We've climbed a steep hill to find we've reached the top of the world."

Will drew her closer still. Her arms slipped about his waist as they stood there silently viewing the magnitude of this glorlous place, comparable to no other either of them had ever seen, or would again see.

The Bay, the lagoons, lakes, ponds, marshes, springs and tulle swamps all shimmered jewel-like in the brilliance of the noonday sun. The bright blue sky was profuse with birds, gulls, geese, pelicans, swan, ducks and egrets. Nature was at its most exquisite and prolific, seemingly untouched from the day of creation. In reality, mankind had already commenced to ravage the richness of its sea and Bay, purging its wildlife. In the late part of the last century, in four years time, the Spaniards had shipped sea otter skins valued at over three million dollars to China by way of the Manila Galleon. In 1803 four New England ships, the Hazard, Alexander, O'Cain and Lelia Byrd sailed into each of the California harbors. Feigning sickness and the need for supplies, they circumvented customs to secretly rape the Bays of thousands of skins. This hoard was exchanged at Canton for commodities such as silk and tea, which reaped an even greater profit.

From The Aleutian Islands all the way down to Baja California, the Russians vastly diminished the otters and seals along the pacific coast.

In a years-time eighty thousand skins were taken from Los Frayles alone, pups included.

Britain's Hudson Bay Company had its own designs on California. Each jet-black velvet-soft otter skin sold from eighty to one hundred dollars. China was by far the most ambitious buyer. The whalers also made untold profits. Those wonderful mammals, which were commonly sighted frolicking in the Bays, were beginning to drastically diminish.

Overland, coming through the Oregon Trail were the unrelenting trappers reaping their own kind of fortune from the slaughter of beavers. Ironically, it was the international craze for men's hats that made the skins so prized. Herds of magnificent elk and antelope were also rapidly decreasing.

To Heather and Will, unsuspectingly standing atop Loma Alta, nature appeared to be bounteous and eternal. At the moment, this part of the Pacific Coast lay before them in Arcadian splendor, a pristine world unto itself. The aromatic scent of mint and mustard seed merged with sea breezes were enthralling. Who could guess that the greed of so many nations had begun to despoil the beauty of this pastoral place?

"Well, we made it," Heather smiled breathlessly. "Did we pass a goat along the way? Or did I imagine It.?"

"I noticed some sort of creature munching away at his lunch."

"Why didn't I think to bring a picnic lunch? We could have lay a quilt right there on the grass by the hedge of wild flowers."

"I guess we'll just have to feast ourselves on the fragrances." He smiled.

Suddenly her face reddened. What was she saying? She had indeed meant a picnic, but somehow her words took on a different connotation. He gave her an affectionate squeeze.

For all the joy and lightness of the day, for an instant Will's face grew pensive. This breathtaking vista, which looked out into the infinite reaches of the Pacific then curved into this splendors Bay, was suddenly a sad reminder of Panama. Heartbroken and debilitated he had staggered out of the jungle to be met by the miraculous sight of the ocean, this very same ocean. He stood there in a stupor, staring with disbelief. Was despair and delirium playing games with him? He stumbled to the beach, sighing as his bare blistered feet sunk into the soft hot sand. Blindly driven and off balance, he reached the shoreline and threw himself into the bubbling surf. Exhilarated by the feel of surging water over his frail body, he lay limp and allowed the cool waves to wash over him again and again. It did not matter that the salt water stung at his parched mouth and open sores. He was again a fetus, deliriously wallowing in the comforting waters of his mother's womb.

Will felt Heather's arms tighten about him, somehow sensing his thoughts. He had not meant to regress to Panama. Softly his lips brushed her forehead. If not for Heather, he might well have felt completely alone, even after having been rescued to reach California. It was as though providence had meant them to meet and fall in love.

But why, they of all people? There were things about himself that she should know. Things he wanted to tell her but could not. To do so would be the end of the sweetest thing that had ever happened to him. He sought her lips and kissed them lightly. It was only the second time their mouths had touched. She was more aware of the moment than he. As far as he was concerned, there had always been a closeness between them. They fit so well in each other's arms. Heather had a way of snuggling beneath his chin and laying her cheek upon his chest. She could hear his heart rapidly beat, pulsating with her own. She ached to lie in bed with him, and have him hold her just like this, his lips warm upon her own. She raised her head and looked long and lovingly into his eyes. He kissed her again, fearful of what she might say, sweet committed words, which he too felt, but could only keep in his heart. Releasing her from his embrace, he led her to a sheltered side of the hill, where they sat silently on the lush grass amidst high hedges of wild flowers and rambling aromatic mint. Their hands tightly clasped.

For all that he had told her about himself, about his mother and sisters, of the adventures and pain of Panama, of Gus, she was aware of an even deeper side not yet disclosed. Whatever it was, he must surely know that she would understand and love him unconditionally.

"Will," she finally whispered. "What is it? Please tell me."

He looked at her stunned by her perception. It was a moment before he could answer. "I can't. It would be too much for you to bare."

"Please trust me."

"I do. But this is different."

"How? What in the world could possibly be so terribly that I would not understand?"

"I'd rather you not know. Not now, maybe never."

The tender look in her eyes tore at him so strongly that he had to look away.

"Will, I love you." She blurted out, shocked at her own impetuousness.

He did not answer, but the feel of his hand gripping hers even tighter was in itself an answer.

"I don't want us to end up like them." There was a sob in her voice.

"Them?" He was surprised to see a tear upon her cheek. With the tip of his forefinger he gently wiped it away.

"When we were aboard ship," she haltingly continued, "Tobias told us a story, a beautiful love story that happened right here in Yerba Buena, years ago. It touched me deeply at the time. Now that I'm actually a part of this place, I find myself overcome with heartache for those lovers I never knew and for us."

She lowered her head self consciously realizing she had included Will and herself in that word 'lovers'.

There was hesitancy in his words as he asked. "Tell me, how do those long ago lovers relate to you and me? Are your tears for them or us?"

"Both."

"Both? You say it with such sadness, Heather, as though I will ultimately hurt you. Believe me, I don't want to," He feared for what she was alluding; yet encouraged her to continue. "Come now, tell me the story."

"It is true, you know." she meekly added, a faint sob still in her throat. "It is known and fondly repeated all over California, one day to become a part of its history."

"Go on."

Heather took a deep breath before she began. "Her name was Concepcion Arguello. They called her Concha. She was sixteen. They say she was the greatest beauty in all of California, La Favorita, the favorite. When I first saw Rufina, I imagined what Concha must have looked like. Her hair was the same shiny black, her dark eyes were thickly lashed, and her skin fair with cheeks like roses. The dancing, the picnics, the riding from Rancho to Rancho weren't much different from today." She hesitated careful to recapture the story just as it had been related to her. "Her father was Comandante at the Presidio. One day an American ship, the Juno, sailed into the harbor. What stepped ashore was someone totally different than a Yankee captain." She smiled. "It was a Russian Baron by the name of Nikolai. They say he was tall, handsome, fair-haired and dashingly uniformed. Here was this magnificent stranger, not only from the other side of the world, but worldly."

Again she paused, unable to fully understand what had brought someone of such noble rank to this remote Spanish Colony. He was Baron Nikolai Petrivitch Rezánoff, a widower early on; who had also buried a daughter. His credentials included having been the first Ambassador to Japan, circumnavigator, chamberlain to the tsar of Russia and chief partner in the Russia America Fur Company. He was on a mission to check on the conditions of the Russian colonies in the North Pacific. On the island of Sitka, a supply post, he found two hundred men facing death from scurvy and starvation. Luckily he was able to procure the Juno and set sail for Yerba Buena for provisions. Since it was against California law to trade with foreigners, Nikolai was detained for six weeks while they negotiated. Time enough for Concha and he to fall madly in love. Against all odds, they became betrothed. He being of the Greek Church, promised to go to Spain for a dispensation, then to Madrid for permission from the king, and finally the blessing of his own sovereign. It meant a separation of two years.

There was more to the mission than the consummation of their love. Unbeknownst to the Spanish colonist, was the Russian's grand plan to have a settlement at the mouth of the Colombian river, then move on to the port of San Francisco, a country rich in natural resources and wonderful climate, compared to the dissoluteness and blistering cold of Sitka.

Sadly, Concha watched Rezánoff sail away, to first deliver food and supplies to those suffering in Sitka. His ultimate desire was not only to marry Concha, but also to one day be viceroy of a Russian province on the Bay of San Francisco. Neither of his dreams came to pass. All that remained was their bittersweet love story.

"They had nothing in common compared to us." continued Heather shamelessly seeming to be pleading her cause. "There were so many differences, culture, religion, and she ultimately being separated from her family. Still, they fell in love and became betrothed."

Will's gaze abruptly dropped. She continued, a slight tremor in her voice.

"First he had to go on an important mission, far away. Possibly Concha stood on this very spot watching as The Juno sailed through the gate, tears running down her face. She waited and waited. Months took on years." Her voice faded.

"Did he come back?" Will asked.

"No, you see, he died. No one knew to tell her, or that she even existed, this young girl waiting in this remote Country of California." She sighed. "Plagued with a fever he fell from his horse on the freezing cold steppes of Siberia and died. As incredible as it seems, thirty six years passed before she learned of his death."

Heather became silent, her eyes shifting to the great mountain across the Bay. Having related the story, it took her moments to recover. At last she spoke.

"Concha is still alive," she continued. "She is old now, living as a nun in a convent, teaching children and caring for the sick. She is called Sister Maria Dominica. Imagine it was only two years ago that she learned of Nikolai's death."

"That beautiful young girl could have married and she became a nun instead?" Will sounded outraged.

"Oh, there were many suitors, but she loved him, only him." Heather emphasized. "Tobias says that the story of their love is recited time and again all over California, and with great affection."

"That is a terrible story, a terrible waste!" He sounded exasperated. "What a stupid fool-hearted girl!"

Heather was crushed by Will's reaction. "But she loved him and was promised to him."

"And he let her down."

"Only because he died."

Will was disturbed. "As far as I can see, the girl romanticized the whole damn thing out of proportion. And please don't parallel them with us! I would never hurt you that way. I won't promise you that I'll come back. I can't. You'd be best without me. Just as this Concha would have been, if that confounded Russian had never sailed into this bay! Can't you see that he not only broke her heart but ruined her life as well? Please promise me that you won't be caught up in the some foolish romantic fantasy of what could have been, if I leave and not come back."

"It's too late, Will." Her eyes were full upon him, shimmering brightly from the want of tears. "I'm already too much in love with you to turn back."

Will's palms covered over his face, concealing his eyes, which he could not control from watering. Not seeing his expression she could not guess what was transpiring in his mind. Had she angered him or caused him further anguish? All she wanted was to love him. Her naiveté and desperation had worked against her. She knew that with the arrival of the next ship Will would be gone. It could be tomorrow or months from now, but it would come for certain.

For a long while they sat in silence. Heather's hand touched upon the gold ring hanging on a thin chain beneath the neckline of her dress. Until recently, her mother had reverently worn Papa's ring. For some reason Belle decided that it would be best given to Heather.

That first night in Monterey with Tobias, it somehow ripped away with Belle's clothes. Upon her return to Yerba Buena, she placed it about her daughter' throat. She had chosen to give it to Heather instead of Iris, because her older daughter had been denied too much of her Papa's attention when he was alive.

Now, here on Loma Alta, high above the Bay, Heather reached out for a fragment of assurance, if only to touch upon her father's ring. As she did, Will's hand reached out and fondled hers, his eyes never raising. She was right. He too had come to deeply love her. None of it coincided with his plans. It was difficult to hide his feelings, to have their eyes meet and not reveal his emotion. His touch told her otherwise. Their kisses had been much too brief. What he wanted most was to have her. Of all the women in this damn world, why Heather? She had just vowed her love and he could not answer.

"Miracles do happen," she meekly endeavored as she toyed with her father's ring. "My poor sweet Papa was unrecognizable in that inferno of a fire, but his wedding ring was yet on his finger, gleaming, almost prophetically so, as if to tell us he was still with us, at least in spirit."

Will's mouth fell agape. He dare not ask fearing that she may have been the one to identify the body?

She gave him a sad smile, her voice trembling. "The strangest thing of all, was that Papa had become too thin to wear his ring. He planned to have it sized, and placed it away in his cuff link box. Yet there it was on his hand." She paused. "During those first few days after the fire, I kept sifting though the ashes of the counting room, of the mercantile house where he was employed. It was a huge brick building, yet standing. But the windows and interior were gutted. I sneaked about at dawn. It was a pretty pathetic sight, a young woman wondering through the black shell of a building. Though his body was gone, I continued to search for some remnant of his Bible. It wasn't on his night table in the bedroom, where it was always kept." She sighed deeply managing to contain herself from crying. "Both he and his precious Holy Book perished together."

Will studied her face as she spoke of her father. For whatever man he was, Heather idolized his memory. He could not comment, only to tighten his grasp upon hers.

"When we arrived here," she continued. "It was so strange to hear Kane-Paul recite a quotation out of St. Paul, just as our Papa did. Whenever we left the house, he would always say. 'Walk in Love.' Do you recall Kane-Paul saying the very same thing, as we left the house?"

"I'm not sure if I did," Will mumble.

Heather took a deep breath, endeavoring to avert a break in her voice. "Whatever happens to us, Will, wherever you go, that is my wish for you—that you Walk in Love." The silence of her thoughts continued the sentence. 'With me.'

Chapter 14

Tobias' arm swept around Belle's waist as he drew her tightly against his chest whispering into her ear. "I can't stand not finding you next to me in my bed. I don't know which is worse, the nights or mornings."

"I know," she whispered back, wondering why they were whispering at all. The house was empty, save for the two of them, though Iris had barely been gone. Still they could hear the sound of her chattering as she walked down the path to the front gate, with Jeremy Ethan solicitously at her side.

"Let's go to your room," he suggested.

"We can't chance having someone find us. One of them will return for sure."

"Damn! Why don't we just get married, now?"

"My mourning period is almost over. I promised Johnny and the girls I'd wait until then out of respect."

"It's torture, you know that. Absolute torture." He kissed her so long and passionately that she reeled in his arms. At last pulling away she signed. "Tobias Knight, you're turning me into a wanton woman. Do you realize I am ready to run off to the sand dunes with you? Me, a proper widowed mother."

"The sand dunes? That is wanton. Why didn't I think of it?"

"Enough of this. We are going to sit here in the parlor like two genteel people and calmly have a cup of tea."

"We just had tea, Belle, remember?"

"I could use another cup, couldn't you?"

"No."

The teacart still stood with its tea service and cups and left over pastries. Belle had chosen to play hostess to Iris' caller, glad to have the household to herself.

Today was laundry day and Miguel Pedro and Estrellita left early for the Laguna Pequeña, a carreta filled with baskets of clothes. As always they sang as they drove, their voices melodically harmonizing as they moved past the cow pastures, now a vibrant green, the deep grass half hiding the unsteady calves.

Ironically, the wash was done at the very same lagoon where Maria Inocencia was savagely raped, culminating in her conception. As her mother, Estrellita knelt upon a strip of sand near the shore and washed upon black stones. She too would rest back on her heels to wistfully take in the beauty of the Bay. Except, she was never left to be alone. Miguel Pedro was as a shadow to her. Whenever she went into the village, or to neighbors or to launder, he was there.

Already men where looking at her as a woman. They were enticed by her lithe body and swaying walk, her long black hair that at times hung loosely to her waist, her honey dark skin and distracting blue eyes. Eyes that she herself was forever haunted by, as she looked into a mirror or in the waters as she washed the clothes.

Heather had gone off with Will. She prepared a picnic basket and they climbed up to Loma Alta. For all of Belle's persistence, Heather refused to be present.

"How dare Iris entertain a man when she is supposedly so in love with Don Cristóbal?"

"It's only a hospitable gesture," Belle placated. "After all, he is a Yankee far away from home. Toby says he's a nice young man."

"That's not the point, Mamma. Iris is deliberately carrying on a flirtation with Jeremy just to while away the time. Even better if he becomes smitten with her. It would be another feather in her cap. Well, I refuse to be a part of it."

Heather was going through her own personal anguish. So much so, that she had no tolerance for Iris' lack of integrity. Here she was willing to wait for Will forever, if she must, and Iris, who was incapable of truly caring, had two men bidding for her favor. So what that Don Cristóbal had to go to Monterey. At least he would be returning to her arms, and soon.

Upon opening the front door to greet Jeremy, Iris found herself gaping with delight. "Why, you're really handsome," she screeched.

"Thank you kindly, Miss Bradbury. He beamed.

Jeremy's grin was contagious. Iris could not help but smile. He was attired in his best dark gray suit and matching vest, a white stiff collared shirt and silk burgundy cravat. He stood there his high black hat in hand, his hair combed, his side burns neatly trimmed. The close shave gave added youth and vibrancy to his face. Jeremy Ethan might well be any well to do Easterner coming to call.

Belle found that she not only liked him, but that they were able to share remembrances about places familiar to them all. It pleased her immensely to watch him devour the pastries, a special treat not found in this country. The pastries and bread with real crust not only delighted Jeremy, but also conjured nostalgic memories of home.

With Tobias' persuasive intervention, Kane-Paul finally allowed Belle into his kitchen. It was a bit of a battle with him fleeing from the house, for the entire day. If they were going to commit 'tabu' then he did not want to be a witness to such sacrilege.

Chapter 15

"That's the ugliest horse I've ever seen!"

Iris thoughtlessly remarked, indifferent to the fact that Jeremy had gone through a great deal of trouble to contrive a proper vehicle out of a two-wheel cart, just to take her for a ride.

"I'd agree if the animal where indeed a horse. But it's a mule, which you very well know. A magnificent mule at that!"

"Magnificent!" she sneered. "What could possibly be magnificent about that mangy looking thing?"

"Don't say that about Santa Fe. Might hurt his feelings."

"Santa Fe?"

"Couldn't just call him mule, not after having traveled the Santa Fe Trail together. We started sperately from St. Louis, moved on too Independence, across Kansas to Santa Fe. He was part of a mule drawn wagon that crashed over a ravine. The rest of the team, along with the wagon, was lost. Thank God the family survived. By all rights Santa Fe belonged to them. For some reason he trailed after me, all the way to California." He fondly patted the mule on the neck. "He looks more like a Santa Fe than a Kansas, wouldn't you say?"

"He looks like a dumb mule to me."

"Believe me, he isn't. He's harness trained. If he weren't, this cart would be a heap of toothpicks. I went through a lot of trouble to make up this here Yerba Buena brougham, just for you." Jeremy laughed as he teasingly referred to the most elegantly built carriages of the times.

"I can't figure you, Jeremy Ethan. There are zillions of horses around here. So many that I hear they have to shoot them to diminish the herds. Why bother with a dumb mule?"

"Well, dear lady, it's this or being driven in a carreta pulled by a slow plodding oxen. I am not using a saddle horse to pull a cart and a wild mustang isn't about to be harnessed. Besides it's bigger and a lot more commodious than your regular mule cart. Please note the red cushions on the seat and backboard. That took a bit of Yankee ingenuity. You'll find that Santa Fe is both fast and sure-footed. And of course, the reigns are in my hands." He took her by her elbow. "Shall we go"

Before she had a chance to object, he lifted her up unto the cart, placing her gently on the seat. He stood there a moment admiring her, as she straightened her fashionable blue dress and straw bonnet.

"You sure are a pretty lady." He smiled looking deep into her eyes, then ran around to energetically leap beside her, the reins in his hands. "Ready?"

"Ready for what?"

"Our outing. Consider this our California adventure. One day when we're old, we can sit back on the porch swing and laugh about it."

"What does that mean anyway?"

"It means just what I said. Can't make it any clearer."

"Listen here, Jeremy Ethan, there is never ever going to be anything between us! So accept that."

"Too late. I've made up my mind," he winked.

"How come you haven't claimed yourself an hija del pais and become a Don? You seem to have managed enough of the language to have gotten yourself hired by Mexico."

"I had a little help by way of an interpreter. Spanish words, that wouldn't exactly dazzle a Señorita. There's always a possibility. Except, I didn't come to California to make it my home. Besides, at the moment I happen to be taken with a blue eyed, fiery tempered Yankee."

"You're exasperating," she sighed.

"I'm exasperating?" He shook his head. "Let's have a truce right now. After all, we did share a once in a life time experience."

"What was that?"

"You mean you've forgotten so soon? Who else in this world have you experienced an earthquake with? It was destiny throwing us into each other's arms. Not exactly common place. And you did let me call on you, which is as close to home and family as I've been in years. You see, Missy, we're not all a bunch of dust covered drifters decaying away in Yerba Buena Cove. I grant we could spruce up a bit, which we do, when there is a fiesta or if providence allows a lady in our lives. In reality, we're a decent lot. Take Chester Perkins, the clerk at the merchandising store. He's an upstanding New England boy, who became a sailor only to be abandoned by his ship when he became ill. In fact, there are many highly educated gentlemen in these parts. Businessmen, if not naturalized, then licensed to do business. You have to admit that Thomas O'Larkin is a fine upstanding gentleman. There is a whole list of names. I could go on—"

"Please don't! California, and Yerba Buena Cove in particular, do not exist on the map as far as I'm concerned. As for the worthy men you're trying to extol, forget it."

"What about me," he teased, "and my contribution to this country."

In the course of having tea Belle politely questioned Jeremy about himself. He was a civil engineer who had studied at Columbia College in New York City, a place that also happened to be home. He came to California after having been hired by Mexico to survey the land for Spanish and American land grants. There was a soiled map in Ridley's saloon, with the names of those who had lots granted to them. The owner's names were written on the map, some with Xs.

There was another more creative side of Jeremy that he was quick to disclose. He took pride that he had been taught the Daguerreotype by S.B Morse, who introduced the new method to America. Jeremy carried his equipment with him everywhere, proudly taking pictures along the way. Many of his works were portraits, of natives as well as immigrants traveling through the wilderness to remote settlements. His dream was to one day have his own studio and gallery, a place where he could display a visual record of history as it happened. Dag type, as it was commonly called, was invented by a Frenchman, Louis Jacques Mande Daguerre, a scenic painter and physicist. America immediately fell in love with his invention. The pictures, with their metallic surface, were known even to the tiniest hamlet. It was somewhere in the midst of this conversation that Iris suddenly straightened showing great enthusiasm.

"Do you carry your camera with you?" She sweetly asked, already commencing to work out some manipulative scheme.

"Always."

As disgruntled as she was upon stepping into that atrocious two wheeled cart, drawn by a mule called Santa Fe, the idea of Jeremy being a dag typist quite suddenly changed her mood. She looked to the rear of the wagon; at once sighting something carefully wrapped in soft green felt. Of course, it was his camera obscura.

"Is that your camera back there?" Iris coyly asked.

"How did you guess?"

"You were planning on having me pose for you, weren't you. Without even first asking me?"

"Well, I intended to get around to the subject as we rode along. It's a good six mile drive over the sand dunes to the ocean beach."

"Six miles over sand dunes? You do realize I have seen the ocean before. Enough of it for a life time."

"So now, you can view it from a different perspective, watch the waves break on the shore. And we can talk and get to really know one another. We haven't had a chance to be alone. How am I suppose to court you lady?"

"Six miles over sand in this contraption?" she screamed. "You call that courting?"

He grinned. "Actually a bit over six miles, maybe seven. No matter, once we ride out of Yerba Buena and head west, the ocean will be in full view. We don't have to go as far as the beach. That we will save for another day."

Suddenly she was smugly smiling to herself. "You actually planned on having me pose for you. We'll I'll do it, Jeremy. If that's what you want. There is something I also want. Will you take a certain picture for me, as a surprise for my sister Heather, whom you will soon meet, so keep it a surprise."

"Of course I will?"

"Well, Heather is an artist, you know. Quite often I've heard her comment that she would love to do a portrait of Estrellita, our pretty little mestiza maid. But Estrellita is much too busy to sit at any length so—"

"So I take a dag type of the girl," he enthusiastically finished Iris' thought.

"That's the idea, except we will have to somehow get her alone without Miguel Pedro knowing. He follows her about like a shadow. Of course we want a picture for him also." She lied "I understand he has a birthday coming up shortly."

"What a nice surprise for them both, especially from one sister to another."

"My sentiments exactly."

They had not yet pulled away from the house and already Iris had managed to manipulate Jeremy into her devious plan.

Chapter 16

"There is so much fire in your hair that I wish it were possible to capture it in color. And your eyes," Jeremy enthused. "Your eyes seem bluer than ever. That would be something, wouldn't it? Color?"

Jeremy had driven out of Yerba Buena Cove, coaxing Santa Fe all the way, to choose a special spot high on the sand hills overlooking the ocean beach. This is where Iris now posed, the vast Pacific a wondrous backdrop. He could not help but sigh at the sight of her. She had discarded her bonnet and allowed the wind to ruffle rampantly through her long auburn hair. Her full skirt whipped about her shapely limbs. The white eyelet-trim of her petticoat and pantalets provocatively revealed themselves to him. Mostly he was captivated by her beautiful face.

Iris stood in a frozen pose as Jeremy repeatedly ducked behind the box like contraption perched on a spindly tripod. The large black cloth, attached to the back of the camera, flapped about his head from the wind. Once he removed the cap from the Goliath like lens, and darted behind his camera, Iris remained unmoved. Still, she was aware of his eyes and his smile. She could hear her own heart beat above the wind and the surf.

Jeremy Ethane's presence had a way of drawing upon her. It was disturbing, and not at all in keeping with her plans. Yes, he was good looking, and educated and undoubtedly from a fine family backs East, but this was California. Here, he was nothing. He had his engineering degree and his talent as a Dag Typist both inconsequential compared to the life of a Don.

She was not about to be taken in by his charm. The fact that they spoke the same language and that she felt free to be outspoken with him, was no reason for him to believe that she would one day relent and fall in love with him. Frustrated by the ambivalence of her feelings she finally stirred. Unknowing to Iris he had already taken a half dozen pictures of her.

"Jeremy, I'm getting blown to death!" she screamed. "And the sand is starting to sting at me!"

"Wait til you see the final result. It'll be a work of art. All those little distractions are unimportant when it comes to creativity."

"Oh, pish posh! You're beginning to sound just like Heather. It doesn't go with your over all appearance. Or that dumb mule," she sarcastically added.

"Wait til I have my own studio and people flock by the hundreds to be immortalized."

"I can't wait. And I won't."

"I guess I'd better pack up this paraphernalia."

"You do that."

Iris put on her bonnet then turned to forlornly stare out at the ocean. Jeremy caught a glimmer of sadness in her far away stare. It was a look he both recognized and understood. She was homesick.

"May I escort you to the Fandango?"

She turned at once, distracted by the question. "That's really amusing. A Fandango in Yerba Buena Cove?"

"Doña Juana Briones is giving it in honor of you and your mother and sister. She is known for her hospitality."

Iris shrugged. After three exciting days and nights of fiesta at Uncle Johnny's magnificent Rancho, whatever Doña Juana Briones and her eight children had to offer was at best a joke. How could one possibly compare the two? Doña Briones had a dairy farm, which sat on the lower West Side of Loma Alta. Her cows were known to be so wild that they had to be caught and their legs tied together before being milked. She also raised chickens and vegetable. Aside from the locals, every ship that anchored in the Bay was at once her customer.

The independent Doña Briones had dared to walk away from the abusiveness of a drunken spouse to make a new life for herself and her children in Yerba Buena. Her resourcefulness was continually called upon, to deliver a baby, set a broken bone or administer one of her precious herbal cures. Her casa was an adobe where a small stream flowed in front. The large white washed sala is where many a Fandango took place. The Fandango was an improvised song accompanied by guitars. A man might sing in tribute to a woman, his country or even his horse. Of course there was continuous dancing.

Tobias offered his contribution of victuals and liquor, as well as Kane-Paul's services. Everyone in the hamlet was invited, which meant, mostly men. All of whom would ask Iris to dance, the little Carlson boys included. She gave a sigh at Jeremy's invitation.

"Well, I guess we may as well go together." She feigned indifference. "I didn't think anything ever happened around here."

"Oh, we make do," he teased. "And thank you for doing me the honor."

"Well, I guess we Easterners may as well stick together. Imagine us, being considered foreigners. I hate that!"

"For a so-called foreigner I find myself having been treated far more favorable than most places I've been too."

"Yes," she shrugged, "I have to admit, people have been rather nice."

"Let's hope it all lasts. There's talk of annexation. The Californios have become disenchanted with Mexican rule. Right now, I'd say it's a toss up between John Bull and Uncle Sam taking over. The British have had an eye on this country for a while now. They're more than aware of the riches, having reaped a fortune in furs. There are those that want California to be an independent Republic. As for me, I visualize a coast to coast country. Wouldn't that be something, the East Coast and the West Coast and everything in between, ours? Already overland immigration has increased. It might happen sooner than we think. We could very well find ourselves standing on U.S soil, or sand." He jested.

"What's the difference? We'd still be standing here on the sand dunes looking at an ocean thousands of miles away from home."

He caught a sob in her voice. His hand gently touched her shoulder. "You're family is here, Iris. So that makes it home." He grinned "And I'm here."

She looked up into his eyes and for an instant became caught in their sweet steady gaze. His hands gently cradled over her shoulders drawing her close to his chest. The very nearness of him left her breathless. As his mouth sought hers, she abruptly tore out of his embrace and ran toward the wagon, which had taken on distance. Santa Fe had wandered off to a scraggly patch of grass, some twenty yards further. The swiftness of her movements were at once impeded by the heaviness of sand, each sinking step slowing her pace.

Amused Jeremy watched as she tackled the undulating sand dunes. Without looking back, she was aware of his eyes following her. She could actually see that infectious grin. Defiantly she had run away from him, when what she wanted most was to stay in his arms. This he knew.

Chapter 17

It was almost dawn, but the sky was yet dark. A chilling fog had settled over the village obscuring the stars and moon. An occasional crimson gold flicker from a lantern shone through the mist, as some celebrants found their way home from Doña Briones' Fandango. Way in the distance there were the muted sounds of guitars.

Lantern in hand, Jeremy led Iris through the front gate and up the steps to the porch. Those within were already fast asleep.

It was a far more exciting party than Iris had anticipated. As usual there were tables laden with food and the wine and the aguardiente flowed. Everyone in the hamlet was there dressed in their finest and in great spirits. Many of the guests had ridden in from outlining ranchos, pitching tents to rest between partying.

Iris actually appeared genuinely happy. Jeremy and she found themselves compatible dancing partners especially when it came to the waltz. Too often he had to share her with an anxious line of waiting males, releasing her far more than he wanted. Yet there was an excitement in watching her, beautifully gowned, and uninhibitedly moving to the native dances. The very sight of her stirred his passions. Iris knew too well how to use her eyes and smile and body to entice him, even as he stood on the sidelines, the patient suitor. He smiled to himself. She might very well be an experienced tease, but without a doubt an inexperienced lover. She was fifteen and playing with fire. He not only wanted to save her from herself, but for himself.

Iris was yet giddy when they arrived home, but seem to sober quickly when Jeremy's mouth softly met hers. They were standing on the porch hushing each other for fear of awakening those inside, when their lips came close and they kissed, culminating a fierce urge that had prevailed all through the party.

Each time they touched or even glanced at one another from across the room something seem to ignite. Now that they were at last alone, he did not hesitate in taking her in his arms and kissing her. It was as though the whole affair, the fervor of the music, the singing, the rhythmic beat of heels, the taunting trill of castanets, the wine, had heightened to this very moment.

Iris' arms slipped tightly about his neck and pulled him closer still, provoking an even greater passion. His body commenced to throb against hers, coercing her to pull away. His arms reached for her, even as she turned her back on him, and groped for the door handle.

"You can't kiss me like that, Iris, and then just turn your back on me."

He spun her around to face him. Her expression of passion had turned to coldness.

"Blame it on the alcohol."

"There's no blame, Iris, not where one's feelings are concerned."

"It was a mistake. I don't want to end up mooning over some damn drifter. All caught up in my feelings, like Heather, whose absolutely silly over that moody Will!"

"This is me, Iris. I'm not a drifter, and you know that."

"You're not what I want, Jeremy."

"That remains to be seen. I understand you far better than Don Cristóbal possibly could. All he knows is that you're beautiful and desirable and it would be a real coup to have a blue eyed Bostonian as a wife. If you marry he'd expect you to mother a dozen or more children, and cow tow to his parents, particularly his father, whose word is law. And what happens when you finally speak the same language? Will you find that you have that much in common? Or that you can be friends?"

"Of course we'd be friends. He adores me. Besides, what does friendship have to do with marriage, anyway?"

"Everything."

"Why are we discussing marriage? One kiss and you practically have us betrothed."

"It was more than a kiss, Iris. It told me you care."

"It did not mean that at all!" she snapped. "It just happened. Don't tell me you haven't ever kissed someone because you just wanted to. A women can do the same thing."

He gave her a sly smile. "Admit it, you really do care for me. Don't you. Maybe even love me a little?"

"We are just friends, Jeremy, just friends. Love doesn't come into it at all, not even a little bit. After all, we're both Easterners and we do dance well together."

"First of all, we're a man and a woman, and we can do much more than just dance well together."

"Goodnight Jeremy."

She again turned away from him only to have him spin her around and into his arms, his mouth passionately on hers. Gasping she pulled away, found the front door, yanked it open and quickly shut her herself inside.

There was the opaqueness of the door between them, but each was aware that the other stood but inches apart. Iris was certain that Jeremy was yet standing there. She could hear his breathing. Or was it the sound of her own breath taunting her? There was an absence of steps on either side and she could see a thin ribbon of light from beneath the doorway from Jeremy's lantern. Breathlessly she waited for him to leave. When he at last did, she felt a sinking deep inside herself. It was a feeling she had never before experienced over a man.

The indescribable emptiness of her Papa's death was only now beginning to subside. But why the sudden void because of Jeremy? He would be back to take her to Doña Juana Briones' festivity that very night. He would be at her doorstep with the very first hint of evening. And there would be another week here in the hamlet, before they would depart for Uncle Johnny's Rancho, and the Rodeo. Of course, Don Cristóbal would be anxiously waiting for her.

"Damn you, Jeremy," she angrily mumbled "you're ruining my life!"

The lamps were yet lit guiding her down the hall to her room. Her mother and Tobias had come home early, while Will and Heather had stayed on, not to party, for they always seemed such half-hearted participants, but to continue up to Loma Alta to watch the sunrise.

Iris heard a faint moan from her mother's room, so she gave a light knock, hoping to find her awake. She was so confused about Jeremy that she was not ready to face the emptiness of her room. She knocked again, entering as she did. Belle sat up in bed, rubbing her eyes.

"Heather?"

"No, it's Iris."

"Oh, Missy, I didn't expect you so soon. What time is it? Are you all right?" Her questions spilled out one after the other and not too coherent. "Would you believe, I was fast asleep."

"I'm sorry Mamma, I thought you might still be awake."

Belle detected a sadness in Iris' voice that pulled at her maternal instinct. She might very well have donned her robe and suggested that they have a cup of chocolate together in the parlor, but there was a naked man under her bed.

Tobias and she had come home early and made love so passionately that they both fell asleep before he had a chance to slip into his own room. The slam of the front door and Iris' footsteps awakened them just in time. Tobias dove under the bed, his hair at once becoming caught in the bedsprings. It was a demoralizing dilemma to happen to two grown people, in his own bed in his own house. Belle could feel a skirmishing under the mattress.

"Goodnight Mamma."

"Goodnight Missy." Belle sighed with relief.

Chapter 18

Embracing tightly beneath the warmth of a large patchwork quilt, Heather and Will stood watching the dawn gloomily unfold. A deep gray fog bank stretched across the horizon. The whirring cold wind stung at their faces and tore through their hair.

They had climbed up the High Hill above Doña Juana's house, leaving the sounds of those still partying, far below. The faint refrain of music, as well as the dim flicker of lamplights gave the gray cold morning an ethereal quality.

From the moment they met, they were barely apart, growing consistently closer while forever contemplating a parting. They stood there as one, their hearts painfully filled with each other's presence.

It was an exciting party. There was a certain camaraderie with all those in the village, foreigners like themselves, as well as the very gracious contingency of Californios, whose ebullient dress and gusto for life further enhanced Doña Juana's Fandango. Will danced with Heather far more than expected. It was a way of being in each other's arms, of staring into each other's eyes.

The Bradbury women, who were the guests of honor, were the first to leave; though the appearance of a new day managed to make little difference to the festivity. One by one, guests would excuse themselves to rest up for the next days partying. Tobias was eager to rush Belle home. She was quite convincing at feigning fatigue. After all, she was a mature

Yankee woman unaccustomed to so much activity. What transpired once they were in bed, was something else altogether.

Iris wanted to go home, not only to catch a few hours sleep, but also to contemplate another even more stunning outfit. She had worn her thick auburn hair up high, caught in a tortoise comb with a pink Castilian rose, like an hija del pais. Her black spangled gown with its snug fitting torso and deep ruffled hem, had been a gift from Rufina. Upon departing the Rancho, Uncle Johnny's wife had presented them with untold gifts. Those along with what Tobias had produced from his vast storeroom kept Belle and her daughters in a flurry of costume changes. Heather had worn white lace, her shoulders bare, her hair atop her head, with sprigs of wild flowers.

It was liberating for Belle to throw away all those ugly black outfits, although there was still three weeks left of mourning. No one cared. Why should she? Colon would never have allowed her to wear such a deep cleavage, or bare her arms and shoulders or lift her hem to reveal the shapeliest of ankles. She chose an exquisite blue gown to match the sapphire and diamond necklace and earrings Toblas had given her. The silver lace mantilla, draped modestly about her shoulders, was recklessly cast off after the first tumultuous cord of music.

There was vicariousness in knowing that the woman she now was would have totally appalled her New England friends. How exciting to be a part of this wonderful place. Incredible as it seemed, life was far more exhilarating for her than it was for her beautiful young daughters. She was in love and savoring every moment. It was only a matter of time until she and Tobias would marry.

Her own happiness aside, Belle could not help but worry about her girl's, particularly Heather. It was obvious that she was hopelessly in love for the first time in her life, and yet her heart was breaking, as was Will's. Whatever it was that was tearing at him, no one really knew.

For some reason Will and Heather had made The Hill, as they came to call Loma Alta, their special place The wind, the scent of sea air, the magnitude of the vista was a wondrous excursion. Here, atop Loma Alta, the expansiveness and beauty of nature had a way of minimizing all else. The whipping of the wind drew them even closer. Their bodies meshed into each other's warmth, arms and legs tangling, coercing them to slip down into a bed of high grass and wild flowers, writhing in the wind.

Will arched himself over her body, covering them both with the quilt. His mouth quickly found hers. His face was cold from the early morning chill, but his mouth felt hot and moist. He was kissing her passionately, his tongue probing, finding hers, inducing her to do the same. His hand gently, cautiously, fondled her breast. His fingertips lightly circled her nipple, to at once become aroused by its hardness. He could feel her warm sighs deep within his mouth as he lie full upon her. The sharp stinging cold of the wind and the heat of their bodies were as ambivalent as their desires. He wanted her desperately, but without condition. She wanted him, knowing full well that he would leave.

Right here, from this very spot she would watch him sail away. Suddenly her kiss became a sob. Will could feel a wetness spill upon her cheeks. He raised her face. Her eyelids lowered, endeavoring to hide the tears, which were all too evident.

"My sweet darling Heather? I'm so sorry for having been carried away like that. Please, please give me."

"There is nothing to forgive, I wanted it every bit as much as you." She hesitated.

"I—I've never had anyone before, ever. Not a kiss, not even a touch."

"I know, that's why it's unforgivable of me."

She gave him a look so tender that he felt even more the scoundrel. "I love you Will. It doesn't matter if you ever tell me so or not. I love you and I want you to know before the time comes when we're parted. It would be far more painful if you left and I never told you."

He stared at her at length, her lovely face seeming so pale and fragile in the gray light of early morning. Her long hair was wildly strewn upon the grass. It had come undone in the wind, the flowers having blown away. He too felt like crying. When he at last spoke his words were almost a whisper.

"I love you, Heather, more than anything in life. I don't want to lose you."

She could not answer. Both joy and relief were compelling her to cry all the more. His kisses were tender and soothing, as they brushed upon her face and brow, upon her eyelids.

"I love you." There was a joy in his voice, as she had never heard before. Something had been released in him. "I love you so very much that I can barely keep my hands off of you. But the first time we make love, it will be in our wedding bed. This I promise."

Chapter 19

Don Cristóbal's left arm tightened protectively around Iris' waist as she sat sideways in the saddle in front of him, his right hand gripping the reigns. The magnificent white steed that carried them, haughtily pranced, seeming to emulate its master's pride. As was the custom, each Caballero rode with his chosen lady in his saddle. They rode en mass, the horses suddenly tearing into a gallop, heading miles away to Villa de Branciforte with its resplendent Santa Cruz beach, where a huge family cookout was to take place. There were squeals of laughter and shouts of exhilaration from both men and women as they flew across the landscape.

The swiftness and daring of the ride had Iris' breath catching with fright. Don Cristóbal's dark devouring eyes where upon her time and again. He was brimming over with pride at the thought of having her as his companion. She could feel his heart, as well as her own, throbbing faster and faster with the thundering gallop of his mount. Dozens of riders, along with their ladies reveled in the high spirited pace, passing and cajoling one another, each couple striving to lead the pack. Soft breezes became high winds as the horses soared. They leaped over gullies, yawning gorges, creeks and meandering streams, traveling through redwoods and over rolling slopes, dismounting several times to rest themselves and their horses. Except for Uncle Johnny and Rufina, who rode as one, the Americanos were left in the dust. Iris found herself hanging onto Cristóbal for dear life. The more she clung and cringed, the more he laughed aloud. Although there was no reason to doubt his superb horsemanship, she was terrified.

Though time and distance were of little consequence to these paisanos, to Heather and her mother as well as Will, it seemed an extremely arduous journey merely to picnic at the ocean's shore, commencing at sunset and lasting until dawn. Although they proceeded the others and were afforded the hospitality of a night's lodging at a Rancho midway through their journey, it still seemed an impossible ride.

As Cristóbal and his undaunted companions sped high over coastal grazing lands, the first sight of the Pacific emerged in magnitude. The last traces of a dazzling orange sun was dissolving into the horizon, its reflection a flaming puddle upon the sea. Crimson and gold stratus clouds were defusing into dusk.

Their horse's feverish pace came to an abrupt halt, as they paused to take in the spectacular vista before them. From their vantagepoint they could see the white beach below, its fluorescent roll of waves upon the sand. The water was darkening, still its exhilarating scent and hallow beckoning roar captivated the senses. The thin sliver of a crescent moon with the brilliance of Venus hovering above drew immediate sighs. There was something wonderfully prophetic about a new moon and it enhanced the festivity.

Breaking into a gamely trot, the horses descended the hilly sand dunes patched with scrub oak and chaparral. Following the strains of the guitars, the riders moved closer to the shore where a half dozen cook fires and dozens of lanterns were already lit upon the beach.

A huge assembly of family, extended family and friends were expected to attend a scrumptious cookout on the beach. The very old or those too feeble to ride as well as the smaller children and babies rode in carretas, having left hours before the rest.

A multitude of Indians from Branciforte, in a convoy of lumbering carretas laden with provisions, arrived early to set up the picnic. Large white cloths were spread upon the sands, each with a lantern atop.

Baskets filled with fruit, apples, oranges, pears, peaches, pomegranates, grapes and large luscious strawberries were set upon the cloths, awaiting their arrival.

Delectable aromas from the cook fires quickly intoxicated the nostrils. Appetites were rife. A huge amount of mussels and clams were already on the logs. There were spits of whole roasting turkey and chickens and huge sides of beef, all crackling. A dozen Indian tortilla makers were fast at work.

On a slope paralleling the activity, the men dismounted, then lifted their ladies down from the saddles. Vaqueros quickly took charge of the animals, as the couples ran hand in hand down to the beach.

Exhausted and aching Iris fell into Cristóbal's arms. Compassionately he held her close, his lips brushing her forehead. They stood there against the crimson sunset seeming like two lovers, when in fact Iris was ready to faint.

Throughout the excitement of the last few days, the Rodeo, the balle, tonight's festivity, their meager ability to breach the language had tarnished that first luster of romance. For all of Cristóbal's warmth and charm and attentiveness, something was disturbingly missing. She found herself becoming disenchanted by the vast differences between them. A circumstance that was of little importance to the hijas del pais, who not only favored their blue eyed Anglo-Saxon partners, but were not compelled to change their life style. The truth was that the naturalized citizens became a part of their women's world. Iris was quickly realizing that she was a much more vocal person than her limited Spanish allowed. The sensual looks, the embraces, the love songs at her grill, took a quick turn that day of the Rodeo, with the brutal games that followed.

Although they had missed the grand Rodeo in March, this smaller version was in itself a mammoth display of cattle on their way to be counted and branded. Each year the Ranchos held their Rodeo, to be administered by the juezes del campo, the judges of the plains, appointed by Rancho owners. The branding, the roping of steers were in itself a thrilling event. The skills of the vaqueros were breath taking to watch, as they noosed the most ferocious of steers.

The animals were grass fed and left to run wild on vast ranges of land. The California steer was fast and ready to attack. Its slim legs were lightening swift. Its nose was flat and its horns were widespread and dangerously sharp.

To the vaquero, whose only weapon was a reata, the fiercer the beast the greater the challenge. To think that a well-trained horse and a thirty-foot piece of raw hide lopped at the end could serve as such an adept weapon.

Cristóbal had taken Iris to the Rodeo holding her in the saddle in front of him. She held her red handkerchief to her face, as the dust from the vast moving herd rose up like an ugly brown cloud across the plains. The constant bellowing of bulls disarmed her. Some were frightened others enraged.

The screams of the vaqueros rose above the herds, as they wildly galloped on the sides and rear of the cattle, their reatas whipping. Their huge sharp rowels dug unmercifully into the bellies of their obedient mounts. For all the love and respect afforded the family, as attentive the lover, the Californio shown a brutality towards animals in general, a favorite horse or dog withstanding.

Uncle Johnny as Patrón, proudly rode with his herd at the Rodeo. As excellent a horseman as he was, he did not perform any of the tasks that belonged to the vaqueros. His ferro or brand was quite simple, his initials in block letters overlapping one another.

After the Rodeo, there were the horse races in which Cristóbal excelled, making Iris proud to be his lady. Next came the games, the cockfights, the bull and bear fights, and the cartera del gallo, the roaster pull.

First there was the Bull and Bear fight, where two huge animals were tied tightly together with a reata. In no time each was attacking the other, the bull gouging the bear with its horns, the bear clawing viciously at his face. Blood oozed from their bodies, covering their fur. Each animal let out its own pathetically distinctive cry as it writhed in pain. Iris had covered her face screaming.

This was followed by the carrea del gallo. A live cock was greased and buried up to his neck. One by one horseman dashed by, leaning down from their saddles to loop the head with the end of their reatas. The idea was to triumphantly rip it from its body. At this point Iris had become so revolted that she asked to be taken back to the casa, where she ran to her room and retched.

Now Iris and Cristóbal stood like two lovers on the sand dunes at sunset. Except they were strangers. Iris found herself missing Jeremy. With him she did not have to pretend. She was able to express herself as she pleased. Mostly she missed the fit of his arms and his kiss. Cristóbal gently lifted her face to look deep into her eyes. He realized she was tired, this lovely Bostonian unaccustomed to such a long vigorous ride. He smiled his devastatingly sensual smile.

"Mi querida." He whispered, his mouth softly upon her forehead. With one arm wrapped proudly about her waist, he led her down to the beach. The abundant joy of family and friends coming together made one believe that this was a rare reunion, rather than another celebrations. Already there were those wading, particularly the children. Dogs paddled in the surf, retrieving sticks. Masses of dogs went everywhere, to lap up the carcasses from the feast.

Iris fell upon the sand, Cristóbal solicitously beside her. Indian servants were fast to bring them food and drink. She gulped down some wine and stared vacuously out at the water, too tired to think. The sounds of the fiesta quickly gave way to Iris' enormous fatigue.

An hour's siesta, comfortably covered by a blanket on the sand, helped revive her. She awakened to the sudden awareness of where she was. The music, the singing, the laughter at last coaxed her into a consciousness. She lie there for a moment staring up at a sweeping black sky lavished with stars. The feel and scent of sea breezes caused her to sigh, prompting Cristóbal's gentle touch upon her shoulder.

"Mi amor, my love," came his deep endearing voice. She sat up rubbing her eyes and wondering if her mother and sister had arrived. Though it was dark, and there was a great distance to ride, she felt assured of their safety. They were in the expert care of Hector and his vaqueros.

The food and drink, the music gave her a new vitality. Uncle Johnny, Rufina, their little daughters, accompanied by their Indian nursemaids, and several in laws joined them as they dined. Everything tasted delicious. Iris particularly favored the fresh roasted mussels, and of course the aguardiente, which ultimately had her on her feet dancing barefoot in the rolling surf. Don Cristobal began to again appear more desirable to her, their lips and thighs brushing as they danced.

It was about that time that her mother and sister arrived, exhausted beyond belief. They were ready to collapse onto the sand, when they spotted Iris dancing seductively with Don Cristóbal, waves thrashing about their naked legs.

"That is Iris, isn't it?" squinted Belle. As dark as it was, the campfires caught glints of long reddish hair, loose and wild about her face. The laugh was unmistakable. As well as the outfit which resembled a gypsy.

Her white blouse revealed naked shoulders and a hint of pale round cleavage. The full dark blue skirt was cinched at the waist by a wide red sash. Extravagant pendulous earrings of wired gold hung from her lobs, dangling wildly as she danced. Her boots, shawl and yellow rimmed hat lay on the sand.

"How does she do it, Mamma?" sighed Heather. "We're half dead from our journey, and look at her."

Will and Tobias, though fair horsemen, were equally spent. The two Americano couples' appearance was greeted with jubilant shouts and warm embraces. Johnny met them and led them to their cloth on the sand. After their long hard ride, that first offering of wine was particularly appreciated. There was a quick click of glasses and a fond 'Salud.'

Quite suddenly there was a hush. All reverently watched, standing as two strapping Indians carried an elegant old gentleman onto the beach and seated him in an ornately carved armchair close to the warmth of one of the fires. In moments he was surrounded by all of the guests save for the Bradbury women, Tobias and Will, who remained in awe. Even babies, held by their nursemaids were brought to greet the family patriarch.

Don Cristóbal had escorted Iris to their spot on the beach. Kissing her palm he graciously excused himself to join the throng surrounding the old gentleman. Iris' feelings of dejection were slightly lightened upon knowing her mother and sister were there. Tobias and Will's presence barely received a nod from her. Uncle Johnny and Rufina had also rushed to greet the old gentleman.

"Who's that?" Iris sarcastically asked, failing to hide her disappointment at having the festivity come to a halt. "The pope?"

"He is Don Diego, the Patrón, the father, grandfather and eldest of this very large family." Tobias explained. "As you can see, he is highly respected. Actually revered."

One by one, the sons, daughters, their spouses and children crowded in an orderly fashion to greet him, most kneeling to kiss his hand. The men respectfully removed their hats and both men and women were quick to flick away their cigarillos.

This disturbed Iris who suddenly recalled what Jeremy had told her about a father's word being law. None of them, not even grown parents with children of their own, would dare so much as sit in their father's presence, or drink or smoke, without his permission.

As dire as it seemed, Don Diego had a kind smile and gentle touch for each and every one of them, kissing the young women and children lovingly upon the brow. It had not occurred to Iris that Don Diego was not present at the Santa Clara fiesta. There were almost as many old faces, as there was young, all seeming to be related. He was a widower contemplating a younger wife. Though still active for a man of seventy-four, with thick dark hair, he had not attended because of a fall from a horse. Since he was Patrón of a grand Rancho in Branciforte, close to Mission Santa Cruz, its close proximity to the ocean beach was perfect. When all respects had been given, the festivity continued in high spirits.

As the crowd dispersed Iris noticed a familiar face standing by the firelight. It was cousin Blanquita. She was part of the entourage that had arrived with Don Diego, and the last to leave the old man's side. He was yet grasping her hand, whispering something in her ear. He then raised his hand in a signal to the musicians. A trio of guitars struck an exotic cord. Spontaneously and in unison, a rhythmic clapping commenced. An exquisite male voice became a part of the feverish beat. Iris smugly smiled. It was Don Cristóbal. His eyes sought hers as he moved close to where she lie upon the sand.

No sooner had their eyes met, when a lone woman dancer stood in the opening, the waves splashing behind her, the fire flickering shadows over her lithe young body. Slowly she began to gyrate. Her hands gracefully fluttered about her face and body, then seductively slipped down her torso to rest upon open thighs. Her knees bent slightly as her pelvis slowly rotated in time to the music.

Iris gasped. That young sensual creature, with naked legs and black flowing hair, was Señorita Blanquita. She was now stalking Don Cristóbal, her small high virginal breasts projecting, challenging him like the horns of a bull. As the tempo heightened they came together, writhing as one. Even with the sand beneath their feet, they moved with grace and fire.

Blanquita's swishing skirt at times rose so high that it skimmed her crotch. Her slim immature body curved voluptuously with each movement of the dance. Her long limbs, though lean, were shapely and strong. Her angelic face, with its full pouting mouth and seductive gaze was far too alluring for a mere girl not quite a woman. Her posturing seemed to have enticed Cristóbal into dancing, when in truth they had performed as partners many times. The crowd encouraged them with their shouts and claps and snapping of fingers. Each dancer played off the other.

As far as Iris was concerned, Cristóbal's movements were much too erotic for a man who avowed his affection for her. This might well have been the acceptable custom of dancing in California, but back in Boston it was down right dirty.

Iris felt herself seething with anger. Watching the precious Señorita Blanquita provocatively aligning her body with Cristóbal was the most salacious thing she had ever seen. These so-called cousins perceived each other's every move. The look on their faces was sheer passion, their eyes hypnotized by each other's gaze. Their mouths at once pouted and seductively smiled, at times close enough to kiss.

Under the black night sky, lit only by stars and moon and shadowing flames, Blanquita appeared as dark skinned as Estrellita. Suddenly one could see the Indian that she was.

"I have a little surprise for you, cousin Blanquita," Iris fumed, her eyes narrowing.

Chapter 20

The fiesta ended at daybreak, three days before, but the Bradbury women were still suffering from fatigue. Since every Rancho had its embarcadero, Iris wondered why they could not have had their picnic on the shores of the Bay, instead of taking that impossible journey on horseback. Evidently the Bay could be viewed and enjoyed on any given day. The ocean beach at Santa Cruz, with its closeness to Don Diego was reasons enough.

Although those tumultuous days of celebration seemed to have reached its peak that night on the Pacific shore, those at Isla Del Vagabundo were elated to have Señorita Blanquita ride back with them.

Ironically it was Iris who was most pleased. She had gone through a great deal of scheming to effect her surprise. Wrapped in a silk handkerchief in her valise was a portrait of Estrellita, so resembling Blanquita, that it was startling. Her skin had paled with the noon day sun full upon her face. And those large almond eyes seemed lighter still.

Iris had convinced her to pose; insisting it was a surprise for her father. She pretended to be making amends for her previous insensitivity. Could they be friends?

After conferring with Miguel Pedro, who was most dubious, Estrellita was allowed to supposedly accompany her to the merchandising store, when in fact they met Jeremy at the bridge.

The bridge, which looked out upon the Bay, was a few planks laid across a small salt-water lagoon called Laguna Salada. Upon the arrival of a ship in the harbor, instead of the passengers having to step from the long boat to wade the last few yards to the beach, one could step onto the rocks at the furthest end of the crescent beach. After scrambling onto a ledge at the side of Loma Alta, then walking a distance behind Doña Briones' dairy farm, one would then titter across the bridge to the main street. This was the procedure some months before, when the Skylark sailed through a dense fog to anchor in the Bay. It was frightening stepping onto that slippery shelf of rocks, with unfamiliar hands reaching out of rising mist to welcome them. The lanterns gave a ghoulish look to those helping them ashore. The so-called bridge, though proudly deemed their first by the populace, seemed a precarious journey at best.

This is where Jeremy managed to get that perfect shot of Estrellita. The truth being that every photograph taken of her appeared lovelier than the last. Her features, her high cheekbones and full mouth, her long dark gleaming hair and azure eyes were spectacular.

Iris had studied the portraits at length, at last choosing the one that would most serve her purpose. It was now just a matter of time before it was presented to Blanquita. At the moment Iris was taking her siesta. Her eyes were wide open, her hands behind her head, as she watched Heather brushing her hair before the vanity mirror. She looked curiously happy, Iris thought, too happy. She had noticed a remarkable change in both her sister and Will; always holding hands, dreamily looking into each other's eyes, giggling. There was a decided intimacy between them that bothered Iris. Suddenly she sat up in bed her voice raising.

"You've done it! You let him put his thing inside of you, haven't you?"

Heather spun around, a shocked angry look upon her face. She could hardly speak. "How dare you?"

"Oh, you have, I can tell."

"Stop it, Iris!"

Heather rose, walked over to the bed and stood over Iris, a threatening look in her eyes. "I don't want to hear you say that again! Will and I are very much in love, and we're waiting until we're married to—"

"Married?" Iris screamed. "He asked you to marry him?"

"Yes."

"When did all this happen? Does Mamma know?"

"We wanted to announce it properly, but you had to spoil it for me."

Iris burst into laughter. "No wonder the two of you have been looking so starry eyed. It was an obvious change from all that anguishing. Here we all thought poor Heather would be left behind when Will left. Instead he's proposed." Suddenly she ceased to laugh. "Are you going with him, to live in the East, instead of here with us?"

"I really don't know. It hasn't been fully decided. Does it matter? I love him and am prepared to live wherever he wants."

"Thousands of miles away from Mamma and me?"

Heather sat on the edge of the bed beside Iris. Gently she brushed her sister's hair back from her brow. She was so elated with the idea of marrying Will, that it had not occurred to her that it could separate her from her mother and sister. The three of them had been together as far back as she could recall.

This past year found them clinging to one another even more desperately than ever. Heartbroken they had walked away from Papa's wake, to ultimately sail around the Horn to this strange country of California. To think, that after having journeyed that long distance, that it would be the very thing that would tear them apart.

As much as she wanted Will, only now as she searched the sadness of her sister's eyes, did she realize the sacrifice of loving him. She was but a tot when Iris was born, yet the recollection of that tiny baby in her mother's arms was a memory forever sustained. From that moment she felt compelled to watch after her, grasping her hand wherever they went, as though they were a part of one another. And they were.

Regardless of their indifference, they were blood, each possessing that which was both their mother and father.

Heather's arms slipped about Iris, and for a moment they silently embraced. Each could feel that the other had choked up, their eyes watering. Iris was the first to withdraw, breaking the spell as she did.

"Come on now, tell me for real. Did you do it with Will?"

"No."

Heather's face flushed. They had been so incredibly intimate, passionately touching and kissing, that her meek 'no' seemed a lie.

"You did!"

"No. And I don't want to discuss it any more. Just know that I've never been happier in my life. We'll marry here, of course, with my family around me. I'd like it to be atop Loma Alta, looking out over the bay, wIth the sweet minty smell of the Yerba Buena. And wild flowers in my hair."

"Come on Heather, we'll all get blown to pieces. Our hair will be a mess. More chances than not we'll be fogged in."

"You're so unromantic."

"Unromantic? Can you imagine the whole wedding party and guests trudging up that hill? You should be married right here at the Rancho. Believe me, it will be romantic, and unconventional enough to please your esthetic nature. I hear California weddings are spectacular. Uncle Johnny and Rufina will really put themselves out for the occasion. After all, he'll be giving you away. Who else could take Papa's place?"

"I guess you're right. But we don't want a big ostentatious display. I'm certain it would be too much for Will right now."

"Why? He seems to be coming out of his so-called mood. He did propose."

"Yes, but he's still a very private person. Besides, we haven't announced it yet. You're the first to know, Iris. So far you're the only one. Will and I haven't begun to make arrangements. Just that we're committed to one another."

"Who discusses arrangements with the groom anyway? All he has to do is be there. And I'll get Jeremy to take your wedding picture and—"

"Jeremy and Cristóbal, here together."

"That's not a problem Heather. Why should it be?"

Heather took a deep sigh. "You're getting too far ahead of matters, Missy. I want to tell Mamma first. And let me be the one to tell her. You promise?"

"Yes." Her voice softened and her eyes began to tear. "Please don't go back East to live without us. We've never in our lives been apart. I don't know if I could stand it."

They fell into each others arms weeping, caught up in a moment of deep emotion, such as only sisters understand. Slowly Heather drew back to study the utter sweetness of Iris' face, seeming so child-like, so innocent. Gently she kissed her brow. In the rapture of the moment she suddenly realized how much they did indeed love one another, and how very close they truly were. For the bloodline between siblings is a far closer link than that which relates children to their parents. At the moment, Heather was convinced that for all of Iris' contrariety, she was truly good at heart.

Chapter 21

"Iris Bradbury, you conniving little bitch!"

Uncle Johnny, Don Juan Ricardo Bradbury, the Patrón, had Iris by the shoulders and was fiercely shaking her.

"How dare you!" he shouted. "How dare you contrive to hurt Blanquita in such a ruthless way? How dare you? My own flesh and blood—in my own house?"

Day break had just begun to illumine the darkness, when he came storming into her bedroom, tore back the comforter and pulled Iris bodily from the bed, though she was sound asleep.

Heather awakened in a state of shock to be confronted by the inconceivable sight of her very own uncle accosting her sister. With sibling instinct she leaped from her bed to pleadingly pull at his arm, not realizing the reason for his tirade.

Belle and Tobias attired in their robes came flying from adjoining rooms to follow on Johnny's heels. They too had been jarred awake by the sound of his outburst.

His temper irrupted during the Morning Prayer, and reached explosive proportions by the time he got his hands on Iris.

It was Rufina who detected Blanquita kneeling amidst the servants, her face streaming with tears. Ordinarily she would have been fast asleep, to be later awakened by a servant offering chocolate at her beside.

With her black rebozo and downcast head, she at first went unrecognized. Rufina, who was well acquainted with every member of her enormous household staff, found herself curiously distracted by the familiar but misplaced figure of a light skinned girl among the help. Time and again the Patróna looked back over her shoulder to at last catch that brief instant when Blanquita would raise her head to look upon the Madonna.

She was there most of night, tearfully praying. Her prayers were filled with anguishing questions. Who was she and where did she truly belong? Why was she not told of her twin sister? For that is truly who that girl in the picture was. She immediately sensed it, deep within her soul, the moment she laid eyes upon that hauntingly familiar face. It might well have been her face staring back at her from the silvery surface of the daguerreotype.

Iris had slyly handed it to her just as she was about to enter her room to retire for the night. From out of the shadows she emerged, this beautiful Yankee whom Blanquita had made an effort to like for Cristóbal's sake. From the beginning Blanquita felt an uncomfortable chill whenever they passed. It was an unnerving feeling she tried to dismiss.

That night on the beach, as she and Cristóbal danced, Blanquita could actually feel Iris' eyes drawing upon her, stronger than anyone else in the crowd. It was a foreboding feeling. Iris' seething stare was the menacing warning of what was to later come. In a strange whispering voice, Iris called out her name, at once commanding her presence. Smiling smugly she placed the picture, yet wrapped in the silk handkerchief, in Blanquita's hand.

"Su hermana. Your sister." Iris disdainfully announced, audible enough so only the two of them could hear.

There was a vicariousness in the way Iris abruptly turned her back and ran down the corridor, knowing full well that Blanquita was yet standing there confused.

Blanquita entered her room and lit the lamp before unfolding the handkerchief that unveiled the portrait of Estrellita, as well as the shocking mystery of her own life. She gasped. Stupefied, she stared breathless and unblinking. That girl was herself. Except she was dressed in humble Indian garb. In the background was the Bay of San Francisco and the distance hills of Contra Costa. 'Su hermana.' Iris' words reverberated though her head and heart. How could she deny that this girl was not of her blood? Why was the truth hidden from her for so long? She was the privileged one and her sister the servant? But for the shades of their skins, they were one and the same. Who were her parents, if the mother and father she had always honored were not truly hers? And why did it come to light only now, by way of this jealous young woman?

Blanquita's despair was so consuming that she was unaware of time as she knelt in the cold corridor, deliberately distanced from the revered statue of the blue Madonna. With the first streak of daylight, soft footsteps began to shuffle about her. The place quickly crowded with the Indian servants, with field hands and vaqueros. Surrounded by the encompassing warmth of other bodies kneeling near enough to brush her shoulders was in itself a sequestered place. With her head lowered and her dark rebozo falling about her face, Blanquita could become momentarily lost in her grief.

Doña Rufina's keen eyes at last recognized her. Softly she rose from her own prayers, to step lightly through the mass of servants to gently touch upon Blanquita's shoulder. The Patróna was immediately cognizant of her despair. It was there in the sadness of her eyes, in the uneven heaving of her breasts and her trembling hands clasped in prayer. Rufina knelt beside her, causing those close by to quickly move aside. Compassionately she drew her sweet little cousin into the fullness of her embrace. The sight of the Patróna holding what seemed one of them in her arms caused a subdued stir among the help. For always she prayed at the foot of the Madonna, beside her husband.

Slowly the two of them rose as Rufina led the young girl away. All eyes curiously followed after them. The repetitive drone of the Alba persisted.

Johnny was quick to follow after the two women, at last meeting up with them in Blanquita's bedchamber. As the portrait of Estrellita was shown to them, they also gasped. Not that they were unaware of Estrellita's existence, but that the long guarded secret, had been so cruelly disclosed.

All the while Johnny shook Iris, she tearfully pleaded innocence. Nothing could quell his anger. Even after Tobias finally managed to step between the two, Johnny stood glaring at Iris, his fists clenched.

She immediately ran to Heather's open arms. Her sister was quick to wrap her in a robe and hold her protectively, though still badly shaken by the violence she had just witnessed.

As of yet Heather had not told anyone other than Iris of her impending marriage. All at once the joy of it had been traumatically taken away. Her Uncle Johnny, whom she had grown to adore, was suddenly someone she feared. What had Iris done to Blanquita to affect him so severely?

Belle was staring at Iris with disbelief, all the while attempting to placate Johnny, who was beyond being calmed. As far as he was concerned there was no tolerable excuse for what Iris had done.

"I can't believe that my own brother's daughter can be so evil!" he screamed. "That's what you are, Iris, evil! I will not have you in my house! You can pack your things now and return to the village. Alone for all I care. Your mother and sister will always be welcome. But you, you can go to hell!"

"I didn't mean it at all the way it seems," Iris cried. "It's just that the two of them looked so alike and—and I thought Blanquita would marvel at the resemblance. That's why I asked Jeremy to take the picture of Estrellita as a kind of surprise," she spurted out.

Heather abruptly released Iris from her embrace. "My God, Iris! You didn't!"

"If it was suppose to be such a big secret that the two not know that the other existed, then why didn't someone tell me?" Iris simpered.

"If you had any question along that line, Missy, why didn't you come to me?" Johnny demanded. "I'll tell you why, because your suspicions allowed you a perfect weapon to hurt that sweet unsuspecting girl. You know what my wife told me to do to you? Just what her father or any Patrón in my place would do. Give you a good flogging!"

All three Bradbury women gasped in unison. In a shielding gesture Belle stepped in front of Iris.

"As right as you are at being angry, we don't do things that way, Johnny. The girls and I will leave as soon as possible. Believe me, I am so very sorry, and ashamed. If there is some way that I can make it up to Blanquita, I will."

"There is nothing you can do. The damage is irreversible! The truth is out! My wife and I and our family will deal with it ourselves." He gave Iris a threatening look. "Not a word of this to the girl, Estrellita. Do you understand?"

"Yes," she meekly answered, her knees shaking.

Chapter 22

Don Cristóbal gave Iris a long searing look as she approached him in the corridor, causing her to stop, stunned. Those dark shimmering eyes, that had adoringly devoured her, now shown with contempt. She wanted to run to his arms, but instead found herself hastening to leave the Rancho.

Tobias, her mother, Heather and Will all rode abreast while Iris was confined to the rear closely accompanied by Hector.

As always his mere presence was capable of completely unnerving her. She froze as he moved his horse adjacent to hers; at times riding so close that she could feel the hardness of his thigh muscles ripple against her own. The fullness of her skirt offered little cover against the defiant feel of him. She was overcome with both fear and repulsion as his eyes squinted with disdain, a black cigarillo dangling from the corner of a scoffing smile. Time and again his large dark callused hand reached out to grip her reigns, straightening her spirited steed. The animal, which was used to racing ahead as well as being handled by an adept horseman, reared upon first having her in the saddle.

As much as she loathed Hector, she was at the mercy of his expertise. He was sadistically enjoying her plight. This beautiful haughty Easterner, who had been treated royally by all, was now reduced to a sulking chastised little girl.

Fearing to take her grip off the reigns even for an instant Iris was unable to wipe away the tears, which consistently coursed down her cheeks. Her obvious unhappiness made her feel even more a mockery to this ruthless Indian, who considered her more ruthless than himself.

To no longer be loved and accepted by her Uncle Johnny and his family, to actually be ostracized from his Rancho, was the most humiliating experience of her life. And Cristóbal, whose devotion she counted upon, only added to the shock. His coldness had convinced her that Blanquita meant more to him than one realized, when in truth it was a matter of honor and integrity that was the issue. One did not deliberately hurt one's own kin, not in this country of California.

The idea of fidelity towards family was beyond Iris' comprehension. All her life she had played one member of the household against the other. Papa was the easiest of all to manipulate, and Heather the easiest to hurt. Never before had she set out to be quite so vicious. Nor did she anticipate such angry recourse. It was as though everyone hated her.

Hector and his chosen band of vaqueros, who rode almost everywhere with Uncle Johnny, were very much present that day at Delores when Estrellita made her First Communion. Iris wondered how they felt knowing that Blanquita, who was treated like a blue blood, was in fact Estrellita's double. Yet the darker of the two was brought up as a servant. Did the few Indians who knew take pride in Blanquita's position, or did they resent her? If it was supposed to be a secret, how come so many people seemed to know, while both Blanquita and Estrellita remained oblivious of one another. There was an apparent shielding of both girls, by the paisanos and Indians alike.

Iris felt that she of all people was being treated like an outcast, condemned to Yerba Buena Cove forever. Back to a nothing life, save for Jeremy. My God, Jeremy! Suddenly she felt desperate for him, for the feel of his arms. He would be there waiting for her. Of this she was certain. At least she had him. Or did she? She must get to him first and pacify things before someone else confronted him.

After all, he did take the picture of Estrellita, many of them. There would be questions and God forbid further confrontations for certain. She must not lose Jeremy.

Chapter 23

Belle was conspicuously quiet as they journeyed homeward to Yerba Buena. Beyond her pale, stoic face, was a breaking heart. Tobias, who was aware of her feelings as they rode side by side, often turned to give her a compassionate glance or touch. His concern proved of little comfort. Belle was devastated beyond belief.

Until that moment, the lives of her girls and herself seemed at last destined for ultimate happiness and security. Had her rose hued vantagepoint failed to fully perceive the perverse warning signs? For all the outward show of enjoyment, Iris' irritations had continued to flare. Belle could not help but question her lack of awareness as a mother.

Because she herself was deliriously in love and emotionally secure, all else promised to fall into place. Had she given too much of her time and feelings to Tobias, and far too little to Iris?

She could not bring herself to look at Iris, even after they arrived home. Not only out of anger at her daughter's insensitivity, but because of her own shame. Shame was a feeling she had never before experienced. She could barely look Johnny or Rufina in the eye, though they did not blame her in the least.

Exhausted, they entered the house in Yerba Buena to be immediately greeted by the irony of it all, Estrellita's untimely sweetness. The girl was pleasantly startled to be hugged at length by Señorita Heather, whom she had come to love. Even Iris' sheepish greeting came as a surprise.

Doña Belle had warmly grasped both her hands in her own, before rushing into her room.

They were not expected home for at least another two weeks, perhaps a month. As usual one of the vaqueros raced ahead to alert the household of their coming.

In the interim Kane-Paul had left for New Helvetia, more commonly known as Sutter's Fort. It was a remote settlement on the Sacramento River, built by an ambitious Swiss adventurer and frontiersman known as Don Juan Agustus, Captain John Agustus Sutter.

The Fort was not only the remotest outpost in California, but also the first to welcome weary immigrants. The New Helvetia community, which was under Sutter's complete control, consisted of traders, trappers, run-away sailors, overland immigrants, fifty indispensable Indians and ten Kanakas, two of them woman.

There was one in particular, whom Kane-Paul could not dismiss from his dreams and daydreams. Her name was Lailani. As children, they attended the same Protestant Mission School in the Sandwich Islands. Even then, they would exchange secret glances and giggles. To have found one another again in the remoteness of California was regarded by both as one of destiny's sweetest decisions. Kane-Paul had promised himself that together they would indeed 'walk in love', ecstatically sharing its peripheral pleasures.

Johnny's final words to Iris, on that last day at the Rancho, were not only explicit but also threatening. Estrellita must not know of her sister. The slightest knowledge of Blanquita's existence could not help but have harrowing repercussions, not only to her, but also to Miguel Pedro.

Always she believed him to be her father. What would it do to have her realize that he was not of her own flesh and blood? He above all, had not only held the secret, but had been a crucial part of the duplicity.

If the girls had been full-blooded Indians, the birth of twins would in itself have been an ill omen. According to custom, one twin was automatically killed. But they were a generation removed from their heritage, Catholics, totally subjugated to the dictates of the Padres.

The shock of Maria Inocencia giving birth to two blue eyed girls was not only the ultimate despair for their mother, but for Miguel Pedro, who was prepared to accept the baby as his own. His prayers were filled with the hope that the child would emerge looking more Indian than white. That way they could pretend that the offspring was theirs, ultimately assuming their lives as man and wife. What came from her womb was an aberration too terrible to warrant her living.

With much thought and planning, the lighter skinned child was given to a family in Monterey, the mother having had a stillborn child at the approximate moment. To the grieving parents and Padres alike, God had signaled a way. Estrellita remained at Delores, in the care of one of the soldier's wives. Miguel Pedro was allowed visitations. With Secularization he was gladly given the tiny girl, whom he named Estrellita. To ultimately find a home in Yerba Buena was a blessing. Tobias and Hannah were aware that they were taking a special child into their home. They also knew that her twin was being raised in Monterey, as an hija del pais. Each girl had been content in her own way until now. The truth had been cruelly revealed to one of the twins. At all cost, the other must be protected.

It was dusk when Belle finally appeared from her room, to step out into the garden. The air was crisp; a slight breeze billowed her skirt and shawl. Lethargically she sank onto the bench facing the Bay, her head in her hands. She felt Tobias' arm slip about her shoulders. Still she remained unresponsive to his touch.

"It is our problem Belle." he endeavored to assure, "not just your cross to bear. My love for you has nothing to do with Iris."

"I'm so ashamed."

He could feel her tremble. "You've done nothing. Johnny and Rufina realize this."

Her tear filled eyes lifted to his. "Why, why is she like that? Both girls came from the same loving parents, the same home. How can one of them be so cruel? I'm glad Colon's not alive to be witness to all of this. It would have broken his heart. He adored that girl."

"Colon's gone. I'm here, Belle, remember that."

"I know. But strangely, a part of him persists right now. He took care of things right up to the last. Why couldn't I have been more discerning? How did I allow this to pass right by me?"

"Don't blame yourself."

"I can't help but be tormented by the terrible anguish one of my own has caused. Blanquita's pain must be intolerable at the moment. And what becomes of her now that she knows? I—I can't even look at Iris. Yet, I love her so. How can it be?"

She turned and sobbed uncontrollably in his arms. She had been harboring the hurt all through their journey, at times feeling that she might choke from the pain. Cradled in Tobias' embrace she allowed it to be released. He too could almost weep. Never before had he seen her cry. Perhaps a tear of nostalgia but nothing as overwhelming as now. He was not certain what he would have done if Iris had truly been his own daughter. Even Heather, whose own silence mimicked her mother's seemed unapproachable. At the moment she and Will sat alone in the parlor, close but barely conversing.

Iris rushed to her room shortly after entering the house. She had thrown herself on her bed, her face in her pillow, her profuse sobs and tears of little difference to all but Estrellita. Concerned, the young girl had gently knocked on the bedroom door causing Iris to quickly wipe away her tears with the back of her fists.

"Señorita Iris," It was Estrellita's soft voice. "Are you all right?"

"I just want to be alone," she wept.

Dismayed by the lack of everyone's indifference to Iris' despair, Estrellita was at a loss as what to do. Hesitantly she turned the knob, leaving the door slightly ajar. She peeked through the slim opening to find a most distraught young woman hysterically sobbing into the pillow.

"Can I do something for you, Señorita Iris?"

"Go away."

"Yes, Señorita."

Estrellita shut the door, blankly staring at it for a moment after. Nothing made sense. She could not explain it to herself, but she felt deeply troubled. From the moment all three Bradbury women stepped into the house, Estrellita was instantly aware of a great sadness. Yes, they were drained from their trip, but this was a homecoming akin to no other she had ever seen. Estrellita was certain that something dire had occurred at the Rancho, something that somehow touched upon her own humble life. In her haste Estrellita had forgotten to light the chandelier for Don Tobias' homecoming. A small ritualistic gesture, at best. Why did it seem so foreboding?

Chapter 24

Heather's whispering finally broke the silence. "I can't believe they could have kept such a secret so long without the girls finding out." Her voice saddened. "Now one of them has."

Will bit his lip. "Yes. And what was the good of it?"

He haltingly answered in the same whisper, both of them being extremely mindful of Estrellita's presence somewhere in the house. They sat in the parlor on the settee, their thighs and legs aligned, the fingers of their adjoining hands enmeshed. With the word secret, Heather felt Will's grasp inadvertently tighten. She was aware that he too harbored something painfully secretive that never ceased to haunt him.

To tell her was certain to alienate them forever. He had fallen hopelessly in love with her. There was no turning back. As long as they remained here in this far away place, they had a chance. There were times when he desperately longed to see his family, his mother and sisters. Four of them were married, so there were sons-in-law to take care of his aging mother and two spinster sisters. Considering the banking crisis, and his father's sound investments, the family remained reasonably solvent. Still, it was not the same as having her sons. They in particular had been close to their mother. The fact that Gus and he were so much younger than the girls afforded her more time with them as youngsters. Their father, who was consistently preoccupied with business, took to the boys only after they became men and potential partners. By then, he was dead. Their mother was there the day they sailed away, giving them each inscribed timepieces in gold.

In his solitude, Will would slip the timepiece from his vest pocket and fondly touch upon the inscription. He knew in his heart that his mother, above all, desperately awaited some word from Gus and himself. Except Gus was gone. And there was little left of that smiling robust young man that he was upon setting sail for the Caribbean. How much longer could he postpone writing to her?

Many times he had taken a pen in hand only to feel it tremble in his grasp, coercing the spill of silent tears upon his face. There were no words that could possibly minimize Gus' dying in the jungles of Panama. He was her last child, her baby.

Why did the devastation of losing Gus make his own life seem so inconsequential in comparison? Yet his family would rejoice, even in sorrow, knowing he was alive.

What would Gus have done if he had been the surviving brother? Would he have immediately returned with the Skylark, or continued to pursue the mission that precipitated them traveling to this far away land in the first place? As destiny would have it, Will fell in love. The fact that he met Heather Bradbury and wanted to make her his wife, would in itself be news ill received. Still his family must know the full truth. Too much time had already past. A letter could be sent by the next Yankee ship that came into the Bay. When, was anyone's guess? The closest post office was in Independence Missouri, two thousand miles away. A courier taking the overland pass would first have to brave the Sierra Nevada to reach the Oregon Trail, the main route. He would then be confronted with the Rocky Mountains and the wide Missouri River, before glimpsing Independence. The River was both the beginning and the end of the western most edge of the Constituted United Sates. The Eastern seaboard was still a long hard drive away. An alternate mail route was south to Baja California, taking The Old Spanish Trail that linked up with the Santa Fe Trail and ultimately Independence. All of which had its own brand of danger. Miraculously, mail did arrive, more times than not. Those riders were dauntless. Far braver than Will felt at the moment. He gave a melancholy sigh, which Heather misinterpreted.

"I grant, it's not too happy a prospect having Iris as a sister-in-law. What she did to that girl was unforgivable."

She caught her words, daring not mention Blanquita's name. Uncle Johnny was frightfully adamant in his warning. Yet he and Rufina fondly kissed her and her mother 'goodbye' and warmly hugged Tobias and Will, inviting him back. No matter, Iris was still her sister.

"I want you as my wife, Heather. I love you for you, just as I want you to love me, for me. We can't make ourselves responsible for any members of our family. As dearly as we love them, we are individuals, apart from their actions. Believe me, this thing with Iris, nor anything else in this world, is not going to sway me otherwise. I want you too feel as strongly in your convictions for me."

"I do, you know that."

"I realize our wedding was to be a huge event at the Rancho, but it doesn't matter to me. It hasn't all along. And I don't expect things to subside, because certain things can never be forgotten. I want us to be together now. I spoke to Tobias and he said he'd make arrangements for us to go to Monterey by launch. David Spense can marry us. He's a Justice of the Peace." He tried to jest. "Just think, we'll even be able to understand our own wedding vows."

"Monterey?" she softly questioned.

It seemed the least likely place considering that is where Blanquita and her family lived. Just the idea of a wedding would encourage a fiesta from one faction or another. How could they even consider a celebration in the face of what had happened?

"Isn't it possible to be married by the Alcalde right here in Yerba Buena?" Heather added. "Isn't he also a sort of Justice of the Peace?"

"Possibly. I'll have to look into it."

Her eyes misted. "I love you." She whispered.
"And I love you. Believe me, you'll never know how much."

Chapter 25

Just before daylight, Iris slipped out of bed and dressed, taking pains to cover herself warmly, and to wear her boots. She was determined to find Jeremy. Since they had only been home since late afternoon yesterday, there obviously was not time enough for him to realize she was back, although nothing seem to go unnoticed in this minuscule community.

She did not even know where he lived. It never occurred to her to ask, although he rather she not see the shed of a place he called home. Since she was not about to be running from shack to shack at this ungodly hour pounding on doors, her best option was to head for the merchandising store, where Chester Perkins had his sleeping quarters.

She stepped out of the house to the shocking feel of a sharp chill. The fog and darkness defusing to a gray mist afforded an eerie atmosphere. There was not a single lamp lit anywhere. The occasional rasping cry of gulls echoed overhead. She shivered. Adjusting a large black rebozo over her head and shoulders she proceeded down the steep hill toward the village, often times skidding on the damp ground.

She knocked at both the front and back doors of the store, frantically running around from one place to the other. Though barely discernible through the grimy windows, the dim glow of a single oil lamp weaving its way through the merchandise caught her attention. Upon first hearing the insistent knock, Chester drowsily stumbled from his bed to peek out from behind his shredded curtains. He was taken aback by the sight of a dark outline of a woman at his back door. He tripped twice stepping into his trousers. The idea of a woman seeing his disheveled sleeping quarters prompted him to allow her entrance through the front of the store. It was a shock to find Iris. The light of his lamp close to her face immediately illumined her pale skin and long reddish hair, the rebozo having slipped to her shoulders. Chilled, she quickly stepped into the store.

"Where does Jeremy live!" She sounded troubled and breathless. "I have to find him!"

"He's staying at the cooper's, just two houses down from you."

Iris started to turn away but was halted by his words.

"He's not there. He left for Sutter's Fort about the same time you left for Santa Clara."

"Oh no," she moaned, realizing that she had spent an entire sleepless night anticipating seeing him, and for nothing.

"What is it, Miss Bradbury? Maybe I can help you."

"No. It has to be Jeremy. It has something to do with Estrellita."

"Estrellita? Has something happened to her?"

By the anxiousness of his voice, Iris was at once aware that Chester not only felt concern for the girl, but a deep caring.

He was only three years her senior, a young man alone in this far away country of California. The sight of Estrellita sent his heart racing, though there was seldom a time that she was not accompanied by the Indian claiming to be her father. Miguel Pedro, though at first stern faced, now spoke kindly to him, as did his beautiful daughter. For a long time Estrellita's eyes remained downcast. When she finally raised her gaze to look at him and softly smile Chester felt his heart stop. The blue of her eyes stunned him into a stupor. It took weeks before he could even utter a 'good day' without stammering. He turned ashen at the thought of something having happened to her.

"Estrellita is fine," Iris sighed plopping herself down in a chair. "Better than I am. Now, tell me how do I get to Sutter's Fort?"

He talked through a succession of yawns. "I'm afraid New Helvetia is three bays and a winding river away."

"What are you talking about? What's New Helvetia?"

"Oh, I'm sorry, that's the name of the place. It's just that it's Captain Sutter's domain, so to speak. He had it built in the shape of a fort, with cannons on the outer walls. It sits back on a slope, two miles or so from the bank of the Rio Sacramento, or Rio Jose Maria. Whatever they call it, it's the same river."

"You mean Jeremy just up and sailed away, the first chance he got?"

"He'll be back. It was an opportunity that came along, and he took it. Every so often Sutter's schooner, The Sacramento, comes down here for provisions. And this was one of those times."

Anything made of iron, or manufactured goods were well needed at the fort. Sutter requested a list of a hundred items. House door locks, saws, butcher knives, rifle powder, red and white beads for the Indians. There was always a demand for a certain brown cotton cloth, which his Indians used for their clothing.

"Let me guess," It was Iris. "Jeremy left to take pictures, no doubt."

Chester yawned, finally placing the lamp on the counter. "That's Jeremy. Keeps saying he wants to visually record history. Even has a bunch of dag-types of me in the store. The caption will no doubt read, 'New England greenhorn found stranded in remote Mexican hamlet.'"

Iris remained unfazed by Chester's early morning humor. She was annoyed by the sight of him tugging at his slipping suspenders, the uncombed cowlick on the top of his red crop of hair, and the jagged sleep mark on his cheek. She wondered why she was here. In reality, there was no place else to turn.

"How long does it take to get to Sutter's Fort anyway?"

He shrugged. "Depends. Could be as long as ten days."

"Ten days!" she screamed. "Then there's the trip back. How long does he intend to stay?"

"Hard to guess. The schooner often makes trips to Bodega Bay, and Fort Ross before reaching Sutter's Fort."

"Where in blazes are Bodega Bay and Fort Ross?"

He thought a moment, causing her further impatience. "Well, Bodega's about sixty miles up the coast. It was once a Russian port, set up for fur sealing. It's deserted now. I hear they used to have eighty Aleuts with forty skin boats hunting otters, all along the coast as far as the islands outside the gate, staying clear of our bay. Sixteen miles farther north is Fort Ross. Another empty Russian settlement, large enough to have held four hundred people, Russians, Kodak's and their families. Nothing's left but ghosts I guess."

All movable property had been sold to Sutter. A self contained fortified village was stripped to the timbers. Cannon, livestock, windows, windmill, even the chapel had been shipped to New Helvetia.

"Everything is gone." Chester shrugged. "Still the Russians have managed to leave their mark."

"There's an old nun somewhere in a convent that can attest to that." She retorted sarcastically, angered by the specter of a Russian colony capable of enticing Jeremy and his camera. "Pish-posh on all that Russian stuff," she hissed. "When is Jeremy coming back? Damn dagtype. That's what started all the trouble in the first place."

"Trouble? What trouble?"

"Oh, go back to bed, Chester," she sighed. "I'm sorry I awoke you."

"Well, since I'm up, and about to brew some coffee, wait a bit and I'll fix you a cup."

"Why not?" Iris simpered. "What else is there to do in this God forsaken place?"

Shrugging, he turned and walked toward the potbelly stove to fetch the kettle. He was stopped midway by the deviousness of her question.

"You've really taken a fancy to Estrellita, haven't you?"

He gave her a sheepish grin. "Yes Miss, I have indeed."

"Really? What would your staunch church going New England folks think about you being smitten with a half breed?"

Though it was hard to tell in the semi-light of the store, his face became as red as his hair. "I don't give a hoot who thinks what! Least of all you!"

Chapter 26

Iris ran down hill full force into Jeremy's arms the instant she caught sight of him walking up toward Tobias' house. Both shocked and elated he caught her and lifted her in the fullness of his embrace, crushing the soft broad rimmed hat that had blown from her head to dangle from a sash upon her back. Her arms wrapped tightly about his neck.

"Oh Jeremy, I thought you'd never get here. I've been back a month. It feels like a year! I missed you terribly."

"Enough to kiss me before God and all of creation, right here and now?" He asked not waiting for a reply, his mouth passionately pressing upon hers.

She kissed him back with such ardor that it almost sent them both reeling down hill. With a satisfying sigh he at last placed her on the ground, his arms still warmly embracing her. He was smiling deliriously. This was exactly what he had fantasized time and again on his trip, all the while knowing that there was tremendous competition for her favor.

"Wow, am I dreaming?" He finally caught his breath. "What brought this on? What happened to your Don Cristóbal?"

"Oh him?" she frowned. "That was a mistake. You knew it would be. I don't ever want to go back to the Rancho as long as I live. I don't care about any of them. Uncle Johnny to boot!"

"This sounds serious. You're even mad at you Uncle Johnny? What happened?"

"It's all too troubling to be discussing now when I'm so happy to have you home. I missed you, Jeremy." Her eyelids demurely fell. "Truly I did. I realize how foolish I was to spurn you that last time we were together. But—" She raised her gaze to meet his, her eyes seeming remarkably blue and sincere. "But only because I was afraid of caring for you and ending up in some ramshackle place for the rest of my life."

"You care for me? This no-account drifter?" He was smiling broadly. "You really do?"

"Oh yes—yes. With all my heart."

"Here I thought I'd just about lost all my chances with you. Still I was having the damnedest time ridding myself of the feel of you, of that sweet luscious mouth." He paused to seriously search her face. "As much as you make my heart pound, Missy dear, I'm afraid there's more to all this, isn't there? What happened at the Rancho that makes you never want to return? They are family. And family is truly treasured in these parts."

"Family indeed. They could care less about me. It's just all too weird, this Patrón business. I think it's gone to Uncle Johnny's head. After all, I'm still his niece and a Yankee. I expect to be treated accordingly," she pouted. "It's been so distressing. I want to put it all out of my mind and just be with you." She stood back a bit and studied him a moment. "You look as brown as an Indian, but so beautiful to behold, I could cry."

He drew her close to his chest, softly bestowing soft kisses upon her brow. She felt so small and fragile in his arms, this strong willed, defiant young woman who had soundly rejected him but weeks ago. What happened in the interim he did not want to know. This was too good to be true. He felt himself slightly sway from the sweetness of her scent. Her arms, which were firmly wound about his waist, suddenly slipped away.

"Let's go down to the bridge and just talk." In looking out at the bay, her gaze avoided his. "I want to know all about your trip to Sutter's Fort," she falsely enthused.

Iris hung onto Jeremy's arm all the way to the bridge. They sat themselves on a strip of sand at the edge of the small lagoon, where a profusion of water birds fluttered and glided upon the misty surface. She tore at the sash attached to her hat, recklessly casting the yellow vicuna aside. The nimbleness of her fingers unobtrusively undid the top button of her neckline. How tempting to lie back enmeshed in each others limbs, hidden by high fronds, and make love like some long ago Ohlone lovers, if that indeed is what happened on this very shoreline.

The romance of it all was heavy, even with the dampness of the fog upon their faces and the chill wind off the bay. They kissed long and hard, with Jeremy being the one to withdraw though Iris wanted more of him. He sensed an urgency in her that was more than passion.

"You want me Jeremy, don't you? Kiss me."

Her arms clung about his neck, her mouth ravenously seeking his. Gently he took her hands and pulled them down, firmly holding them in his own. There was a sudden seriousness.

"Tell me, what happened at the Rancho? By the gist of things, I gather it's far more serious than you say. I'm truly taken with you, Missy, you know that. But it's not going to be resolved like this."

"I did miss you, Jeremy. And I do care, honest. And if I seem desperate, it's because the waiting for you just—just took its toll."

"And would you have been just as desperate for me, if things had gone well at the Rancho?"

"How can you doubt my feelings?"

"I don't Iris. There was something between us from the first moment, and definitely after the Fandango. But I won't allow it to be a last resort for you."

"It's like I said I was afraid of caring for you. As soon as I saw Cristóbal again, I wanted you all the more. I realized he and I were from two totally different worlds. We couldn't begin to carry on a conversation. Besides, he turned out to be despicable."

"Despicable? Someone as gallant as Don Cristóbal?"

"Well he was," she insisted.

"What brought it on, Iris? It couldn't have been anything you said." He found himself smiling at his own remark.

"Why I left had nothing to do with Don Cristóbal. Uncle Johnny seems to have forgotten that I am more blood kin to him than all those in-laws and cousins he's accumulated by becoming a Don." She was scowling. "Mountain man that he was, he's suddenly taken up with playing God, that's what!"

Jeremy thought a moment, his eyes failing to blink as they stared into hers.

"It's hard to believe that your own uncle would run you off. It must have been something pretty serious."

"He didn't exactly run me off," she pouted. "Jeremy, you must believe me," she continued convincingly, "when I tell you that you've been uppermost in my mind ever since we parted, regardless of what happened with Uncle Johnny."

Jeremy was not totally convinced, but too enamored to pursue the topic. He was captivated by the sweetness of her voice and the lovable look on her face. An exquisite face with a delectable mouth yearning to be kissed. Patiently he listened to her lamentations.

"This last month, waiting for you, here in Yerba Buena was a nightmare," she continued almost in tears." There is nothing here, just nothing!"

"I grant it can seem pretty dismal to a young woman like yourself."

"It's not only the place itself, but also the cursed weather. It's so unpredictable. Where are the seasons? It's still supposed to be summer, isn't it? Here we are shrouded in fog."

"It'll burn off by noon."

"I keep hearing that phrase and I hate it."

He smiled. "Feels exhilarating to me. It got to be pretty hot up the river, from eighty to a hundred degrees. And the mosquitoes were monstrous."

"You're here now Jeremy, and Yerba Buena is at last bearable. There is nothing to do other than just sit around hearing everyone talking about the past, like it was yesterday."

"Talking is an important pastime in any small community. Fond memories make for a feeling or camaraderie."

"Community? This place isn't a community! It's an outhouse. I've heard all the stories, ten times over. You'd think that stupid forth of July party just happened yesterday. Who cares?"

She was referring to the celebration of the first wooden structure built in Yerba Buena, by an Ohio merchant called Jacob Lees. It was a rambling redwood house completed on July fourth, 1836. The American flag was hoisted for the first time in California, furling alongside of the Mexican flag above the Lees house. The three or four American ships in the harbor sent out Launches and Schooners to all the Ranchos around the Bay. The three days and nights of festivity with fireworks and the constant salutes fired from the ships were yet to be rivaled. The Lees house eventually belonged to the Hudson's Bay Company. Still, that long ago event continued to be recanted.

"What I'm really interested in knowing," Iris eyes widened, "is about the festivities that are forever taking place right now, at all those Ranchos around the bay."

"That's understandable."

"I now realize that most of those prominent families were aboard the Skylark that day of our fiesta. You know, the Estudillos, the Perdita's, Castros, and Martinez families." She sighed. "I was so green and engrossed in Uncle Johnny, that I paid little heed to anyone else. These are real Dons, whose ancestors came with the Anza Expedition. The King of Spain gave their land grants to them. Not like those later day Dons who married hijas del pais," she sneered,

Jeremy was quick to catch the scorn in alluding to her Uncle Johnny. He passed over her remark by offering an account of his trip.

"Well, we did stop at two Rancho's along the way."

"Where?" She anxiously questioned.

He had to smile at having so easily perked her interest. "We first docked just across the bay, at Whaler's Harbor, Puerto de Balleneros," he added in Spanish. "And were at once welcome to Rancho Sausalito. Means little grove of willows." He smiled realizing he was acting the interpreter, though she could care less. "It is owned by Captain Richardson, Don Antonio." His smile could not help but broaden. "He was probably the first to marry an hija del pais. Maria Antonia Martinez was young, beautiful and her father was Comandante of the Presidio."

Richardson who arrived in 1822, was a mate on the English whaler Orion. It was uncertain if he jumped ship or was deliberately left ashore. His carpentry and boat building skills immediately ingratiated him with the Californios.

"As the story goes. Yes, another story." Grinning Jeremy continued. "He got himself baptized, married and became a Don."

"I think I've heard that one before. I just wasn't paying attention. At least now I know that it's possible to go to Rancho Sausalito as well as all the other Ranchos and not be at the mercy of Uncle Johnny, or stuck here in this awful hamlet."

"I wouldn't say that to Don Antonio, if I were you."

"You mean Don Antonio, Captain Richardson? Why?"

"Actually, it was he, not Lees, who built the first structure in Yerba Buena. Three years before that famous 4th of July party, Richardson put up a shanty with a sailcloth roof." He pointed. "Right there on the sand hills overlooking the bay. I'm guessing he has a fondness for the place."

"Why didn't he just leave it to the coyotes and bears?"

"How else would we have ever met, Iris?" he teased.

"So what happened at Rancho Sausalito?" she persisted.

"Well, we had barely boarded the Sacramento when we were there across the bay, dancing up a storm."

"I was gone a day and already you were dancing?"

"You know how it is in these parts," he smiled. "Broken heart and all, you dance." His hands gently squeezed hers. "I did manage to have a nice talk with Doña Maria Antonia. She confided that she fell in love with her husband at first sight. One look at that tall, blonde, blue eyed Englishman, and she instantly decided that she was going to marry him. So there they are, across the Bay, living happily with their beautiful children. It's a story I intend to pass on to our grandchildren."

His staring caused her to suddenly shiver, but it was not because of the morning chill. She quickly changed the subject.

"So what was the other Rancho you visited?"

"That of Don Ignacio Martinez, of Pinole. He invited us to stay over night. In no time we were in the midst of a Fandango. Don Ignacio, who is incredibly charming, is a man pushing sixty. He out danced and out sang us all." He grinned. "With a bit of agaurdiente under my belt, I made an off key fool of myself praising my beautiful Bostonian, with her copper hair, blue eyes and delectable proportions. And they cheered."

"You're teasing me, Jeremy."

"Honest. You were my love song. And I can't even sing."

"Your love song?" Her flush suddenly took on a grudging expression. "Delectable proportions indeed. You still danced with all those Señoritas."

"My heart was with you, Iris. You know that."

This she knew. It was evident in his eyes and voice, in the tenderness of his touch. She smiled sweetly at him. For the moment she felt assured of herself. There was still the matter of Estrellita and Blanquita and the picture he had taken at her request. Somehow she must tactfully find a way to tell him, before someone else did. More likely it would be Tobias, and soon.

She humored Jeremy by pretending interest in his trip to Sutter's Fort. In reality, she was burning with curiosity about life on other

Rancho's besides her Uncle Johnny's. There had to be something to look forward to besides the dreariness of this awful place.

Quite suddenly he took her in his arms and was kissing her. The inclination was to lie back, hidden by the thick tall fronds and make love. For all her inexperience, Iris wanted Jeremy, right then and there. The wildness in her was evidenced in her wanton kisses, the sensual sliding of her taut young breast across his chest, and her firm lean limbs tightly tangling themselves with his.

It had been a long time since he had a woman, and far longer someone whom he loved. As aroused as he was he was not about to take this desirable young virgin in the rushes. His maturity and caring convinced him to temper his passions. Yet it was not his chivalry that quelled the fire, but the harrowing scream that abruptly shrilled from Iris. There crawling over her shoulder was a huge ugly gray rodent, the size of a cat. Jeremy leaped up with such alacrity that the rat fell belly up before running off with lightening speed. He was quick to lift Iris in his arms and carry her away. She sobbed hysterically into his chest. Even he had to shiver at the sight of it perched upon her shoulder, inches from Iris' beautiful face.

"It's all right, sweetheart, it's all right now. "He soothed, still holding her protectively in his arms.

"I hate this place!" she cried in his chest. "I hate it!"

"I'll take you home."

"No! No! I want to stay with you."

She clung to him. Her response to his suggestion that he take her home was as hysterical as her reaction to the rat. Iris was intent on stopping him from going to Tobias' house, for fear of encountering anyone who knew about the dag-type of Estrellita. She had to tell him first. She clung to him tighter still.

Suddenly Jeremy broke out in laughter. "For all the snakes, coyotes and mountain lions that I've faced in the wilds, how did I manage to get undone by a waterfront rat? Now, there's another story we can tell our grandchildren."

She was strangely subdued by his last remark, at last raising her head to look into his eyes. "You keep referring to our grandchildren as though it were inevitable."

"Now, what makes you think it isn't?" He teased.

"Will you take me away from here?"

"Is that a yes?"

"Yes to what? You haven't really proposed."

"Shall I get down on one knee?"

"No!"

She was yet frightened of the rodent, knowing full well that it was but one of many scurrying through Yerba Buena Cove.

"Don't you dare let go of me!"

"I won't."

"I mean ever, no matter what. Promise me."

"I promise."

Chapter 27

It was summer yet it felt like spring. There was a warm fragrant breeze upon their faces. It was now noon. Iris and Jeremy rode their saddle horses across the undulating hills and valleys called El Potrero de San Francisco, which ran from the Mission Bay to the Bay. This was the road that led to Santa Clara. One that Iris recognized, but which they only intended to ride a short distance to picnic.

Everything was a bright green and in full bloom, particularly the poppies, which carpeted the landscape with their iridescent orange. A profusion of flitting butterflies, with sheer opalescent wings, herald the resplendence of the day. Scores of shimmering rivulets and springs spilled their way downward to the bay. To their right the land rose and diminished far into the distance, hills crowned with thick columns of trees, with pine and redwoods.

They reigned their mounts, stopping to take in the sight of the magnificent view of the water. As Jeremy promised, the fog had lifted. The unruffled blue-green bay glistened from the sun directly overhead. From this vantagepoint they could take in its full stretch of thirty miles, commencing at the anchorage, to at last merge with a round lake-like bay, called San Pablo.

The desolate El Potrero with its meandering loose stone walls rising four feet high, was where the Mission horses were once raised. The most beautiful and prized horses seen by man. The cream colored Arabians with silver black manes were particularly favored. Don Juan Bradbury had such an animal.

The vast grazing lands that lay before them had also once belonged to Delores. It remained empty of livestock. A herd of three hundred and fifty cattle for the purpose of breeding had come with the Anza expedition. Eventually their numbers had grown into hundreds of thousands. With secularization, a vast amount of the Mission herd was deliberately killed on the spot and skinned, the bloody carcasses left scattered across the fields. Dried bones could be found everywhere, now sunk in seasons of high grass and wild flowers. Fences were ingeniously constructed from those bones. Great sharp wide horns decorated many a high gate.

They had been together since early morning. She begged that he not bring her home. Jeremy went to the grocer's with a basket and come out with what resembled a picnic. There were also wild strawberries to be found and fresh spring water, although he had brought a bottle of wine and two glasses. Jeremy lifted her down from her horse. For a moment their bodies were aligned coercing them to kiss. Reluctantly he kept it brief. He gestured that she step aside as he placed a red and white checkered clothe on a patch of grass, the basket in the middle.

"Behold! Our own Yankee picnic."

Exhausted, Iris sank down upon the edge of the cloth. She took off her yellow vicuna hat and the red kerchief around her throat. Jeremy sat beside her, at once susceptible to her sadness. She was unusually quiet as they rode, almost lethargic. Aside from that initial passion, Iris' mood had gone progressively downhill. Although obviously undone by the sight of that disgusting rat in the midst of the most impassioned of kisses, there was something else that was troubling her. His hand gently trailed over her shoulder and down her arm.

"What is it, Iris?"

She endeavored to brighten her expression by feigning a smile. "I'm just tired."

He moved closer to her still. "Too tired for this?"

His lips grazed hers. What was to be a brief kiss became prolonged and passionate. Sighing, Iris at last withdrew.

"Jeremy?" her voice was child like. "There is something I have to tell you."

"What is it?"

Her breath caught. How could she tell him?

"We'll, I'm all ears." He jested, very much interested to hear what she had to at last say.

"Well—well, you never did tell me about Sutter's Fort. It seems like you were gone forever. What was it like?"

"You're stalling, Iris. There is something you've been wanting to tell me all day, so say it"

"First, tell me about your trip. I really want to know."

"Do you?" He was unconvinced.

"Of course." She endeavored to sound enthused. "All I've gotten out of you is that you attended two fiesta's along the way. Did you take dag-types of the festivities?"

"Of course," he smiled.

"Good," she smugly retorted. "Now I'll know who you were with."

He gave her a wink. "Maybe I'd best get on with my story. I did tell you we were on the schooner, The Sacramento?"

"I know that."

"And that it used to be called The Constantine, when it was owned by the Russians."

"Oh, the Russians again." She sighed "I know. I kept looking for it. And when you finally arrived last night, I was disappointed to hear you'd gone right home to sleep."

"Just as well. I was dog tired and dirty."

"At that point I wouldn't have cared."

He gave her a tender look. "But I would have. I'm courting you lady. As impossible as it is in this far-away outpost, I have to at least try to look like a knight in shining armor."

Her eyes started to water. She immediately caught herself. "So two fiestas later, where were you?"

"We left the Martinez Rancho, which fronts the Carquines Straits, sailed Eastward through the straits to Suisun Bay, where the water gradually became fresh. Continuing eastward, we passed small islands, tulles and swamp. We came upon a channel that led us to the mouth of the Sacramento River. Our next two stops were to pick wild blackberries along the bank." He smacked his lips. "By the way, they were delicious."

"Just so you don't say that about some Señorita."

Pleasantly taken by the remark, he teased. "You sure are a jealous wench. Ask Kane-Paul. He was there."

"I know. Mamma went crazy having the kitchen all to herself."

"Hush. We're still working our way up the river. After untold turns we reached Sutter's embarcadero. It's set on the confluence of two rivers, the Sacramento and The American. Two and a half land miles more, and there was the Fort. I tell you, it's a shock suddenly having this huge settlement loom out of the wilderness. Eighteen-foot high adobe walls with a cannon at the main gate and an Indian sentry, in uniform yet. The whole ominous look of it was tempered by an exquisite rose garden, of at least two acres, right outside the structure." He shook his head, "Unbelievable."

"And this Captain Sutter? Is he an army captain, a sea captain, what?"

"He says he served in the Swiss Guard of Charles X of France. Who's to question? He could have made himself a general if he wanted. Anyway, he's a big broad man in his early forties, blue eyes, and gray hair. I found him to be pleasant, very talkative, hospitable, and extremely busy controlling every aspect of his colony." Suddenly he was laughing. "Would you believe, he has a saddle mule called Katy, whom he's extremely fond of. A man after my own heart."

"Now you're teasing."

"I'm not, I swear. Anyway, while I was there, several wagon trains of American immigrants arrived from overland. A more exhausted, bedraggled and grateful bunch you can't imagine. I found myself embracing total strangers, feeling I had met up with kin. Wait til you see what I caught on camera. It's going to take days of developing."

She gave him a thin smile.

"You can't imagine what it feels like to capture the expressions on an immigrant's face upon at last reaching a civilized outpost. Everyone that comes to California makes it a point to reach Sutter's Fort."

She sighed. "You do have a talent for portraits, Jeremy."

He looked at her askance for a moment. There was something telling in her sigh and in that remark. Still he continued.

"We were well fed, at a big common table." He gave a slight shiver. "Yet I couldn't help but be sickened by the sight of his Indian help being fed like animals, hunched over a trough, eating with their hands. It's hard to understand how these native people who are able to perform so many skills, can be treated as less than human. My God! They have feelings and a soul. That's the one thing that bothered me deeply."

Iris' eye lids quickly dropped. Telling him about the twins was suddenly going to be excruciatingly difficult. She remained almost breathless as he continued.

"A Captain John Fremont was there with a party of explorers and United States soldiers, about fifteen of them. They were resting up after a harsh winter coming across the Sierra Nevada. The illustrious Kit Carson was their guide. We had some pretty interesting conversations at the table. Another arrival, a carpenter by the of name James Marshall sat at my left. A very quiet man, with few words, although he and Sutter briefly discussed the building of some sawmill or something. One of the reasons I took so long getting back was that I also visited Fort Ross and Bodega Bay. Two Russian—"

"Jeremy," she interrupted. Though his attention was immediately hers, she could not speak. Distraught, her hands covered over her face.

"Sweetheart, what is it?" His arms were fast about her.

"I—I did something terrible," she blurted out her eyes avoided his.

"What? Tell me."

"Promise you won't hate me. Promise."

"This sounds dire," he jested.

Slowly she raised her head, not quite looking him in the eye. "I didn't mean it to turn out so terrible, honest Jeremy. In fact, I thought I might be doing something nice." She paused.

"Go on." Jeremy insisted.

"Remember that picture you took of Estrellita?"

"As a surprise for Heather?" There was a tone of skepticism in his voice.

"It wasn't really for her. It was for Blanquita."

Jeremy frowned. "Who's Blanquita?"

"Oh God. It's so complicated," she mumbled.

"Look at me, Iris."

With difficulty she made eye contact. Her voice was trembling. "I lied when I said it was for Heather."

"Why did you lie to me?"

"I—I thought maybe you wouldn't agree to take it."

"Could very well be, Iris." He looked stern.

She took a deep breath and continued. "I met Blanquita the first time we went to the Rancho. She's a cousin from Monterey. Except—except she's the spitting image of Estrellita. The same height, age, the same blue eyes, except she's much fairer. It seems that they've been passing her off as a blue-blood, 'sangre azul', when all along she was really Estrelllta's twin. It was a secret. Neither of them knew about the other until—"

"Until you showed Blanquita the picture!" He angrily finished the sentence, his sweet easygoing countenance taking on a frightening look.

"I brought it with me when I went to the Rancho. Estrellita knows nothing. She's never to know! Uncle Johnny forbade it."

He sat there stunned for a moment. Finally his deep voice bellowed out, seeming to ricochet through the hills and valleys.

"Damn you Iris! You manipulated me! You knew damn well what you were doing. Don't try to pretend otherwise!"

"It was supposed to be a surprise."

"And it was, wasn't it? "He was on his feet, his fists clinched at his sides. "Why? Why were you so intent on destroying that girl? Ruining her life? Because that's what you did. It had something to do with Don Cristóbal didn't it? Did you decide to get even because he paid attention to her? Is that it? Damn! You're so transparent I can't believe it! I can imagine how your Uncle Johnny reacted to all this, as well as your mother and sister and Tobias. My God! And I took the picture, Iris! Indirectly, I am to blame."

"No! No. You're not!" With both arms she clung to his leg only to be pushed away. "Jeremy, please listen to me!"

"I've heard enough!"

"Jeremy, please don't hate me! You're all I have! I didn't mean it! I swear!" She was crying.

"How could I have thought I loved someone so ruthless! You're a conniving bitch, Iris! How foretelling to find a rat crawling over you! Making love to you would have been like lying down with vermin!"

He spat on the ground then turned to retrieve his grazing horse. With one swift leap he was in the saddle, his spur angrily digging into the animal's belly. It reared, then wildly raced away, frenzied by the rage of its rider.

"Jeremy! Don't leave me like this! I really do love you! I'm sorry! I'm sorry!"

He could hear her desperately screaming after him, but he refused to look back.

Chapter 28

Kane-Paul solemnly walked into the parlor carrying a bible in his hand. Without a word he stood before Doña Belle, his large outstretched hand offering her the book. She looked up at him from the settee where she was quietly working on her needlepoint.

Since her return from the Rancho, she had endeavored to remain as busy as possible, somehow distracting her thoughts from the miserable turn of events. Now that Kane-Paul was back, though barely a day, the kitchen was again his domain. There was a catching in her chest, at the somberness of his expression. It was seldom that he did not have a broad beaming smile.

"What is this?" She asked, taking the book into her hands.

"A Bible."

"Yes, I realize that."

She answered all the while pondering his reason for giving it to her. It looked like it had been through the ravages of a battle. The black cover was so worn that the gold embossed title was but a faint outline. She was confused.

"Is there some particular passage out of Saint Paul you want me to read?"

He shook his head 'no'.

"What is it?"

"Lady looky page-fly."

She smiled. "You mean the fly-page."

He nodded 'yes'. Though perplexed, she was quick to comply as this hulk of a Sandwich Islander waited, his demeanor seeming more that of a boy than a man. There was an automatic air of reverence as her fingers daintily flapped to the dog-eared fly page. Curiously enough, there was an inscription written on the upper right hand corner, in a woman's handwriting. She gasped. It was hers. And it read. 'To my dear husband Colon Anthony Bradbury, on our wedding day. May God forever bless our union. From your loving and devoted spouse, Belle Clarissa Bradbury.'

Kane-Paul was quick to catch the Bible as it dropped from her trembling grasp.

"Oh God! No! No! It can't be! It can't be!" Belle broke into uncontrollable sobs. As big a man as he was, Kane-Paul was completely shaken by the sight of this consistently poised lady in tears. What had he done by giving her the Bible? It bore her name. That's all he knew.

Lailani slipped it to him to read on his voyage homeward. In his haste, he forgot his own Bible, which he always carried with him whenever he left Yerba Buena. She had received it from one of the recent immigrants a young woman, traveling with her husband and two small children. Like most foreigners coming to California their journey began in Independence Missouri. Books had a way of changing hands many times over, being traded or borrowed. Bibles in particular were cherished. When both body and spirit seemed beaten from the insurmountable hardships, where else was there to turn, but God?

Belle last saw her husband's Bible in their Boston home, by his bedside. The pages were as pristine as the day it was printed. Suddenly like Colon, it ceased to exist. Grimy hands, tears and the rigors of nature had damaged the book she held in her hands. Somehow it managed to make its way across the Great Plains and the Sierra Nevada, through parched days, pelting rains and snow. Colon Bradbury was buried for almost a year now, and yet an ephemeral part of him had traversed thousands of miles from his humble Boston grave site to bear its own cryptic message.

Upon hearing her anguished outburst, Miguel Pedro and Estrellita rushed into the parlor, the young girl fast on her knees beside Belle.

"Doña Belle, what is wrong? Why do you cry as though your heart were breaking?"

Belle was too choked up to answer. Seeing the distress her sobbing had caused, she endeavored to calm herself, but the tears continued to streak down her face. As Estrellita comforted her, Miguel Pedro raced from the house to find Tobias who had walked down to the Custom House. In no time the two of them were running up hill. Yet out of breath, Tobias rushed into the house to find Belle lying prostrate upon the bed. He slid beside her, and drew her into his arms. She could feel his heart racing beside the ponderous beat of her own.

"Belle, darling, what's wrong?"

It was moments before she could answer. "Didn't Kane-Paul tell you, about Colon's Bible?"

"I came running back as fast as I could. I haven't spoken to anyone, except for Miguel Pedro. He urged me to come home quickly. What do you mean Colon's Bible? Are you talking about Colon Bradbury, your dead husband?"

"Yes. Kane-Paul gave it to me just moments before you arrived. I didn't even ask where he got it. I guessed from his trip to Sutter's Fort."

"Are you sure it's Colon's?"

"Yes." she sobbed "There is an inscription in it from me, written on our wedding day. How did it end up here, thousands of miles away, on the pacific coast? It's frightening. So frightening. Especially now, that my morning period is almost over. Now that we're set to marry." She again began to cry, somehow more freely comforted in his arms. "There has to be something prophetic about all this. I just know it."

"It's a bizarre coincidence that's all. Someone going overland probably traded it with someone else, who traded it with someone else, all the way down the line. It is possible."

"But not probably. There's something more to this. I just know it. His Bible disappeared about the time he died."

"A great many things went. You said so yourself. Maybe it was accidentally sold with a box of things you may have disposed of at the time. If some peddler got hold of it, why wouldn't it end up heading for California?"

Belle raised her head and looked into his face. "I want to believe your explanation but it's such a cruel coincidence. How could I possibly tell the girls?"

"You don't. There's no reason for them to know. Why upset them with something that concerns their father? It would be too much of a blow right now. We just went through that scene at the Rancho. I want you to dry your tears." He handed her a handkerchief from the inside pocket of his jacket. "We have a wedding coming up, ours. You can cry then, but only out of joy."

Her mouth was upon his with soft kisses. "I love you Tobias Knight, as I never thought it possible to love a man. Nothing in this world can ever change that. Nothing."

He responded with such fervor, that for a moment they forgot that the door was slightly ajar. Quite suddenly it softly clicked closed. Miguel Pedro had wisely complied. He had also taken Colon's Bible and quickly hidden it the closest place possible, as Heather and Will were approaching the house. He lifted the piano top and dropped it inside.

Chapter 29

Jeremy lie on a narrow cot in the room he shared with a cooper by the name of Dave. It seemed an eternity since he slept in a bed that fit his size. He could not help but recall the one he had at home, in his parent's house. It had a large feather mattress with two feather pillows, soft white linen, and a down patchwork comforter. The coarse gray blanket rumpled beneath him was more suited for a horse than a human.

Suddenly he was gripped with longing for his parents and siblings, for the large commodious house that was home. He missed the sight of their sweet familiar faces and the distinctive sound of each of their voices, and their laughter. Strangely enough, he even felt nostalgic for all those subtle scents that pervaded the house. The cedar lined chests and armoires, the fragrance of flowers in the parlor, the laundry fresh from the line, the faint spring-like fragrance of his mother's cologne, the rose sachets in the dresser drawers, and his father's pipe. Of all the scents, the ones most prevalent in his mind were the aromas that consistently wafted from their wonderful kitchen with its cozy hearth. What was it about the smell of fresh baked bread that tugged at the boy inside of him, so that a lone tear trickled down his cheek?

Why was he thinking of food when he had no appetite? Aside from a foul cup of coffee that morning, his last meal was a light snack before retiring last night. If anything, his entrails were afire. He had been lying there for an hour anguishing over the situation. As much as he tried, he could not stop his thoughts from regressing back to Iris. She was everywhere.

His head slightly spun from the alcohol he had taken on an empty stomach. For an instant he became mesmerized by a spider, diligently spinning its web in a corner of the window frame, a tedious, beautifully patterned web to ultimately catch its prey.

"I won't compare you to Iris," he sardonically spoke aloud. "That would be an insult. A spider devours its prey for sustenance, survival of the fittest. That bitch Iris Bradbury just happens to like the taste of blood. Damn it all!"

Here he was thousands or miles away from home, heartbroken over a no—account woman, and talking to a spider. One of many in this God forsaken shack, along with the rats and the roaches and the pestilent fleas.

It was time to move on. He was both homesick and heartsick. Unfortunately, more the latter. He could still hear Iris' voice desperately crying out after him as he rode away, leaving her sprawled on the ground on the El Potrero. For a moment he almost turned back. Instead he dug his heels even harder into the horse's belly as he raced toward Yerba Buena. With one thought only, and that was to state his piece with Belle and Heather Bradbury and Tobias Knight.

Inadvertently he felt responsible for Iris' actions. Without the existence of that dag-type of Estrellita, none of this could have occurred. Needless to say their understanding of the situation offered little solace. He felt guilt ridden because an innocent young woman was ruthlessly hurt. Upon arriving at Tobias' house and having Estrellita greet him at the door, was in itself a blow he had not anticipated. Only then was he hit with the reality of what had happened. My God! Of course, there were two or them!

Belle was yet in her room distraught over having discovered Colon's Bible. By the look on Jeremy's face, Tobias immediately realized why he was there, and without Iris. They took a short walk away from the house and talked.

After conferring with Toblas, Jeremy headed for Ridley's saloon, where he downed three quick slugs of hundred proof whiskey which quickly added to his depression. He sat in on a game of Faro, but was unable to concentrate. His next stop was to the merchandising store, were Chester had helped him set up a room for storing his equipment and developing his plates. Chester, who at once took an interest in dag-type, became his first apprentice. Always Jeremy had been able to lose himself in his work.

From the first moment he set eyes on a daguerrotype, he became instantly enamored. The idea of reproducing a lasting image so intrigued him, that he incorporated it with his engineering assignments. A slivered copper plate was treated with iodine fumes, then placed in the camera obscura, where it was exposed to natural light let in through a lens. Once developed over vapors of heated mercury fixed with common salt, the exposed plate became a permanent picture.

He had been anxious to see the developed plates of his trip, which began from the moment he boarded the schooner Sacramento. Suddenly none of it mattered. Not for one instant in all the time he had taken dag-types, had it occurred to him that one of them could be used so destructively. How true that a picture was far more real than words. The very thing that first captured his creativity now hung upon him like a monstrous weight.

With his camera he had caught both bleak and extraordinarily beautiful landscapes. He had immortalized the expressions on a multitude of faces, of different races and circumstances. To have his work used as a vehicle for vengeance, by someone he loved, was a double-edged sword smack to the heart.

He slammed his fist against the hard planked wall alongside his cot, unaware that it ripped at his knuckles, drawing blood. Hot tears welled up in his eyes.

"You bitch!" He screamed aloud. "You two-faced rotten little bitch!"

He had left her on the El Potrero not wanting to ever lay eyes on her again. She could rot out there with all those dried up carcasses for all he cared. It was definite. He was going home. For now he was going to sleep. Emotionally spent and slightly inebriated he passed out. An urgent pounding at the door awakened him. A shaft of sun through the dusty pane told him it was still daylight. Since doors were never locked, a knock was a matter of courtesy, though the anxious fist upon the door was at once ominous. Upon opening the door Jeremy was surprised to find Heather and Will. The look on their faces registered their concern for Iris. What else would have brought them here? He stepped outside, quickly shutting away the dilapidated interior of the shack.

"We're worried about Iris." Heather was first to speak.

Jeremy had to gather his wits a moment before answering. "I left her about noon on the El Potrero."

"It's almost four thirty." Will anxiously added. "Do you think she got lost?"

"I don't know how?" Jeremy shook his head. "Unless she's been hurt. I was so angry that I left her. I guess I shouldn't have."

"Tobias told us you came by the house?" Heather offered. "I can understand your anger. We're all distraught about what happened at the Rancho, and ashamed." The words commenced to choke in her throat. "I can't help but worry. She's still my sister. Missy is so unpredictable. Who knows where she headed or what sort of wild animal she may have met up with."

Wills arm slipped about her waist. She leaned against him. "We haven't much time before dark." Will offered "I suggest we get a few men together and find her."

"You do that Will, but I'm on my way right now. It was my responsibility in the first place to bring her home, no matter how I felt."

Quickly he saddled his horse and was galloping up the sand hill that led toward the El Portrero. Although he was cursing her all the while, his heart was pounding with fear for her safety.

Chapter 30

To Jeremy's relief, the chestnut mare Iris was riding was at The Mission, its reigns haphazardly tethered to the stay-pole. The highly spirited mount that she rode home from the Rancho was replaced by a passive mare; one referred to as sobrepaso, describing its gentle nature. Sure enough, it was patiently waiting for her.

Although hours had passed, Jeremy first hastened to the spot where he left her on the El Potrero. The cloth was yet on the ground, along with the ravaged remains of their picnic basket, the work of some wild animal. Her large-brimmed yellow hat and red scarf were on the ground where she had discarded them. He felt a pulling in his chest. As angry as he was with Iris, he could not help but chastise himself for leaving her alone. Not only was she hysterical, but totally inexperienced in the saddle and in protecting herself against the elements. She had completely relied on him, having no reason to carry a weapon. Now her family and the whole of the hamlet were in an uproar. And it was his fault. His anxiety was suddenly eased when he spotted her horse's tracks, which headed toward the Mission.

After a long spell of heaving sobs and disconsolate tears, Iris raised herself from her prone position on the grass and wiped her eyes with the hem of her skirt. All the crying and ranting in the world was not about to bring Jeremy back. Alone on the undulating hillside overlooking the grandeur of the bay, she felt completely abandoned and unloved, by everyone. If only her Papa were alive. She ached for his fond embrace and the sweet way he called her 'Missy'. If only she was home again in Boston, she could go to his grave and bring flowers and speak to him. At that moment she wanted him so desperately that her heart felt like it might burst. And she wanted Jeremy, but he was lost to her forever.

In her utter despair she went to Delores, to the neglected cemetery to the left of the Mission church, now overgrown with weeds and wild flowers. She wondered through the rows of wooden crosses, most hidden beneath years of overgrowth. Aimlessly she searched for something that might beckon out to her and offer comfort. Suddenly there it was, a familiar name, almost obscured, but somehow there for her to see. It was the grave of Capitán Don Luis Antonio Arguello. His epitaph was carved in fanciful Spanish. It read that he was the first Governor of Alta California, born in June of 1784 and died March 1830. It was here that Jeremy found her, kneeling on the ground, pathetically talking aloud, her delicate hand holding back the tall thorny weeds that all but hid the surface of the cross.

"Heather told me about Concepcion," she sadly simpered. "She's an old woman now. I heard she once wanted to cut off her beautiful long eyelashes, but the padre stopped her. Who will stop me from cutting off all my hair and my wrists? Who will even care?" she sobbed. "Do you know my Papa? Papa was so good and kind that he must surely be an angel. Tell him I miss him more than life itself. Tell him to help me." She paused to quizzically study the simple wooden cross. "You are in heaven, aren't you? You must have been a good man having been buried here in this churchyard. Even if you weren't, you received the Last Sacraments for sure. I hear that in your church it can save you from hell at the last minute." Her sobs became deeper. "I don't want to go to hell, but I do want to die. I want to die and be with my Papa!"

Jeremy could not bear to stand in the sidelines and hear her a moment longer. He called out her name. Startled she looked up.

"Jeremy! Is it really you?"

"I've come to take you home. Your family is worried sick about you." His voice was stern, though the sight of her had softened him.

"Why would they worry? They all hate me! Everyone hates me!"

"Maybe it's because you're so hateful." He answered flatly, concealing all emotion.

"And you, you hate me most of all, don't you?"

"I'm not certain what I feel anymore, Iris. It's been a difficult day. Let's go home."

"I don't want to go home."

"Regardless of what you want, your family loves you. Out of respect, you mustn't cause them any more worry. Now come on."

With both his hands on her shoulders he lifted her to a standing position. She did not help him at all, weakening into a rag doll in his arms.

"No!" she choked out. "I can't go back!"

He was yet firmly holding her by the shoulders, looking down into those captivating blue eyes, bright with tears.

"You'll face them, just as you are facing me. I never wanted to see you again, Iris. I was leaving this country for good. But I'm here. God knows why, because you're not worth it!"

"Not even a little bit?" Tears spilled down her cheek.

He was adamant. "I want to get you home before dark."

"I know you won't believe me. But the one thing in the entire world that's true, is that I really love you Jeremy. Honest."

He did not answer. They emerged from the graveyard a solemn looking couple. To the few Indians lazing in the shade of the corridor, the young Americano couple might well be in mourning. In truth, it had been years since anyone was buried in the Mission cemetery. Still, there was no recording of the death. Occasionally a priest would came to bless the graves. The Books of Burial, with all those who had died at Delores, were now in Santa Clara. Considering all the deaths since the beginning of the Mission in 1776, not one father had died or been buried there.

Jeremy lifted Iris into the saddle, all the while torn by her sobs. To his own chagrin, he was actually beginning to feel sorry for her. Even worse, he believed her when she said 'I love you.'

Chapter 31

Everyone in the household became exceptionally quiet after Iris' return. Jeremy stepped into the parlor with her in tow, and sheepishly apologized for not having brought her home in the first place. As courteous as he was, he departed without giving Iris the slightest glance. Her heart ached as he walked away. His straight, swift stride out the door had a message of its own. She was convinced that he would pack up his gear and ride away forever.

Contrary to his own pronouncements, he decided to remain in Yerba Buena Cove long enough to develop the many plates he had accumulated during his Sacramento sojourn. To Jeremy's astonishment, Iris' face kept emerging again and again. How could he have forgotten that wonderful session on the sand hills overlooking the Pacific?

She had rushed him into taking and developing Estrellita's pictures. He was so smitten with Iris that he allowed himself to be manipulated into believing there was an urgency in having the dag-type in her hand before departing for the Rancho. Then there was his sudden decision to go to Sutter's Fort. Even so, how had that glorious day of picture taking escape his mind?

Yet there she was, appearing more beautiful, more appealing, as each metallic surface manifested itself into her face and form. The lighting could not have been more perfect. Those already lovely features were rendered flawless. She looked more the child than he realized, a combination of innocence and coquetry. Her long thick hair glistened like silk in the sunlight. At times it blew wildly about her head, or seductively swathed her throat and breasts. Mostly, he was spell-struck by her gaze. Those large luminous eyes not only stared back at him, but through him. Her incredibly sweet smile, with its perfect teeth, were equally taunting. He had captured a certain aura only apparent in the utter stillness of each new pose. Or was it simply his own perceptions playing games with him? As captivated as he was, he must accept the truth of the matter. Iris Bradbury was a vain, despicable, traitorous young woman. Whether time and maturity would make a difference in her, he could care less. It was over.

It was difficult enough avoiding her in so small a hamlet. But he did, leaving and returning to his shack with great haste, his eyes hastily scanning the dirt road that led up to Tobias' house. He also avoided the comments of the men that quickly saddled their mounts to join Will in finding Iris. Jeremy did not know if he was the bastard or the hero, only that the incident prompted extra drinks at the bar.

He need not have concerned himself. Iris had become unusually reclusive, almost morbidly so, hiding away in her room, with the red cat called Scamp. She actually allowed him to slip in and sleep at the foot of her bed. Iris, who hated cats, was finding solace in this purring compliant creature. His round attentive green eyes pretended to listen as she softly sobbed out her despair.

Time and again Estrellita would lightly rap upon the door, peeking in to offer her an 'algo', a little something. Usually it was chocolate, which she brought on a small silver tray with a warm tortilla. The flat bread, which once tasted disgustingly bland to Iris, was all she wanted. Never before had she felt heartsick over a suitor. Also the remorsefulness of her actions was taking its toll. As desperate as she felt, she could not help but be unnerved by Estrelllta's solicitude, by her patience and caring, considering she had never been kind to the girl from the moment they met. Iris could not help but wonder what Estrellita's reactions would be if she knew what she had done. Thank God that would never happen.

It was past noon and most everyone in the household was taking a siesta, when Hector arrived seeking Don Tobias. Estrellita slipped barefoot from her bed to answer the door. It was an unusually soft knock for Hector. He gave her a long compassionate look, which she sweetly responded to, but could not quite decipher. For some strange reason his sudden arrival sent a shiver up her spine. It was not his presence, but her intuitiveness that told her he brought some ominous news.

Tobias quickly arose to confer with him in the front garden, close to the gate, both their voices a whisper. Hector rode off with great alacrity, as though Don Tobias had hastened him with a message.

As Tobias entered the house, it was Estrellita whom he beckoned out into the back garden, where he bid her to be seated on a bench close to the shrine of the Madonna. He sat besides her grasping both her hands in his. It took moments before he could muster the words. Her large lucid eyes were anxiously upon him, studying him. It was obvious that Don Toby was troubled. Thoughtfully he weighed his words before speaking.

"Estrellita, my dear, shortly there will be a visitor to the house. Someone quite special will be coming to see you."

She looked surprised. There was no one in the world she could imagine coming to Yerba Buena to see her. Was it Father Santillian? He had officiated at her First Communion at Mission Delores. Was there something more? Yes that was it. She smiled.

"It is a young woman."

She looked confused.

Tobias tactfully continued, knowing full well what he was about to say would change her life forever.

"Her name is Blanquita. She—she is your sister. Your flesh and blood sister and a twin."

"Dios mio?" she gasped. "I have a sister? Why did I not know Don Tobias?"

His large hands gently tightened over hers, which were now trembling. He realized that he had clumsily blurted out the most startling of disclosures. There was little time for tact. Hector had raced ahead to announce that Blanquita, along with Don Cristóbal, were on their way.

Once having recovered from the shock of knowing she had a sister, Blanquita refused to return to Monterey without meeting Estrellita. To do so would be to forever have a void in her heart. Suddenly she found herself yearning and grieving for her twin. Time and again she stared at her own likeness in the Daguerreotype and sobbed. To think that a part of her existed and she never knew.

Tears now filled Estrellita's eyes, spilling like tiny rivulets upon her face.

"She did not know that you existed until recently." Tobias continued. "She wants very much to meet you."

"Dios mio!" She sobbed. "I truly have a sister, a flesh and blood sister? I can hardly believe what I hear." She straightened a smile upon her face. "There is much to do. She mustn't see me crying like a baby. What about my father, has he been told she is coming?" For a moment her face dropped and she asked. "Why did he not tell me about Blanquita? Was she separated from us for some terrible reason?"

"Yes," he softly answered "There was a reason. And it will be difficult for him. You must understand."

"My poor Papa," she briefly sobbed, her voice suddenly lightening. "It is truly a miracle, the three of us being united. God is Good!"

Tobias felt his throat tighten. In a moment Blanquita and Cristóbal would be at the door. They rode equally as fast as Hector, and were on the outskirts of the village when they sent him ahead. He must quickly tell her the rest of the story. Or as much as he could to temper the shock of Estrellita being confronted with the fairness of her twin. It was Miguel Pedro's place to tell the girls the truth about their mother, Maria Inocencia, and about himself. Tobias attempted a brief explanation.

"Blanquita was taken away to be raised in Monterey. Apart from you, because to have been born a twin in those days meant that one of you could have been killed."

Estrellita somberly nodded, having heard the ways of the past, and of her people.

"But there is more," Tobias continued, his voice seeming to have lost all strength. "Though you are identical, the same in every way, she is much fairer than you. It was decided that she pass as a 'sangre azuel.' This revelation will no doubt affect her more than you."

"While I knew I was Indian, she did not?"

Tobias nodded, somehow relieved that it was all out, and that this sweet young girl had at once understood the gravity of it all.

"She has been loved and indulged." Estrellita softly offered. "This I understand. But only now will she know her own father, but never as I have. How sad that she has missed having his love all these years. I have been the fortunate one, haven't I Don Tobias?"

He again nodded, except this time he could not look at her. She was about to learn that Miguel Pedro was not truly her father. What would it do to her? There was not a moment more to ponder the thought. He must alert the Indian of what was about to happen. There was no doubt that he would be devastated. In Miguel Pedro's heart, he and he alone had always been Estrellita's father. Maria Inocencia was the love of his life and his bride. There was no other way for him but to love her child. Except now the truth would be known, and all would be shattered.

"Wipe away the tears," Tobias gently suggested. "I want you to stay right here in the garden. When Blanquita arrives I will send her to you. It must be a private meeting between two sisters." He rose and hurried toward the house.

"Don Tobias," she called after him, causing him to pause in his haste and fondly look back at her. Estrelllta's lovely face was upturned and smiling, a sweet ethereal smile.

"Amor a Dios."

Chapter 32

Her heart fiercely pounding, Estralleta jumped up at the first glimpse of a young woman stepping into the garden. Although she knew it to be Blanquita, from the distance of twenty feet, she could not make out her features.

She appeared an elegantly groomed Señorita, dressed in a fawn colored riding outfit and hat, a red gold-fringed scarf at her throat, and elaborately tooled red and gold boots. Her tilting wide-brimmed hat cast a shadow across her face. A long shiny black braid, laced with red ribbon, fell over one breast down to her waist. Her slow graceful steps, her baring shown breeding. Blanquita in turn set eyes on a humble serving girl, dressed in common Indian attire, blue skirt and white blouse. Her long black hair hanging loosely to the waist.

Hesitatingly they each moved toward the other, as though struggling through a dream. But paces apart, they were instantly stunned to recognize each other's face. It was Estrellita who made the first gesture, rushing forward to fall upon her knees at her sister's feet. Emotionally she grasped Blanquita's outstretched hand, placing soft tearful kisses in her trembling palm. Her beautiful slender hand that felt like silk had never experienced a moment's toil.

"Please rise, you are my sister, not my servant." Blanquita compassionately pleaded in eloquent Spanish. Their voices had the same sweet pitch.

Slowly Estrelllta's raised her eyes to fully view her twin. My God! She did look every bit the 'sangre azuel.' Her skin was the color of alabaster, the cheeks as pink as roses. Those large almond eyes, were the very shape and color of her own. Her full perfectly shaped mouth with its sadly faint smile was hers exactly.

They could not help but stare at each other speechless, tears streaming down their faces. In unison they fell into each other's arms. To think, that the last time they embraced was in their mother's womb, their hearts beating as one. Even now, as they clung to one another, there was a synchronous pulsation of hearts. In that instant each suddenly understood that certain wrenching void that had manifest itself for no reason, in fleeting spells throughout their lives. There had been a spiritual connection all along that culminated at the very moment they touched. Together they cried for reasons too deep to comprehend.

It was Blanquita who took a small step back endeavoring to calm them both. She pulled out a white lace handkerchief from inside her cuff and wiped both their tears, as though she had done so many times before.

She was the first born by three minutes, the one to be a great shock to her mother, as well as the Indian mid wife. Maria Inocencia had cringed refusing to take her baby, yet the labor persisted bringing forth the second girl. For a breathless moment Estrellita's dark skin allowed Maria Inocencia to believe that she was the infant they could keep. She had taken her to her breast. With this child, she and Miguel Pedro could at least have a chance. The infant's eyes opened revealing the same startling blue of her twin. To Maria Inocencia all was forever lost. If possible, somewhere deep within their subconscious, these two young women were yet haunted by the memory of their Indian mother's despairing cries upon beholding her babies.

Whatever the reason, this moment of reunion caused them to cleave far more desperately than each had anticipated. In half embraced they walked to the Madonna shrine and knelt before it in silent prayer.

Almost as one they quietly rose to sit upon the adjacent bench, their hands clasped. Blanquita was first to speak.

"Now that we have found one another, we must never again be parted."

"At least not in spirit, my Señorita," Estrellita softly answered.

"Call me Blanquita."

Estrellita's voice choked in her throat. "It is difficult. You are such a fine noble lady and—"

"You are my sister, remember that." She had to clear her own voice before speaking. "I grant that it was difficult for me to reconcile to the fact that I am part Indian. I have been treated otherwise. They loved me as their own, and still do. For some unknown reason I was my grandfather Don Diego's favorite. Yet like my adopted parents, he knew. He knew I was not born of his blood, yet he loved me and protected me. I was their chosen child." She paused. "While you have been compelled to led such a humble life, merely because of the shade of your skin. Yet we are the same, so incredibly close in spirit, that I ache for the years we were separated." She raised Estrelllta's hand and tenderly kissed the back of her palm. "We must never again be apart. As much as I love my family, in truth you are my only family."

"I am not the only one, my sister. There is Miguel Pedro, our father. He is the dearest man in the entire world. One who has silently suffered great pain. Now that the truth is at last out, he can finally feel the joy of having both of us together again."

Blanquita's expression was most confusing to her sister. The idea of Miguel Pedro being her father had not quite occurred to her. She barely noticed him as they entered the house. Not seeing her face, he had no hint of who she was, nor she him.

It was only now, as the two girls sat in the garden, that Tobias took Miguel Pedro aside. As he so often did, he fondly addressed him as 'Miguelito'. The astute Indian at once discerned the seriousness of what was about to be said. Painfully Don Toby told him what must be done.

Maria Inocencia's twin daughters had found one another, and were anxiously awaiting his presence in the garden.

It was a heart wrenching moment having to witness the expression on Miguel Pedro's face. The proud, stoic, Indian seemed to pale and sway. For a moment he ceased to breathe, his black eyes staring lifeless. The short palpitating breathes that finally came were rife with pain. Tobias embraced him warmly, like a brother.

"It must be done Miguelito," Tobias gently advised. "They must know the truth, that their mother was truly their mother. And you, my dear friend, are the one man she loved most in the entire world. Those beautiful twin girls were entrusted to you and you did right by them in every way. They cannot help but love you. Now go. Amor a Dios."

Miguel Pedro felt his heart stop as he stepped lightly into the garden and at once cast his eyes upon Maria Inocencia's twin daughters, sitting as one on the bench, their hands affectionately clasped. The last time he saw them together they were babies, barely born, lying side by side in a large basket, ready to be forever separated. He could not contain the tears then or now. But he must, for the girls warranted his strength and his love.

Estrellita immediately rose and ran to embrace him. There was such joy in her face, that he felt slightly strengthened. But only for an instant, because shortly she would know the secret he had harbored all her life. In telling her he would be relinquishing his daughter. She was all he had in the world, all that remained of his sweet little wife. Estrellita could feel him tremble in her embrace.

"It is all right Papa, it is all right. God has been good to us. Blanquita is at last a part of our lives."

Smiling she stepped aside, allowing Miguel Pedro and Blanquita full view of one another. Where Estrellita shown pride and joy Blanquita could only feel deep disappointment. She yet sat upon the bench, having become frightfully still at the sight of the Indian standing beside her sister. Dressed in his baggy white pants and white loose top, tied with a rope, he might well be one of numerous farm hands in their Rancho in Monterey. She shivered. This man could not be her father. Her father was Don Rigoberto, a man of pride and position, of inherent nobility. His speech and baring, his clothes, even the prized Arabian he rode had an air of elegance. It took little for Miguel Pedro to read her thoughts. Humbly he turned his gaze away from her and to Estrellita.

"Go mi hijita, go sit beside your sister."

She studied him fearfully. There was no joy in his face, only heartache. Slowly she walked back to the bench and sat beside Blanquita, their hands instinctively touching. The moment had come for them to know the truth.

Miguel Pedro stepped in close enough to be heard, yet not too close. It seemed important that he distance himself from them. He could barely breathe, much less speak. Those two beautiful faces totally focused upon him as though he was about to disclose the secret of life itself. And perhaps he was. Estrellita looked so radiant and her sister so sad. He would not falter a moment longer.

"I loved your mother deeply. When she died a part of me also died." He hesitated. "I was her husband, but not your father."

Estrellita gasped. Blanquita at once felt her shock. The twin's hands tightened into a knot of tangled fingers. Stunned, they allowed him to continue without question.

"I knew her as a child and loved her even then. She was a Mission Indian like myself, a full-blooded Indian. She was impregnated against her will, by a white man, a trapper no one even remembers. It happened right here in Yerba Buena, one morning when she was all alone washing clothes at the Laguna Pequeña. Yes, mi hijita, the very place where you so often have knelt on the shoreline to also do the wash." His eyes began to water.

Estrellita's hands went to her face. Her sister's arms were fast about her. Tenderly he eyed Estrellita.

"Mi hijita, I could not have loved you more if you were my own flesh and blood. You were all I had left of your mother and I could not give you up." His gaze compassionately shifted to Blanquita. "You too are your mother's child. You have had a good life Señorita. I am so sorry that the truth may bring a great change for you. For reasons we must accept, God has chosen this moment to give you back to one another," he faltered "and chosen to take away my daughter."

"No Papa!"

Estrellita leaped up and ran into his startled embrace. She sobbed so hard that he could barely make out the words, but they were there warm and assuring.

"You are my father for all of life. I will never give you up or stop loving you. We will always have each other, always. I love you Papa. I love you Papa." she repeated again and again.

Blanquita sat there frozen, yet full with the pain of her twin's emotions. She well understood the bond between Estrellita and Miguel Pedro. In that instant, she too wanted to be in her parent's arms. Loving them and assuring them, and in turn feeling comforted by their love. Never could she compromise the family who had made her theirs.

Upon first meeting Estrellita, Blanquita promised that they would never again be parted. Estrellita had referred to her as a fine lady. What she wisely meant, was that there was no revising of roles. Though twins, they each became what destiny had determined. Where Blanquita felt instantly humbled, Estrellita was imbued with a new sense of worth. As a whole, her life had been the exception when compared to most Mission Indians. Still the idea of being a twin to one who had always been regarded as a blue blood, was an exciting revelation.

Though spiritually bound, it would be impossible for either one of them to assume the lifestyle of the other. The dye had long been cast. They would meet on occasion and rejoice in their togetherness, but nothing more. There would be moments in their life, when each would feel the other's thoughts. At last there would be sweet remembrances.

Unfortunately there would also be the disturbing specter of the man who was their natural father. The one who raped their mother? Who was he? This man who had crudely satiated himself then walked away uncaring of the consequences.

How unjust that he should remain oblivious of the destruction he had wrought. What did he care about that sweet Indian girl wistfully doing her wash? What did it matter that she slashed her wrists? And what of the two beautiful half-breed daughters separated at birth? And the husband who had loved and lost his wife?

How many others had this man destroyed along the way? Sadly misplaced children like themselves, all joined by a common bond. These were the questions Blanquita and Estrellita would ask themselves time and again throughout their lives.

Chapter 33

Iris rose from her siesta and sauntered barefoot into the parlor, her hair wildly about her head, her dress crumpled. She stopped, stunned in her steps to see Don Cristóbal sitting there with her mother and Tobias. All of them looked uneasy at the sight of her. Don Cristóbal defiantly rose, gave her a long scorching look, then angrily stormed from the house, his steps heavy, the metallic ring of his spurs grating at her senses.

She flinched. "Well, talk about rudeness. What is he doing here anyway?"

Iris acted annoyed, though she was mortified at having to face him again and looking her worst. At that same instant Heather entered with a tray of refreshments, which Kane-Paul had quickly prepared. To her dismay she caught Don Cristóbal's wrathfully sizing up Iris, then indignantly walking away.

"Just put the tray down on the tea table" Belle instructed her daughter. "Iris, sit down. I want to speak with you." Her tone was firm.

Though supportively by her side, Tobias remained quiet. Iris plopped herself down in her father's rocker, which had been crowded in a corner of the parlor. Contemptuously she chose to sit in his favorite place, her fingers anxiously twisting at a long strand of hair as she annoyingly rocked.

"You want to know why Don Cristóbal is here?" It was Belle. "He came with Blanquita to meet her sister."

"Why?" Iris frowned, "Why? That was suppose to be kept a secret. We promised Uncle Johnny!"

"Well it's not a secret anymore. It was Blanquita's choice. She wanted to meet her sister. The girls are together now in the garden, with Miguel Pedro."

"That's stupid! Why couldn't she leave well enough alone? Now everyone is really going to be mad at me. This thing is never going to end, never. And that Indian will kill me for sure. I may as well wish myself dead right now!"

"Stop it, Missy!" Heather interjected. "They're liable to hear you. Just keep your mouth shut!"

"Don't you tell me what to do, miss sanctimonious. You're just too sure of yourself because you have Will. And Mamma has him." Her eyes narrowed as she looked at Tobias, then to her mother. "Who do I have? Nobody. I want to go back home to Boston." She wailed.

"That's not possible at this time, Iris." Tobias coolly added.

"Why?" She snapped back at him. "Because you say so? Well you're not my father yet. Nor will you ever be. Why, why did Papa have to die?" Her tears were genuine and spilled non-stop. She had worked herself into a state of hysterics.

"Señorita Iris." A gentle hand slipped a handkerchief into her palm. The voice belonged to Blanquita. Her sudden appearance left Iris staring at her, mouth agape. She solemnly stood by and watched as Iris meekly wiped her face. Iris could not know that now all three of their tears had touched that handkerchief.

"I'm sorry, so sorry. Please—please forgive me" Iris blurted out in broken Spanish.

"So am I, for you, Señorita Iris," came Blanquita's soft response.

What she wished to say remained in the silence of her thoughts. 'Pain has different depths, Señorita. Your tears can be wiped away and eventually forgotten. Ours are forever.'

Iris eyes followed as Blanquita turned to Estrellita and Miguel Pedro, standing as one at the parlor door. She stretched out her arms to her twin, who was quick to fill her embrace. It was startling seeing these two young women, who so resembled one another, react with such rapport. Those watching felt a tightening in their throats.

Blanquita then moved to Heather, Belle and Tobias, lightly kissing each upon the cheek. She had made her peace. It was time to return home, to the parents and siblings she had always loved. Each girl expressed the desire for her life to remain the same. Estrellita would stay in Yerba Buena to remain the daughter of Miguel Pedro, the father whom she would never cease loving. Blanquita would of course return to Monterey to a family that anxiously awaited her return. There would be times when they would meet and rejoice in their togetherness. Destiny though seemingly cruel, had indeed been a blessing.

Chapter 34

Everyone in the house seemed to sit up in bed at once, having been startled into awakening. In the eerie gray of the early morning piano cords sounded from the parlor. The solemn rendition was immediately recognized as SAVING GRACE, a piece associated with Estrellita. The playing grew consistently louder, those slim tapering fingers seeming to have been imbued wlth surprising strength. Yesterday's shocking revelation could not help but provoke this kind of delayed reaction.

Though the discovery of a twin had been a bittersweet happening, the reality of Miguel Pedro not being her father was shattering. If anything, her feelings for him had compounded. She felt the fierceness of his pain as he traumatically disclosed the truth about their mother and the faceless man that was their father.

"The girl's gone mad," Iris hissed out to her sister as they jumped from their bed and fumbled for their robes.

"What did you expect?" Heather snapped back."

"It all worked out, didn't it" Iris countered.

"Did it?"

"Of course it did. Wouldn't you want to know you had a sister?"

Heather deliberately did not answer. Too often of late, she had disowned Iris in her mind.

One by one, each member of the household headed for the parlor. Miguel Pedro and Kane-Paul rushing from their bunk house. Only one of them thought to take in a lantern to lighten the semi-darkness of the room. With a simultaneous gasp they realized that Estrellita was carrying the lantern. Who was that strange figure at the piano?

There was an automatic hush among them as they moved into the parlor, stopping a discreet distance from the unrelenting piano player. To their shock, it was a thin scraggly looking old man. His sparse snow-white hair hung in uneven strings to his shoulders. His long whiskers and matted mustache were equally white and stringy. Aware that he was being watched, he stopped playing and turned to take stock of the small, stunned audience. His faded eyes scanned the group, stopping at Belle.

"Good morning, my dear. I could use a cup of tea."

Belle and the girls gasped in horror. It was Colon Bradbury. The voice and eyes were unmistakably his, and he had said Belle's name. Aside from that, he remained unrecognizable. His baggy buckskins and patched plaid shirt were totally incongruous with the meticulously dressed Bostonian that went daily to the mercantile house.

Suddenly Iris shrieked out and ran to him, falling to her knees to embrace him, her cheek upon his chest. Heather was beside her also fondling their father. He held them both, kissing them upon the brow many times.

"Papa, is it really you?" Iris finally managed. "It's a miracle! You're all I've thought about for days and nights, and now you're here, alive. How could it be, when we buried you?"

"It had to be done that way, Missy, for us to have a life together."

"Oh, my poor Papa," Iris cried. "What has happened to you? You look so changed."

"I'll tell you everything after I have rested a bit. We made it, didn't we girls? Didn't we Belle? We're all here together, just as I planned. We're a family again."

He looked to his wife, who remained in a state of shock, Tobias at her side, his hand fiercely clutching hers. He was not about to leave go of the woman he loved.

Close behind them stood Estrellita, the lamp yet glowing in her hand. Miguel Pedro and Kane-Paul stood at her side, all stunned, all aware of Belle and Tobias's relationship and pending wedding.

The Bible that preceded Colon's appearance was carefully removed from inside the piano by Miguel Pedro and given to Belle. After sadly contemplating what to do, she hid it away in a trunk in her bedroom fearing that its existence would devastate her daughters. Never did she dream that Colon himself would come forth, like Lazarus from the dead.

She had claimed his charred body, identifying the wedding ring on his finger. She made the funeral arrangements, having him modestly buried because of lack of funds. No, this could not be real. She had been too happy with Tobias to digress into that loveless mundane life of before. Not here in California, nor anywhere, ever.

Kane-Paul at once recognized Colon Bradbury as a man he met at Sutter's Fort. Along with two Aleuts and a Swede, he returned with them to Yerba Buena aboard the Sacramento. Ironically, Colon had commented about Kane-Paul's reading of the Scriptures, not once recognizing the Holy Book he had traded for a pistol, early on in his journey.

Jeremy had taken dag-types of all of them along the way. For some strange reason, he was intrigued by Colon's face. He found him an interesting study. The wispy, platinum white hair became gossamer in the sunlight, and the craggy face a configuration of deep shadows. Never did he dream that the old man that captured his creativity was Iris' father. Even now a daguerreotype of Colon hung on the wall in a shed in back of the merchandising store that served as Jeremy's studio.

Belle remained breathless, fearing that she might faint at any moment. Tobias felt her weight upon his arm. Steadying herself she moved apart from him, her hand slowly slipping from his grasp. As unbelievable as it was, that old man, holding their daughters in his embrace, was in reality her husband. She owed him respect. Slowly she stepped toward him; her heart aching for the love she must leave behind. She was too choked up to speak. Colon's voice came quite calm.

"Where is our room, Belle? I would like to lie down now."

He paused to study Tobias standing there tense and ready to bound forward to swoop Belle away from this decaying old man. He discerned a subtle madness about Colon, which was not yet apparent to his wife and daughters.

What Tobias perceived was a man who cunningly staged his own death. Prior to his contrived demise, he had booked passage for his wife and daughters aboard the Skylark. Without regard for their safety, he allowed them to travel clear around the Horn, to a remote Mexican hamlet. Three women alone to fend for themselves. Whatever the reason, short of madness, he was wrong to abandon them. Tobias was adamant in his thinking. Belle no longer belonged to Colon, to administer to his aging aliments and obvious dementia. She was a beautiful, sensual woman who needed to be loved and made loved to. He was not about to let her go.

"Thank you for taking care of my little family," Colon addressed Tobias. "You will excuse Belle and myself as we go to our room. It's been a very hard journey and a very long time since I've been alone with my wife. You do understand."

Dismayed Tobias looked to Belle, as did everyone else in the room. She had paled and her hands were trembling. Tobias stepped forward ready to intervene, but was quickly stopped by her subtle look and gesture of the hand.

Chapter 35

Belle's assuring glance was not enough to keep Tobias from pacing back and forth in the parlor while she remained closed in her room with Colon. Her daughters, though elated beyond belief to see their father alive, were quick to discern the precariousness of the situation. Toby, who was not only younger and more vigorous, was a man of affluence and respected. He made their mother deliriously happy. Colon had come to them a specter of himself. Even at his best, he was no match for the likes of Tobias Knight. Though it was difficult to admit, especially for Iris, they realized that their parents were no longer suited to again live as husband and wife.

Yet there she was, alone with him in the bedroom, acting more maternal than spousal. She covered him with a comforter and drew the curtains, as daylight had begun to brighten the room. His eyes followed her as she moved about, seeming more beautiful than he remembered.

"Come lie down with me Belle."

"I think you should try to get some sleep Colon," she gently offered, shivering at the request.

"Please, I've missed you so."

Reluctantly she sat on the edge of the bed and pretended to be solicitous by drawing the comforter close to his face. His hand caught hers. It felt so course and bony. Maybe it always was. There had never before been a comparison. His dry callused mouth brushed the back of her hand. She cringed.

"You're a good woman Belle. I trusted you to make it here safely. You didn't fail me." He smiled thinly. "It was thoughtful of you to bring my piano. Yes, it was very astute of you my dear. Knowing how I enjoy playing."

She looked at him dumbfounded. Why was he going on about the piano, when that was the first thing they sold while he was yet alive? What was she thinking? He did not die. Someone else was in that coffin. Who? Until that moment she had acted calmly. Suddenly she could not contain herself.

"Why Colon, why did you pretend to die like that? It was a horrible thing to do to us."

"That was the way it had to be, for all our own good. Surely you understand that everything I ever did was for our family."

She shook her head. "I don't understand at all. Not at all." She pulled her hand away from his. "It changed all our lives forever."

"Nothing has changed Belle. We're still a family. And I'm still your husband."

He again took her hand and could feel it tremble in his. Suddenly she hated his touch, so awkward and blatant. But that is the way it always was, something she was compelled to accept.

"Slip under the covers with me. Please."

"I can't."

"Yes you can. You have always been a dutiful wife Belle. This I remember most about you. And the conjugal pleasure I received from you. I thought of it often in my long journey overland."

She bit her lip so hard that she could actually taste blood. Her voice was sharp.

"Rest now Colon. You need your rest."

"The most difficult part of all was being without you and the girls. I was there at my own funeral, watching the three of you at a distance. I felt your pain, but I knew it was only temporary." He squeezed her hand.

"It was a proper burial, considering there were little or no funds. You did well. I'm proud of you."

She gasped. "You were there watching us mourn?"

"I couldn't be found out."

"My God! Who was it that we buried?"

"Someone who deserved to die," he said in a matter of fact manner.

"I've never heard you speak like this before, so cold. What about the wedding ring? You put it on his finger, after he was dead." She gasped. "My God! I wore it around my neck. Now Heather has it around hers. To think it was on a corpse we did not know."

"He was a much bigger man than myself, so it never got past the knuckle, though I did try."

Repulsed Belle kept shaking her head in disbelief.

"Actually it worked out differently then first intended," he continued. "I had brought a goodly amount of arsenic and laudanum to the counting room, to kill myself. I wanted to die Belle, but away from the house, so as not to upset you any more than I had to. It truly was planned as a suicide. Except someone else appeared prematurely. We fought." He paused, his eyes becoming unfocused. "You see, he was destined to die instead of me. When it happened, I went home and got my wedding ring, placed it on his finger, then pored kerosene from the lamp all over his body and the counting room, and set it afire. It couldn't have turned out better if I had planned it."

"I can't believe what I'm hearing. You killed a man Colon, and are actually pleased at the outcome?"

"It was really all an accident that worked in our favor. They were going to incarcerate me for my debts. What could be more shameful for all of us than that? But then he came into the counting room and things took on a different turn."

"Who came into the counting room Colon? For God's sake! Who did we bury?"

"It's not important anymore. Justice has been done. It's over. We're here now, together, thousands of miles away. I don't want to discuss it anymore Belle. It's over." His voice softened. "Now get under the covers woman. I want you to touch me, like you used to, down there, the way I like."

Belle leaped up from the edge of the bed and stood back across the room, her back hugging the wall. She was shaking uncontrollably as she stared down at the insidious man beneath the comforter in her bed. The bed where she and Toby had made rapturous love.

Whatever law or vow or duty prevailed, she would defy them all. 'Yes', she thought 'we're thousands of miles away from home, except this is my home, where I intend to live without you. I don't want to be your wife anymore, Colon. I don't have to.'

Chapter 36

Tobias caught Belle in his arms as she ran out of the bedroom into the parlor. He could feel her sobs against his chest. They were both yet in their robes, more husband and wife and lovers than each had ever before experienced. There was not the slightest consideration in either of their minds that Belle would go back with Colon. The foremost question was what were they going to do with him? Tobias did not hesitate a moment in summoning Don Juan Ricardo, Johnny Bradbury.

The girls went back to their room to dress. Estrellita brought them a breakfast tray, which they failed to touch. They were both yet dazed by the appearance of their father, a man strangely apart from the memory that they so fondly cherished. As much as they loved him, they did not know him.

"It's not going to work, Iris." Heather sadly argued. "Papa's not the man Mamma married. Nor can it ever be the same between them again?"

"We'll take care of him and make him well," Iris insisted. "He's been through hell. You can see it in his face. He's so thin and old. God only knows what he's encountered along the way, or what awful thing drove him to do what he did. But he got here for us, and that in itself is a miracle," she sobbed.

"What about Mamma," Heather reasoned," She's in love with Tobias. I can't see them giving each other up for—"

"For Papa?" Iris fumed. "She's his wife, damn it! She promised to stay with him forever, for better or worse. How can you even consider her leaving him for Tobias?"

"She already has, whether she meant to or not. She thought she was widowed and made a new life for herself, just as she thought Papa wanted. Now what?"

"I think it's disgusting that Mamma couldn't wait out her mourning period. She was barely on board ship when she took up with Tobias. Don't try to pretend they haven't slept with one another. They have trouble staying out of each other's arms. Now it's over. Papa's here and he doesn't have to know any of it. They can just resume their lives as before."

"Nothing is as it was before, Missy. We've all changed. Papa most of all."

"I don't care what you say, he's still our flesh and blood father. Now he can give you away when you marry, instead of that—that."

"That man? Tobias was there from the moment he saw us, three lost ladies. He's not only taken care of us, but truly cares for us. It's no one's fault that he and Mamma fell in love. And she's been happier than I've ever seen her in my whole life. The fact that I understand what she must be going through doesn't mean I don't love our Papa, because I do, with all my heart. And I'm going to do everything I can to help him. But I don't expect Mamma to stop loving Tobias, because it can't happen. I know, because I couldn't stop loving Will. And I did try."

"So go to him! That's all you think about anyway. You don't give a damn about me or Papa or what happens to us."

"Oh, Missy," she spoke tenderly. "Don't say that. I love you both dearly. And I care very much what happens. I just don't know what to do about it right now. Everything has been such a shock."

"Go to Will. Go on," Iris angrily goaded. "That's what you want to do. You tell him every little thing. Tell him about how our Papa suddenly showed up like a crazy man. How he was supposed to be dead and buried a year ago, and suddenly there he is playing the piano in the parlor. So what do we do with him? There are no loony bins in California."

"Please Iris, stop It. I love Papa, no matter what. And I'll take care of him. I promise."

"What a wonderful wedding gift for Will," she sneered. "This should really test his great love for you."

Chapter 37

"My father's alive!" Heather's words breathlessly spilled out upon first seeing Will. He was on his way to the Custom House when he heard her voice anxiously calling out his name from a distance. He rushed to meet her half way up the hill from her house. What she said so stunned him that he just stood there frozen, staring at her without a word.

"My father's alive," she repeated more calmly. "He didn't die in the fire. It was someone else. He came overland and is here, now."

He did not respond. She became frightened by the look on his face. An expression she had not seen before.

Her hands were on his. "Will, did you hear me? My father's alive."

"I heard what you said." He sternly answered. His head dropped, his eyes avoiding hers. "I wish I hadn't."

She could not believe his words. "What are you saying?"

He at last lifted his gaze to look into hers. There was anguish in his eyes. His voice was an unfamiliar monotone. "Whatever happens, I want you to know that I do love you. And I'm sorry."

"Sorry? What is there to be sorry about? I don't understand."

He took a deep breath. "I think its best I get it over with now. I'm going back home with you to face this thing head on."

"Will, what are you talking about? You're frightening me."

He did not answer. His jaw tensed revealing a rippling muscle that had not been apparent before, though she thought herself familiar with his every expression. His tan face paled and his dark eyes took on a coldness that was frightening. Grabbing her firmly by the arm he led her back up the hill to Tobias' house. She could barely keep pace with his long reckless strides. Not once did he pause or look back at her as she stumbled along the way.

Already emotionally wrought from the shock of seeing her father, Heather allowed herself to be pulled along like a submissive child. Once inside the house, Will's hands dropped to his sides, his fists clenched. He sharply refused to sit down, or accept a cup of chocolate, which Estrellita graciously offered. Miguel Pedro, who was quick to abide by Will's request, hastened Belle and Tobias from the garden to the parlor. Iris was also summoned from her room.

"Heather tells me her father is here." Will singled out Tobias, feeling that it was fitting to first address the man of the house.

"Yes."

"I want to see him." He was adamant.

"Why?" Came the three Bradbury women in unison, struck by the intensely angry look on Will's face.

Will's eyes remained focused on Tobias. "I want to see him now."

"The man is resting, Will." Tobias' voice came slow and modulated, endeavoring to convey calmness, though he too suspected the worst.

"I don't give a damn," Will harshly responded.

"Will, what is this all about?" Heather pleaded.

She grasped his forearm with both her hands. She could feel the tenseness of his muscles. He remained rigid to her touch. Worse, he would not look at her. Last night between passionate kisses, and tender promises, they had talked of a future together. The man beside her was a stranger. The change came instantaneously with mention of her father. Heather could feel her heart pulsating in her throat and ears, pounding in her head. She could barely breathe. There was some frightful link between her father and the man she loved. Will truly tried to spare her, by at first denying his feelings for her. Still, that deep foreboding secret continued to be concealed. The moment of truth was here and she did not want to know. Her palms covered over her ears in a gesture that denoted fear. It was Colon's voice that came before any other. He had slipped from the bedroom to make himself seen.

"What do you know, it's Will." Came Colon's surprisingly congenial voice.

"You know this man, Papa?" It was Iris.

"Yes, he's Will Kramer. He worked for a short time with me in the counting room."

"No, no," Heather was panic-stricken. "You're mistaken, Papa. His name is Will Medina,"

"No, it's not." Will looked at Heather, his eyes and voice slightly softening. "Medina was my mother's maiden name. I used it just in case anyone recognized the name Kramer."

"Franz Kramer?" Belle gasped. "You're Franz Kramer's son? We never met, but I do know he was Colon's employer. And one of the partners in the mercantile house that burnt down."

Will addressed Belle, his eyes glaring. "My father was the one who perished in that fire."

"Oh, my God! No." Heather could no longer choke back the tears. She ran to her mother's arms. Belle too had gasped.

Alone in the bedroom, she had questioned Colon as to the identity of the corpse. He had avoided the issue. The truth coming from Will was too devastating to hear. It affected them all. Heather was in love with him and planned to be his wife. Already they regarded him as family. How could they not feel his pain? Why did it have to happen because of Colon? Staid, hard working, religious, family oriented Colon Bradbury was a killer in this young man's eyes. Mother and daughters could only cling to one another.

"We know our father went to the mercantile house that night." Will explained, pausing to take a breath." He never returned home. It took us awhile to figure out what happened. Suddenly it came to us. Gus and I had the body in Colon Bradbury's grave exhumed. It measured taller and broader than Colon. There was a deep indentation on the side of the skull." He had to gulp. "There were too many inconsistencies with his so-called suicide story. When we found out that passage had been booked for his wife and daughters to California, we knew he would eventually make his way here. Who could know that Gus would die in that damned Jungle."

"Your brother Gus is dead?" It was Colon, almost childlike in his question. "I am so terribly sorry to hear that. He was such a nice young man."

"You're sorry?"

Will had managed to contain his rage until that point. Suddenly he rushed toward Colon, raising his fist in his face. Tobias moved between the two men. Although his sympathy was entirely with Will, he could not allow this frail, deranged old man to be physical assaulted, especially before the ladies. Belle and the girls were quick to group themselves around Colon, Iris throwing her arms around her father.

"Papa is incapable of killing anyone." Iris screamed out at Will. "It had to be an accident. It just had to. Tell him, Papa, tell Will what happened."

"Allow the man his piece." Tobias gently advised, his hand firmly on Will's shoulder.

Will stood there, shaken and staring, tears threatening to spill down his face. He and Gus had traveled from one coast to another, braving an impenetrable jungle in between, for this very moment. Except Gus had died. He lost a father and a brother because of Colon Bradbury. That in itself demanded the ultimate in revenge.

Except the sight of him now, a blank-eyed shrunken figure of a man with three frightened women clinging protectively at his side, was a scene Will's rancor had failed to foresee. Because now, that they were at last face to face, he did not know what to do.

Through it all he remained haunted by Heather's face, by the beseeching sadness in her eyes. How well he had come to know the gentleness of her heart. He had not wanted to fall in love with her. Perhaps he fooled himself into believing that the whole matter would go away. But there it was in front of him. Tobias calmly asked him to hear the man out. As if anything could ever appease the enormous loss he had suffered. His speechlessness prompted Tobias to again ask.

"Will, please listen to what he has to say?"

Will did not answer.

"He intends to kill me." Colon soberly interjected. "Isn't that the reason you're here Will? To do me in?"

Colon questioned him, and all Will could see were Heather's eyes staring at him, brimming with tears.

"How was it an accident?" Will asked, "I want to hear your version. I'll allow you that."

Colon's head teetered as he talked. His voice cracked. "At your father's coaxing I gave him a strong box filled with hard cash to invest. It was my life savings. He invested it in his own name, in a more lucrative venture. All the while allowing me to believe that it was a losing transaction. A gamble, he called it. I wasn't the only one he duped. There were a lot of small investors like myself, who were wiped out. It eventually came to light in the books. My indebtedness would have had me arrested and imprisoned. I was going to kill myself, Will, the very night of the fire. Unexpectedly Franze came into the counting room. We had a terrible confrontation. He struck me and I fell. While I was down, he came at me again. There next to me on the floor was the brass doorstop. I hit him in the head as hard as I could. And he fell dead. I could not believe what I had done."

He had recanted every detail as though it had been playing itself again and again in his mind through the past year. Suddenly the somberness of his expression morbidly turned to glee.

"All at once, it was a way out. I went home and got my wedding ring, and a few belongings. I put the ring on his finger, dosed him in kerosene and set him on fire so they couldn't identify the body. The note I left my wife at home and the empty bottles of arsenic on the counting room floor would imply suicide. I could have caused the fire having knocked over the lamp as I fell. So that's how it was staged. I had planned to die Will, but it was your father who died instead, because of the blow to the head. It wasn't meant to kill him, but it did." Those glazed eyes looked to Will with compassion. "I'm sorry for you son. Truly I am."

There was barely a breath as Colon told his story. No one knew what to say, least of all Will. He had suspected his father of underhanded dealings. Even so, the murder of one's father warranted revenge. To rationalize that he had brought it on himself was too difficult an assumption for a son to make.

Suddenly Will's hands became limp at his sides. He looked to Heather one last time. It was a long, anguishing look. He then walked from the house.

Chapter 38

Tobias was quick to follow after Will, reaching out to grasp his shoulder, before he hastened through the garden gate. In truth, the sum of Tobias' emotions remained inside the house with Belle and the girls. It was difficult to stand by with restraint and watch as they rallied about Colon. They were his family, how else could they possibly react? It took everything he had to not step forward and tear Belle away from that pathetic old man that was her husband. Tobias was not beyond feeling compassion for Colon's ordeal of the past year, but not enough to relinquish Belle.

Johnny's presence seemed their only solution at the moment. It might well be another day before he arrived at Yerba Buena, that is if he was at his Rancho and not in Monterey which he frequented. Their departure from Santa Clara was distressing enough, now this. Colon's sudden appearance was related in a message sent with one of his fastest vaqueros.

The problem concerning Colon's fateful connection with Will's father was another matter altogether that awaited Johnny. From the moment they picked Will up at Panama, a sun scorched emaciated shell of a man, Tobias had assumed a responsibility towards him. He included him in his business dealings, at once recognizing the young man's knowledge of books and ledgers. The camaraderie that grew between them took on added meaning upon realizing they were destined to become in-laws.

Will arrived in Yerba Buena physically and emotionally spent, only to find himself falling in love with Heather. An unthinkable circumstance, but it happened. The sweetness of those past few months with Heather had abruptly merged into a nightmare. The ambivalence of his feelings so twisted at his heart that he could actually feel the pain. The thought of never seeing her again was too excruciating to ponder. Yet how could they possibly ever be together?

With heavy steps and heart he walked from the house, only to brace himself at the gate where Tobias caught up with him. Tears already choking in his throat Will welcomed his friend's embrace.

"You're not alone, Will." Tobias compassionately assured. "Somehow it will work out. I'm not giving Belle up, nor should you walk away from Heather. She loves you. Possibly more than ever, because you knew who she was from the start and still wanted her."

"I must have been as mad as her old man thinking it could work for us. That I could keep the truth from her indefinitely. And from myself."

"You fell in love in spite of everything, because Heather Bradbury was worth it to you." He searched Will's face a moment before continuing. "I realize it is a difficult situation. But try to remember that Colon is a weak little man, who inadvertently made a terrible mistake. I can't tell you how sorry I am to learn that it was your father who died. For some reason I believe him, when he said it was an accident."

"You also believed his wife was a widow, when all the while it was my father's charred body six feet under." Will shot back.

"We met and fell in love, just as you and Heather. But only because Colon Bradbury booked their passage on the Skylark. For some providential reason, we were all thrown together on that long voyage, and because of him.

Will's voice was a repressed sob. "What about Gus? How do I ever forget that he is buried at the base of some mule steps deep inside a foreign jungle?"

"You don't forget. He'll always be with you. Nothing is easy. Life has so many hardships. That's why I gravitated to this place, because here I have found peace and joy. Even so, tragedy had its way. I buried my only child, a tiny baby girl, and then my wife. At the foot of Loma Alta there is a small immigrant cemetery. That is where they are, their tomb stones lost amidst the weeds and wild flowers."

Tobias had to swallow before continuing. It was a story he seldom told, though he still visited those two humble graves, one so small, that the very sight of it brought tears.

"One day, a miracle happened," he smiled "I met Belle and fell desperately in love. Colon Bradbury nor anyone else is going to stand in my way. The poor man is to be pitied. Can't you see that?"

Will was silent for a long time, his chin on his chest. At last he looked up.

"Perhaps you're right I don't know. I'm not sure of anything any more."

He took a deep breath, bracing himself as he did. Tobias was undoubtedly right. Yet all the words in the world could not pacify the pain of losing his brother. And there was the matter of his father. Why did it have to be Heather, of all people, who made him feel whole again, made him feel loved when he was at his lowest? They had become so close. Even now he could feel the strength of her thoughts reaching out to him. As he walked away his strong youthful carriage became slow and a stoop. One did not have to see his face to realize the look of anguish.

"What I am going to do right now." He told Tobias before leaving. "Is go to Ridley's and get good and drunk, and then get good and sick."

Chapter 39

Estrellita gently placed a shawl about Heather's shoulders. In doing so, she startled her. Realizing whom it was Heather fell sobbing into her embrace. Heather had climbed up Loma Alta, where Estrellita found her, at the summit, a lone figure immersed in the cold gray of the day. Her clothes and hair blew wildly in the chilling wind. She stood there dazed staring out at the bay and the distant mountains. The water was choppy and muddy green and a great sheet of fog had blown in throw the gate. Swaths of mist clung about the base of Tamal Pais making it appear surreal, like a huge floating island.

"Come home, Señorita Heather. Kani-Paul has made a nice thick soup for lunch. It will warm and nourish you. After, you can take a siesta. You need your strength now more than ever."

"I am not hungry," Heather finally managed between sobs. "Thank you for bringing my shawl." She was shivering, even in her voice.

"Don Juan Ricardo, your uncle shall be here soon. He will make it all better."

"How? For God's sake, how? Our presence has caused him nothing but grief."

"Do not blame yourself for Iris' actions. My sister and I will be fine Señorita. We have found a part of ourselves that was lost. Don Juan Ricardo will feel the same as I upon seeing his brother. You must believe that with all your heart."

Heather shook her head. It was far more complicated than Estrellita could possibly understand. As often as she had longed for her father and revered his memory, never did she dream that his resurrection would cause so much pain. She had lost the only man she had ever loved, because of him. Right here, on this hilltop, she related the bittersweet story of Concepcion and Nikoli to Will. At the time she feared that her own love would be unrequited. Like those long ago lovers, who were to be married, Will too would be sailing away. She could not stop crying. Estrellita drew her closer to her embrace soothing her as she wept.

"The day is not done Señorita Heather. Wait til your Uncle comes."

Slowly Heather lifted her head and wiped her tears with the hem of her shawl. She steadied herself. Her voice sounded a bit stronger.

"I must stop thinking of myself. Poor Papa needs all of us right now. Especially me, because of Will."

"I am so sorry for all of you and for Don Toby."

"What is going to happen? I can't believe what my Papa has been through. He has always been so gentle and caring and forthright." Her voice caught. "How could it be that he of all people killed—"

"Please Senorita Heather, it was an accident."

"I can't think of anything more devastating to have come between Will and me. I am suffering for them both."

"I understand Señorita. I too have felt my father's pain."

Heather at once recognized the look in Estrellita's eyes, as she mentioned Miguel Pedro. Her own shock at finding a twin and learning that her father was not truly her father, gave the young women instant rapport.

Suddenly they were truly wrapped in each other's arms, two women drawn together not only by the poignancy of their pain, but by a certain sisterhood that touches the soul, eclipsing color or blood or station.

Chapter 40

The daguerreotype of Colon Bradbury taken on the schooner Sacramento had come to haunt Jeremy for a second time. Realizing he was Iris' father was shock enough, but knowing he had killed Wills' father was too much to take.

Will appeared at Ridley's shortly after having left Tobias. Supporting himself at the long polished bar, he downed two quick shots of whiskey, hardly taking a breath between drinks. Sensing his despair, Jeremy stood beside him, choosing not to imbibe so early in the day. With a bit of gentle probing, Will's story began to spill forth. Yerba Buena being but a hamlet, the two men had met early on. The night of Doña Briones' Fandango they felt a warm rapport. They were two Yankees completely enamored with Bradbury sisters, although Will had strong misgivings about Iris. He was quick to empathize with Jeremy upon realizing that Iris' blot against Blanquita had also been at his expense. That warranted another drink.

Having ended up at the merchandising store, where Jeremy worked at his developing, the two men were caught up in another coincidence. Each, in a bizarre way, had met up with Colon. Jeremy, who was proud of the old man's portrait, was quick to tear it from the wall and place it face down on a table strewn with dag types of his trip.

Mostly there were captivating shots of Iris. Instead of destroying them, he found himself studying her lovely chiseled features and form, both cursing her and wanting her. He pretended to be indifferent to their presence, although Will had scanned the pile of copper plates upon entering. Iris' face too often resembled her sister. Thoughts of Heather rushed back to him again and again. Finally Jeremy asked the obvious.

"What about Heather? What do you think all this is doing to her?"

"She's hurting." Will meekly replied.

When she first told him that her father was alive, it was like being hit full force in the heart. He could feel himself reel from the staggering emotional blow. Only moments before he was warmed by the sight of her running down the hill to meet him, calling his name. Their elation was short lived. In that instant, as she blurted out her good news, fate took a ruthless turn. Heather rushed to him to share her joy, only to be left shattered by his reaction.

He had emotionally braced himself to affirm his love for her, no matter what. And he did love her, but his words failed to ring true as he stormed from the house after confronting Colon.

"I do love her" Will continued, "But somehow nothing is the same. There will always be this thing hanging over us."

"Wasn't it there all along? You knew the truth even before Colon emerged. You were aware that he was alive, otherwise you and Gus would have never braved Panama. Why does it make a difference now? Your feelings for Heather are the same, aren't they?"

Will paused silently weighing his feelings. "Now she knows, and that makes a difference. How do we as a couple live it down." He was beginning to mumble, "Our children will have a grandfather who killed their grandfather."

"Neither of you are at fault."

"Colon Bradbury is alive and my brother and father are dead." He almost wept. "Gus above all, I miss."

"Still you allowed yourself to fall in love with Heather, because of who she is. That part hasn't changed, has it?"

Will shook his head 'no'. "But everything else has. That wretched pathetic little man is alive. His wife and daughters grieved for him at his grave, my father's grave, and here he was alive all along. I can't get over it Jeremy, nor can I look him in the face again. It'll always be that way. What about Belle and the girls? In their minds my father provoked the whole thing. Maybe what I feel is shame. Shame for my father. If what Colon says is true, then my father precipitated the whole matter out of greed. Being his son, I don't want to admit it. But Gus is dead. We chased a sorry soul across a Continent for nothing—for nothing," his voice trailed.

Will solemnly turned to study the rising sand hills that faced the back of Jeremy's studio. The door was wide open and the room was beginning to take in sand. He leaned against the door frame and stared out at the tan undulating hills traced with scrub oak and chaparral. The wildness of the afternoon winds caused the dunes to dance before his eyes. Dejectedly he shook his head. Enough was said. Nothing was resolved, nothing.

Suddenly Chester came tearing out of the back of the merchandising store in shock. "A man just shot himself on the sand dunes!"

Will and Jeremy looked at one another. Without a word they knew who it was.

Chapter 41

Colon Bradbury was buried in the small cemetery at the foot of Loma Alta, but paces from Hannah and her baby girl. The fog had cleared and the sun shone brightly causing the bay to sparkle. The green hills were brimming with wild flowers, the flaming orange poppies in abundance.

Every member of Yerba Buena came to the funeral, mainly because of Belle and the girls. Aside from his family, no one knew the old man in the pine box. They stood in small clusters as the Alcalde offered a prayer at the simple grave site.

Johnny Bradbury arrived too late. He never got to see his brother alive. As he entered the house Heather and Belle were quick to run to his embrace. Iris stood there frozen, aching for his arms now more than ever. Her Papa was dead and this was his brother. He knew too well that she was apprehensive. What he saw was a pale reed of a girl, having had suffered enough. She too was family and she needed him. With a nod he beckoned her to come to him. He held all three women, as he had that first night they met, here in this house.

After a separation of twelve years, he dearly anticipated seeing his brother. More so than he first realized. Living here in the country of California, family had come to mean a great deal to him. Elated he rode full speed, his vaqueros fast behind him. What he found was a wizen old man in a make shift casket. Colon's body was laid out in the parlor, adorned with an abundance of flowers and candles. Johnny did not recognize the corpse as being his brother. Perhaps if he were alive something in his voice would have been familiar. He could not help but weep. He knew too well what length Colon had gone through to come to California. That overland trip might have done him in, this already frail figure of a man. Still he made it, to meet his wife and daughters and to ironically face his accuser.

His letter to Johnny did not disclose the full reason why he decided to send his wife and daughters to California. Only that they were in dire circumstance because of financial reversals. The last line of Colon's letter read, 'I look forward to seeing you one day in the future. With deep affection, Colon.'

It came as a shock to Johnny to hear Colon had killed himself in the counting room. Even then there were doubts. Perhaps that is why he prevailed upon Belle to fulfill her morning period. Now, none of it mattered. His brother truly was dead.

Even in his madness, Colon was aware that he did not belong. As it was, he had become debilitated beyond belief. He could not go on a moment longer. How ironic, that his precious Bible had been traded for a pistol meant to save his life, not end it. Pretending to retire to his room, he instead fled from the house. He did not know where he was headed, only that he wanted to die.

The immense undulating sand dunes that reached out to a mammoth ocean was where Colon decided to put a bullet in his heart, a deeply broken heart. He made up his mind before the day had a chance to darken.

Johnny dressed flamboyantly like the Don that he was, wept as he spaded mounds of dirt over the face of Colon's coffin. Belle and the girls huddled together crying. How could they be going through this for a second time? How was it possible for Colon to die twice? Again they buried him and mourned, wondering which loss, which heartache was the greater.

Tobias stood beside them, his eyes endearingly upon Belle. She was now his, but what a terrible way to have won her. Belle could no help but feel guilt ridden for the freedom that was now hers. If Colon had lived, she would have definitely left him for Tobias. Her husband never had a chance. Somehow he knew. Heather and Iris seemed closer than ever, tightly holding each other, sharing a kind of despair only sisters could understand.

Estrellita, Miguel Pedro and Kani-Paul stood close behind, offering solace in their own quite manner. Will and Jeremy remained in the rear of the mourners. They had both met the man in the pine coffin, each under different circumstances.

Suddenly Will moved forward, slowly stepping through the small gathering until he reached the Bradbury women. Unknowing to them, he silently stood behind. Catching Tobias' eye, he motioned that he wished to stand next to Heather, who stood close to her mother, Iris being on her other side. Tobias drew Belle closer, allowing Will to step through. He remained quietly beside Heather. His height and breadth were not immediately obvious to her, though she was unconsciously aware of some change having happened in the space beside her. His staring at last coerced her to look up at him. Startled she gasped. He softened at the sight of her. Grief was all over her face, a part of which he caused. He wanted to take her in his arms. He mouthed something that caused her heart to leap with joy, even at that most ominous occasion. It was, 'I love you.' His hand grasped hers, fondling it close to his heart.

Iris felt Heather's warmth slightly slip away from her. She then caught sight of Will. With her mother and Tobias standing there in half embrace, and Will and Heather tenderly adjoined, she felt more lost than ever. Overcome with anguish she slightly reeled. A man's gentle hand gripped her shoulder. She looked up to find Jeremy.

Chapter 42

Don Juan Ricardo and his vaqueros galloping horses, already emulating thunder, charged forth even harder upon coming into view of the Rancho. If Johnny ever appreciated his home and family more, it was now. All he could think of, as they raced non-stop from Yerba Buena, was holding his wife and daughters in his arms.

The last few days at the village had manage to culminate many things, both sad and uplifting. Though it was a day of mourning, an aura of love quietly accompanied the small group gathered at Tobias' house after the funeral. Tobias and Belle, Heather and Will, and even Iris and Jeremy has made their own private peace.

Colon Bradbury, unassuming man that he was, inadvertently affected the lives of every one of them. Observing his sister-in-law and his nieces and the men they had fallen in love with, Johnny concluded that it was all for the better.

In California where love of family was uppermost, Johnny never thought to give the same connotation to his own New England roots. His brother's desperate act had somehow touched all their lives, causing them to be more closely connected.

Or was it Franz Kramer's greed that started the chain of events? The Bradbury women had sailed around the Horn to arrive at Yerba Buena, to ultimately find love. As did Will, whose obsessive trek through the jungle culminated in love rather than revenge. As for Johnny, there was that last 'good bye' to his brother. He was filled with regret for having arrived too late to save Colon from himself. What then would the outcome have been?

What else was there for Johnny to do but go home and revel in his blessings? Indeed, for a one time wayward Yankee, he had it all. John Richard Bradbury was now and forever Don Juan Ricardo. There was but one small shadow in the vast brightness of his life. He realized that he was the last of his line. What did a name matter? Colon had two daughters also, whom he dearly loved. They were there for him at the end. Johnny felt warmed by the thought of his own precious little girls, both as beautiful and loving as their mother. What else could he possibly want?

His heart filled with joy at the sight of Rufina galloping toward him, her waist long hair loose and flying like a black satin mantel about her head and shoulders. Sighting him in the distance she leaped upon her mount, the train of her white dress whipping at the ground as she swiftly rode; her shapely naked legs at times exposed, her red flat shoes heeling at her horse's side. At high speed they both raced toward each other. The vaqueros deliberately slacked behind.

As Rufina's face came into focus, it was shockingly absent of the joy Johnny had anticipated all the way home. What he saw in its place was rage, a look totally unfamiliar to him. It was then that she began to weld the bullwhip curled in her right hand. With a fierce snapping of the wrist she lashed out at Johnny, so close that his horse reared. He was horrified to find that her anger was directed at him.

"My god, woman, what has come over you?" He shouted.

"You beast!" she spat "I could have ripped off your head if I wanted. How dare you call yourself a Don? You have no idea what the title means. My father and his father before him were real Dons, proud and honorable. You have disgraced our good name, by marrying me under deception!"

"What deception? I love you. You are my very soul." In Spanish his words bore even greater emotion.

"Tell it to the woman who awaits you at the house. The Indian woman who claims to be your wife."

Johnny felt his heart sink. He did not want to believe what he heard. "I was certain she was dead," he gasped.

"Tell me now, that the good Lord has decreed a season of resurrections." She did not know that Colon had died and been buried. He spade every last shovel of dirt, which was more sand than dirt.

"So it seems," he mumbled incoherently.

It all came back to him, like some long forgotten dream. Almost seven years had passed since he had seen the Indian girl he called Gentle Wind Woman. They were as man and wife. Those days were gone. He was now Don Juan Ricardo.

"I became baptized and married in your faith," he argued almost pleading. "It was a Christian marriage. You are my only wife. That other union no longer exists."

"Do you have the courage to tell her that, when she has walked untold miles searching for you? I want to hear that you did not mingle your blood with hers."

Johnny lowered his head. He could not answer. There had been a simple Shoshone ceremony followed by a rowdy celebration given by his fellow trappers. The bonding of the spirit and the flesh between Gentle Wind Woman and himself was far more than concupiscence. He had loved her and she him. Many a Hudson Bay man, even the head of a company, took an Indian wife, some more than one, from different tribes. The red women were stolen or bought or taken at will. Confused, the Indians could not understand why in turn they could not take a white woman.

Johnny was at once attracted to Gentle Wind Woman, a chaste girl of fifteen years. He took her into his life and ultimately into his heart. They lived together at the Hudson's Bay settlement at Fort Hall in Idaho, near the Snake River. In those days he wore fringed buckskins like an Indian and had a beard and hair to the waist. He was one with a ruthless group of mountain men, trailblazers who opened the way through the wilderness. The Hudson Bay Company trappers liked to brag that HBC meant 'here before Christ.'

They might well have been a lonely lot of frustrated bachelors if it were not for the red women that became their mates. They were a great asset to their men. As well as being artisans, they were conditioned to doing all the work, no matter how arduous, for their partners were considered the hunters. Fort Hall was a community of white trappers, Indian women and half blood children.

Life in the wilds brought Johnny and Gentle Wind Woman together, only to abruptly tear them apart. As they made their way from Fort Hall to Fort Vancouver, a Hudson's Bay trading post in the northwest, they found themselves caught in the fiercest winter they had ever seen. Almost having perished himself, Johnny believed she had died. Unable to find him she finally trekked back to Fort Hall. It was years later that news came that Johnny was spotted at Fort Vancouver, following that brutal winter when each thought the other was dead. What she did not know, was that he had made his way down the Columbia River to Oregon with a group of trappers, then to California.

With renewed hope Gentle Wind Woman resumed her search. She commenced her long journey to Fort Vancouver on a high spirited pinto, with several loose horses, only to learn that Johnny was long gone. Gentle Wind Woman's journey carried her down river by Mackinaw. She continued on foot reaching the remote Hudson's Bay trading post in Yerba Buena, or what remained of it. Once there, she was directed to Johnny's Santa Clara Rancho. The last leg of her long journey was on a carreta, driven by a Spanish speaking Indian. Neither understood the other's tongue.

Through the years she carried a handwritten note in English, scrawled by a trapper back at Fort Hall. It read, 'I am bound to find John Richard Bradbury of the Hudson Bay Company.' That one faded line led the way. At last they were to meet.

"She is in the patio waiting for you." Rufina announced. Her initial anger turned into sad resignation. She realized how well she knew this man that was her husband. She felt his ambivalence and his pain. Rufina reminded herself that the Indian girl was from a time remote from their lives together as Patróne and Patróna. She moved her horse adjacent to his, their thighs touching. When she again spoke there was a softness to her voice.

"She refused to come into the house. I offered her food and drink, which she gratefully accepted. I sensed a great deal of pride in that woman. You must meet with her Johnny."

"I don't want to lose you." He reached out, grasped her hand, raised it to his lips and tenderly kissed her palm.

"Amor a Dios," she whispered.

She solemnly watched as he raced ahead to the house. For an instant he looked back over his shoulder to see Rufina sitting straight and proud in her saddle. She was an enigmatic picture in white, her dark shimmering hair flowing about her head. His vaqueros had slowly moved their horses in a semi-circle behind her. The land that surrounded them on all sides, as far as the eye could see, reminded him of who he was, Don Juan Ricardo.

Gentle Wind Woman, though here upon this very land was but a minuscule footprint of the past. Wherever she walked, the seasons would cover her steps, as though she did not exist. Nothing ever again could bring back the sweet memory of their love. Or so he thought.

Chapter 43

Johnny walked haltingly through the house to the inner garden. It seemed unbelievable, all of it. Blanquita and Estrellita, Colon, and now Gentle Wind Woman. Perhaps this was the most shocking of all.

His life here in the Rancho with Rufina had obliterated whatever memory he might have sustained of the wild man that he was. There was no comparison between the two lives, as well as the two women. How was he to face the Indian wife who had been so diligent in her search for him, never giving up? When they were together, she walked faithfully at his side. In those passing years Gentle Wind Woman could have easily taken up with another trapper, which was more a possibility than not. Why was she here? He remembered her as being devoted and passionate. Wildly they had made love under the night skies filled with stars, in the heat and glare of sunlight, under a canopy of tress, besides waterfalls and on verdant hillsides, wherever and whenever he was so inclined. The recollection caused him to shiver in the warmth of the day.

The patio was empty. Those who usually congregated there, sewing, shelling peas or playing their guitars, even the small scampering children and animals were gone. It was Doña Rufina's request. Aside from the unusual dissoluteness, the garden seemed exceptionally beautiful. The abundance of multicolored flowers, the citrus tress in blossom, the splashing fountain with birds soaring and warbling, the sweetness of their song, were a welcoming sight. Still there was sadness.

The spirit of Gentle Wind Woman proceeded her presence. She was not there for him to immediately see, but he could feel her. Suddenly she stepped out from the shadowy archway. Although he knew at once it was she, he was shocked not to recognize her. She was dressed in deerskin, with beaded and braided leggings and moccasins. Her thick black hair was worn in two braids that hung over her breasts to her waist. Her proud stance and unfaltering gaze did not at all resemble the California Indian, who for decades had endured a kind of slavery. The pride Rufina at once discerned in this Shoshone Indian was long ago beaten from the neophytes, who in their Mission days often stared blankly and unsmiling.

What remained concealed were the scars on her arms and legs. As was the custom, in mourning his death, she had unmercifully slashed herself. Gentle Wind Woman had been a white man's wife. She lived comfortably in a community of integrated half bloods. Aside from the leggings, she dressed in white woman's clothes.

She looked far thinner than he remembered. Her deep copper colored skin was as weather worn as old hide. She was Rufina's age, yet her high cheekbones and classic features, once beautiful, could not rival his wife's flawless face. Gentle Wind Woman would be old before her time. Still she would carry the pride of her ancestors to her grave.

For all her beauty and self-esteem as well as her ability on a horse and with a reata and bullwhip, in truth Doña Rufina was a pampered woman. She was consistently protected by the men in her life, from her father and brothers to her husband.

Her exquisite clothes were meticulously washed and ironed. She wore large-rimmed hats to protect her skin from the sun. Her graceful hands felt like silk, never to be toil worn. Her house was in perfect order, the food scrumptious and bountiful. Her horse was richly caparisoned. Her babies were hers to love and joy over, but cared for by others. Above all, she was loved and revered as a wife. She would remain lovely and happy all the days of her life.

Gentle Wind Woman gasped at the sight of Johnny. His face was smooth and beardless, making him appear far younger than she remembered. He discarded his large brimmed hat, revealing smooth shinny hair, cropped to his shoulders and drawn back in a queue. His elaborate clothes embroidered with gold threads and his exquisitely tooled boots announced that he was Patrón of this great Rancho. He had leagues of land, great herds of cattle and horses, and above all, a beautiful wife. What could each of them possibly have to say to the other? Once they had shared a life together, intimate and joyful. Now they were strangers.

Her deep black eyes looked at him unfaltering. Eyes that could be incredibly tender and then cold as she steeled herself from the heartache that could easily spill forth. He recognized the stoic granite look that was capable of concealing anguish. Once he would have taken her in his arms and bedded her without a word, and it would have been enough for both of them. Their time together was gone. He fought to address her in her own tongue, though she had learned a modicum of English at the Fort. She spared him the effort by speaking first.

"It has been a long time."

"Yes." He meekly nodded.

"Now that I have found you, I will leave you to your new life."

"Let me help you. Our Father Above has been good to me." He did not say The Great Spirit because it was the white man's label.

"Yes, He has been good to you. Even more than you know."

She turned toward the archway and gave a slight nod. From out of the shadows emerged an Indian boy of six years and some months. Aside from his Indian attire, Johnny at once recognized him as a half blood. His dark skin was more golden than red and his eyes shone like amber. His long loose hair was several shades lighter than his mother's and with a slight wave. He rushed to her side his arms clinging to her waist.

Johnny at once felt a gripping in his heart. The child's golden eyes brightened as they met his.

"It is time that the boy be with his father." She softly announced.

"My son?" Johnny choked. "I didn't know."

"Nor I, when we were lost to one another. He knows all about you and is proud."

Johnny knelt before the boy, his large hands gently upon his lean shoulders. Aside from his mother's high cheekbones and coloring, his features were unmistakably that of a Bradbury. As they stared at one another, a smile simultaneously crossed their faces. One and the same smile. To his son, Johnny Bradbury was even more than his mother had described. The boy had hidden quietly in the shadows and watched as his father stepped into the garden. He stood even taller and straighter than he imagined. And when he walked, it was with pride. His skin and hair were fair, as were his eyes. And he was clean-shaven, not at all like the other Hudson Bay men. Compared to the trappers at the Fort, his father's attire was truly magnificent. As was this great Rancho with its leagues of land. The multitude of horses alone told the boy that Don Juan Ricardo was rich and powerful. His mother had brought him a very long way to meet him. This towering white man that sired him must surely be some sort of chief. Yes a great chief.

Johnny fought back the tears, all the while wanting to laugh aloud with joy. The boy's smile was so much like his own, wide and infectious, his teeth seeming even whiter against the deep gold of his skin. He took him into his arms, the son he thought he would never have, and held him at length.

At last Johnny's eyes raised to Gentle Wind Woman. "Thank you." He emotionally whispered.

She nodded. "My son is with his father. He knows why we traveled this long distance, and why I must now go without him. There is no place for me in your life."

She raised her hand thwarting what she knew would be Johnny's objections. Still he would not allow her to depart without insisting that her thread worn clothes be replaced and that she be geared with proper provisions, as well and two of his finest horses. Included would be a pouch full of ten dollar eagle gold pieces and Spanish and Mexican coins of gold and silver. After all, she was his son's mother, a woman he had once loved. For all of his well meant intentions, he realized that Gentle Wind Woman was right. She did not belong in his life nor could she take their son with her, wherever that was. Not back to the wilds, not now that he had met his father living here in this wondrous place.

All through that long arduous journey Gentle Wind Woman had dreamt of the three of them being together. By the night fires she had told her son stories about his father, the great trailblazer and hunter that he was. She described his light hair and eyes and his wonderful laugh, that at times echoed through the forest. It was not meant to be. All the love in her heart was not enough. She would leave not truly knowing her destination, or if she would choose to live. For now, she was truly a widow and childless. She looked lovingly at her son, their gaze silently seeming to embrace. The boy's amber eyes glimmered gold, as though he might cry, but he would not. To have at last found his father meant giving up his mother. This, he intuitively knew. There was a long disturbing silence among the three of them, each feeling the other's emotions.

She was first to speak, addressing Johnny. "Your son's name is John Richard Bradbury."

Epilogue

January 1850

Heather and Will stood atop the grassy summit of Loma Alta, their small son between them, clasping each of their hands. They had carefully made their way up to join an anxious crowd awaiting the arrival of a mail ship in the Bay.

As they ascended the Hill they found themselves stepping past a community of tents, crowded one after the other. Haphazard clotheslines were pinned with tattered shirts, pants and long johns waving in the breeze. There was the revolting stench of garbage and excretion combined with cooking. The stray goats had stayed on gorging themselves on refuse as well as grass.

Will peered into his spyglass searching the vast Pacific Ocean. There was no vessel on the horizon. What finally focused in was the devastating change that had taken place in Yerba Buena Cove, now called San Francisco.

The word GOLD had managed to electrify the world. The profusion of poppies on the hillsides shown like an auspicious omen to the thousands of would be miners arriving in California, by land or sea. The first stop before heading for the 'placer' was here, in this once peaceful hamlet.

Fifty miles north of Sutter's Fort, on the south fork of the American River, in the land of the Coloma Indians, gold was discovered. It was where Sutter and James Marshall choose to build their sawmill. On

January 24, 1848, the quite man who sat next to Jeremy at the long table at Sutter's Fort, accidentally came upon a glittering in the tailrace. This was the beginning of what became an unrelenting orgy for gold.

Loma Alta was now called Spyglass Hill, also Prospect Hill, Signal Hill, Goat Hill, Tin Can Hill, and Wind Mill Hill, because of the windmill that was now a part of the silhouette.

Doña Briones had moved away, along with her dairy farm, her wonderful fiestas and Fandangos, and her brood of children, most now grown.

Only one month before, on Christmas Eve, Tobias' fine house had burnt to the ground, along with everything East of the Plaza. It was not yet dawn when fire bells began to frantically clang. Fanned by the gusty winds from the bay, a fire that commenced near the Plaza suddenly roared out of control. There was not enough water and the abundance of mud made every effort an impossibility. Ironically there were pelting rains nonstop for days just before the fire. In fact, the rains were so fierce that mining operations came to a halt, and now, no water. People ran to the hills, the flames vicariously lapping after them. A miraculous shifting of the winds and the use of gunpowder finally contained the blaze.

There was over a million dollars worth of destruction. Yet no sooner had the ashes cooled when new waves of tents and shakes replaced those lost in the fire. They spread a mile across the waterfront and all over the hillsides, like wild mushrooms bursting out of the earth after a spring shower.

The El Dorado and the Bella Union, the largest of the hundreds of gambling saloons, were fast to put up their tents, a hundred oil lamps blazing overhead, their bands cheerfully playing as though nothing had occurred. Pouches of gold dust and nuggets were again on the tables. Twenty thousand on the turn of the card was commonplace. A complete bust would only mean going back to the minds for more, as if there were no satiating the earth and rivers of its riches.

There were times when there was barely a dozen men in town, everyone seeming to have crowded on launches, lighters and schooners, anything that was sailing to Sacramento. A few lone woman were left behind, occasionally wondering through empty gambling saloons, betting, having a drink and a cigar. Women were such a rarity that they were indulged with gold for the smallest favor, even a smile.

As sentimental as they were about Tobias' San Francisco house, none of them had lived there in the past few years. All the furnishings, the chandelier in the parlor and even the Madonna in the garden, were moved to a beautiful hillside Rancho above Carmelo Bay. Their lovely new home sat among the pines with the sound and scent of the sea, the silent mist a reminder of their Yerba Buena days.

A succession of marriages followed. There was Belle and Tobias, Heather and Will, Cristóbal and Blanquita, Estrellita and Chester, and surprisingly Iris and Jeremy. 'But for the grace of God and Jeremy' Belle sighed 'Iris might well have lost her head.'

She was referring to the enormous horde of men, some forty thousand, that descended upon the city in 1849 alone. They were would be miners from every walk of life, from every country, most averaging the age of twenty-five.

The inhabitants of California were the first to reach Coloma. In those initial six weeks they extracted the gold with knives. Their claims yielded most of them three to five pounds a day. It was one success story after another. Since it was 1848, they were in fact the forty-eighties, whose camaraderie and honesty was sadly lacking in the masses that arrived in forty-nine.

Jeremy, Will and Chester were quick to leave for the first dry diggings at Kelsey's; Kelsey's Digs, later called Placerville. Santa Fe was heavily packed with base mining supplies. Most important was a wagon carrying Jeremy's camera equipment. They were among three hundred men, digger Indians, sailors and soldiers, who for four months dug at Kelsey's. The excitement of it all managed to revive the adventurer in

Johnny, who joined them at the diggings. They were so prosperous, that as a whole the Californios did not return to the mines. Kane-Paul, who had headed for Sutter's Fort and Lailani, found himself at the right place at the right time when gold was discovered.

Lost in the mesmerizing rush for gold was the sad prediction of the end of an era. The days of the Dons were about to slip into history.

Miguel Pedro, who remained an indispensable part of Tobias and Belle's household, continued to be close to Estrellita, who never ceased to be his daughter. She and Chester lived near the Carmelo River, which was only a matter of miles from Monterey and Blanquita.

Babies were suddenly being born from every faction. To her astonishment, Belle became a mother of a boy, and a grandmother of a girl, but days apart when Iris gave birth. Iris was the greatest surprise of all. Motherhood and maturity had evoked a new feeling for family. She continually overcompensated for the hurt she once caused those who were her kin. She showed sincere affection for the little cousins that were off springs of Estrellita and Blanquita. She felt a particular fondness for little Johnny, the half Shoshone son of her Uncle Johnny. He not only resembled his father, but in a strange way, her own Papa. He came into their lives the day of Colon's burial. He was a Bradbury and deeply loved. In her more willful days, Iris might have insisted on following Jeremy to the diggings, not caring if she was the only woman there. Instead there was complacency and a glow about her. She was content to stay home with her children, of whom there were now two, knowing that there would be a passionate reunion with her husband.

There were many changes since the Bradbury women first stepped onto the shores of Yerba Buena Cove, but none so traumatic as the Gold Rush. New names quickly replaced the old. The small main thoroughfare, where the bay lapped upon the shore was now called Montgomery Street, after Commander John B. Montgomery of the U. S. sloop of war Portsmouth. On July 8, 1846, awaiting news of war between the U. S. and Mexico, the imposing naval ship dropped anchor in the bay. The next morning a contingent of sailors and marines marching behind a fife and drum made their way to the Plaza and raised the Stars and Stripes. What followed was a great ball. The residents of Yerba Buena were quick to celebrate, realizing that they were now on U. S. soil.

The Plaza was renamed Portsmouth Square, though it was still referred to as the Plaza. The old custom of the paseo, the leisurely stroll, had turned into a milling congestion of nationalities. The Senorans made up the greatest mass, followed by Chileans and scores of Americans shabbily dressed in plaid shirts and baggy pants. They were quickly infiltrated by fur clad Russians, Chinese in blue frocks and long queues, Sandwich Islanders, sailors from Fiji, New Zealanders and tattooed Malaysians. To think that once a potato patch grew in this very square, in front of the old adobe Custom House.

Ridley's was also gone. In its place was the Portsmouth Hotel. The hotels were where the well-heeled Argonauts could afford to stay. Though high priced, flea infested, damp and crowded, it was better than sleeping in a miserable wind blown tent propped up on a slushy hillside.

The two churches, Grace Church and Trinity Church were made of sheet iron. A two thousand-foot pier called the Long Wharf and another called Central Pier, stretched out into the bay, receiving the overflow of wares as well as the ships that consistently sailed up the Sacramento.

Huge loads of sand from the sand hills were crated down to fill in the bay. These added parcels were little more than expensive water lots. A more filthy, congested, muddy, rat infested waterfront had yet to be seen. Two hundred rotting deserted sailing ships, squeezed side by side, rocked on their anchors. Some slowly sank into mud, others were converted into warehouses and businesses. The profusion of masts reached up to the skies like great a skeletal forest. Horses were in the hundreds, sinking deep into dust or mud, depending on the weather.

Crime of every possible nature existed, and gangs. The most ruthless were the Sydney Ducks, ex convicts from English prisons in New South

Wales. Everyone took to wearing Bowie knives or pistols for protection. Here in a place where once no one thought to lock their doors.

Colon Bradbury had shot himself on the sand dunes, not realizing that he had set the pace for many a despairing miner. Fortunes were made by sweat, blisters and aching backs and quickly lost at the gambling tables.

Those who never stepped out of their stores were the real winners. This is where Tobias Knight and later Will really prospered. Everything was excessively expensive. An egg cost one dollar, a shovel ten times its worth. It was nothing to see a grubby, bearded man in shredded clothes carrying a bag of gold, unable to purchase anything, or even find lodging. What did it matter? They were rich. Gold fever had managed to obscure the senses.

If anyone paused to scan the verdant hills across the bay or East to the Contra Costa, it was indeed rare. Tamal Pais, which loomed majestically and untouched across the water, was unromantically referred to as Table Mountain. The name had first cropped up several decades before on the navigational chart of an English vessel. With so many ships now coming around the Horn, the name took hold.

To the true residents of the country, it forever remained Tamal Pais, a beautiful and spiritual reminder of a once glorious past. To the handful of aged Ohlone Indians yet alive, the mountain was where the spirits dwelled. There upon the summit, at times enveloped in mist, the great God Coyote reigned. Even now, he viewed with sadness the city across the bay. From the beginning, when man first laid eyes on this pastoral place, he was determined to ravage it.

From atop of what was once Loma Alta Heather and Will stared solemnly down upon the strange new city of San Francisco. Its joyous and promising inception did not befit the gentle saint whose name it bore.

Will tenderly embraced Heather. His grip gently tightened over the small hand of their four-year-old son. Another baby was due and barely discernible in her belly. They hoped to be back East before it was born. It was time to present his little family to his mother and sisters, to their spouses and nieces and nephews. Too much time had passed. In the passing, deep wounds were healed.

"Is our ship coming today, daddy?" asked the sweet faced little boy, with his father's dark hair and his mother's blue eyes.

Will softly smiled. It seemed that every vessel that came around The Horn was at once abandoned by a frantic crew bent on rushing to the diggings. The mail ship, which was greatly anticipated by every bedraggled, homesick miner, was not even a blur on the horizon. There was also a steamer that left twice a month for Panama. It was supposedly due back shortly. But that remained to be seen.

For some providential reason they were meant to go to Panama, to again feel a closeness with Gus, who often became forgotten as their own life ensued. Will had to choke back the tears remembering Gus buried in a grave deep inside a steaming jungle. Once they stepped onto Panamanian shores, perhaps he could somehow touch upon his brother's spirit. The steamer was their only hope of reaching the East Coast. It would again be a grueling ride through that snaking jungle river, this time with a pregnant wife and child. God willing, fate would be kinder than it was for those two dauntless brothers bent on vengeance. This time it would be different. This time there was love. Besides, there was great support in numbers, for many others were making the voyage with them.

Once in their Eastern home, no matter how happy, their thoughts would often turn back nostalgically to this mystical place on the Pacific shore. To the way they had first seen it from atop Loma Alta. The way mankind would never see it again, pristine and beautiful.

One day, when all the madness for gold was gone, they would return to their California family.

"Soon Gus" Will at last answered his son. "Soon."

About the Author

Margot Dolgin is a California Author and Artist. Her genre is Historical Fiction. Her first novel ALL ELSE IS SHADOW is a bittersweet love story that transcends time. Although it takes place when America is in the midst of an Industrial Revolution and the throes of a Spiritual Revival, there are aspects that touch upon her own life. WALK IN LOVE is set in Yerba Buena (San Francisco) prior to the Gold Rush. It evolved from the author's kinship with the city of her birth. The Bay and topography remain a pervading view of another time. Her research unearthed provocative details of that era. There is romance, adventure and a thread of mystery. FAYREMORN, which is set in Georgian England, is perhaps the most powerful in its dramatic story line. There is love, hate, poignancy, cynicism, hope and again a sense of mystery. Her latest novel NAKED IN THE WIND, is set on the California Coast. It is a contemporary story that required a substantial amount of research. There is love, hate, pathos and a dramatic double twist ending. There are glimpses of early Carmel By The Sea, San Francisco in 1906, in the late 40's and 1971. Each novel promises a surprise ending. The Author also created the covers of her books.

0-595-15018-7